DEXTER
IS
DELICIOUS

ALSO BY JEFF LINDSAY

Darkly Dreaming Dexter

Dearly Devoted Dexter

Dexter in the Dark

Dexter by Design

JEFF LINDSAY

DEXTER IS DELICIOUS

A NOVEL

Doubleday

NEW YORK · LONDON · TORONTO · SYDNEY · AUCKLAND

DOUBLEDAY

All rights reserved. Published in the United States by Doubleday, a division of Random House, Inc., New York, and in Canada by Random House of Canada Limited, Toronto.

www.doubleday.com

DOUBLEDAY and the DD colophon are registered trademarks of Random House, Inc.

Library of Congress Cataloging-in-Publication Data
Lindsay, Jeffry P.
Dexter is delicious : a novel / Jeff Lindsay. — 1st ed.
p. cm.
1. Morgan, Dexter (Fictitious character)—Fiction. 2. Forensic scientists—Fiction. 3. Serial murderers—Fiction. 4. Police—Florida—Miami—Fiction. 5. Miami (Fla.)—Fiction. I. Title.
PS3562.I51175D48 2010
813'.54—dc22
2010013405

ISBN 978-0-385-53235-8

PRINTED IN THE UNITED STATES OF AMERICA

1 3 5 7 9 10 8 6 4 2

First Edition

For Hilary, as ever.

Acknowledgments

It would not be possible to write these books without the generous help of some wonderful people who work in forensics. In particular I would like to thank Samantha Steinberg, Sharon Plotkin, and Lisa Black. If I got something wrong, it's because I didn't ask them.

I am also grateful for the continued support of my U.S. editor, Jason Kaufman, whose wise guidance and patient encouragement with these books have been essential, and very much appreciated. And Dexter would never have happened at all without my agent, Nick Ellison; thank you, Saint Nick.

As always, life support and general well-being were provided by Bear, Pookie, and Tink, who make it all worthwhile.

DEXTER
IS
DELICIOUS

ONE

THIS PART OF THE HOSPITAL SEEMS LIKE FOREIGN COUNTRY
to me. There is no sense of the battlefield here, no surgical
teams in gore-stained scrubs trading witty remarks about
missing body parts, no steely-eyed administrators with their clip-
boards, no herds of old drunks in wheelchairs, and above all, no
flocks of wide-eyed sheep huddled together in fear at what might
come out of the double steel doors. There is no stench of blood, anti-
septic, and terror; the smells here are kinder, homier. Even the colors
are different: softer, more pastel, without the drab, battleship utili-
tarianism of the walls in other parts of the building. There are, in
fact, none of the sights and sounds and dreadful smells I have come
to associate with hospitals, none at all. There is only the crowd of
moon-eyed men standing at the big window, and to my infinite surprise, I am one of them.

We stand together, happily pressed up to the glass and cheerfully making space for any newcomer. White, black, brown; Latin,
African-American, Asian-American, Creole—it doesn't matter. We
are all brothers. No one sneers or frowns; no one seems to care about
getting an accidental nudge in the ribs now and again, and no one,

wonder of all, seems to harbor any violent thoughts about any of the others. Not even me. Instead, we all cluster at the glass, looking at the miraculous commonplace in the next room.

Are these human beings? Can this really be the Miami I have always lived in? Or has some strange physics experiment in an underground supercollider sent us all to live in Bizarro World, where everyone is kind and tolerant and happy all the time?

Where is the joyfully homicidal crowd of yesteryear? Where are the well-armed, juiced-up, half-crazed, ready-to-kill friends of my youth? Has all this changed, vanished, washed away forever in the light from yonder window?

What fantastic vision beyond the glass has taken a hallway filled with normal, wicked, face-breaking, neck-snapping humans and turned them into a clot of bland and drooling happy-wappys?

Unbelieving, I look again, and there it is. There it still is. Four neat rows of pink and brown, tiny wiggling creatures, so small and prunish and useless—and yet it is they who have turned this crowd of healthy, kill-crazy humans into a half-melted splotch of dribbling helplessness. And beyond this mighty feat of magic, even more absurd and dramatic and unbelievable, one of those tiny pink lumps has taken our Dark Dabbler, Dexter the Decidedly Dreadful, and made him, too, into a thing of quiet and contemplative chin spittle. And there it lies, waving its toes at the strip lights, utterly unaware of the miracle it has performed—unaware, indeed, even of the very toes it wiggles, for it is the absolute Avatar of Unaware— and yet, look what it has done in all its unthinking, unknowing wig-glehood. Look at it there, the small, wet, sour-smelling marvel that has changed everything.

Lily Anne.

Three small and very ordinary syllables. Sounds with no real meaning—and yet strung together and attached to the tiny lump of flesh that squirms there on its pedestal, it has performed the mightiest of magical feats. It has turned Dexter Dead for Decades into something with a heart that beats and pumps true life, some-thing that almost feels, that so very nearly resembles a human being—

There: It waves one small and mighty hand and that New Thing inside Dexter waves back. Something turns over and surges upward into the chest cavity, bounces off the ribs and attacks the facial muscles, which now spread into a spontaneous and unpracticed smile. Heavens above, was that really an emotion? Have I fallen so far, so fast?

Yes, apparently I have. There it goes again.

Lily Anne.

"Your first?" says a voice beside me, and I glance to my left—quickly, so as not to miss a single second of the spectacle on the far side of the window. A stocky Latin man stands there in jeans and a clean work shirt with MANNY stitched over the pocket.

"Yes," I say, and he nods.

"I got three," he says, and smiles. "I don't get tired of it, either."

"No," I say, looking back at Lily Anne. "How could you?" She is moving her other hand now—and now both at the same time! What a remarkable child.

"Two boys," he says, shaking his head, and adds, "and at last, a girl." And I can tell from the tone of his voice that this thought makes him smile and I sneak another glance at him; sure enough, his face is stretched into an expression of happy pride that is nearly as stupid-looking as my own. "Boys can be so dumb," he says. "I really wanted a girl this time, and . . ." His smile stretches even wider and we stand together for several minutes in companionable silence, contemplating our bright and beautiful girls beyond the glass.

Lily Anne.

Lily Anne Morgan. Dexter's DNA, living and moving on through time to another generation, and more, into the far-flung future, a day beyond imagination—taking the very essence of all that is me and moving it forward past the clock-fingered reach of death, sprinting into tomorrow wrapped in Dexter's chromosomes—and looking very good doing it. Or so it seems to her loopy father.

Everything has changed. A world with Lily Anne Morgan in it is so completely unknown: prettier, cleaner, neater edges, brighter colors. Things taste better now, even the Snickers bar and cup of vending machine coffee, all I have had for twenty-four hours. The candy bar's flavor was far more subtle than I had known before, and the coffee tasted of hope. Poetry flows into my icy cold brain and trickles down to my fingertips, because all is new and wonderful now. And far beyond the taste of the coffee is the taste of life itself. Now it is something to nurture, protect, and delight in. And the thought comes from far out beyond bizarre that perhaps life is no longer something to feed on in the terrible dark frenzy of joy that has defined me until this new apocalyptic moment. Maybe Dexter's world should die now, and a new world of pink delight will spring from the ashes. And the old and terrible need to slash the sheep and scatter the bones, to spin through the wicked night like a thresher, to seed the moonlight with the tidy leftovers of Dexter's Dark Desiring? Maybe it's time to let it go, time to let it drain away until it is all gone, vanished utterly.

Lily Anne is here and I want to be different.

I want to be better than what I have been.

I want to hold her. I want to sit her on my lap and read her Christopher Robin and Dr. Seuss. I want to brush her hair and teach her about toothpaste and put Band-Aids on her knees. I want to hug her in the sunset in a room full of puppies while the band plays "Happy Birthday," and watch her grow up into wonderful beautiful cancer-curing symphony-writing adulthood, and to do that I cannot be who I have always been—and that is fine with me, because I realize one more important thing.

I don't want to be Dark Dexter anymore.

The thought is not so much a shock as a completion. I have lived my life moving in one direction and now I am there. I don't need to do those things anymore. No regrets, but no longer necessary. Now there is Lily Anne and she trumps all that other dancing in the dark. It is time to move on, time to evolve! Time to leave Old Devil Dexter behind in the dust. That part of me is complete, and now—

Now there is one small and very sour note singing in the choir of Dexter's happiness. Something is not quite right. Somewhere nearby some small gleam of the old wicked life flashes through the rosy glow of the new and a dry rattle of scales grates across the new melody.

Someone is watching me.

The thought comes as a silky whisper only one step removed from a chuckle. The Dark Passenger, as ever, is amused at the timing as well as the sentiment—but there is truth in the warning, too, and I turn very casual-careful, smile now stitched in place in the old fake way, and I scan the hallway behind me: first to the left, toward the vending machines. An old man, his shirt tucked into pants pulled much too high, leans against the soda machine with his eyes closed. A nurse walks by without seeing him.

I turn and look to the right, down to where the hallway ends in a "T" that goes one way to a row of rooms and the other way to the elevators. And there it is, as plain as a blip on any radar screen, or what is left of the blip, because someone is going around the corner toward the elevators, and all I can see is half his back as he scuttles away. Tan pants, a greenish plaid shirt, and the bottom of one athletic shoe, and he is gone, and he does not leave any explanation at all of why he was watching me, but I know that he was, and this is confirmed by the cheesy smirk I feel oozing from the Passenger, as if to say, *Oh, really, we're leaving* what *behind?*

I know of no reason in this world, or any other, why anyone would be interested in little old me. My conscience is as clean and empty as it can possibly be—which means, of course, that I have always tidied up carefully, and in any case, my conscience has the same hard reality as a unicorn.

But someone very definitely was watching me and this is oh-so-more-than-slightly bothersome, because I can think of no wholesome and happy reason why anyone would want to watch Dull-as-Dishwater Dexter, and I must now think that whatever threatens Dexter might also be a danger to Lily Anne—and this is not a thing that I can allow.

And of course the Passenger finds this highly amusing: that moments ago I was sniffing the bright buds of spring and forswearing the way of all flesh, and now I am once again up on point and eager to slay—but this is different. This is not recreational homicide. This is protecting Lily Anne, and even after these very first moments of life, I will quite happily rip the veins out of anything that comes near her, and it is with this comforting thought that I stroll to the corner of the hall and glance toward the elevator.

But there is nothing there. The hallway is empty.

I have only a few seconds to stare, barely enough time to enjoy my own slack-jawed silence, and my cell phone begins to vibrate on my hip. I draw it from its holster and glance at the number; it is Sergeant Deborah, my own adopted flesh and blood, my cop sister, no doubt calling to coo over the arrival of Lily Anne and offer me sibling best wishes. So I answer the phone.

"Hi," I say.

"Dexter," she says. "We got a shit-storm and I need you. Get down here right away."

"I'm not on duty right now," I say. "I'm on paternity leave." But before I can reassure her that Lily Anne is fine and beautiful and Rita is in a deep sleep down the hall, she gives me an address and hangs up.

I went back and said good-bye to Lily Anne. She waved her toes, rather fondly, I thought, but she didn't say anything.

T W O

THE ADDRESS DEBORAH GAVE ME WAS IN AN OLD PART OF
Coconut Grove, which meant there were no high-rises or
guard booths. The houses were small and eccentric, and all
the trees and bushes spread up and out into an overgrown riot of
green that hid almost everything except the actual road. The street
itself was small and darkened by the canopy of overhanging
banyans, and there was barely room for me to steer my car through
the dozen or so official vehicles that had already arrived and
claimed all the parking spots. I managed to find a crevice beside a
sprawling bamboo plant about a block away; I wedged my car in
and took the long hike back, lugging my blood-spatter kit. It seemed
much heavier than usual, but perhaps it was just that being so far
from Lily Anne sapped my strength.

The house was modest and mostly hidden by plant life. It had a
flat, tilted roof of the kind that had been "modern" forty years ago,
and there was a strange and twisted chunk of metal out front that
was probably supposed to be a sculpture of some kind. It stood in a
pool of water, and a fountain squirted up next to it. Altogether it
was the very picture of Old Coconut Grove.

I noticed that several of the cars parked in front looked rather federal motor pool–ish, and sure enough, when I got inside there were a couple of gray suits in among the blue uniforms and pastel guayaberas of the home team. They were all milling about in clusters, a kind of colloidal motion made up of groups—some doing question and answer, some forensics, and others just staring around for something important to do to justify the expense of driving over here and standing at a crime scene.

Deborah was in a group that could best be described as confrontational, which was no surprise to those who know her and love her. She was facing two of the suits, one of them a female FBI agent I knew, Special Agent Brenda Recht. My nemesis, Sergeant Doakes, had sicced her on me when an attempted kidnapping of my stepkids, Cody and Astor, had gone down. Even filled with the good sergeant's helpful paranoia she had not managed to prove anything against me, but she had been deeply suspicious, and I was not looking forward to renewing my acquaintance with her.

Standing beside her was a man I can only describe as a generic fed, with a gray suit and white shirt and shiny black shoes. They were both facing my sister, Sergeant Deborah, and another man I didn't know. He was blond, about six feet tall, muscular, and absurdly good-looking in a rugged, masculine way, as if God had taken Brad Pitt and decided to make him *really* handsome. He was staring off to the side at a floor lamp while Deborah snarled something forceful at Special Agent Recht. As I approached, Deborah glanced up and caught my eye, turned back to Special Agent Recht, and said, "Now keep your goddamned wingtips out of my crime scene! I have real work to do," and she turned away and took my arm, saying, "Over here. Take a look at this."

Deborah dragged me toward the back of the house, muttering "Fucking feds" to herself, and because I was so very much filled with love and understanding from my time in the maternity ward I said, "Why are they here?"

"Why are they ever here?" Debs snarled. "They think it's kidnapping, which makes it federal. Which also makes it impossible for me to do my fucking job and find *out* if it's kidnapping, with all those assholes in their goddamned Florsheims clomping around. Here," she said, switching gears very smoothly and propelling me into a room at the end of a hall. Camilla Figg was already there, crawling across the floor very slowly on all fours on the right side of the room and avoiding the left side altogether. That was a very good idea, because the left side of the room was so spattered with blood that it looked like a large animal had exploded. The blood glistened, still moist, and I felt a twitch of unhappiness that there could be so much of the awful stuff.

"Does that look like a fucking kidnapping to you?" Deborah demanded.

"Not a very efficient one," I said, looking at the huge smear of blood. "They left almost half of their victim behind."

"What can you tell me?" Deborah said.

I looked at her, feeling mildly annoyed at her assumption that I would know what had happened instantly, on first look, by some kind of instinct. "At least let me read the tarot cards," I said. "The spirits have to come a long way to talk to me."

"Tell them to hurry," she said. "I got the whole fucking department breathing down my neck, never mind the feds. Come on, Dex; there must be something you can tell me. Unofficially?"

I glanced at the largest splotch of blood, the one that started in the middle of the wall over the bed and went in all directions. "Well," I said, "unofficially, it looks more like a game of paintball than a kidnapping."

"I *knew* it," she said, and then frowned. "What do you mean?"

I pointed at the red splat on the wall. "It would be very difficult for a kidnapper to inflict a wound that did that," I said. "Unless he picked up his victim and threw him at the wall at about forty miles an hour."

"Her," Deborah said. "It's a her."

"Whatever," I said. "The point is, if it's a child small enough to throw, then she lost so much blood here she has to be dead."

"She's eighteen years old," Debs said. "Almost nineteen."

"Then assuming she's average size, I don't think we want to try to catch somebody who could throw her that hard. If you shoot him, he might get very annoyed and pull off your arms."

Deborah was still frowning. "So you're saying this is all fake," she said.

"It looks like real blood," I said.

"Then what does it *mean*?"

I shrugged. "Officially, it's too soon to tell."

She punched my arm. It hurt. "Don't be a jerk," she said.

"Ow," I said.

"Am I looking for a body, or a teenager sitting at the mall and smirking at the dumb-ass cops? I mean, where would a kid get this much blood?"

"Well," I said hopefully, not really wanting to think about that, "it might not even be human blood."

Deborah stared at the blood. "Sure," she said. "Of course. She gets a jar of fucking cow blood or something, throws it at the wall, and takes off. She's scamming her parents for money."

"Unofficially, it's possible," I said. "At least let me analyze it."

"I got to tell those assholes something," she said.

I cleared my throat and gave her my best Captain Matthews imitation. "Pending analysis and lab work, there is a very real possibility that, uh, the crime scene may not be. Um. Evidence of any actual crime."

She punched my arm again, right in the same spot, and it hurt even more this time. "Analyze the fucking blood," she said. "Fast."

"I can't do it here," I said. "I have to take some back to the lab."

"Then *take* it," she said. She raised her fist for another devastating arm punch, and I was proud of the nimble way I skipped out of her reach, even though I nearly crashed into the male model who had been standing beside her while she talked to the feds.

" 'Scuse me," he said.

"Oh," Deborah said, "this is Deke. My new partner." And she said the word "partner" in a way that made it sound like "hemorrhoid."

"Pleased to meet you," I said.

"Yeah, sure," Deke said. He shrugged and moved off to the side, where he could stare at Camilla's rear end as she inched along the floor, and Deborah gave me a very eloquent look that said many four-letter things about her new partner.

"Deke has just come down from Syracuse," Deborah said, in a voice pleasant enough to peel paint. "Fifteen years on the force up there, chasing stolen snowmobiles." Deke shrugged again without looking. "And because I was careless enough to lose my last partner, they decided to punish me with him." He held up one thumb and then bent over to see what Camilla was doing. She immediately began to blush.

"Well," I said, "I hope he works out better than Detective Coulter." Coulter, Deborah's previous partner, had been killed as part of a performance art piece while Deborah lay in the hospital, and even though his funeral had been very nice I was sure the department was watching Deborah very carefully now, since they frowned on cops who developed the habit of carelessness with partners.

Deborah just shook her head and muttered something I didn't quite catch, although I heard several hard consonants in it. So because I always try to bring cheer wherever I go, I changed the subject. "Who is that supposed to be?" I said, nodding at the gigantic bloodstain.

"The missing girl is Samantha Aldovar," she said. "Eighteen, goes to that rich kids' school, Ransom Everglades."

I looked around the room. Aside from the blood spatter, it was not a remarkable room: desk with chair, a laptop computer that seemed to be a few years old, an iPod dock. On one wall, happily unmarked by blood, was a dark poster of a pensive young man. Underneath was labeled, TEAM EDWARD, and below that, TWILIGHT. There were some nice-looking clothes hanging in the closet, but nothing extraordinary. Neither the room nor the house it was in seemed like it belonged to somebody wealthy enough for a fancy prep school, but stranger things have happened, and there were no bank statements pasted up on the walls that I could see.

Was Samantha faking her own kidnapping to get money from her parents? It was a surprisingly common ploy, and if the missing girl had been surrounded by rich kids all day it might have created pressure on her to come up with some designer-label jeans of her own. Kids can be extremely cruel, bless them, especially to someone who can't afford a five-hundred-dollar sweater.

But the room didn't tell me enough either way. Mr. Aldovar might be a reclusive billionaire able to buy the entire neighborhood while flying to Tokyo for sushi. Or perhaps their financial means really were modest and the school gave Samantha financial aid of some kind. It didn't really matter; all that mattered was to make sense of that horrible wet splat of blood and get it cleaned up.

I realized that Debs was staring at me expectantly, and so rather than risk another knockout punch to my triceps, I nodded at her and exploded into vigorous action. I put my kit down on the desk and opened it. My camera was right on top, and I snapped a dozen pictures of the stain on the wall and the area around it. Then I went back to my kit, took out a pair of latex gloves, and pulled them on. I grabbed a large cotton swab from a plastic bag and a jar to hold it, and carefully approached the glistening splat of blood.

I found a place where it was thick and still wet and twirled the head of the swab slowly through it, lifting enough of the awful stuff to make a useful sample. Then I carefully pushed the swab into the little jar, sealed it, and stepped away from the mess. Deborah was still staring at me as if she were looking for a soft spot to punch, but as I watched, her face softened slightly. "How's my niece?" she said, and the dreadful red splat on the wall faded to a wonderful soft pink background.

"She's beyond amazing," I said. "All fingers and toes in the right place and absolutely beautiful."

For just a moment something else fluttered across my sister's face, something that seemed slightly darker than the thought of a perfect niece. But before I could say what it was, Deborah's same old on-duty grouper face swam back into place.

"Great," she said, and she nodded at the sample in my hand. "Get that analyzed, and don't stop for lunch," she said, and turned away.

I closed up my kit and followed Debs out the bedroom door and down the hall to the living room. Off to the right, Captain Matthews had arrived and planted himself where everyone could see that he was on the scene and relentlessly pursuing justice.

"Shit," Deborah said. But she squared her jaw and marched over to him anyway, possibly to make sure he didn't step on a suspect. I would have loved to watch, but duty sounded its clarion call, so I turned away for the front door, and found Special Agent Brenda Recht standing in my path.

"Mr. Morgan," she said, tilting her head and raising an eyebrow as if she were not quite sure whether to call me that or something more familiar, like "Guilty."

"Special Agent Recht," I said, pleasantly enough, considering. "What brings you here?"

"Sergeant Morgan is your sister?" she said, which did not really answer my question.

"That's right," I said anyway.

Special Agent Recht looked at me, then stared across the room to where Deborah was talking to the captain. "What a family," she said, and walked past me to rejoin her generic-looking partner.

I thought of several very good comebacks that would have put her neatly in her place, but after all, her place was actually several rungs above mine on the food chain, so I just called out, "Have a nice day," to her back and headed out the door to my car.

THREE

THE TEST I NEEDED TO RUN TO FIND OUT IF THE BLOOD was human was a fairly basic one, simple and relatively quick, so I stopped for lunch even though Deborah had told me not to. Just to keep things righteous, it was only a take-out sandwich, but after all, I had nearly starved myself at the hospital, and I had rushed away from Lily Anne to work on a day off, so one small Cuban sandwich did not seem like too much. In fact, it seemed like almost nothing at all, and I finished it in the car before I even got off I-95, but I arrived at my little laboratory in a much better mood.

Vince Masuoka was in the lab staring at something under a microscope. He looked up at me when I entered and blinked several times. "Dexter," he said. "Is the baby all right?"

"Never better," I said, a combination of truth and poetry that pleased me more than it should.

Apparently Vince did not agree; he frowned at me. "You're not supposed to be here," he said.

"The pleasure of my company was requested," I said.

He blinked again. "Oh," he said. "Your sister, huh?" He shook his head and then ducked back down to the microscope. "There's fresh coffee," he said.

The coffee may have been freshly made, but the grounds had apparently been sitting in a vat of toxic chemicals for several years, because the stuff was as close to undrinkable as something can be and still be liquid. Still, life is a series of trials, and only the tough survive them, so I sipped a cup of the wretched stuff without whimpering as I ran the test on the blood sample. We had several vials of antiserum in the lab, so it was only a matter of adding my sample to one of them and swirling the two together in a test tube. I had just finished when my cell phone began to chime. For a brief, irrational moment, I thought it might be Lily Anne calling, but reality reared its ugly head in the form of my sister, Deborah. Not that her head is actually ugly, but she is very demanding.

"What have you got," she demanded.

"I think I may have dysentery from the coffee," I told her.

"Don't be an asshole," she said. "I'm getting enough asshole from the Fibbies."

"I'm afraid you may have to put up with some more," I said, looking at my test tube. A thin line of precipitate had formed between the antiserum and the sample from the crime scene. "It looks like it's human blood."

Deborah was silent for a moment, and then said, "Fuck. You're positive?"

"The cards never lie," I said, in my best Gypsy accent.

"I need to know whose blood it is," she said.

"You're looking for a thin man with a mustache and a limp. Left-handed and wearing black, pointy shoes," I said.

She was silent for a second, and then she said, "Fuck you. I need some help here, goddamn it."

"Deborah, there's only so much I can do with a blood sample."

"Can you at least tell me if it belongs to Samantha Aldovar?" she said.

"I can run another test and find out the blood type," I said. "You'll have to ask the family what hers is."

"Do it," she snarled, and hung up.

Have you noticed how difficult it is just to get along in the world? If you're no good at all in your job, people treat you badly and eventually you will be unemployed. And if you're a little better than competent, everyone expects miracles from you, every single time. Like most of life, it's a no-win situation. And if you dare to mention it, no matter how creatively you phrase your complaints, you are shunned as a whiner.

In truth, I do not mind being shunned. If only Deborah had shunned me, I would still be at the hospital admiring Lily Anne and her blossoming motor-control skills. But I could not risk being shunned full-time, not with the economy as bad as it is, and a growing family to think about. And so with a world-weary sigh, I bent my aching back to the dreary task at hand.

It was late afternoon when I called Deborah with the result of my test. "It's type O," I said. I did not expect her to respond with flowery gratitude, and she didn't. She simply grunted, said "Get your ass back over here," and hung up.

I got my ass back into my car and drove it south to Coconut Grove and the Aldovars' house. The party was still going when my ass got there, and my parking spot by the bamboo-on-steroids was gone now. I circled the block one time, wondering if Lily Anne missed me. I wanted to be there with her, not here in the dull and deadly world of blood splatter and Deborah's temper. I would run in, tell Debs I was leaving, and get back to the hospital—assuming I could find a place to put my car, which I could not.

I circled again, and finally found a place twice as far away, beside a large Dumpster in the yard of a small and empty house. Dumpsters are one of the new and fashionable lawn ornaments in South Florida, and they spring up all over our town like mushrooms after a summer rain. When a house goes into foreclosure, which they do quite often nowadays, a crew arrives with the Dumpster and empties the house into it, almost as though they picked it up by one side and poured everything out. The former occupants of the house presumably find a nice freeway overpass to live under, the bank resells the house for ten cents on the dollar, and everyone is happy— especially the company that rents the Dumpsters.

I took the long hike back to the Aldovars' house from my charming Dumpster-view parking spot. The walk was not as horrible as it might have been. The day was cool for Miami, with the temperature only in the low eighties and the humidity no more than a steam bath, so there were still several dry spots left on my shirt when I pushed through the swarming flock of reporters gathered in front of the house and trudged on in.

Deborah stood in another group that looked like they were facing off for a tag-team wrestling match. Clearly the main event would be Debs versus Special Agent Recht; they were already nose-to-nose and exchanging rather heated opinions. Their respective partners, Deke and the Generic Fed, stood to one side of the main couple like good wingmen, glaring at each other coldly, and to Deborah's other side was a large, distraught woman of around forty-five who was apparently trying to decide what to do with her hands. She raised them, and then dropped one, and then hugged herself, and then raised the left one again, so I could see that she was clutching a sheet of paper. She fluttered it, then dropped both hands again, all in the span of the three seconds it took me to cross the floor to join the happy little group.

"I don't have time for you, Recht," Debs was snarling. "So let me say it for you in one-syllable words: If I got that much blood, I got assault and attempted murder at the least." She glanced at me, and then back to Recht. "That's what my expert says, and that's what my experience says."

"Expert," Recht said, with very nice federally provided irony in her voice. "You mean your brother? He's your expert?" She said "brother" as if it was something that ate garbage and lived under a rock.

"You got a better one?" Debs said with real heat, and it was very flattering to see her go to bat for me.

"I don't need one; I have a missing teenage girl," Recht said, with a certain amount of her own heat, "and that's kidnapping until further notice."

"Excuse me," the fluttering woman said. Debs and Recht ignored her.

"Bullshit," Deborah said. "There's no note, no phone call, nothing but a room full of blood, and that's not kidnapping."

"It is if it's her blood," Recht said.

"Excuse— If I . . . Officer?" the fidgeting woman said, fluttering the piece of paper.

Deborah held her glare on Recht for a moment, then turned to face the woman. "Yes, Mrs. Aldovar," she said, and I looked at the woman with interest. If she was the missing girl's mother, it would explain the eccentric hand movements.

"This could . . . I . . . I found it," Mrs. Aldovar said, and both of her hands went up helplessly for a moment. Then the right one fell to her side, leaving the left in the air with the sheet of paper.

"You found what, ma'am?" Deborah said, already looking back at Recht as if she might lunge forward and grab the paper.

"This is . . . You said to look, um . . . medical report," she said, and she twitched the piece of paper. "I found it. With Samantha's blood type."

Deborah made a wonderful move that looked like she had been playing professional basketball her whole life. She stepped between the woman and the feds and got her backside directly in front of Recht, effectively screening her out from any chance of seeing the paper, all while reaching out and plucking the paper politely from Mrs. Aldovar's hand. "Thank you, ma'am," she said, running a finger down the page. After only a few seconds she looked up and glared at me.

"You said type O," she said.

"That's right," I said.

She flipped the page with a fingertip. "This says AB positive."

"Let me see that," Recht demanded, trying to lurch forward and get at the paper, but Deborah's NBA butt-block was too much for her.

"What the fuck, Dexter," Deborah said accusingly, as if it were my fault the two blood types were different.

"I'm sorry," I said, not at all sure what I was apologizing for, but quite certain from her tone of voice that I should.

"This girl, Samantha—she has AB-positive blood," she said. "Who has type O?"

"Lots of people," I reassured her. "It's very common."

"Are you saying—" Mrs. Aldovar tried to say, but Deborah plowed on.

"This is no help," Debs said. "If it's not her blood in there, then . . . who the hell flings somebody else's blood on the wall?"

"A kidnapper," Special Agent Recht said. "Trying to cover his tracks."

Deborah turned and looked at her, and the expression on her face was truly wonderful to see. With just a few rearranged facial muscles and one small raised eyebrow, Debs managed to say, *How is it possible that someone this stupid can tie her own shoes and walk among us?*

"Tell me," Deborah said, looking her over with disbelief, "is 'special agent' kind of like 'special education'?" Deborah's new partner, Deke, give a vacuous syllable of laughter, and Recht blushed.

"Let me see that paper," Recht said again.

"You went to college, didn't you?" Deborah went on, very conversationally. "And that fancy FBI school in Quantico."

"Officer Morgan," Recht said sternly, but Deborah waved the paper at her.

"It's Sergeant Morgan," she said. "And I need you to get your people off my crime scene."

"I have jurisdiction with kidnapping—" Recht started to say, but Deborah was gaining steam now and cut her off without any real effort.

"Do you want to tell me that the kidnapper threw that much of his own blood on the wall, and was still strong enough to take away a struggling teenager?" she said. "Or did he bring some blood in a mayonnaise jar and say, '*Splat*, you're coming with me'?" Deborah shook her head slightly and added a small smirk. "Because I can't see that either way, *Special* Agent." She paused, and she was on such a roll that Recht apparently didn't dare speak. "What I see," Deborah said, "is a girl pranking us and faking her own kidnapping. And if you have evidence that this is anything else, now is the time to whip it out."

"Whip it out," Deke said with a goofy chuckle, but nobody apparently noticed except me.

"You know very well—" Recht began, but once again she was interrupted—this time by Deborah's new partner, Deke.

"Hey," he said, and we all turned to look at him.

Deke nodded at the floor. "The lady fainted," he said, and we all turned to look where he had nodded.

Mrs. Aldovar, as advertised, was out cold on the floor.

FOUR

OR A VERY LONG MOMENT WE ALL STOOD IN A FROZEN tableau of hostile indecision. Debs and Recht stared at each other, Deke breathed through his mouth, and I tried to decide whether assisting the fallen woman was technically within my jurisdiction as a blood-spatter analyst. And then there was a clatter at the front door and I heard a minor commotion behind me.

"Shit," a male voice called out, quite clearly. "Shit, shit, *shit*."

It was impossible to argue with the general sentiment, but nevertheless I turned around to see if I could gather some specifics. A middle-aged man hurried toward us. He was tall and soft-looking and had close-cropped gray hair and a matching beard. He slid to one knee beside Mrs. Aldovar and picked up her hand. "Hey, Emily? Honey?" he said as he patted her hand. "Come on, Em."

I have spent my entire career working with first-rate professional investigators, and some of it must have rubbed off on me, because I almost immediately deduced that this had to be Mr. Aldovar. And my sister is no slouch, either, because she had arrived at the same startling conclusion. She managed to rip her gaze away from Recht and look down to the man on the floor.

"Mr. Aldovar?" she said.

"Come on, honey," he said, hopefully not to Deborah. "Yes, I'm Michael Aldovar."

Mrs. Aldovar opened her eyes and wobbled them from side to side. "Michael?" she muttered.

Deborah knelt down beside them, apparently thinking that conscious parents are more interesting than the fainted kind. "I'm Sergeant Morgan," she said. "I'm investigating your daughter's disappearance."

"I don't have any money," he said, and Deborah looked startled for a moment. "I mean, if there's a ransom, or— She knows that. Samantha can't think— Has there been any phone call?"

Deborah shook her head as if trying to shake water off. "Can you tell me where you've been, sir?"

"There was a conference in Raleigh," Mr. Aldovar said. "Medical statistics. I had to— Emily called and said Samantha had been kidnapped."

Deborah looked up at Recht and then quickly back to Mr. Aldovar. "It wasn't kidnapping," she said.

He didn't move at all for a second, and then he looked directly at Deborah, still holding his wife's hand. "What are you saying?" he said.

"Can I talk to you for a moment, sir?" Deborah said.

Mr. Aldovar looked away, then down at his wife. "Can we get my wife into a chair or something?" he said. "I mean, is she all right?"

"I'm fine," Mrs. Aldovar said. "I just . . ."

"Dexter," Debs said, jerking her head at me. "Get some smelling salts or something. You and Deke help her up."

It's always nice to have a question answered, and now I knew. Apparently, it actually was within my jurisdiction to help women who faint at a crime scene.

So I squatted down beside Mrs. Aldovar, and Deborah led Mr. Aldovar off to one side. Deke looked at me anxiously, reminding me very much of a large and handsome dog who needs a stick to fetch. "Hey, you got some of that smelling stuff?" he said.

Apparently it had become universally accepted that Dexter was the Eternal Keeper of the Smelling Salts. I had no idea where that baffling canard had come from, but in truth, I was completely without.

Luckily, Mrs. Aldovar apparently was not interested in sniffing anything. She gripped my arm, and Deke's, and murmured, "Help me up, please," and the two of us heaved her to her feet. I looked around for a horizontal surface uncluttered by law enforcement where we could deposit her, and spotted a dining table complete with chairs in the next room.

Mrs. Aldovar did not need a great deal of help getting into the chair. She sat right down as if she had done the same thing many times before.

I looked back into the next room. Special Agent Recht and her generic companion were edging their way toward the door, and Deborah was very carefully not noticing them. She was instead busy chatting with Mr. Aldovar. Angel Batista-No-Relation was standing on the patio, just outside a sliding glass door, dusting the glass for fingerprints. And I knew that just down the hallway, the huge bloodstain still hung on the wall, calling for Dexter. This was my world, the land of violence, gore, and mayhem. Both personally and professionally, this was where I had lived my whole life.

But today it had lost the rosy glow that had for so many years kept me enchanted. I did not want to be here, browsing through the residue of someone else's happy frolic—and even more, I did not want to be off on a carefree romp of my own. I needed different vistas today. I had come to the old turf unwillingly, out of duty to Deborah, and now I wanted to go back to my new country, where all was bright and beautiful, the Land of Lily Anne.

Deborah glanced up at me without any real recognition and then back to Mr. Aldovar. I was scenery to her, part of what a crime scene looked like, Dexter as Background. Enough: It was time for me to leave, to go back to Lily Anne and Wonder.

And so without lingering for any awkward farewells, I slid out the door and walked back to my car, where it still sat nestled in by the Dumpster. I drove to the hospital in the prelude to evening rush hour, a magical time when everyone on the road felt empowered and entitled to all the lanes at once because they had left work early, and in my past life I had taken great joy in the sight of so much naked contempt for life. Today it left me cold. These people were endangering others, not something I could tolerate in a world where I would soon be driving Lily Anne to ballet lessons. I drove at a careful ten miles per hour over the speed limit, which only served to enrage most of the other drivers. They flew past me on both sides, honking and extending their middle fingers, but I held firm to my safe and sane course, and soon I arrived at the hospital, without any actual exchange of gunfire.

As I came off the elevator on the floor for maternity I paused for a second as the faint echo of a whisper rattled off the back wall of Dexter's Dark Subbasement. This was where I had almost seen somebody who might have been watching me for some reason. But the thought came out sounding so ludicrous that I could do no more than shake my head and send a distant *Tut-tut* to the Passenger. "Almost Somebody" indeed. I moved on past, turning the corner to the nursery.

All my new friends at the nursery window were gone, replaced by a new crop, and Lily Anne, too, was no longer visible on the other side of the glass. I had a moment of crippling disorientation—where had she gone?—but then logic reasserted itself. Of course—it had been several hours. They would not leave her there alone and on display for so long. Lily Anne would be with her mother, feeding and growing closer. I felt a small surge of jealousy. Rita would have this important and intimate bond with the baby that I could never know—a head start on Lily Anne's affections.

But happily for all, I heard the soft and mocking chuckle that lives inside, and I had to agree. *Come now, Dexter: If you suddenly choose to feel emotions, is breast envy the best one to start with? Your role is just as important: to provide firm and loving guidance on the thorny path through Lily Anne's life.* And who better than me, who had lived on the twisted trail, savoring the thorns, and who now wanted nothing more than to help her through the thickets unharmed? Who better, in short, than No-Longer-Demented Daddy Dexter?

It was all so neat and logical. I had lived the wicked life in order to know how to steer Lily Anne into the light. Everything made sense at last, and although bitter experience has taught me that if everything makes sense you are looking at it wrong, I nevertheless felt great comfort from the notion. There was a Plan, a True Pattern, and at long last Dexter knew what it was and could actually see his feet on the game board. I knew why I was Here—not to harry the wicked, but to shepherd the pure.

Feeling greatly enlightened and uplifted, I walked briskly past the nurses' station and down to Rita's room at the far end of the hall, right where it was supposed to be. Even better, Lily Anne was there, sound asleep on her mother's chest. A large bouquet of roses sat on the bedside table, and all was right with the world.

Rita opened her eyes and looked up at me with a tired smile. "Dexter," she said. "Where have you been?"

"There was an emergency at work," I said, and she looked at me blankly.

"Work," she said, and she shook her head. "Dexter, I— This is your newborn child here." And right on cue, Lily Anne wiggled slightly and then continued sleeping. She did it very well, too.

"Yes, I know," I said reassuringly.

"It's not— How can you just wander off to work?" she said, and she sounded very peeved, in a way I had never heard before. "When your brand-new baby is— I mean, work? At a time like this?"

"I'm sorry," I said. "Deborah needed me."

"So did I," she said.

"I'm really very sorry," I said, and weirdly enough, I really was. "I'm very new at this, Rita." She looked at me, shaking her head again. "I'll try to get better," I added hopefully.

Rita sighed and closed her eyes. "At least the flowers you sent were nice," she said, and a tiny bell began to ring in the dark back-seat of Dexter's wicked wagon. I had not sent any flowers, of course. I was not experienced enough at all the many subtle hypocrisies of married life to think of such a clever ploy—I had not even realized that responding to an emergency at work was wrong, let alone that I needed to apologize with flowers. Of course, Rita had many friends who might have sent them, and I knew several people who were theoretically friends—even Deborah might have had a moment of sensitivity, unlikely as that seemed. In any case, there was absolutely no reason a few fragrant blossoms should set off any kind of alarm.

But they did. They definitely did—a steady, annoying *ding-ding-ding* of an alarm that very definitely meant all was not what it should be. So I leaned casually over and pretended to sniff the roses, while actually trying to read the accompanying card. Again, there was nothing at all unusual about it, just a small tag that said, *Congratulations to us!* and scribbled in blue ink underneath was, *An admirer*.

From the same general region that provided the little alarm bell, I heard a soft and wicked chuckle well up. The Dark Passenger was amused, and no wonder. Dexter is many things, but "admirable" is not one of the top ten. As far as I knew, I had no admirers. Anyone who really knew me well enough to admire me was theoretically already dead, dissected, and disposed. So who would sign the card like that? I knew enough about humans to know that a friend or family member would sign their own name to make absolutely sure they got credit for the flowers. An ordinary human, in fact, would already have called on the telephone to say, "Did you get *my* flowers? I wanted to be sure because they're so expensive!"

Clearly, no such call had come, since Rita assumed the roses were from me. Just as clearly, there was nothing really threatening about such a minor mystery.

So why did I feel small and icy feet walking up the back of my neck? Why was I so certain that some hidden danger threatened me and, therefore, Lily Anne? I tried to be logical, which is something I had once been very good at. Of course, I told myself reasonably, it was not merely the anonymous flowers—I also had the alarm from the possible sighting of a potential someone earlier on. And when I added it all up, I realized what I had: a very strong possible maybe something or not, which might or might not be an actual threat or not. Or something.

Put that way, in clear and logical form, it made perfect sense for me to feel uneasy. Lily Anne was being stalked by an idiot.

Me.

FIVE

I SPENT AN HOUR SITTING WITH RITA AND WATCHING LILY Anne sleep, fuss, and feed. Objectively speaking, it was not really a great deal of activity, but it was far more enjoyable and interesting than I would have imagined. I suppose it is no more than a form of egotism to find your own baby so very fascinating—certainly, I had never found other babies compelling—but whatever it might say about me, I did it now and I liked it. Rita dozed, waking only once when Lily Anne twitched and kicked for a few seconds. And then a few minutes later, Rita frowned, opened her eyes, and looked at the clock on the wall above the door.

"The kids," she said.

"Yes," I said, watching as Lily Anne reacted to Rita's voice by curling and uncurling one tiny hand.

"Dexter, you have to pick up Cody and Astor," she said. "At the after-school program."

I blinked. It was true: The program closed at six, and the young women running it began to get very cranky by quarter past. The clock said ten minutes of six. I would just make it.

"All right," I said, and I stood up, reluctantly tearing myself away from my baby watching.

"Bring them back here," Rita said, and she smiled. "They need to meet their new sister."

I headed out the door, already imagining the wonderful scene: Cody and Astor stepping softly into the room, their little faces lit up with love and amazement, seeing for the first time the tiny wonder that was Lily Anne. The scene was crystal clear in my mind, rendered with the combined genius of Leonardo da Vinci and Norman Rockwell, and I found myself smiling as I ambled down the hall to the elevator. It was a *real* smile, too. An actual, unfaked, spontaneous human expression. And surely Cody and Astor would soon be wearing the same fond smile, gazing down at their new sister and realizing as I had that a life on the Dark Path was no longer necessary.

For Cody and Astor had also been condemned to walk in shadows, monsters like me, flung into the darkness by the savage abuses of their biological father. And I, in my own wicked pride, had promised to steer their little feet onto the Harry Path, teaching them to be safe and Code-abiding predators, as I was. But surely the coming of Lily Anne had changed all that. They, too, would have to see that everything was new and different. There was no longer any need to slink and slash. And how could I, in this brave new world, even think of helping them spin away into that dreadful abyss of death and delight?

I could not; everything was new now. I would lead them to the light, set their feet on the path to the Good Life, and they would grow to be decent, upstanding human beings, or the best possible imitations. People can change—wasn't I already changing, right before my very own eyes? I had already had an emotion and a real smile; anything was possible.

And so with a true surge of genuine human confidence that all would soon be rose petals, I drove to the after-school program, which was at a park near our house. The traffic was in full rush-hour, homicidal flow, and I had a new insight into what made Miami drivers tick. These people weren't angry—they were anxious. Each one of them had someone waiting for them at home, someone they hadn't seen all miserable workday long. Of course they got upset if another driver slowed them down. Everyone had a Lily Anne of their own to get home to and they were understandably eager to get there.

It was a dizzying image. For the first time I felt a real kinship with these people. We were connected, one great ocean of humanity bound together by a common goal, and I found myself humming a pleasant tune and nodding with forgiveness and understanding toward each upraised middle finger that came my way.

I made it to the park only a few minutes late, and the young woman standing anxiously at the door gave me a relieved smile as she handed Cody and Astor over to me. "Mr. Um Morgan," she said, already fishing for keys in her purse. "How is, um . . . ?"

"Lily Anne is doing very well," I said. "She will be in here finger-painting for you in no time."

"And Mrs. Um Morgan?" she said.

"Resting comfortably," I said, which must have been the correct cliché, because she nodded and smiled again and stuck the key into the door of the building.

"All right, kids," she said. "I'll see you both tomorrow. Bye!" And she hurried off to her car, at the other end of the parking lot from mine.

"I'm hungry," Astor said as we approached my car. "When is dinner?"

"Pizza," Cody said.

"First we're going back to the hospital," I said. "So you can meet your new sister."

Astor looked at Cody, and he looked back, and then they both turned to me.

"Baby," Cody muttered, shaking his head. He never said more than two or three words at a time, but his eloquence was astounding.

"We wanna eat first," Astor said.

"Lily Anne is waiting for you," I said. "And your mother. Get in the car."

"But we're hungry," Astor said.

"Don't you think meeting your new sister is more important?" I said.

"No," Cody said.

"The baby isn't going anywhere, and it isn't really *doing* anything except lying there, and maybe pooping," Astor said. "We've been sitting in that dumb building for *hours* and we're *hungry*."

"We can get a candy bar at the hospital," I said.

"*Candy* bar?!" Astor said, making it sound like I had suggested she eat week-old roadkill.

"We want pizza," Cody said.

I sighed. Apparently rosy glows were not contagious. "Just get in the car," I said, and with a glance at each other and a surly double stare for me, they did.

The drive back to the hospital theoretically should have been about the same distance as the trip in from the hospital to the park. But in fact it seemed to be twice as long, since Cody and Astor sat in complete and sullen silence the whole way—except that, every time we passed a pizza place, Astor would call out, "There's Papa John's," or Cody would say quietly, "Domino's." I had been driving these streets my entire life, but I'd never before realized how completely the entire civilization of Miami is devoted to pizza. The city was littered with the stuff.

A lesser man would certainly have weakened and stopped at one of the many pizza parlors, especially since the smell of hot pizza somehow drifted into the car, even with the air-conditioning on, and it had been several hours since I had eaten, too. My mouth began to water, and every time one of the kids said, "Pizza Hut," I was sorely tempted to park the car and attack a large with everything. But Lily Anne was waiting, and my will was strong, and so I gritted my teeth and kept to the straight and narrow of Dixie Highway, and soon I was back in the hospital parking lot and trying to herd two unwilling children into the building.

The foot dragging continued all the way across the parking lot. At one point, Cody even stopped dead and looked around as if he had heard someone call his name, and he was very reluctant to move again, even though he was not yet standing on the sidewalk.

"Cody," I said. "Move along. You'll get run over."

He ignored me; his eyes roved across the rows of parked cars and fixed on one about fifty feet away.

"Cody," I said again, and I tried to nudge him along.

He shook his head slightly. "Shadow Guy," he said.

I felt small and prickly feet on my spine and heard a cautious unfolding of dark leathery wings in the distance. Shadow Guy was Cody's name for his Dark Passenger, and although it was untrained it could not be ignored. I stopped and looked at the small red car that had caught his attention, searching for some clue that might resonate with my own inner sentinel. Someone was half-visible through the windshield of the car, reading the *New Times*, Miami's weekly alternative paper. Whoever it was gave no sign of interest in us, or anything else besides the cover story, an exposé of our city's massage parlors.

"That guy is watching us," Astor said.

I thought of my earlier alarm, and the mysterious bouquet of roses. It was the flowers that decided me; unless there was a slow-acting nerve toxin in the roses, there was no real threat hovering around me. And while it was possible that the person in the car really was a predator of some kind—this was Miami, after all—I felt no twinge of warning that he was focused on us.

"That guy is reading the paper," I said. "And we are standing in the parking lot wasting time. Come on."

Cody turned slowly to look at me, an expression of surprised peevishness on his face. I shook my head and pointed at the hospital; the two of them exchanged one of their patented looks, and gave me a matching expression that said they were disappointed but not sur-prised at my substandard performance. Then they turned together and began to walk again toward the hospital door. Cody glanced back at the car three times, and finally I did, too, but there was nothing to see except a man reading the paper, and eventually we got inside.

Dexter is nothing if not a man of his word, and I led them straight to the vending machine for the promised candy bar. But once again they dropped into sullen silence, staring at the vending machine as if it was some kind of torture device. I began to fidget with impatience—another real human emotion, making two of them so far, and I had to say I was not enjoying my transformation to the species. "Come on," I said. "Just pick one."

"But we don't *want* one," Astor said.

"Would you rather be hungry?" I said.

"Rather have pizza," Cody said softly.

I could feel my jaw beginning to tighten, but I maintained my icy control and said, "Do you see pizza in this vending machine?"

"Mom says that too much candy can make you have diabetes," Astor said.

"And too much pizza makes you have high cholesterol," I said through clenched teeth. "And going hungry is actually good for you, so let's forget the candy bar and go upstairs." I held out my hand to them and half turned toward the elevator. "Come on," I said.

Astor hesitated, mouth half-open, and we stood that way for several long seconds. Then Cody finally said, "Kit Kat," and the spell was broken. I bought Cody his Kit Kat, Astor chose a Three Musketeers, and at last, after what had seemed as long and painful as major surgery, we all got into the elevator and headed upstairs to see Lily Anne.

We made it all the way to Rita's room without a word about pizza or diabetes, which I regarded as a miracle, and in my new human optimism I actually thought we might get through the door and into Lily Anne's presence. But Astor stopped dead just outside the closed door, and Cody trickled to a halt behind her. "What if we don't like her?" Astor said.

I blinked; where does this stuff come from? "How can you not like her?" I said. "She's a beautiful little baby. She's your sister."

"Half sister," Cody said softly.

"Jenny Baumgarten has a little sister and they fight all the time," Astor said.

"You're not going to fight with Lily Anne," I said, appalled at the thought. "She's just a baby."

"I don't like babies," Astor said, a stubborn expression growing on her face.

"You're going to like this one," I said, and even I was surprised at the tone of firm command in my voice. Astor looked at me uncertainly, and then at her brother, and I took advantage of their hesitation and seized the moment. "Come on," I said. "Inside." I put a hand on each one and herded them both through the doorway.

Not much had changed in the tableau; it was still Madonna and Child, with Lily Anne lying on her mother, who held her with one arm. Rita opened her eyes sleepily and smiled as we came in, but Lily Anne simply twitched a little and kept sleeping.

"Come meet your sister," Rita said.

"You both keep saying that," Astor said. She stood there looking peevish until Cody pushed past her and walked over to stand beside the bed. His head was just about level with Lily Anne's, and he studied her for a long moment with apparent interest. Astor finally dribbled over to stand next to him, seemingly more interested in Cody's reaction than in the baby. We all watched as Cody slowly put a finger out toward Lily Anne and very carefully touched her tiny curled-up fist.

"Soft," Cody said, and he stroked her hand gently. Lily Anne opened up her fist and Cody let her grasp his finger. She closed her hand again, holding on to Cody, and wonder of all, Cody smiled.

"She's holding me," he said.

"I wanna try," Astor said, and she tried to get around him to touch the baby.

"Wait your turn," he told her, and she took a half step back and jiggled impatiently until he finally took his finger away from Lily Anne's fist and let Astor have a turn. Astor moved right in to repeat what Cody had done, and she smiled, too, when Lily Anne clutched her finger, and the two of them took turns at this new game for the next fifteen minutes.

And for a whole half hour we didn't hear a single word about pizza.

S I X

I T WAS VERY ENJOYABLE FOR ME TO WATCH THE THREE children—*my* three children!—bonding with one another. But of course, any child could have told me that when you are enjoying yourself within sight of a grown-up it is only a matter of time before the fun ends. And Rita, as the only real grown-up in the room, did not let us down. After a short while she looked at the clock and then spoke up. "All right," she said, adding the dreaded words, "it's a school night."

Cody and Astor exchanged another of their eloquent looks, in which no sound was made but a great deal was said. "Mom," Astor said, "we're playing with our new sister." She said it as if it were in quotation marks, so Rita couldn't possibly object. But Rita was an old hand at the game, and she shook her head.

"You can play with Lily Anne more tomorrow," she said. "Right now, Dex—Daddy—has to take you home and put you to bed."

They both looked at me as if I had betrayed them, and I shrugged. "At least there's pizza," I said.

The kids were nearly as reluctant leaving the hospital as they had been going in, but somehow I managed to herd them out the door and into my car. Rather than repeat the horrors of the trip over and reel from the fumes of pizza all across town, I let Astor use my phone to order as we drove, and we had only been home for ten minutes or so when our dinner was delivered. Cody and Astor tore into the pizza as if they hadn't eaten in a month, and I felt lucky to get two small slices without losing an arm.

After we ate we watched TV until bedtime, and then plunged into the familiar rituals of brushing teeth, putting on pajamas, and climbing into bed. It was a little bit strange for me to perform the ceremony; I had witnessed it often enough, but Rita had always been the High Priestess of bedtime, and stupidly enough, I felt a little anxious that I might do some part of it wrong. But I kept thinking of what Rita had said in the hospital, when she had verbally stumbled and called me "Dex—Daddy." I truly was Dex-Daddy now, and all this was my turf. Soon I would perform the same rites with Lily Anne, guiding her, and her siblings, through the treacherous shoals of night time and safely into bed, and I found this an oddly comforting thought. In fact, it sustained me all the way up to the time when I finally had Cody and Astor tucked in and I reached for the light switch.

"Hey," Astor said. "You forgot prayers."

I blinked, suddenly very uncomfortable. "I don't know any prayers."

"You don't have to *say* it," she said. "Just listen."

I suppose that anyone with even a little bit of self-awareness will eventually feel like a complete hypocrite in the company of children, and this was my time. But I sat down with a very solemn face and listened to the singsong nonsense they recited every night. I was reasonably sure they didn't believe any of it any more than I did, but it was part of the procedure, and therefore it had to be done, and we all felt better when it was over with.

"All right," I said, standing up and turning off the light. "Good night."

"Good night, Dexter," Astor said.

"Night," Cody said softly.

In the normal course of things, I would probably sit down on the couch with Rita and watch another hour of television, just for the sake of disguise maintenance; but tonight there was no need to subject myself to the ordeal of pretending the programs were funny or interesting, so I didn't return to the living room. Instead, I went down the hall to the small room that Rita called my study. I had used it mostly for research connected to my hobby. There was a computer for me to track down those special individuals who deserved my attention, and there was a small closet where I could store a few harmless items like duct tape and fifty-pound-test fishing line.

There was also a small filing cabinet, which I kept locked, that contained a few folders holding notes on prospective playmates, and I sat at my little desk and opened this up. There wasn't a great deal there at the moment. I had two possibilities, but due to the press of events I had not really pursued either of them, and now I wondered if I ever would. I opened a folder and looked inside. There was a murderous pedophile who had twice been released because of a convenient alibi. I was fairly sure I could break the alibi and prove his guilt—not in the legal sense, of course, but enough to satisfy the strict standards my cop adoptive father, Harry, had poured into me. And there was a club in South Beach that was listed as the last place where several people had been seen before disappearing. Fang, it was called, a truly stupid name for a club. But in addition to the missing-persons reports, the club had turned up in a few INS documents. Apparently, they had an alarmingly high rate of turnover in their kitchen staff, and someone at INS suspected the dishwashers were not all running home to Mexico because the Miami water tasted wrong.

Illegal immigrants are a wonderfully easy target for predators. Even if they vanish there is no official complaint; family, friends, and employers don't dare complain to the police. And so they do vanish, in numbers that no one can really guess, although I believe it is high enough to raise a few eyebrows, even in Miami. And someone at this club was clearly taking advantage of the situation— probably, I thought, the manager, since he would have to be aware of the turnover. I flipped through my file and found his name: George Kukarov. He lived on Dilido Island, a very nice Beach address not too far from his club. A handy commute for work and play: balance the books, hire a DJ, kill the dishwasher, and home for dinner. I could practically see it—a lovely setup, so clean and convenient that it almost made me envious.

I set down the file for a moment and thought about it. George Kukarov: club manager, killer. It made perfect sense, the kind of sense that got Dexter's inner hound up on point and salivating, whining eagerly, quivering with the need to be out and after the fox. And the Passenger fluttered in agreement, stretching its wings with a sultry rustle that said, *Yes, he is the one. Tonight, together, Now . . .*

I could feel the moonlight coming through the window and pouring through my skin, slicing deep inside me, stirring the dark soup of my center and making these wonderful thoughts float up to the top, and as the smell of the simmering broth drifted up and out on the night air I could picture him taped to the table, squirming and curdling with the same sweaty terror he had sautéed from who knows how many, and I could see the happy knife go up—

But the thought of Lily Anne drifted in, and now the moonlight was not so bright, and the whisper of the blade faded. And the raven of Dexter's newborn self croaked, *Nevermore,* and the moon went behind the puffy silver cloud of Lily Anne, the knife went back in its sheath, and Dexter came back to his small suburban life as Kukarov skittered away into freedom and continued wickedness.

My Dark Passenger fought back, of course, and my rational mind sang harmony. *Seriously, Dexter,* it crooned with oh-so-sweet reason. *Could we really let all this predatory frolicking go unchallenged? Let monsters wander through the streets when it is well within our power to stop them in a final and very entertaining way? Could we really and truly ignore the challenge?*

And I thought again of the promise I had made in the hospital: I would be a better man. No more Demon Dexter—I was Dex-Daddy now, dedicated to the welfare of Lily Anne and my fledgling family. For the first time human life seemed rare and valuable, in spite of the fact that there was so much of it, and for the most part it consistently failed to prove its worth. But I owed it to Lily Anne to change my ways, and I would do it.

I stared at the file folder in my lap. It sang softly, seductively, pleading with me to sing along and make lovely music in the moonlight—but no. The grand opera of my brand-new child covered it over, overture swelling, and with a firm hand I fed the folder into the shredder and went to bed.

I got to work just a little bit later than usual the next morning, since I had to deliver Cody and Astor to school first. In the past this had always been Rita's task. Now, of course, everything was different; it was Year One of the Lily Anne Golden Epoch. I would be dropping the two older children at school for the foreseeable future, at least until Lily Anne was a little bit older and could safely ride around in a car seat. And if it meant that I no longer got to work with the first robins of the day, it seemed like a very small sacrifice.

The sacrifice seemed slightly larger, however, when I finally got to the office and found that someone other than Dutiful Dexter had actually brought in doughnuts—and they were all gone, leaving only a tattered and stained cardboard box. But who needs doughnuts when life itself is so sweet? I went to work anyway, with a smile in my heart and a song on my lips.

For once there was no frantic call for me to rush off to a crime scene, and I managed to get through a great deal of routine paperwork in the first ninety minutes of the day. I also called Rita, mostly to make sure that Lily Anne was doing well and had not been kidnapped by aliens, and when Rita had reassured me in a sleepy voice that all was well, I told her I would come to visit that afternoon.

I ordered some supplies, filed some reports, and got my whole professional life almost entirely squared away, and although that did not quite make up for the doughnuts, it nonetheless made me feel very pleased with myself; Dexter dislikes disorder.

I was still wrapped in my pink cloud of satisfaction a little before ten o'clock, when the phone on my desk rang. I stepped over and picked it up with a cheerful, "Hello, Morgan!" and was rewarded with the surly voice of my sister, Deborah.

"Where are you?" she said, rather unnecessarily, I thought. If

I was talking to her from a phone attached to my desk by a long wire, where would I be? Maybe cell phones really do destroy brain tissue.

"I'm right here, on the other end of the telephone," I said.

"Meet me in the parking lot," she said, and hung up before I could protest.

I found Deborah beside her motor pool car. She was leaning impatiently against the hood and scowling at me, so in a fit of strategic brilliance I decided to attack first. "Why do I have to meet you out here?" I said. "You have a perfectly good office, and it has chairs and air-conditioning."

She straightened up and reached for her keys. "My office is infested," she said.

"With what?"

"Deke," she said. "The smarmy dim-witted son of a bitch won't leave me alone."

"He can't leave you alone," I said. "He's your partner."

"He's making me nuts," she said. "He leans his ass on my desk and just sits there, waiting for me to fall all over him."

It was a striking image, Deborah falling up out of her desk chair and all over her new partner, but however vivid the picture, it made no sense to me. "Why would you fall all over your partner?"

She shook her head. "Maybe you noticed he is like *stupid* good-looking?" she said. "If you haven't, you're the only one in the entire fucking building. Including especially Deke."

I had noticed, of course, but I didn't see what his ridiculous good looks had to do with anything under discussion. "Okay," I said. "I noticed. So what?"

"So he thinks I'm going to throw myself at him, like every other chick he's ever met," she said. "Which is nauseating. He's dumber than a box of rocks, and he sits there on the corner of my desk flossing his perfect fucking teeth and waiting for me to tell him what to do and if I have to look at him for two seconds longer I'm going to blow his fucking head off. Get in the car," she said.

Deborah had never been one to disguise her real feelings, but even so, this was quite an outburst, and I just stood for a moment and watched her as she climbed into the car and started the engine. She revved it for a moment and then, to make sure I got the message that she was in a hurry, she hit the siren in a brief *whoop* that startled me out of my reverie and into the passenger seat. Before I even had the door closed she had put the car in gear and we were rolling out of the lot and onto the street.

"I don't think he's following us," I said as she hit the gas hard and accelerated out into traffic. Deborah didn't reply. She simply swerved around a flatbed truck piled high with watermelons and sped away from the station and her partner.

"Where are we going?" I asked, clinging for dear life to the armrest.

"The school," she said.

"What school?" I asked her, wondering if the roar of the engine had hidden an important part of our conversation.

"The rich kids' school Samantha Aldovar went to," she said. "What's it called, Ransom Everglades."

I blinked. It didn't seem like a destination that required this much haste, unless Deborah thought we were late for class, but here we were, hurtling through traffic at a dangerous pace. In any case, it seemed like good news that, if I survived the car trip over there, I would face nothing more life-threatening than a possible spitball. And of course, considering the school's economic and social status, it would almost certainly be a very high-quality spitball, which is always a consolation.

So I did no more than grit my teeth and hang on tightly as Deborah raced across town, turned onto LeJeune, and took us into Coconut Grove. A left on US 1, a right on Douglas, and a left on Poinciana to cut through to Main Highway, and we were at the school, in what would certainly be record time, if anybody kept track of that sort of thing.

We went through the coral rock gate and a guard stepped out to stop us. Deborah showed her badge and the guard leaned in to examine it before waving us through. We drove around behind a row of buildings and parked under a huge old banyan tree in a spot that said RESERVED FOR M. STOKES. Deborah shoved the car into park and climbed out, and I followed. We walked down a shaded walk-way and into sunlight, and I looked around at what we had all grown up thinking of as "the rich kids' school." The buildings were clean and looked new; the grounds were very well kept. The sun shone a little brighter here, the palm fronds swayed just a little more gently, and altogether it seemed like a very nice day to be a rich kid.

The administration building ran sideways across the center of the campus, with a breezeway in the middle, and we stopped at the reception area inside. They had us wait for the assistant something-or-other. I thought about our assistant principal in middle school. He had been very large, with a Cro-Magnon forehead that looked like a knuckle. And so I was somewhat surprised when a small and elegant woman came in and greeted us.

"Officers?" she said pleasantly. "I'm Ms. Stein. How can I help you?"

Deborah shook her hand. "I need to ask you some questions about one of your students," she said.

Ms. Stein raised an eyebrow to let us know that this was very unusual; the police did not come around asking about *her* students. "Come into my office," she said, and she led us a short way down the hall and into a room with a desk, a chair, and several dozen plaques and photographs on the walls. "Sit down, please," Ms. Stein said, and without even a glance at me Deborah took the one molded plastic chair opposite the desk, leaving me to look for a spot on the wall free from framed memories so I could at least lean in comfort.

"All right," Ms. Stein said. She settled into the chair behind the desk and looked at us with a polite but cool expression. "What's this about?"

"Samantha Aldovar is missing," Deborah said.

"Yes," Ms. Stein said. "We heard, of course."

"What kind of student is she?" Deborah asked.

Ms. Stein frowned. "I can't give you her grades, or anything like that," she said. "But she is a pretty good student. Above average, I would say."

"Does she have financial aid to come here?" Debs asked.

"That's confidential information, of course," Ms. Stein said, and Deborah gave her a hard look, but amazingly, Ms. Stein did not seem to wither. Perhaps she was used to intimidating glares from the wealthy parents. It was clearly an impasse, so I decided to help out.

"Does she take a lot of teasing from the other kids?" I said. "You know, about money or anything?"

Ms. Stein glanced at me and gave me a that's-not-really-funny half a smile. "I take it you think there might be a financial motive for her disappearance," she said.

"Does she have a boyfriend, that you know of?" Debs said.

"I don't really know," Ms. Stein said. "And if I did, I'm not at all sure I should tell you."

"Miss Stern," Debs said.

"It's *Stein*," Ms. Stein said.

Deborah waved that off. "We are not investigating Samantha Aldovar. We're investigating her *disappearance*. And if you stonewall us, you're keeping us from finding her."

"I don't really see—"

"We'd like to find her *alive*," Deborah said, and I was proud of the cold and hard way she said it; Ms. Stein actually turned pale.

"I don't . . ." she said. "The personal stuff, I really don't know. Perhaps I could get one of her friends to talk to you. . . ."

"That would be very helpful," Deborah said.

"I think she's closest to Tyler Spanos," Ms. Stein said. "But I would have to be present."

"Go get Tyler Spanos, Miss Stein," Deborah said.

Ms. Stein bit her lip and stood up, heading out the door without nearly as much cool composure as she'd had coming in. Deborah settled back in her chair and squirmed a little, as if trying to find a comfortable way to sit in it. There wasn't one. She gave up after a minute and sat up straight, crossing and uncrossing her legs impatiently.

My shoulder was sore, and I tried leaning on the other one. Several minutes went by; Deborah looked up at me two or three times, but neither one of us had anything to say.

Finally, we heard voices drifting in through the door, rising in pitch and volume. That lasted for about half a minute, and then there was relative quiet again. And after several long minutes in which Deborah recrossed her legs and I switched back to leaning on the original shoulder, Ms. Stein hurried back into her office. She was still pale, and she did not look happy.

"Tyler Spanos didn't come in today," Ms. Stein said. "Or yesterday. So I called her home." She hesitated, as if she were embarrassed, and Deborah had to urge her on.

"She's sick?" Debs said.

"No, she . . ." Again, Ms. Stein hesitated and chewed on her lip. "They . . . She was working on a class project with another student," she said at last. "They said she's, ah, in order to work on it . . . they said she's been staying with the other girl."

Deborah sat bolt upright. "Samantha Aldovar," she said, and it was not a question.

Ms. Stein answered it anyway. "Yes," she said. "That's right."

SEVEN

ETWEEN THE LAWS THAT ANY SCHOOL CAN CALL UPON to protect its students from official harassment and the clout that the parents and alumni of a school like Ransom Everglades could muster, it could have been very difficult for us to gather any information on what was now a double disappearance. But the school chose to take the high road and use the crisis as an exercise in community activism. They sat us down in the same office with the cluttered walls while Ms. Stein hustled around alerting teachers and administrators.

I looked around the room and noticed that there were still the same number of chairs. My leaning spot on the wall no longer seemed terribly inviting. But I decided that our significance in the grand scheme of things had gone up several notches when two of the school's students turned up missing, and, in short, I was now far too important to lean against the wall. And there was, after all, one more perfectly good chair in the room.

I had just settled into Ms. Stein's chair when my cell phone rang. I glanced at the screen, which told me that the call was from Rita. I answered. "Hello?"

"Dexter, hi, it's me," she said.

"That was my first guess," I told her.

"What? Oh. Anyway, listen," she said, which didn't seem necessary, since I was. "The doctor says I'm ready to come home, so can you come get us?"

"You're what?" I said, completely astonished. After all, Lily Anne had just been born yesterday.

"Ready," she repeated patiently. "We're ready to come home."

"It's much too soon," I said.

"The doctor says it's not," she said. "Dexter, I've done this before."

"But Lily Anne—she might catch something, or the car seat," I said, and I realized I was so filled with panic at the thought of Lily Anne leaving the safety of the hospital that I was talking like Rita.

"She's fine, Dexter, and so am I," she said. "And we want to come home, so please come pick us up, okay?"

"But Rita," I said.

"We'll be waiting," she said. "Bye." And she hung up before I could come up with any kind of rational reason for why she shouldn't leave the hospital yet. I stared at the phone for a moment, and then the thought of Lily Anne actually outside, in a world full of germs and terrorists, galvanized me into action. I slammed the cell phone into its holster and jumped to my feet. "I have to go," I said to my sister.

"Yeah, I got that," she said. She threw me her car keys. "Get back here as fast as you can."

I drove south in pure Miami style, which is to say fast, moving smoothly in and out of traffic as if there were no real lanes. I did not usually drive so flamboyantly; I have always felt that, contrary to the true spirit of our city's roads, getting there is just as important as maintaining a forceful image along the way. But the moves came naturally to me—I grew up here, after all, and the current situation seemed to call for all the haste and macho firmness I could muster. What was Rita thinking? And more, how had she persuaded the doctors to go along with it? It made no sense: Lily Anne was tiny, fragile, terribly vulnerable, and to send her out into cold hard life so quickly seemed to be complete and callous madness.

I stopped at home just long enough to grab the brand-new infant car seat. I had been practicing for weeks, wanting to be perfect with it when the time came—but the time had come too soon, and I found that my fingers, usually so deft, were icy blocks of clumsiness as I tried to fumble it into place with the seat belt. I couldn't get it through the slot in the back of the thing at all. I pushed, pulled, and finally cut my finger on the molded plastic and flung the whole thing down as I sucked at the cut.

This was supposed to be safe? How could this protect Lily Anne when it attacked me so aggressively? And even if it worked as it should—and nothing ever did—how could I keep Lily Anne safe in a world like ours? Especially so soon after birth—it was madness to send her home now, one day old. Typical medical arrogance and indifference; doctors think they're so smart, and all because they passed organic chemistry. But they don't know everything—they did not see what a father's heart so clearly told me. It was much too soon to fling Lily Anne out and into the cold cruel world, merely to save a few dollars for the insurance company. This could never end well.

I finally got the car seat in place, and then rushed on to the hospital. But contrary to my perfectly logical fears, when I arrived I did not find Rita standing outside the hospital, dodging bullets while Lily Anne played with used syringes in the trash. Instead, Rita was in a wheelchair in the lobby, a tightly wrapped bundle of baby in her arms. She looked up at me with a loose smile when I rushed in and said, "Dexter, hi, that was very fast."

"Oh," I said, trying to register the fact that somehow everything was fine. "Well, actually, I was sort of nearby."

"You're not going to drive us home that fast, are you?" she said. And before I could point out that I would never drive fast with Lily Anne in the car and in any case I thought she should stay here a little longer, a cheerful and hairy young man hustled over to us and grabbed at the handles on the back of Rita's wheelchair.

"Hey, here's Daddy," he said. "You folks ready to go?"

"Yes, that's— Thank you," Rita said.

The young man blinked and then said, "All righty then," and he stomped down to release the wheel brake and began to push Rita toward the door. And since at some point even I have to cooperate with the inevitable, I took a deep and resigned breath and followed along behind.

At the car I took Lily Anne from Rita and placed her carefully in the aggressive car seat. But for some reason, all the practicing I had done with Astor's old Cabbage Patch doll did not quite translate to the real baby; finally Rita had to help me get Lily Anne properly fastened in place. And so it was a completely helpless, all-thumbs Dexter who finally climbed behind the wheel and started the engine. And with many anxious glances in the mirror to make sure that the car seat had not burst into flames, I nosed the car out of the parking lot and onto the street.

"Don't drive too fast," Rita told me.

"Yes, dear," I said.

I drove slowly home—not slowly enough to risk the heavily armed outrage of my fellow citizens, but within spitting distance of the speed limit. Each blast of a horn, every thump of an overcranked car stereo, seemed new and threatening, and when I stopped at red lights I found myself glancing anxiously at the nearby cars to see if any automatic weapons were pointed our way. But somehow, miraculously, we got home safely. Undoing the straps of Lily Anne's car seat was not nearly as complicated as fastening them, and in no time at all I had her and Rita inside the house and comfortably ensconced on the couch.

I looked at the two of them, and suddenly everything seemed so different now, because for the first time they were here, at home, and just seeing my new baby in this old setting seemed to underline the fact that life was new and wonderful and fragile.

I dawdled shamelessly, soaking it up and reveling in the utter wonder of it all. I touched Lily Anne's toes, and ran the back of my finger over her cheeks; they were softer than anything I had ever felt before, and somehow I thought I could smell the pink newness of her right through my fingertips. Rita held the baby and slid into a smiling semidoze as I touched and sniffed and looked, until at last I glanced at the clock and saw how much time had passed, and I remembered that I was here in a borrowed car whose owner had been known to verbally behead people for far less.

"You're sure you're all right?" I asked Rita.

She opened her eyes and smiled, the ancient smile Leonardo did so well, mother with wonder child. "I've done this before, Dexter," she said. "We'll be fine."

"If you're sure," I said, with a brand-new sensitivity that I actually felt.

"I'm sure," she said, and very reluctantly, I left them there.

When I got back to the Ransom Everglades campus with Debs's car I found that she had been assigned a room in an old wooden building with a view of the bay, as a sort of temporary interrogation room. The Pagoda, as the building was called, perched on a bluff above the athletic field. It was a rickety old wooden building that didn't look like it could survive a single summer storm, and yet somehow it had stood long enough to become a historical landmark.

Deborah was talking to an exceedingly clean-cut young man when I came in, and she just glanced up at me and nodded without interrupting the boy's response. I settled into the chair next to her.

For the rest of the day, both students and faculty came into the rickety old building one at a time to tell us what they knew about Samantha Aldovar and Tyler Spanos. The students we saw were all bright, attractive, and polite, and the teachers all seemed to be smart and dedicated, and I began to appreciate the benefits of a private school education. If only I'd had the opportunity to attend a place like this, who knows what I might have become? Perhaps instead of a mere blood-spatter analyst who slunk away at night to kill without conscience, I could have become a doctor, or a physicist, or even a senator who slunk away at night to kill without conscience. It was terribly sad to think of all my wasted potential.

But private education is expensive, and it had been far beyond Harry's means—and even if he could have afforded it, I doubt that Harry would have gone for it. He had always been wary of elitism, and he believed in all of our public institutions. Even public school—or perhaps especially public school, since it taught a brand of survival skills he knew we would need.

It was clearly a set of skills the two missing girls could have used. By the time Debs and I finished the interviews, around five-thirty, we had learned some very interesting things about both of them, but nothing that suggested they could survive in the wilds of Miami without a credit card and an iPhone.

Samantha Aldovar remained a little bit of a puzzle, even to those who thought they knew her well. The students were aware that she got financial aid, but it seemed to be no big deal to anybody. They all said she was pleasant, quiet, good at math, and had no boyfriend. No one could think of any reason why she would stage her own disappearance. No one could remember ever seeing her hanging around with any kind of disreputable character—except Tyler Spanos.

Tyler was apparently a true wild child, and on the face of things, the friendship between the two girls was extremely unlikely. Where Samantha got a ride to and from school with her mother in a four-year-old Hyundai, Tyler drove her own car—a Porsche. While Samantha was quiet and shy, Tyler seemed to be the original Good Time Charlene, a perpetual loud party just looking for a place to happen. She did not have a boyfriend only because she could not limit herself to one boy at a time.

And yet a close friendship had developed over the last year or so and the two girls were almost always together at lunch, after school, and on weekends. Not only was this puzzling, it was the one thing that bothered Deborah more than any other. She had calmly listened and asked questions, put out a BOLO on Tyler's Porsche, and (with a shudder) sent her partner, Deke, to talk to the Spanos family, and none of these things had caused so much as a ripple on the face of the Sea of Deborah. But the strange friendship between the two girls had, for some reason, caused her to come up on point like a cocker spaniel sniffing steak.

"It makes no fucking sense," she said.

"They're teenagers," I reminded her. "They're not supposed to make sense."

"Wrong," Deborah said. "Some things *always* make sense, especially with teenagers. Nerds hang with nerds; jocks and cheerleaders hang with jocks and cheerleaders. That never changes."

"Perhaps they have some kind of secret mutual interest," I suggested, glancing casually at my watch, which told me that it was very close to time for me to go home.

"I'd bet on it," said Debs. "And I'd bet that if we find it, we find out where they are."

"Nobody else here seems to know what it might be," I said, even though I was actually trying to construct a graceful exit line.

"What the hell is wrong with you?" Deborah said abruptly.

"Excuse me?"

"You keep squirming around like you have to pee," she said.

"Oh, um, actually," I said, "it's almost time for me to go. I have to pick up Cody and Astor before six."

My sister stared at me for what seemed like a long time. "I never would have believed it," she said at last.

"Believed what?"

"That you'd be married, kids, you know. A family man, with all you got going on."

And by that I knew she meant my darker side, my former role as Dexter the Avenger, the lone blade in the moonlight. She had found out about my alter ego, and had apparently become reconciled with it—and just in time for me to abandon the persona. "Well," I said, "I don't suppose I would have believed it either. But . . ." I shrugged. "Here I am with a family."

"Yeah," she said, and she looked away. "And before me."

I watched her face working to rearrange itself back to her usual mask of perpetual grumpy authority, but it took several moments, and in the interval she looked shockingly vulnerable.

"Do you love her?" she said suddenly, swinging back to face me, and I blinked with surprise. Such a blunt and personal question was very unlike Deborah, which was one reason we got along so well. "Do you love Rita," she repeated, leaving me no wiggle room whatsoever.

"I . . . don't know," I answered carefully. "I'm, uh, used to her."

Deborah stared and then shook her head. "*Used* to her," she said. "Like she's an easy chair or something."

"Not that easy," I said, trying to inject a little levity into what had suddenly become a very unsettling conversation.

"Do you even feel love at all?" she demanded. "I mean, can you?"

I thought of Lily Anne. "Yes," I said. "I think so."

Deborah watched my face for several long seconds, but there was really not much to see, and she finally turned away and looked out through the old wooden window frame at the bay. "Shit," she said. "Go home. Go get your kids and hang out with your easy-chair wife."

I had not been human for very long, but even so, I knew something was not quite right in the Land of Deborah and I could not leave her on that note. "Debs," I said. "What's wrong?"

I saw her neck muscles tense, but she continued to look away, out over the water. "All this family shit," she said. "With these two girls and their fucked-up families. And your family with fucked-up you. It's never what it should be, and it's never right but everybody gets it except me." She took a deep breath and shook her head. "And I really want it." She swung back at me with ferocity. "And no goddamn jokes about the biological clock, all right?"

To be completely honest, which I am when I have to be, I was far too deeply shocked by Deborah's behavior for any jokes, whether about clocks or anything else. But joke or no, I knew I had to say something, and I cast about for the right thing and could only come up with a question about Kyle Chutsky, her live-in boyfriend of several years. I had seen the approach on a daytime drama a few years back. I liked to study them for clues on how to act in ordinary situations, and it looked like that was going to pay off here. "Is everything okay with Kyle?" I said.

She snorted, but her face softened. "Fucking Chutsky. Thinks he's too old and beat-up and useless for a nice young thing like me. Keeps saying I can do better. And when I say maybe I don't want to do better, he just shakes his head and looks sorrowful."

It was all very interesting, a truly riveting look into the life of someone who had been a human being much longer than I had, but I was all out of ideas for constructive commentary, and I felt very much the pressure of the clock—the one on my wrist, not the biological one. So, floundering about for something to say that would be properly comforting and yet hint at my need for immediate departure, all I could come up with was, "Well, I'm sure he means well."

Deborah stared at me long enough to make me wonder if I had really said the right thing. Then she sighed heavily and turned to face out the window again. "Yeah," she said. "I'm sure he means well, too." And she looked out at the bay and didn't say anything but, worse than any words she could have uttered, she actually sighed.

This was a side of my sister I had not seen before, and it was not a side I wanted to see a great deal more of. I was used to Deborah being full of sound and fury, signifying arm punches. To see her soft and vulnerable and roiling with self-pity was unsettling in the extreme. Even though I knew I should say something comforting, I had no idea where to begin, and so I stood there awkwardly, until finally the need to leave was stronger than my sense of obligation.

"I'm sorry, Debs," I said, and oddly enough, I was. "I have to get the kids now."

"Yeah," she said without turning around. "Go get your kids."

"Um," I said, "I need a ride, back to my car."

She turned slowly away from the window and looked over at the building's door, where Ms. Stein was hovering. Then she nodded and stood up. "All right," she said. "We're done here." She walked past me, paused only to thank Ms. Stein with flat politeness, and led the way back to her car in silence.

The silence lasted almost all the way to my car and it was not very comfortable. I felt like I should say something, lift the mood a bit, but my first two attempts fell so flat that I stopped trying. Debs pulled into the parking lot at work and stopped beside my car, staring straight ahead through the windshield with the same look of unhappy introspection she'd been wearing for the whole trip. I watched her for a moment, but she didn't look back.

"All right," I said at last. "See you tomorrow."

"What's it like?" she said, and I paused with the door half-open.

"What's *what* like?" I said.

"When you held your baby for the first time," she said.

·I didn't have to think very hard to answer that. "Amazing," I said. "Absolutely wonderful. It's not like anything else in the world."

She looked at me, and I couldn't tell whether she was going to hug me or hit me, but she didn't do either, and finally she just shook her head, slowly. "Go get your kids," she said. I waited for a second, to see if she would say anything else, but she didn't.

I got out of the car and as she drove slowly away I stood and watched, trying to fathom what was going on with my sister. But it was clearly something far too complicated for a newly minted human, so I shrugged it off, got into my car, and went to get Cody and Astor.

EIGHT

TRAFFIC WAS HEAVY AS I DROVE SOUTH ON OLD CUTLER
Road to pick up Cody and Astor, but for some reason everyone seemed to be very polite in this part of town tonight.
A man driving a large red Hummer even paused to let me in when
the lanes merged and I had to get over, which I had never seen
before. It made me wonder if perhaps terrorists had slipped something into the Miami water system to make us all soft and lovable.
First I had resolved to quit my Dark Ways; then Debs had thrown a
fit of near-weeping—and now a Hummer driver in rush hour was
polite and thoughtful. Could this be the Apocalypse?

But I saw no flaming angels on the remainder of the drive to the
park where Cody and Astor were interred, and once again I got
there just before six o'clock. The same young woman was waiting
by the door with Cody and Astor, jiggling her keys and practically
dancing with impatience. She very nearly flung the children at me
and then, with a mechanical smile that was not in the same league
as one of my fakes, she vaulted for her car at the far end of the parking lot.

I loaded Cody and Astor into the backseat of my car and

climbed behind the wheel. They were relatively silent, even Astor, and so, in my role of new human father I decided I should open them up a little bit. "Did everybody have a good day?" I said with immense synthetic good cheer.

"Anthony is such an asshole," Astor said.

"Astor, you shouldn't use that word," I told her, mildly shocked.

"Even Mom says that word when she's driving," she said. "And anyway, I heard it on the radio in her car."

"Well, you still shouldn't use it," I said. "It's a bad word."

"You don't have to talk me to like that," she said. "I'm ten years old."

"That's not old enough to use that word," I said. "No matter how I talk to you."

"So you don't care what Anthony did?" she said. "You just want to make sure I don't use that word?"

I took a deep breath and made a special effort not to ram the car in front of me. "What did Anthony do?" I said.

"He said I wasn't hot," Astor said. "Because I don't have any boobs."

I felt my mouth open and close a few times, all by itself, and just in time I remembered that I still needed to breathe. I was clearly in far over my head, but just as clearly I had to say something. "Well, I-I, um, ah," I said, quite distinctly. "I mean, very few of us do have boobs at ten."

"He's such a butt-head," she said darkly, and then, in a very syrupy-sweet tone, she added, "Can I say butt-head, Dexter?"

I opened my mouth again to stammer something or other but before I could utter a single meaningless syllable Cody spoke up. "Somebody's following us," he said.

Out of reflex I glanced in the rearview mirror. In this traffic, it was impossible for me to tell if somebody was, in fact, following us. "Why do you say that, Cody?" I asked. "How can you tell?"

In the mirror I could see him shrug. "Shadow Guy," he said.

I sighed again. First Astor with her barrage of forbidden language, and now Cody with his Shadow Guy. Obviously, I was in for one of those memorable evenings parents have now and then. "Cody, the Shadow Guy can be wrong sometimes," I said.

He shook his head. "Same car," he said.

"Same as what?"

"It's the car from the hospital parking lot," Astor interpreted. "The red one, where you said the guy wasn't looking at us but he really was. And now he's following us even though you think he isn't."

I like to think I am a reasonable man, even in unreasonable situations, like most of those involving kids. But at this point, I felt I had let unreality intrude just a little too far, and a small lesson was called for. Besides, if I was going to follow my resolve to cross over to the sunny side of the street, I had to start weaning them away from their dark imaginations at some point, and this was as good a time as any.

"All right," I said. "Let's see if he really is following us."

I moved into the left lane and signaled for a turn. Nobody followed us. "Do you see anybody?" I said.

"No," Astor said, very grumpily.

I turned left down a street beside a strip mall. "Is anybody following us now?"

"No," said Astor.

I accelerated down the street and turned right. "How about now?" I called cheerfully. "Anybody behind us?"

"Dexter," Astor grumbled.

I pulled over in front of a small and ordinary house much like ours, putting two wheels on the grass and my foot on the brake. "And now? Anybody following us?" I said, trying not to gloat audibly at making my point so dramatically.

"No," Astor hissed.

"Yes," Cody said.

I turned around in the seat to scold him, and stopped dead. Because through the rear window of the car I could see that a few hundred feet away, a car was nosing slowly toward us. There was just enough light from the setting sun to see a quick flash of red color from the small car, and then it was crawling toward us through the shadows of the tree-lined street. And as if awakened by those shadows, the Dark Passenger carefully uncoiled and spread out its wings and hissed a warning.

Without thinking I stepped down hard on the gas, even before I turned back around to face front, and I left a small patch of torn grass behind me and narrowly missed plowing into a mailbox as I looked forward again. The car skidded slightly as it regained the pavement. "Hold on," I told the kids, and with some something far too close to panic I raced down the street and turned right, back toward US 1.

I could see the other car behind me, but I was well ahead by the time I got back to the highway, and I turned right quickly into heavy traffic. I began to breathe again, just once or twice, as I powered across three lanes of rapidly moving cars and into the far left lane. I gunned it through a light just as it changed to red, and sped up the street for a half mile before I saw an opening in the oncoming traffic and screeched through a left-hand turn and down another quiet residential street. I drove through two intersections and then turned left again so that I was now running parallel to US 1. The street was dark and quiet and there was no sign of anything at all behind us now, not even a bicycle.

"All right," I said. "I think we lost him."

In the mirror I saw Cody staring out the back window, and he turned around and caught my eye, and nodded.

"But who was it, Dexter?" Astor said.

"Just some random lunatic," I said, with more reassurance in my voice than I actually felt. "Some people get off on scaring people they don't even know."

Cody frowned. "Same guy," he said. "From the hospital."

"You can't know that," I said.

"Can," he said.

"It's just a coincidence. Two different crazy people," I told him.

"Same," he said dismissively.

"Cody," I said. But I could feel the adrenaline draining out of me and I really didn't want an argument, so I let it go at that. He would learn as he grew that the greater Miami area was filled with a varied and impressive collection of wackos and predators, and many that were half of each. There was no way to know why someone had followed us, and it didn't really matter. Whoever it was, they were gone now.

Just to play it safe I continued to drive on the side streets all the way home, in case our follower was watching the highway. Besides, with the sun going down it was easier to see somebody behind us in darker house-lined streets, away from the bright orange glow of the lights along US 1. And there was nobody to see; once or twice headlights flared in the rearview mirror, and each time it was simply a homeward-bound commuter, turning down his own street and parking in his driveway.

We came finally to the cross street that took us to our own little bungalow. I turned onto it and edged up to US 1 carefully, looking in all directions. There was nothing to see but traffic, and none of it looked sinister, and when the light finally changed to green I crossed the highway and drove through the two more turns that took us to our street.

"All right," I said, as our little patch of heaven heaved into sight. "Let's not say anything about this to your mom. She'll just worry. Okay?"

"Dexter," Astor said, and she leaned forward against the back of the front seat, pointing ahead to our house. I slid my gaze along her outstretched arm and hit the brakes hard enough to rattle my teeth.

A small red car was parked directly in front of the house, nose pointed at us. The lights were on and the motor was running and I could not see inside it, but I did not need to see in order to feel the rapid beat of dark leathery wings and the angry hiss of a wide-awake Passenger.

"Stay here, doors locked," I told the kids, and I handed Astor my cell phone. "If anything happens call nine-one-one."

"Can I drive away if you're dead?" Astor said.

"Just stay here," I said, and I took a deep breath, gathering the darkness—

"I can drive," Astor said, unsnapping her seat belt and lurching forward.

"Astor," I said sharply, and there was an echo of the other voice, the cold commander, in my own. "Stay put," I said, and she settled back into her own seat almost meekly.

I got out slowly and faced the other car. There was no way to see inside, and no sign of anything dangerous; just a small red car with the lights on and the engine running. I felt the equivalent of a long drumroll from the Passenger—ready for action but no hint of what; it could be flaming chain saws; it could be a pie in the face.

I stepped toward the car, trying to plan what to do, which was impossible because I did not know what they wanted, or even who they were. It was no longer believable that it was merely a random crazy—not if he knew where I lived. But who was it? Who had any reason to act like this? Among the living, I mean, because there were plenty of former victims who might have loved to come after me, but they were all far beyond any sort of action at all, other than decomposition.

I walked forward trying to be ready for everything, another impossibility. Still no sign of life in the other car, and nothing at all from the Passenger except a puzzled and cautious flutter of wings.

And when I was about ten feet away the driver's window slithered down and I stopped in my tracks. For a long moment nothing happened, and then a face came out the window, a familiar face, wearing a bright fake smile.

"Wasn't that fun?" the face said. "When were you going to tell me I'm an uncle?"

It was my brother, Brian.

N I N E

I HAD NOT SEEN MY BROTHER SINCE THAT MEMORABLE evening several years earlier when we had met, for the first time as adults, in a storage container at Port of Miami, and he had offered me a knife so I could assist him in the vivisection of his chosen playmate. As it had happened, I had not been able to bring myself to do so, odd as it sounds. That may be because he had chosen Deborah, and Harry's long-dead hand had squeezed my hypothetical soul so strongly I was unable to hurt her—even though she was not my blood relation, and Brian was.

In fact, he was my only biological relative, as far as I knew, although considering the little I had uncovered about our round-heeled mother, anything was possible. For all I knew, I could have a dozen half brothers and sisters living in a trailer park in Immokalee. At any rate, far more important than the bond of blood we shared was—well, another kind of bond of blood altogether. Because Brian had been forged in the selfsame fire that had turned me into Dexter the Dark, and it had also given him an inarguable need to slice and dice. Unfortunately, he had grown to maturity without the restraints of Harry's guiding Code, and he was very happy to practice his art on anyone, provided they were youngish and female. He had been working his way through a string of Miami prostitutes when our paths had first crossed.

The last time I had seen him, he had been staggering off into the night with a bullet in his side, the only head start I could give him, considering that Deborah was there and somewhat anxious to speak with him in an official capacity. Apparently he'd found medical attention, because he looked quite healthy now; a little older, of course, but he still looked a lot like me. He was very close to my height and build, and even his features looked like a crude and battered imitation of my own, and the bright empty mockery I remembered was in his eyes as he looked up at me from his little red car.

"Did you get my flowers?" he asked, and I nodded, moving forward.

"Brian," I said, leaning onto the car. "You look good."

"As do you, dear brother," he said, still smiling. He reached out and patted my stomach. "I believe you've put on a little weight— your *wife* must be a good cook."

"She is," I said. "She takes very good care of me. Body and, um, soul."

We chuckled together at my use of that fairy-tale word, and I thought again how good it was to know somebody who really understood me. I'd had a brief and tantalizing glimpse of this all-accepting bond on that one night we were together, and now I realized just how much I had given up—and perhaps he did, too, because here he was.

But of course, nothing is ever that simple, especially not with us residents of the Dark Tower, and I felt a small flutter of suspicion. "What are you doing here, Brian?"

He shook his head with pretended self-pity. "Already feeling suspicious? Of your own flesh and blood?"

"Well," I said, "I mean, really. Um, considering . . . ?"

"True enough," he said. "Why don't you invite me in and we'll talk?"

The suggestion was like sudden ice water flung on my neck. Invite him in? Into my house, where my other carefully separate life lay nestled in its bed of clean white cotton? Let a dribble of blood spatter onto the pristine damask of my disguise? It was a terrible idea and it sent a surge of horrid discomfort right through me. Besides, I had never even mentioned to anyone that I had a brother, and in this case the "anyone" was Rita, and she would certainly wonder at the omission. How could I invite him in—into the world of Rita's pancakes, Disney DVDs, and clean sheets? Invite him inside, by all that was unholy, to the Inner Sanctum of Lily Anne? It was not right. It was sacrilegious, a blasphemous violation of . . .

Of what? Wasn't he my very own brother? Shouldn't that cover over everything else in a blanket of sanctimony? Surely I could trust him—but with everything? With my secret identity, my Fortress of Solitude—and even Lily Anne, my Kryptonite?

"Don't drool, brother," Brian said, interrupting my flight of panicked musing. "It's so very unbecoming."

Without thinking, I dabbed at the corner of my mouth with my sleeve, still floundering desperately for some kind of coherent response. But before I could even arrive at a single syllable, a car horn bleated nearby, and I turned to see Astor's peevish face glaring through the windshield of my car. Cody's head was right next to hers, silent and watchful. I could see Astor squirming and mouthing the words, *Come on, Dexter!* She beeped again.

"Your stepchildren," Brian said. "Charming little sprats, I'm sure. May I meet them?"

"Um," I said, with really impressive authority.

"Come on, Dexter," Brian said. "I won't *eat* them." He gave a strange little laugh that did nothing to reassure me, but at the same time I realized that he was, after all, my brother—and Cody and Astor were far from helpless, as they had shown several times. Surely there could be no harm in allowing them to meet their, ah, stepuncle?

"Okay," I said, and I waved back at Astor, beckoning her to come and join us. With very commendable speed they both scrambled out of the car and came over to us, allowing Brian just barely enough time to clamber out of his car and stand beside me.

"Well, well," he said. "What handsome children!"

"He's handsome," Astor said. "I'm just cute until I grow my boobs, and then I'm going to be hot."

"I'm sure you are," Brian said, and he turned his attention to Cody. "And you, little man," he said. "Are you . . ." And he trickled to a halt as he met Cody's gaze.

Cody stood looking up at Brian, his feet spread apart and his hands hanging stiffly at his sides. Their eyes locked together and I could hear the leathery unfolding of wings between them, the dark and sibilant greeting of twin interior specters. There was a look of belligerent wonder on Cody's face, and he just stared for a long moment and Brian stared back, and finally Cody looked at me. "Like me," he said. "Shadow Guy."

"Amazing," Brian said, and Cody turned back to meet his gaze. "Brother, what have you done?"

"Brother?" Astor said, clearly demanding equal time in the spotlight. "He's your *brother*?!"

"Yes, my brother," I said to Astor, and added to Brian, "I didn't do anything. Their biological father did."

"He used to beat us up really bad," Astor said matter-of-factly.

"I see," Brian said. "Thus supplying the Traumatic Event that spawns us all."

"I guess so," I said.

"And what have you done with this wonderful untapped potential?" Brian said, his eyes still on Cody.

I was now in very uncomfortable territory, considering that my plan had been to train them in Harry's Way, a course I was now just as determined to avoid, and I found that I really didn't want to talk openly about this, not at this point in time. "Let's go inside," I said. "Would you like a cup of coffee or something?"

Brian turned slow and empty eyes away from Cody and onto me. "I'd be delighted, brother," he said, and with another glance at the children, he turned and walked toward my front door.

"You never said you had a *brother*," Astor said.

"Like *us*," Cody added.

"You never asked," I said, feeling strangely defensive about the whole thing.

"You should have said," Astor said, and Cody looked at me with an equal, unspoken accusation, as if I had violated some basic trust.

But Brian was already standing at the front door, so I turned away and followed. They came along behind, clearly fuming, and it occurred to me that this would not be the last time I heard similar words. What would I say to Rita when she asked the same thing, as she certainly would? I mean, of course I had never told them I had a brother. Considering that Brian was just like me but without any of Harry's restraints on him, a kind of Dexter Unbound, what could I possibly say? The only really appropriate introduction would be, "This is my brother—run for your life!"

And in any case, I had not anticipated ever seeing him again after that one brief and dizzying encounter. I had not even known if he would survive. He clearly had—but why had he come back? I would have thought it made more sense to stay far away; Deborah would certainly remember him. Theirs had not been the sort of encounter one forgets, and she was, after all, exactly the kind of person who took great professional satisfaction from arresting people like him.

I knew very well, too, that he had not come back because of any kind of sentimental feelings for me, either. He did not have sentimental feelings. So why was he here, and what did I do about it?

Brian reached the front door and turned to look at me, raising one eyebrow. Apparently, the first thing I had to do about it was to open the door and let him in. I did; he gave me a small bow and entered, and Cody and Astor trooped in after him.

"What a lovely home," Brian said, looking around the living room. "So very *homey*."

There were heaps of DVDs lying across the tattered couch, and a pile of socks on the floor, and two empty pizza boxes on the coffee table. Rita had been in the hospital for nearly three days, and naturally enough she had not had the energy to clean up since she returned this morning. And although I do prefer a neat environment, I had been far too distracted myself to do anything about it, and the place really was not at its best. In fact, it was a frightful mess.

"I'm sorry," I said to Brian. "We've been, um—"

"Yes, I know, the blessed event," he said. "Into each life some domesticity must fall."

"What does that mean?" Astor demanded.

"Dexter?" Rita called from the bedroom. "Is that— Is somebody with you?"

"It's me," I said.

"His *brother* is here," Astor said belligerently.

There was a pause, replaced by the sound of panicked rustling of some kind, and then Rita came out, still brushing at her hair with one hand. "Brother?" she said. "But that's— Oh." And she stumbled to a halt, staring at Brian.

"Dear lady," Brian said with knife-edged mocking joy, "how lovely you are. Dexter always did have an eye for beauty."

Rita fluttered her hands at her head. "Oh, my God, I'm such a mess," she said. "And the house is— But, Dexter, you never even said you had a brother, and this is—"

"It certainly is," Brian said. "And I apologize for the inconvenience."

"But your *brother*," Rita repeated. "And you never said."

I felt my jaw muscles moving, but no matter how carefully I listened, I did not hear myself saying anything. Brian watched me with real enjoyment for a moment before he finally spoke up.

"I'm afraid it's all my fault," he said at last. "Dexter thought I was long dead."

"That's right," I said, feeling like one of the Three Stooges picking up a bobbled line cue.

"Still," Rita said, still fussing absently with her hair. "I mean, you never— You said you were— I mean, how could you not . . . ?"

"It's very painful," I said tentatively. "I don't like to talk about it."

"Still," Rita repeated, and even though there was no guidebook for the territory we had entered, I knew I had not heard the last of this. So, hoping to maneuver us back onto firmer terrain, I blurted out the only words I could find.

"Could we have a cup of coffee?" I said.

"Oh," Rita said, her peevishness changing at once to a look of startled guilt. "I'm sorry—would you like— I mean, yes, here, sit down." And she moved to the couch and removed the assorted litter that blocked it with a rapid series of precision moves that did us all proud, domestically speaking. "There," she said, piling the armful of clutter beside the couch and waving at Brian. "Please—sit down, and— Oh! I'm Rita."

Brian stepped forward with brittle gallantry and took her hand. "My name is Brian," he said. "But please sit down, dear lady; you should not be on your feet so soon."

"Oh," Rita said, and she was actually blushing. "But the coffee, I ought to—"

"Surely Dexter is not so hopeless that he can't make coffee?" Brian said, arching one eyebrow at her, and she giggled.

"I suppose we'll never know unless we let him try," she said, and she actually simpered at him as she sank onto the couch. "Dexter, would you please— It's three scoops for six cups, and you put the water into the—"

"I think I can manage," I said, and if I sounded a little surly, who had a better right? And as Brian sat beside my wife, on my couch, I stalked into the kitchen to make coffee. And as I clattered through the motions of filling the pot from the sink and pouring the water into the machine, I heard from deep inside a quiet settling of bat wings as the Passenger stood down. But from the icy coils of Dexter's allegedly powerful brain I heard only stammers of confusion and uncertainty. The ground seemed to be turning under my feet; I felt exposed and threatened and assailed by all the wicked armies of the night.

Why had my brother returned? And why did that make me feel so terribly insecure?

T E N

A FEW MINUTES LATER I HAD POURED THE COFFEE INTO mugs and set them on a tray with the sugar bowl and two spoons. I carried it carefully to the doorway into the living room, and stopped dead. The picture I saw was one of domestic bliss, charming in every aspect—except for the fact that it did not include me. My brother had settled onto the couch with Rita as if he had always lived there. Cody and Astor stood a few feet away looking at him with fascination, and I froze in the kitchen door and stared at the tableau with a growing sense of discomfort. Seeing Brian here, on my couch, Rita leaning toward him as she spoke, and Cody and Astor watching—it was just too weirdly surreal. The images did not quite mesh, but they were very unsettling, as if you had entered a cathedral for high mass and found people copulating on the altar.

Brian, of course, seemed completely undisturbed. I suppose it is one of the great advantages of being incapable of feeling things; he looked as comfortable on my couch as if he had grown there. And just to emphasize the fact that he apparently belonged there more than I did, he saw me lurking with the coffee and waved a hand at the chair next to the couch.

"Sit down, brother," he said. "Make yourself at home." Rita jerked upright, and Cody and Astor swung their heads to me and watched as I approached with the coffee.

"Oh!" Rita said, and to me she sounded a little guilty. "You forgot the cream, Dexter." And before anyone could speak she was gone into the kitchen.

"You keep calling him *brother*," Astor said to Brian. "How come you don't use his name?"

Brian blinked at her, and I felt a surge of kinship. It wasn't just me—Astor had reduced him to mere eye movements, too. "I don't know," he said. "I suppose it's because the relationship is such a surprise to both of us."

Cody and Astor swung their heads to face me in perfect unison.

"Yes," I said, and it was very true. "A complete surprise."

"Why?" Astor said. "Lots of people have brothers."

I had no idea how to explain, and I stalled by putting down the tray and sinking into the chair. And once again it was Brian and not me who jumped into the silence.

"Lots of people have families, too," he said. "Like you two. But brother—Dexter and I did not. We were, ah, abandoned. Under very unpleasant circumstances." He gave her the bright smile again, and I am quite sure I only imagined that there was some real glint behind it this time. "Especially me."

"What does that mean?" Astor said.

"I was an orphan," Brian said. "A foster child. I grew up in a whole bunch of different homes where they didn't like me and didn't really want me, but they were paid to keep me."

"Dexter had a home," Astor said.

Brian nodded. "Yes, he did. And he has another one now."

I felt cold talons on my back and did not know why. Surely there was no threat in Brian's words, but still—

"You two need to realize how very lucky you have been," Brian said. "To have a home—and even somebody who understands you."

He looked at me and smiled again. "And now, *two* somebodies." And he gave them a horrible fake wink.

"Does that mean you're going to hang around with us?" Astor said.

Brian's smile grew a fraction. "I just might," he said. "What else is *family* for?"

Brian's words jerked me into action, and I leaned toward him as if somebody had burned me on the back. "Are you sure?" I said, and I felt the words turn into cold and clumsy lumps in my mouth. Nonetheless, I stammered on. "I mean, you know, um, it's wonderful to see you and all, but—there's a certain amount of risk involved."

"What risk?" Astor demanded.

"I can be very careful," Brian said to me, "as we both know."

"It's just, you know, Deborah might come around here," I said.

"She hasn't come around for the last two weeks," he said. And he raised a mocking eyebrow at me. "Has she?"

"How do you know that?" Astor said. "Why does it matter if Aunt Deborah comes around?"

It was very interesting to hear that "two weeks," and know exactly how long Brian had been watching us, and we both ignored Astor's interruption because it quite clearly mattered a great deal. If Deborah were to see Brian here, we would both be in unspeakably hot water. But what Brian said was true: Deborah did not come around very often lately. I hadn't really thought about why that might be, but perhaps in light of her recent meltdown on the subject of my having a family before she did, I could assume that she found it painful in some way.

Luckily for me, I was spared another lesson in family dynamics, as Rita came bustling in bearing a small milk pitcher, and even a plate of cookies. "There," she said, putting down her load and arranging things in a more perfect display. After all, she was Rita the Mighty, absolute Ruler of the Domestic and All Things Kitchen. "We had some of that Jamaican blend left that you said was so good, Dexter. Did you use that?" I nodded mutely as she moved things around on the coffee table. "Because after all, you liked it so much, maybe your *brother* would like it, too." And she loaded the word "brother" with so much extra weight that I was very sure I had not heard the last of it.

"It smells absolutely wonderful," Brian said. "I can already feel myself perking up."

Brian's words were so patently fake that I was sure Rita would turn on him with a raised eyebrow and a curled lip. Instead, she actually blushed a little as she sank back onto the couch and pushed a cup toward him. "Do you take milk and sugar?" she said.

"Oh, no," Brian said, smiling right at me. "I like it very dark."

Rita turned the cup's handle toward him and placed a small napkin beside it. "Dexter likes a little sugar," she said.

"Dear lady," Brian gushed, "I would say he's found it."

I don't know what terrible suffering had turned Brian into the Fountain of Phoniness I now saw sitting on my couch, but I can only believe it was a very good thing that he was incapable of feeling shame. I have always prided myself on being smooth and somewhat plausible; he clearly never learned either. His compliments were coarse, obvious, and quite clearly fake. And as the evening went on—through more coffee, then a pizza, because naturally my *brother* had to stay for dinner—he heaped it on higher and deeper. I kept waiting for the heavens to open up and shatter him with lightning, or at least for some great voice to urge him to put a sock on it, as Harry would have said. But the more outrageous Brian's flattery and flummery got, the happier it made Rita. Even Cody and Astor simply watched him in an admiring silence.

And to cap off my discomfort, when Lily Anne began to fuss in the next room, Rita brought her into the living room and put her on display. Brian obliged with the most exorbitant display yet, praising her toes, her nose, her tiny perfect fingers, and even the way she cried. And Rita absolutely ate it up, smiling, nodding, and even unbuttoning her shirt to feed Lily Anne right there in front of us all.

Altogether, it was one of the most uncomfortable evenings I had spent since—well, quite honestly, since the last time I had seen

Brian. It was all made worse because there was truly nothing I could say or do—and this was partly because I did not know what I found objectionable. After all, as Rita took such pleasure in saying at least three times, we were all family. Why shouldn't we sit around together and trade cheerful lies? Isn't that what families do?

When Brian finally got up to go at around nine o'clock, Rita and the kids were all thrilled with their new relative, Uncle Brian. Their old relative—battered and anxious Daddy Dexter—was apparently the only one who felt nervous, uneasy, and uncertain. I walked Brian to the front door, where Rita gave him a large hug and told him to please come around as often as possible, and Cody and Astor both shook his hand in what must be described as a fawning manner.

Of course I'd had no chance at all to speak with Brian privately, since he had been surrounded by the admiring crowd all night. So I took the chance to walk him out to his car, firmly closing the door on his groupies. And just before he climbed into the little red car, he turned and looked at me.

"What a lovely family you have, brother," he said. "Domestic perfection."

"I still don't know why you're here," I said.

"Don't you?" Brian said. "Wasn't I obvious?"

"Painfully obvious," I said. "But not at all clear."

"Is it so hard to believe that I want to belong to a family?" he said.

"Yes."

He cocked his head to the side and looked at me with perfect emptiness. "But isn't that what brought us together the first time?" he said. "Isn't it completely natural?"

"It might be," I said. "But we're not."

"Alas, too true," he said with his usual melodramatic flair. "But nevertheless, I found myself thinking about it. About you. My only blood relative."

"As far as we know," I said, and to my surprise I heard him say the same words at the same time, and he smiled broadly as he realized it, too.

"You see?" he said. "You can't argue with DNA. We are stuck with each other, brother. We're family."

And even though the same thought had been repeated endlessly all evening, and even though it was still ringing in my ears as Brian drove away, it did nothing to reassure me, and I went to bed still feeling the slow creep of uneasy toes along my spine.

ELEVEN

I T WAS A FRETFUL NIGHT FOR ME, WITH PATCHES OF SLEEP separated by deep bogs of restless wakefulness. I felt assailed by something I could only think of as nameless dread, a terrible lurking thing egged on by a voiceless unease from the Passenger, who seemed for once to be absolutely uncertain, just as flummoxed as I was. I might possibly have flogged this beast into its cage and found a few hours of blissful unconsciousness—but then, there was also Lily Anne.

Dear, sweet, precious, irreplaceable Lily Anne, the heart and soul of Dexter's new and human self, turned out to have another wondrous talent far beyond her more obvious charms. She had, apparently, a wonderfully powerful set of lungs, and she was determined to share this gift with all of us, every twenty minutes, all night long. And by some quirk of malignant nature, every time I managed to slide into a brief interlude of real sleep, it coincided exactly with one of Lily Anne's crying spells.

Rita seemed completely undisturbed by the noise, which did nothing to raise her stock with me. Every time the baby cried, she would say, "Bring her to me, Dexter," apparently without waking up, and then the two of them would drift off into sleep until Rita, again without opening her eyes, would say, "Put her back, please." And I would lurch to the crib, put Lily Anne down and cover her carefully, and silently beg her to please, *please*, sleep for just one small hour.

But when I returned to bed, even in the dark and temporary silence sleep eluded me. As much as I despise a cliché, I did, in fact, toss and turn, and neither option gave me any comfort. And in the few real moments of sleep that came to me, for some reason I dreamed, and they were not happy dreams. I do not, as a rule, dream at all; I believe the act may be connected to having a soul, and since I am quite sure I don't have one, for the most part I am blissfully brain-dead when I go to sleep, without any disturbance from the subconscious.

But in the sweaty depths of this night, Dexter dreamed. The images were as twisted as the bedsheets: Lily Anne holding a knife in her tiny fist, Brian collapsing into a pool of blood while Rita breast-fed Dexter, Cody and Astor swimming through that same awful red pool. Typical for such nonsense, there was no real meaning in any of it, and yet it still made me vastly uncomfortable on the bottom shelf of my inner cabinet, and when I finally staggered out of bed the next morning I was very far from rested.

I made it into the kitchen unaided, and Rita thumped a cup of coffee in front of me, with not nearly the care she had shown arranging Brian's cup. And even as I had this unworthy thought, Rita picked up on it, as if she were reading my mind.

"Brian seems like such a great guy," she said.

"Yes, he does," I said, thinking to myself that *seeming* is very far from *being*.

"The children really like him," she said, adding to my undefined sense of discomfort, which my pre-coffee partial consciousness had done nothing to dispel.

"Yes, um . . ." I said, taking a large slurp and silently willing the coffee to work quickly and get my brain back online. "Actually, he's never really been around kids before, and—"

"Well, then, this will be good for all of us," Rita said happily. "Has he ever been married?"

"I don't think so," I said.

"Don't you know?" Rita said sharply. "I mean, honestly, Dexter—he is your brother."

Perhaps it was my newfound human *feeling* erupting, but irritation at last pushed its way through my morning fog. "Rita," I said peevishly, "I know he's my brother. You don't need to keep telling me."

"You should have said something," she said.

"But I didn't," I said, quite logically, though admittedly still a bit cranky. "So can we change the channel, please?"

She looked like she had a lot more to say on the subject, but she very wisely held her tongue. She did, however, undercook my fried eggs, and so it was with a sense of real relief that I finally grabbed Cody and Astor and fled out the door. And of course, life being the unpleasant business that it is, they were stuck on the same page as their mother.

"How come you never told us about Uncle Brian, Dexter?" Astor demanded as I pushed the car into gear.

"I thought he was dead," I said, with what I really hoped was a note of finality in my voice.

"But we don't have any other uncles," she said. "Everybody else does, and we don't. Melissa has five uncles."

"Melissa sounds like a fascinating individual," I said, swerving to avoid a large SUV that had stopped in the middle of the road for no apparent reason.

"So we like having an uncle," Astor said. "And we like Uncle Brian."

"He's cool," Cody added softly.

Of course, it was very good to hear that they liked my brother, and it really should have made me happy, but it did not. It simply added to the sense of mean-spirited tension that had been rising in me ever since he had appeared. Brian was up to something—I knew it as well as I knew my own name—and until I knew what that something was I was stuck with my sense of lurking dread. It had not gone away by the time I dropped the kids at school and headed into work.

For once there were no freshly discovered headless bodies lying in the streets of Miami and frightening the tourists, and as if to underline this great mystery, Vince Masuoka had even brought in doughnuts. Considering the ragged assault my home life was making on me, this was very welcome indeed, and it seemed to me to call for some positive reinforcement. "Hail, doughnut, well brought," I said to Vince as he staggered in under the weight of the pastry box.

"Hail, Dexterus Maximus," he said. "I bring tribute from the Gauls."

"French doughnuts?" I said. "They don't put in parsley, do they?"

He flipped open the lid to reveal rows of gleaming doughnuts. "No parsley and no escargot filling, either," he said. "But they do include Bavarian cream."

"I shall ask the Senate to declare a triumph in your honor," I said, quickly grabbing one. And in a world built on the principles of love, wisdom, and compassion, that would have marked an end to the very uncomfortable course my morning had been following. But of course, we live in no such blissful world, and so the doughnut had barely had a chance to settle happily into my stomach where it belonged, when the phone on my desk began to rattle for my attention, and somehow, just from the way it sounded, I could tell it was Deborah.

"What are you doing?" she demanded without saying hello.

"Digesting a doughnut," I said.

"Do it up here in my office," she said, and hung up.

It is very difficult to argue with someone who is already off the line, as I am certain Deborah knew, so rather than go through the huge physical effort of redialing, I headed to the Homicide area and Deborah's desk. It was not, to be fair, actually an office at all but more of an area within a partition. Still, she seemed in no mood for the quibble, so I let it lie.

Deborah was in her chair at the desk clutching what looked like an official report. Her new partner, Deke, stood over by the window with a look of detached and vacuous amusement on his unreasonably handsome face. "Look at this," Deborah said, smacking the pages with the back of her hand. "Can you believe this shit?"

"No," I said. "That's because from this far away I can't even read that shit."

"Mr. Chin Dimple," she said, indicating Deke, "went to interview the Spanos family."

"Oh, hey," Deke said.

"And he found me a suspect," Debs said.

"Person of interest to the investigation," Deke said very seriously in official reportese. "He's not really a suspect."

"He's the only fucking lead we've got, and you sit on it all night," Debs snarled. "I have to read it in the goddamn report at nine-fucking-thirty the next morning."

"I had to type it," he said, sounding slightly hurt.

"With two teenage girls missing, the captain on my ass, and the press about to blow up like Three Mile Island, you type it and don't tell me first," she said.

"Hey, well, what the fuck," Deke said with a shrug.

Deborah gnashed her teeth. I mean, really; it's something I'd only read about before, mostly in fantasy stories, and I'd never believed it happened in real life, but there it was. I watched, fascinated, as she gnashed her teeth, started to say something very forceful, and instead threw the report on her desk. "Go get some coffee, Deke," she said at last.

Deke straightened up, made a clicking noise as he pointed a finger at her, and said, "Cream and two sugars," and sauntered away toward the coffeepot down the hall.

"I thought you liked your coffee black," I said as Deke disappeared.

Deborah stood up. "If that's his last fuckup, I am the happiest girl in the world," she said. "Come on."

She was already moving down the hall in the opposite direction from Deke, and so once again any protest I might have made was largely irrelevant. I sighed and followed, wondering if Deborah had learned this kind of behavior, perhaps from a book called *The Management Style of Bulldozers*.

I caught up with her at the elevator and said, "I suppose it would be too much to ask where we're going?"

"Tiffany Spanos," she said, hammering at the "down" button a second time, and then a third. "Tyler's older sister."

It took me a moment, but as the elevator doors slid open I remembered. "Tyler Spanos," I said, following her into the elevator. "The girl who's missing with, um, Samantha Aldovar."

"Yeah," she said. The doors slid shut and we lurched down. "Nimnut talked to Tiffany Spanos about her sister." I assumed Nimnut meant Deke, so I just nodded. "Tiffany says that Tyler has been into that Goth shit for a while, and then she met this guy at a party who was, like, Goth squared."

I suppose I lead a very innocent life, but I had thought that "Goth" was a sort of fashion statement for teenagers with bad complexions and a particularly repulsive form of angst. As far as I knew, the whole thing involved cultivating a look of black clothes and very pale skin, and perhaps listening to Euro-tech pop music while looking longingly at a DVD of *Twilight*. It seemed to me something that would be very hard to conceive of squared. But Deborah's imagination knew no such boundary.

"Am I allowed to ask what 'Goth squared' means?" I said humbly.

Deborah glared at me. "Guy's a vampire," she said.

"Really," I said, and I admit I was surprised. "In this day and age? In Miami?"

"Yeah," she said, and the elevator doors slid open. "Even had his teeth filed," she said, heading out the door.

I hurried after her again. "So we're going to see this guy?" I asked. "What's his name?"

"Vlad," she said. "Catchy name, huh?"

"Vlad what?" I said.

"I don't know," she said.

"But you know where he lives?" I said hopefully.

"We'll find him," she said, stalking toward the exit, and I finally decided that enough was enough. I grabbed her arm, and she turned to glare at me.

"Deborah," I said, "what the hell are we doing?"

"One more minute with that brain-dead bag of muscles and I'm going to lose it," she said. "I gotta get out of here." She tried to pull away, but I held on.

"I am as willing as anyone to flee in terror from your partner," I said. "But we are going to find somebody and we don't know his full name or where he might be. So where are we going?"

She tried again to jerk her arm away from my grip, and this time she succeeded. "Cybercafé," she said. "I'm not stupid." Apparently I was, because once again I was playing follow the leader as she stormed out the door and into the parking lot.

"You're paying for coffee," I said rather feebly as I hurried after.

There was an Internet café only about ten blocks away, and so in no time at all I was sitting at a keyboard with a very good cup of coffee and an impatient Deborah fidgeting at my elbow. My sister is an excellent shot with a pistol, and no doubt has many other sterling character traits, but putting her in front of a computer is like asking a donkey to do the polka, and she very wisely left all her Googling to me. "All right," I said. "I can search for the name 'Vlad,' but—"

"Cosmetic dentistry," she snapped. "Don't be an asshole."

I nodded; it was the smart move, but after all, she was the trained investigator. Within minutes I had a list of dozens of dentists in the Miami area, all of whom practiced cosmetic dentistry. "Shall I print it out?" I said to Debs. She looked at the long list and chewed on her lip so hard I thought she might well need a dentist herself soon.

"No," she said, grabbing for her cell phone. "I got an idea."

It must have been a very secret idea, because she didn't tell it to me, but she called a number she had on speed dial and in just a few seconds I heard her say, "This is Morgan. Gimme the number for that forensic dentist." She scribbled a hand in the air, indicating that she wanted a pen, and I found one beside the keyboard and passed it to her, along with a scrap of paper from the nearby trash can. "Yeah," she said. "Dr. Gutmann, that's the guy. Uh-huh." She wrote the number down and disconnected.

She immediately punched in the number she'd written down and after a minute of talking to a receptionist and then, judging by the way she began to tap her toe, listening to elevator music, Gutmann came on the line. "Dr. Gutmann," Deborah said. "This is Sergeant Morgan. I need the name of a local dentist who might sharpen a guy's teeth so he looks like a vampire." Gutmann said something and Deborah looked surprised. She scrabbled for the pen and wrote as she said, "Uh-huh. Got it, thanks," and then flipped the phone closed. "He said there's only one dentist in town stupid enough to do that. Dr. Lonoff on South Beach."

I found it quickly on the page of dentists I had called up on the computer. "Just off Lincoln Road," I said.

Deborah was already out of her chair and moving toward the door. "Come on," she said, and once again Dutiful Dexter lurched up and followed along.

TWELVE

D R. LONOFF'S OFFICE WAS ON THE FIRST FLOOR OF A RELA-
tively old two-story building on a side street two blocks from
Lincoln Road Mall. The building was one of those semi-Deco
buildings South Beach had once been infested with, and it had been
nicely restored and painted a very light lime green. Deborah and I
went in past a sculpture that looked like a geometry lesson having
sex in a hardware bin and we walked straight to the back, where a
door announced, DR. J. LONOFF, DDS: COSMETIC DENTISTRY.

"I think this is it," I said, trying to sound like David Caruso.

Deborah just gave me a quick and mean look and opened the
door.

The receptionist was a very thin African-American man with a
shaved head and dozens of piercings in his ears, eyebrows, and
nose. He was wearing raspberry-colored scrubs and a gold necklace. A sign on his desk said, LLOYD. He looked up as we entered,
smiled brightly, and said, "Hi! Can I help you?" in a way that
sounded like, *Let's start the party!*

Deborah held up her badge and said, "I'm Sergeant Morgan,
Miami-Dade Police. I need to see Dr. Lonoff."

Lloyd's smile got even bigger. "He's with a patient right now. Can you wait just a couple of minutes?"

"No," Deborah said. "I need to see him now."

Lloyd looked a bit uncertain, but he didn't stop smiling. His teeth were large, very white, and perfectly shaped. If Dr. Lonoff had done Lloyd's teeth, he did really good work. "Can you tell me what this is about?" he said.

"It's about me coming back with a warrant to look at his drug register if he isn't out here in thirty seconds," Deborah said.

Lloyd licked his lips, hesitated for two seconds, and then got to his feet. "I'll tell him you're here," he said, and he vanished around a curved wall and into the back of the office.

Dr. Lonoff beat the thirty-second deadline by a full two seconds. He came huffing around the curved wall, wiping his hands on a paper towel and looking frazzled. "What the hell are you— What's this about my drug register?"

Deborah just watched him as he skidded to a stop in front of her. He seemed young for a dentist, maybe thirty, and in all honesty he looked a little too buff, too, as though he had been pumping iron when he should have been filling cavities.

Deborah must have thought so, too. She looked him over from head to toe and said, "Are you Dr. Lonoff?"

"Yes, I am," he said, still a little huffish. "Who the hell are you?"

Once again Deborah held up her badge. "Sergeant Morgan, Miami-Dade Police. I need to ask you about one of your patients."

"What you need to do," he said with a great deal of medical authority, "is to stop playing storm trooper and tell me what this is about. I have a patient in the chair."

I saw Deborah's jaw stiffen, and knowing her as well as I did I braced myself for a round or two of tough talk; she would refuse to tell him anything, since it was police business, and he would refuse to let her at his records, because doctor-patient records were confidential, and they would go back and forth until all the high cards were played, and meanwhile I would have to watch and wonder why we couldn't just cut to the chase and break for lunch.

I was just about to find a chair and curl up with a copy of *Golf*

Digest to wait it out—but Deborah surprised me. She took a deep breath and said, "Doctor, I got two young girls missing, and the only lead I have is a guy with his teeth fixed so he looks like a vampire." She breathed again and held his eye. "I need some help."

If the ceiling had melted away to reveal a choir of angels singing "Achy Breaky Heart," I could not have been more surprised. For Deborah to open up and look vulnerable like this was completely unheard-of, and I wondered if I should help her find professional counseling. Dr. Lonoff seemed to think so, too. He blinked at her for several long seconds, and then glanced at Lloyd.

"I'm not supposed to," he said, looking even younger than his thirty or so years. "The records are confidential."

"I know that," Deborah said.

"Vampire?" Lonoff said, and he peeled his own lips back and pointed. "Like here? The canines?"

"That's right," Deborah said. "Like fangs."

"It's a special crown," Lonoff said happily. "I have them made by a guy in Mexico, a real artist. Then it's just a standard crown procedure, and the result is pretty impressive, I gotta say."

"You've done that to a lot of guys?" Deborah said, sounding a bit surprised.

He shook his head. "I've done about two dozen," he said.

"A young guy," Deborah said. "Probably not more than twenty years old."

Dr. Lonoff pursed his lips and thought. "Maybe three or four of those," he said.

"He calls himself Vlad," Deborah said.

Lonoff smiled and shook his head. "Nobody by that name," he said. "But I wouldn't be surprised if they all call themselves that. I mean, it's a kind of popular name with that crowd."

"Is it really a crowd?" I blurted out. The idea of a large number of vampires in Miami, whether actual or fake, was a little bit alarming—even if only for aesthetic reasons. I mean, really: all those black clothes? So very New York–last year.

"Yeah," Lonoff said. "There's quite a few of them. They don't all want their fangs done," he said with regret, and then he shrugged. "Still. They have their clubs, and raves, and so on. It's quite a scene."

"I only need to find one of them," Deborah said with a little bit of her old impatience.

Lonoff looked at her, nodded, and unconsciously flexed his neck muscles. His shirt collar didn't quite pop. He pushed his lips out and then in, and, suddenly reaching a decision, he said, "Lloyd, help them find that in the billing records."

"You got it, Doctor," Lloyd said.

Lonoff held out his hand toward Deborah. "Good luck, ah— Sergeant?"

"That's right," Deborah said, shaking his hand.

Dr. Lonoff held on a little too long, and just when I thought Debs would yank away her hand, he smiled and added, "You know, I could fix that overbite for you."

"Thanks," Debs said, pulling her hand away. "I kind of like it."

"Uh-huh," Lonoff said. "Well, then . . ." He put a hand on Lloyd's shoulder and said, "Help them out. I've got a patient waiting." And with a last longing look at Deborah's overbite, he turned around and disappeared into the back room again.

"It's over here," Lloyd said. "On the computer." He pointed to the desk he'd been sitting at when we came in, and we followed him over.

"I'm going to need some parameters," he said. Deborah blinked and looked at me, as if the word were in a foreign language—which I suppose it was, to her, since she did not speak computer. So once again, I stepped into the awkward void and saved her.

"Under twenty-four," I said. "Male. Pointy canine teeth."

"Cool," Lloyd said, and he hammered at the keyboard for a few moments. Deborah watched impatiently. I turned away and looked at the far side of the waiting room. A large saltwater fish tank sat on a stand in the corner next to a magazine rack. It looked a little crowded to me, but maybe the fish liked it that way.

"Gotcha," Lloyd said, and I turned around in time to see a sheet of paper come whirring out of the printer. Lloyd grabbed it and held it out to Debs, who snatched it and glared at it. "There's just four names," Lloyd said with a touch of the same regret Dr. Lonoff had shown, and I wondered if he got a commission on the fangs.

"Crap," said Deborah, still looking at the list.

"Why crap?" I said. "Did you want more names?"

She flicked the paper with a finger. "First name on here," she said. "Does the name Acosta mean anything to you?"

I nodded. "It means trouble," I said. Joe Acosta was a major fig-ure in the city government, a sort of old-school commissioner who still carried the kind of clout you might have found fifty years ago in Chicago. If our Vlad was his son, we might be in for a fecal shower. "Different Acosta?" I asked hopefully.

Deborah shook her head. "Same address," she said. "Shit."

"Maybe it's not him," Lloyd said helpfully, and Debs looked up at him, just for a second, but his bright smile vanished as if she'd hit him in the crotch.

"Come on," she said to me, and she whirled away toward the door.

"Thanks for your help," I told Lloyd, but he just nodded, one time, as if Debs had sucked all the joy out of his life.

Deborah was already in the car with the motor running by the time I caught up with her. "Come on," she called out the window. "Get in."

I climbed in beside her and she had the car in gear before I got the door closed. "You know," I said, fastening my seat belt, "we could leave Acosta for last. It could just as easily be one of the others."

"Tyler Spanos goes to Ransom Everglades," she said. "So she hangs with the upper crust. The fucking Acostas *are* the upper crust. It's him."

It was hard to fault her logic, so I said nothing; I just settled in and let her drive too fast through the midmorning traffic.

We drove over the MacArthur Causeway and let it take us onto the 836 all the way to LeJeune, where we went left into Coral Gables. Acosta's house was in a section of the Gables that would have been a walled community if it was built today. The houses were large, and many of them, like Acosta's, were built in the Spanish style out of large blocks of coral rock. The lawn looked like a putting green and there was a two-story garage on the side, attached to the house by a breezeway.

Deborah parked in front of the house and paused for a moment after turning off the engine. I watched her take a deep breath, and I wondered if she was still going through the same strange molecular meltdown that had lately made her seem so soft and emotional. "Are you sure you want to do this?" I asked her. She glanced at me, and she did not really look like the fierce and focused Deborah I knew so well. "I mean, you know," I said. "Acosta could make your life pretty miserable. He's a commissioner."

She snapped back into focus like she'd been slapped and I saw the familiar sight of her jaw muscles working. "I don't care if he's Jesus," she snarled, and it was very good to see the old venom return. She got out of the car and began to stride up the sidewalk to the front door. I got out and followed, catching up to her just as she pushed the doorbell. There was no response, and she shifted her weight impatiently from foot to foot. Just as she reached a hand up to ring a second time, the door swung open, and a short, square woman in a maid's uniform peered out at us.

"Yes?" the maid said in a thick Central American accent.

"Is Robert Acosta here, please," Deborah said.

The maid licked her lips, and her eyes darted from side to side for a moment. Then she shivered and shook her head. "Why you wan' Bobby?" she said.

Deborah held up her badge and the maid sucked in her breath loudly. "I need to ask him some questions," Debs said. "Is he here?"

The maid swallowed hard, but said nothing.

"I just need to talk to him," Debs said. "It's very important."

The maid swallowed again, and glanced past us out the door. Deborah turned and looked, too. "The garage?" she said, turning back to the maid. "He's in the garage?"

At last, the maid nodded. "*El garaje*," she said, softly and very fast, as if she was afraid she would be heard. "Bobby *vive en el piso segundo.*"

Deborah looked at me. "In the garage. He lives on the second floor," I translated. For some reason, in spite of being born and bred in Miami, Debs had chosen to study French in school.

"Is he here right now?" Deborah asked the maid.

She nodded her head jerkily. "*Creo que sí,*" she said. She licked her lips again and then, with a sort of spasmodic lurch, she pushed the door closed, not quite slamming it.

Deborah looked at the shut door for a moment, then shook her head. "What was she so scared of?" she said.

"Deportation?" I said.

She snorted. "Joe Acosta wouldn't hire an illegal. Not when he can get a green card for anybody he wants to."

"Maybe she's afraid to lose her job," I said.

Deborah turned and looked at the garage. "Uh-huh," she said. "And maybe she's afraid of Bobby Acosta."

"Well," I said, but Deborah jerked into motion and headed around the corner of the house before I could say any more. I caught up with her as she got to the driveway. "She's going to tell Bobby we're here," I said.

Deborah shrugged. "It's her job," she said. She came to a halt in front of the double-size garage door. "There's got to be another door, maybe some stairs," she said.

"Around the side?" I offered, and I took two steps farther toward the left side when I heard a rumbling sound and then the garage door began to roll up. I turned back around and watched. I could hear a muted purring coming from inside and it got louder as the door opened wider, and when it was up far enough to see into the garage, I saw that the sound came from a motorcycle. A thin guy of twenty or so sat on the bike, letting it idle and looking out at us.

"Robert Acosta?" Deborah called to him. She took a step forward and reached to grab her badge to show him.

"Fucking cops," he said. He revved the engine once, and then kicked it into gear, very deliberately aiming the bike right at Deborah. The motorcycle leaped forward, straight at Deborah, and she barely managed to dive to one side. Then the bike was into the street and accelerating away into the distance, and by the time Deborah got back onto her feet, it was gone.

THIRTEEN

IN THE COURSE OF MY WORK WITH THE MIAMI-DADE POLICE Department, I had heard the phrase "shit-storm" used on more than one occasion. But in all honesty, I would have to say that I had never truly seen the actual meteorological event until after Debs called in a BOLO for the only son of a powerful county commissioner. Within five minutes we had three squad cars and a TV news van pulled up in front of the house next to Debs's car, and at the six-minute mark Debs was on the phone with Captain Matthews. I heard her say, "Yes, sir. Yes, sir. No, sir," and not much else in the course of a two-minute conversation, and by the time she put the phone away her jaw was locked shut so tight I didn't think she could ever again eat solid food.

"Shit," she said through her tightly clenched teeth. "Matthews pulled my BOLO."

"We knew this was coming," I said.

Debs nodded. "It's here," she said, and then, looking past me to the road, she added, "Aw, shit."

I turned and followed her gaze. Deke was climbing out of his car, hitching up his pants, and giving a big smile to the woman who stood in front of the news van brushing her hair and setting up a shot. She actually stopped brushing for a moment and gaped back at him, and he nodded to her and sauntered toward us. She watched him go for a moment, licked her lips, and went back to her hair with renewed vigor.

"Technically, he is your partner," I said.

"Technically he's a brain-dead asshole," she said.

"Hey," Deke said as he strolled up to us. "Captain says I should keep an eye on you, make sure you don't fuck nothing else up."

"How the hell are *you* going to know if I fuck up?" Debs snarled at him.

"Oh, hey, you know," he said, shrugging. He looked back at the TV newswoman. "I mean, just don't talk to the press or something, right?" He winked at Deborah. "Anyway, I got to stay with you now," he said. "Keep this thing on track."

For a moment I thought she would let loose a blast of seven separate killing remarks that would drop Deke where he stood and singe the Acostas' manicured lawn, but Debs had clearly received the same message from the captain, and she was a good soldier. Discipline won out and she just looked at Deke for a long moment and finally said, "All right. Let's check the other names on this list," and walked meekly to her car.

Deke pulled up his pants again and watched her go. "Well, all right," he said, and followed her. The TV newswoman watched him go with a somewhat distracted expression, until her producer almost smacked her with a microphone.

I got a ride back to headquarters with one of the squad cars, driven by a cop named Willoughby who seemed obsessed with the Miami Heat. I learned a great deal about point guards and something called the pick and roll by the time I got out of the car. I am sure it was wonderfully useful information, and someday it will come in handy, but I was nevertheless very grateful to climb out into the afternoon heat and trudge back to my little cubicle.

And there I was, left to my own devices for most of the rest of the day. I went to lunch and tried out a new place not too far away that specialized in falafels. Unfortunately, it also specialized in dark hairs swimming in a vile sauce, and I came back from my break with a very unhappy stomach. I went through some routine lab work, filed a few papers, and enjoyed the solitude until about four o'clock, when Deborah wandered into my cubicle. She was carrying a thick folder and she looked as distressed as my stomach. She hooked a chair out with her toe and slouched into it without speaking. I put down the file I was reading and gave her my attention.

"You look beat, sis," I said.

She nodded and looked at her hands. "Long day," she said.

"You checked out the other names on the dentist's list?" I asked her, and again she just nodded, and so, because I wanted to help her be a little more socially adept, I added, "With your partner, Deke?"

Her head jerked up and she glared at me. "That fucking idiot," she said, and then she shrugged and slumped again.

"What did he do?" I asked.

She shrugged again. "Nothing," she said. "He's not totally terrible at the routine stuff. Asks all the standard questions."

"So why the long face, Debs?" I asked.

"They took away my suspect, Dexter," she said, and once again I was struck by the weary vulnerability that crept into her voice. "The Acosta kid knows something; I know it. He may not be hiding those girls, but he knows who is, and they won't let me go after him." She waved a knuckle toward the hallway. "They even have that asshole Deke babysitting me to make sure I don't do anything that might embarrass the commissioner."

"Well," I said, "Bobby Acosta may not be guilty of anything."

Debs showed me her teeth. It would have been a smile if she were not so clearly miserable. "He's guilty as shit," she said, and she held up the folder in her hand. "He's got a record you wouldn't believe—even without the stuff they blacked out when he was a minor."

"A juvie record doesn't make him guilty this time," I said.

Deborah leaned forward, and for a moment I thought she was going to hit me with Bobby Acosta's file. "The hell it doesn't," she said, and then, happily for me, she opened the file instead of swinging it at my head. "Assault. Assault with intent. Assault. Grand theft auto." She looked up at me apologetically as she said "grand theft" and shrugged before dropping her eyes back to the folder. "Twice he was arrested because he was caught on the scene when somebody died in suspicious circumstances, and it should have been manslaughter at the very least, but both times his old man bought him out of trouble." She closed the folder and slapped it with the back of her hand. "There's a lot more," she said. "But it all ends the same way, with blood on Bobby's hands and his father bailing him out." She shook her head. "This is one bad, fucked-up kid, Dexter. He's killed at *least* two people, and there is absolutely no doubt in my mind that he knows where those girls are. If he hasn't already killed them, too."

I thought Debs was probably right. Not because a record of past crimes always meant present guilt—but I had felt a slow and sleepy stir of interest from the Passenger, a speculative raising of inner eyebrows as Deborah read from the file, and the old Dexter would very definitely have added the name of Bobby Acosta to his little black book of potential playmates. But of course, Dexter 2.0 didn't do those things. Instead, I merely nodded sympathetically. "You may be right," I said.

Deborah jerked her head up. "*May* be," she said. "I *am* right. Bobby Acosta knows where those girls are, and I can't fucking *touch* him because of his old man."

"Well," I said, acutely conscious of speaking a cliché but unable to think of anything else worth saying, "you really can't fight city hall, you know."

Deborah stared at me for a moment with an absolutely blank face. "Wow," she said. "Did you think that up by yourself?"

"Well, come on, Debs," I said, and I admit I was a little peevish. "You knew this would happen, and it happened, so why should it bother you?"

She blew out a long breath, and then folded her hands in her lap and looked down at them, which was somehow much worse than the snarling comeback I'd expected. "I don't know," she said. "Maybe it's not just this." She turned her hands over and looked at the back side. "Maybe it's . . . I don't know. Everything."

If *everything* really was bothering my sister, it was much easier to understand her weary misery; being in charge of *everything* would be a crushing burden. But in my small experience with humans, I have learned that if someone says they are oppressed by *everything*, it usually means one small and very specific *something*. And in my sister's case, even though she had always acted like she was in charge of everything, I thought this would hold true; some particular *something* was eating at her and making her act like this. And remembering what she had said about her live-in boyfriend, Kyle Chutsky, I thought that was probably it.

"Is it Chutsky?" I said.

Her head jerked up. "What. You mean does he beat me up? Is he cheating on me?"

"No, of course not," I said, holding up a hand in case she decided to hit me. I knew he wouldn't dare cheat on her—and the idea of anybody trying to beat up my sister was laughable. "It's just what you were saying the other day. About, you know—tick-tock, bio clock?"

She drooped over again and looked at her hands in her lap. "Uh-huh. I said that, didn't I," she said. She shook her head slowly. "Well, it's still true. And fucking Chutsky—he won't even talk about it."

I looked at my sister, and I admit that my feelings did me no credit, because my first truly conscious reaction to Deb's outpouring was to think, *Wow! I really am feeling empathy with an actual human emotion!* Because Deborah's continuing descent into a soft pudding of self-pity had actually reached me, deep down on the brand-new human level recently opened by Lily Anne, and I found that I did not have to search my memory for a response from some old day-time drama. I really *felt* something, and that was very impressive to me.

So without actually thinking it through at all, I got up from my chair and went over to her. I put a hand on her shoulder and squeezed gently and said, "I'm sorry, sis. Is there anything I can do?"

And naturally enough, Deborah stiffened and slapped my hand away. She stood up and looked at me with something that was at least halfway back to her natural snarl. "For starters, you can stop acting like Father Flanagan," she said. "Jesus, Dex. What's got into you?"

And before I could utter a single syllable of completely logical rebuttal, she stalked out of my office and disappeared down the hall.

"Glad to help," I said to her back.

Maybe I was just too new to having feelings to really understand them and act accordingly. Or maybe it was just going to take Debs a little time to get used to the new, compassionate Dexter. But it was starting to seem even more likely to me that some terribly wicked person or persons had put something sinister in the Miami water supply.

Just as I was getting ready to leave for the day, the weirdness went up one more notch. My cell phone rang and I glanced at it, saw that it was Rita, and answered. "Hello?" I said.

"Dexter, hi, um, it's me," she said.

"Of course it is," I said encouragingly.

"Are you still at work?" she said.

"Just getting ready to leave."

"Oh, good, because— I mean, if, instead of picking up Cody and Astor?" she said. "Because you don't have to tonight."

A quick mental translation told me that I didn't have to pick up the kids for some reason. "Oh, why not?" I said.

"It's just, they're already gone," she said, and for one terrible moment, as I struggled to understand what she meant, I thought that something awful had happened to them.

"What— Where did they go?" I managed to stammer.

"Oh," she said. "Your brother picked them up. Brian. He's going to take them for Chinese food."

What a wonderful world of new experiences I was having with being human. Right now, for example, I was struck speechless with astonishment. I felt wave after wave of thoughts and feelings wash over me: things like anger, amazement, and suspicion, ideas like wondering what Brian was really up to, why Rita would ever go along with it, and what Cody and Astor would do when they remembered that they didn't like Chinese food. But no matter how copious and specific my thoughts were, nothing at all came out of my mouth, except, "Uhk," and as I struggled for coherent sounds, Rita said, "Oh. I have to go. Lily Anne is crying. Bye." And she hung up.

I'm sure it was only a few seconds that I stood there listening to the sound of absolutely nothing, but it seemed like a very long time. Eventually I became aware that my mouth was dry, since it was hanging open, and my hand was sweaty from where I had clamped the cell phone into my fist. I closed my mouth, put the phone away, and headed for home.

Rush hour was in full swing as I headed south from work, and oddly enough, all the way home I saw no acts of random violence, no violent swerving or fist waving, no shots fired. The traffic inched along as slowly as ever, but nobody really seemed to mind. I wondered if I should have read my horoscope—perhaps that would explain what was going on. It could well be that somewhere in Miami really knowledgeable people—druids, perhaps—were nodding their heads and murmuring, "Ahhh, Jupiter is in a retrograde moon of Saturn," and pouring another cup of herb tea while they lounged around in Birkenstocks. Or maybe it was a group of the vampires Debs was chasing—was it called a flock? Perhaps if enough of them sharpened their teeth a new age of harmony would dawn for us all. Or at least for Dr. Lonoff, the dentist.

I spent a quiet evening at home watching TV and holding Lily Anne whenever I could. She did a lot of sleeping, but it worked for her just as well if I was holding her at the time, so I did. It seemed to me to indicate a remarkable degree of trust on her part. On the one hand, I hoped she would grow out of that, since it was not terribly wise to trust others so much. But on the other tiny, perfect hand, it filled me with a sense of wonder and a resolve to protect her from all the other beasts of the night.

I found myself sniffing Lily Anne's head frequently—certifiably odd behavior, I know, but, from what I could gather, completely in keeping with my new human persona. The smell was remarkable, unlike anything else I had ever smelled. It was an odor that was almost nothing at all, and it did not really fit into any category like "sweet" or "musty," although it contained elements of both—and more, and neither. But I sniffed and was unable to say what the smell was, and then I sniffed again just because I wanted to, and then suddenly a new odor welled up from the region of the diaper, one that was quite easy to identify.

Changing a diaper is really not as bad as it sounds, and I didn't mind it at all. I am not suggesting that I would embrace it as a career choice, but at least in the case of Lily Anne's diaper it was something that did not actually cause me any suffering—in some ways it was even enjoyable, since I was doing a very specific and necessary service for her. I got further pleasure from seeing Rita swoop in like a dive-bomber, probably to make sure I didn't accidentally boil the baby, and then pause and just watch when she saw my quiet competence, and I felt a warm glow of satisfaction when I finished and she took the baby off the changing table, saying only, "Thank you, Dexter."

While Rita fed Lily Anne, I returned to the TV and watched a hockey game for a few minutes. It was disappointing; in the first place, the Panthers were already down by three goals, and in the second place, there were no fights. I had originally been attracted to the game because of the honest and laudable bloodlust the players showed. Now, however, it occurred to me that I really ought to frown on that sort of thing. The New Me, Diaper Daddy Dexter, was strongly opposed to violence and could not possibly approve of a sport like hockey. Perhaps I could switch to bowling. It seemed awfully boring, but there was no blood, and it was certainly more exciting than golf.

Before I could reach any decision, Rita came back with Lily Anne. "Would you like to burp her, Dexter?" she said with a Madonna-like smile—the Madonna in the paintings, not the one with the fancy bra.

"I would like nothing better," I said, and weirdly enough, I meant it. I placed a small towel over my shoulder and held the baby facedown on it. And once again, for some reason it was not at all awful, even when Lily Anne made her delicate barfing noises and small bubbles of milk came out and onto the towel. I found myself murmuring quiet congratulations to her with each little *blarp* she made, until finally she drifted back into sleep and I switched her around to the front position, holding her to my chest and gently moving her from side to side in a rock-a-bye motion.

I was in this position when Brian brought Cody and Astor home at around nine o'clock. Technically, this was pushing the envelope a bit, since nine o'clock was bedtime and now the kids would be at least fifteen minutes late climbing into their beds. But Rita didn't seem to mind, and it would have been churlish of me to object, since everyone had so clearly had a very good time. Even Cody was almost smiling, and I made a note to find out what conceivable Chinese restaurant Brian might have taken them to in order to get that kind of reaction.

I was at a bit of a disadvantage, since I was holding Lily Anne, but as Rita hustled the two older kids off to pajamas and teeth brushing I stood up for a friendly word with my brother. "Well," I said as he stood by the door with an air of quiet satisfaction, "they look like they had a good time."

"Oh, they did," he said with his dreadful fake smile. "Remarkable children, both of them."

"Did they eat the spring rolls?" I asked, and Brian looked extremely blank for a moment.

"The spring— Oh yes, they devoured everything I put in front of them," he said, and there was such an ominous happiness in the way he said it that I was absolutely certain we were not talking about food.

"Brian," I said, but I got no further as Rita came whirling out.

"Oh, Brian," she said, snatching Lily Anne from my arms. "I don't know what on earth you did, but the children had a wonderful time. I've never seen them like this."

"It was entirely my pleasure," he said, and it made small icicles blossom along my spine.

"Won't you sit for a few minutes?" Rita said. "I could make some coffee, or a glass of wine . . . ?"

"Oh, no," he said happily. "Thank you very much, dear lady, but

I really must be going. Believe it or not, I have an appointment this evening."

"Oh!" Rita said with a guilty blush. "I hope you didn't— I mean, with the children, and you might have— You shouldn't—"

"Not at all," Brian said, as if it had all made sense. "I have plenty of time. But I must take my fond farewells now."

"Well," Rita said, "if you're sure that— And I really can't thank you enough because it's—"

"Mom!" Astor called from down the hall.

"Oh, dear," Rita said. "Excuse me, but—thank you so much, Brian." And she leaned in and kissed him on the cheek.

"Entirely my pleasure," Brian said again, and Rita smiled and hurried away to Astor and Cody.

Brian and I looked at each other for a moment, and while there was a great deal I wanted to say to him, I did not really know what it was specifically enough to say it. "Brian," I said again, but it stopped there, and he smiled that terrible fake, knowing smile.

"I know," he said. "But I really do have an appointment." He turned and opened the front door, and then glanced back at me. "They truly are remarkable children," he said. "Good night, brother."

And he was out the door and gone into the night, leaving me with no more than the afterglow of his dreadful smile and a very uncomfortable sense that something very wrong was going on.

FOURTEEN

I WAS MORE THAN A LITTLE CURIOUS TO FIND OUT WHAT HAD actually gone on with my brother and the kids, but Rita hustled them into bed before I could speak to them. I went to sleep unsatisfied, and in the morning there was no chance to speak to them away from their mother. This was a very necessary condition, since if anything had happened other than Chinese food, I most certainly didn't want Rita to hear about it. And the kids had probably been warned not to say anything, if I knew Brian—which I really didn't, come to think of it. I mean, I thought I knew how he would think and act in certain matters, but beyond that—who was he? What did he want from life, beyond the occasional slash-happy play session? I had no idea, and I did not find one in spite of pondering it all the way through breakfast and the drive to work.

Happily for my self-esteem, I did not get a great deal more time to worry about my inability to figure out my brother, because when I arrived at work the second floor where Forensics was located was buzzing with the kind of whacked-out frenzy that only a really interesting crime can cause. Camilla Figg, a square forensics tech in her mid-thirties, went dashing past me clutching her kit and she barely even blushed as she brushed against my arm. And when I walked into the lab, Vince Masuoka was already jumping about stuffing things into his bag.

"Have you got a pith helmet?" he called to me.

"Thertainly not," I said. "Thilly quethtion."

"You may want one," he said. "We're going on safari."

"Oh, Kendall again?" I said.

"Everglades," he said. "Something really wild went down last night."

"Ungowa," I said. "I'll pack the bug spray."

And so only an hour later I climbed out of Vince's car and stood beside Route 41 in the Everglades, just a couple of miles from Fortymile Bend. Harry had brought me camping in the area when I was a teenager, and I actually had some happy memories here involving several small animals that had contributed to my education.

Aside from the official vehicles parked by the road, there were two big vans pulled onto the small dirt parking area. A little trailer was hooked onto one of them. A flock of about fifteen teenage boys and three men in Boy Scout uniforms huddled uncertainly around the vans, and I saw two detectives talking to them, one at a time. There was a uniformed cop standing beside the road, waving the traffic to keep moving, and Vince tapped him on the shoulder.

"Hey, Rosen," Vince said. "What's up with the Scouts?"

"They're the ones that found it. Got here this morning for a camping trip," Rosen said, adding, "Keep moving," to a car that had slowed down to look.

"Found what?" Vince asked him.

"I just wave at the fucking cars," Rosen said sourly. "You're the ones that get to play with the bodies. Keep moving, come on," he said to another gawker.

"Where do we go?" Vince said.

Rosen pointed to the far side of the parking area, and turned away. I guess if I had to stand in the traffic while someone else got to play with the bodies, I would have been surly, too.

We walked toward the trailhead, past the Scouts. They must

have found something awful out there, but they didn't look terribly shocked or frightened. In fact, they were chuckling and shoving one another as if this were a special kind of holiday, and it made me sorry I had never joined the Boy Scouts. Perhaps I could have earned a merit badge for body-part recycling.

We went down the trail that led south into the trees, and then curved around to the west for about half a mile until it came out into a clearing. By the time we got there, Vince was sweating and breathing heavily, but I was almost eager, since a soft voice had been whispering to me that something worth seeing was waiting for me.

But at first glance, there seemed to be very little to see except a large trampled-down area surrounding a fire pit and, to the left of the fire, a small heap of something or other that I could not quite see past Camilla Figg's hunched-over form. Whatever it was, it caused a leathery whir of interest from the Dark Passenger, and I moved forward with just a trace of eagerness—forgetting for the moment that I had forsworn such Dark Pleasures.

"Hi, Camilla," I said to her as I approached, "what have we got?" She instantly blushed furiously, which was, for some reason, her usual habit when I talked to her.

"Bones," she said softly.

"No chance they're from a pig or a goat?" I asked.

She shook her head violently and, in one gloved hand, held up what I thought I recognized as a human humerus, which was not all that funny. "No chance," she said.

"Well, then," I said, noticing the charred marks on the bones and listening to the happy sibilant chuckle from within. I could not tell if they had been burned after death, as a way to get rid of the evidence, or—

I looked around the clearing. The ground had been stamped flat; there were hundreds of footprints, indicating a large party, and I didn't think it could have been the Scouts. They had arrived only this morning, and hadn't had time to do something like this. The clearing looked like a lot of people had been very active for several hours. Not just standing here, but moving around, jumping up and down, getting rowdy. And all centered around the fire pit, where the bones were, as if—

I closed my eyes, and I could almost see it as I listened to the rising tide of reptilian sound from my soft and deadly inner voice. *Look,* it said, and in the small window it showed me I saw a large, festive group. A solitary victim tied up by the fire. Not torture, but execution, done by one person—while all the others watched and partied? Was that possible?

And the Passenger chuckled and answered. *Yes,* it said. *Oh, absolutely.* Dancing, singing, carrying on. Plenty of beer, plenty of food. A good old-fashioned barbecue.

"Hey," I said to Camilla, opening my eyes. "Is there anything on the bones that looks like teeth marks?"

Camilla flinched and looked around at me with an expression that was very close to fear. "How did you know?" she said.

"Oh, just a lucky hunch," I said, but she did not look convinced, so I added, "Any guess at the gender?"

She stared at me for a moment longer, and then appeared to hear my question at last. "Um," she said, turning back to the bones with a jerk. She raised a gloved finger and pointed it at one of the larger bones. "Pelvic girdle indicates a female. Probably young," she said.

A little something clicked inside the mighty supercomputer that was Dexter's brain and a card slid into the out-tray. *Young female,* the card read. "Oh, um, thanks," I said to Camilla, backing away to look at this small and interesting idea. Camilla just nodded and bent over the bones.

I looked around the clearing. Over where the trail disappeared deeper into the swamp I saw Lieutenant Keane, chatting with a man I recognized from FDLE, the Florida Department of Law Enforcement, which is sort of a state-level version of the FBI; they have jurisdiction everywhere in Florida. And standing with them was one of the largest men I have ever seen. He was black, about six and a half feet tall, and at least five hundred pounds, which on him did not look particularly fat somehow—possibly because of the focused ferocity of his stare. But since the FDLE guy was talking to him and not calling for backup, I had to assume he belonged here, too, although I had no idea why. If he was representing either the Sheriff's Department or Broward County I was sure I would have seen him before, or at least heard rumors about someone that large.

But as interesting as it was to see a real giant, it was not enough to hold my attention, and I looked to the other side of the clearing. Across from the small clot of cops there was a clean area of the clearing, where several detectives were standing around. I went there and set my kit down, thinking hard. I knew of a young female who was missing, and I knew someone looking for a young female who would be very interested in making this connection. But what was the right way to do this? I am not really a political animal, although I understand it well enough—politics is just a way to indulge in my former hobby using metaphorical knives instead of real ones. But it seemed like no fun at all to me. All the careful maneuvering and backstabbing were so obvious and pointless and didn't really lead to anything all that exciting. Still, I knew it was important in a structured environment like the Miami-Dade Police Department. And Deborah was not very good at it, although she usually managed to bull her way through with a combination of toughness and good results.

But Deborah had been so very unlike herself of late, with her pouting and self-pity, and I didn't know if she was up to a confrontation that was likely to prove extremely political—a different detective was leading on this, and for her to try to yank it away would be difficult, even when she was at her best. Still, maybe a good challenge was just what she needed to bring her back to herself. So perhaps the best thing to do was simply to call her and tell her—let loose the dogs of war and let the chips fall where they may. It was a wonderfully mangled metaphor, which made it seem even more convincing, so I stepped away from the group of cops and reached for my cell phone.

Deborah let it ring several times; again, this was very unlike her. Just when I was ready to give up, she answered. "What," she said.

"I'm in the Everglades at a crime scene," I said.

"Good for you," she said.

"Debs, I think the victim was killed, cooked, and eaten in front of a crowd."

"Wow, awful," she said, with no real enthusiasm, which I found a little bit irritating.

"Did I mention that this victim appears to be young and female?" I said.

She didn't say anything at all for a moment. "Debs?" I said.

"I'm on my way," she said, with a little bit of the old fire in her voice, and I closed my phone with satisfaction. But before I could put it away and get to work, I heard someone behind me scream, "*Fuuuuuck!*" and then a volley of gunshots broke out. I ducked down and tried to hide behind my blood-spatter kit, rather difficult considering it was about the size of the average lunch box. But I took what cover I could get and peeked over the top toward the gunfire, half expecting to see a horde of Maori warriors charging at us with their spears raised and their tongues out. What I saw instead was almost as unlikely.

The officers who had been standing around a moment earlier were now all crouched in combat firing position and frantically shooting their weapons into a nearby bush. Contrary to the very best of established police procedure, their faces were not set in cold and grim masks, but looked wild and wide-eyed. One of the detectives was already ejecting an empty clip from his pistol and frantically trying to fumble in a spare, and the others just kept firing with berserk abandon.

And the bush they were apparently trying to kill began to thrash about spastically, and I saw the glint of something silver-yellow. It flashed in the sunlight one time, and then was gone, but the officers kept firing for several more seconds, until finally Lieutenant Keane ran over, yelling at them to hold their fire. "What the fuck is wrong with you idiots?!" Keane yelled at them.

"Lieutenant, I swear to God," one of them said.

"A snake!" said the second guy. "Fucking huge snake!"

"A snake," Keane said. "You want me to step on it for you?"

"You got really big feet?" the third guy said. " 'Cause it was a Burmese python, about eighteen feet long."

"Aw, shit," Keane said. "Are those protected?"

I realized I was still crouched down, and I stood up as the FDLE man sauntered over. "Actually, they're thinking about a bounty on those bad boys," the FDLE guy said, "if any of you Wyatt Earps was lucky enough to hit it."

"I hit it," the third guy said sullenly.

"Bullshit," said one of the others. "You couldn't hit shit with a shoe."

The giant black man wandered over to the bush and looked, then turned to the group of nonmarksmen, shaking his head, and, realizing that the excitement was over, I picked up my kit and went back to the fire pit.

There was a surprising amount of blood spatter for me, and in just a few moments I was happily at work, making sense of the nasty stuff. It was not yet completely dry, probably because of the humidity, but a great deal of it had soaked into the ground, since it had not rained for quite some time, and in spite of the moisture in the air, things on the ground were relatively parched at the moment. I got a couple of good samples to take back with me for analysis, and I also began to get a picture of what had probably happened.

The majority of the blood was in one area, right by the fire pit. I cast about in ever-widening circles, but the only traces of it I found more than six feet away appeared to have been tracked there on someone's shoes. I marked these spots in the forlorn hope that somebody might be able to get an identifiable footprint from them and went back to the main spatter. The blood had *poured* out of the victim, not spurted, as it would have from a slash wound. And there were no secondary splashes anywhere nearby, which meant that there had been only one wound, like bleeding out a deer—nobody else in the crowd had jumped in and stabbed or slashed. This had been a slow, deliberate killing, a literal butchering, performed by one person, very controlled and businesslike, and I found myself reluctantly admiring the professionalism of the work. That kind of restraint was very difficult, as I well knew— and with a crowd watching, too, presumably shouting drunken encouragement, offering rude suggestions. It was impressive, and

I took my time, giving it the kind of reciprocal professionalism it deserved.

I was on one knee, just finishing an examination of a last probable footprint, when I heard raised voices, threats of unpleasant and intimate dismemberment, and assorted profane expressions of anatomical impossibility. It could only mean one thing. I stood up and looked over toward the trailhead, and sure enough, I was right.

Deborah had arrived.

FIFTEEN

IT WAS A PRETTY GOOD FIGHT, AS THESE THINGS GO, AND IT would have lasted a whole lot longer if not for the FDLE man. He was a guy I knew about by reputation, named Chambers, and he literally stepped in between Deborah and the other detective, a large man named Burris. Putting one hand out onto Burris's chest, and the other politely in the air in front of Deborah, Chambers said, "Cut it out." Burris shut up immediately. I saw Debs take a breath to say something, and Chambers looked at her. She looked back and held her breath, and then just let it out silently.

I was impressed, and I edged around to get a better look at the man from the FDLE. He had a shaved head and he was not tall, but as he swung around I could see his face, and I knew why Debs had buttoned her lip, even without the small warning flutter from the Passenger. The man had gunfighter's eyes, the kind you see on the old pictures of Wild West lawmen. You did not argue with those eyes. It was like looking into two cold, blue pistol barrels.

"Lookit," Chambers was saying. "We want to solve this thing, not fight about it." Burris nodded, and Deborah said nothing. "So let Forensics finish up, try to get an ID on the victim. If the lab work says it's your girl," he said, nodding at Deborah, "it's your case. If not"—and he tilted his head to Burris—"go crazy. It's all yours. Until then"—he looked straight at Debs and, to her great credit, she looked back without whimpering—"you stay quiet and let Burris work. All right?"

"I get access," Deborah said sullenly.

"Access," Chambers said. "Not control."

Debs looked at Burris. He shrugged and looked away. "All right," she said.

And so the Battle of the Everglades was over, ending happily for everyone—except, of course, for Dexter the Drudge, because Debs apparently interpreted "access" to mean following me around and peppering me with questions. I was almost finished anyway, but it did not make things easier to have a shadow, especially one like Deborah, who was likely to attack me with one of her agonizing arm punches at any moment if I failed to answer her satisfactorily. I filled her in on what I knew and what I had guessed as I sprayed my Bluestar in a few final spots, looking for any last traces of blood. The spray would reveal even the tiniest hint of blood, down to the smallest droplet, and it did not affect the DNA of the sample.

"What is it?" Deborah demanded. "What did you find?"

"Nothing," I said. "But you're standing on a footprint." She stepped aside guiltily and I got my camera out of my bag. I stood and turned back around, bumping squarely into Deborah. "Debs, please," I said. "I really can't do this with you attached to my hip."

"Fine," she said, and she stalked away to a spot opposite the fire pit.

I had just taken a last picture of the main blood spatter when I heard Deborah calling. "Dex," she said. "Hey, bring your spray over here." I looked over to where she stood. Vince Masuoka was kneeling and taking a sample of something. I got my Bluestar and joined them.

"Spray it right here," Deborah said, and Vince shook his head.

"It's not blood," he said. "It's the wrong color."

I looked down at the spot he was examining. There was a flattened area, as if a heavy object had stood there backed up against a row of vegetation. The leaves were wilted from heat, and on them, as well as at the edge of the depression, there were a few small brown stains. Something had spilled out from some kind of container that had been there.

"Spray it," Deborah said.

I looked at Vince, who shrugged. "I got a clean sample already," he said. "It's not blood."

"All right," I said, and I sprayed a small spot on one of the bushes.

Almost immediately a very faint blue glow was visible. "Not blood," Debs said scornfully. "So what the fuck is that?"

"Shit," Vince mumbled.

"It's not much blood," I said. "The glow is too faint."

"But it's *some* blood?" Debs demanded.

"Well, yes," I said.

"So it's some other kind of shit, with blood *in* it," she said.

I looked at Vince. "Well," he said. "I guess so."

Deborah nodded and looked around. "So you got a party," she said. She pointed at the fire pit. "And way over there you got the victim. And way over here on the other side of the party you got this." She glared at Vince. "With *blood* in it." She turned to me. "So what is it?" she demanded.

I should not have been surprised that this was suddenly my problem, but I was. "Come on, Debs," I said.

"No, *you* come on," she said. "I need one of your special hunches here."

"I have a special hunch back at the station," Vince said. "His name is Ivan."

"Shut up, dickless," Deborah said. "Come on, Dexter."

Apparently there was nothing for it, so I closed my eyes, took a deep breath, and listened. . . .

And almost immediately got a very amused answer from the Passenger. "Punch bowl," I said, snapping my eyes open.

"What?" Deborah said.

"It's the punch bowl," I said. "For the party."

"With human blood in it?" she said.

"Punch?" Vince said. "Jesus' tits, Dex, you're a sick fuck."

"Hey," I said innocently, "I didn't drink any of it."

"You're fucking crazy," Deborah added helpfully.

"Debs, look," I said. "It's away from the fire, and we got this dent in the ground." I knelt next to Vince and pointed to the depression in the dirt. "Something heavy, stuff spilled out to the sides, lots of footprints around it—you don't have to call it punch if that makes you nervous. But it's the beverage."

Deborah stared at the spot I pointed to, looked across the clearing at the fire pit, and then back to the ground at her feet. She shook her head slowly, dropped into a squat beside me, and said, "Punch bowl. Fuck."

"You're a sick fuck," Vince repeated.

"Yeah," Debs said. "But I think he's right." She stood up. "I bet you a dozen doughnuts you find some kind of drug traces in there, too," she said with a very noticeable note of satisfaction.

"I'll check it," Vince said. "I got a good test for ecstasy." He gave her his hideous sex leer and added, "Would you like to take the ecstasy test with me?"

"No, thanks," she said. "You don't have the pencil for it." She turned away before he could try one of his awful comebacks, and I followed. It took me only three steps to realize that something about her was very wrong, and when it registered I stopped dead and turned her to face me.

I looked at my sister with surprise. "Debs," I said. "You're actually smiling."

"Yeah," she said. "Because we just proved that this is my case."

"What do you mean?"

She punched me, hard. It may have been a happy punch for her, but it still hurt me. "Don't be stupid," she said. "Who drinks blood?"

"Ouch," I said. "Bela Lugosi?"

"Him and all the other vampires," she said. "You want me to spell 'vampire' for you?"

"So what— Oh," I said.

"Yeah, oh," she said. "We turn up a vampire wannabe, Bobby

Acosta. And now we got a whole fucking vampire frat party. You think that's a coincidence?"

I didn't think so, but my arm hurt too much to say so. "We'll see," I said.

"Yes, we will," she said. "Get your stuff; I'll drive you back."

It was definitely lunchtime when we got back to civilization, but none of the subtle hints I threw out to Debs seemed to register, and she drove straight back to headquarters without pausing, in spite of the fact that Route 41 turns into Calle Ocho, and we could easily have pulled over at a number of excellent Cuban restaurants. Just thinking about them made my stomach growl, and I imagined I could smell the *plátanos* sizzling in the frying pan. But as far as Deborah was concerned, the wheels of justice were already in motion, grinding their inexorable way toward a guilty verdict and a safer world, which apparently meant that Dexter could very well do without lunch for society's sake.

And so it was a very hungry Dexter who made his weary way back to the forensics lab, chivvied every step of the way by his sister's demands for rapid identification of the victim from the Everglades scene. I unpacked my samples and flung myself into my chair, searching for answers to the burning question: Should I drive all the way back to Calle Ocho? Or simply head to Café Relampago, which was much closer and had excellent sandwiches?

Like most important questions in life, this one had no easy answer, and I thought hard about the implications. Was it better to eat quickly, or well? If I chose instant gratification, did that make me a weaker person? And why did it have to be Cuban food today? Why not, for example, barbecue?

The moment that thought popped into my head, I began to lose my appetite. The girl in the Everglades had been barbecued, and for some reason that troubled me a great deal. I could not get the pictures out of my mind: the poor girl lashed in place, slowly bleeding out as the flames reached higher, the crowd howling, and the chef dabbing on barbecue sauce. I could almost smell the cooking flesh, and that drove all thoughts of *ropa vieja* and lunch completely out of my head.

Was this the way life was going to be from now on? How could I do my job if I felt actual human empathy for the victims I saw every day? Worse, how could I stay in a job that came between me and lunch?

It was a terribly sad state of affairs, and I let the self-pity wash over me for a few minutes. Dexter in the Dumps, an absurd figure. I, who had sent dozens of the deserving into the afterlife, was now mourning the loss of one insignificant girl, and merely because whoever killed her had not wasted the meat.

Preposterous; and in any case, the mighty machine that was me needed some kind of fuel. So I brushed away the unhappy thoughts and trudged down the hall to the vending machines. Looking through the glass at the meager selection of snack foods brought me no joy, either. At the hospital a Snickers bar had seemed like manna from heaven. Now it looked like punishment. Nothing else called out to me and promised fulfillment, either. In spite of all the bright wrappers and gleeful slogans, all I could see was a case filled with preservatives and chemically enhanced colors. It was all artificially flavored with genuine synthetic replicas, and it seemed about as appetizing as eating a chemistry set.

But duty called, and I needed to eat something to function at the necessary high level. So I settled on the least offensive choice— crackers with a substance in the middle that claimed to be peanut butter. I fed in some money and pushed the button. The crackers dropped out into the tray, and as I bent to pick them up a small and shadowy figure in the dark basement of Castle Dexter opened a door and stuck its head out. I froze for a moment in the bent-over position and listened. I heard nothing except the silken fluttering of a tiny warning flag, that things were not what they should be, and I stood up slowly and carefully and turned around.

There was nothing at all behind me: no maniac with a knife, no semi truck careening toward me out of control, no turbaned giant with an assegai—nothing. Still, the small voice whispered at me to beware.

Clearly, the Passenger was playing with me. Perhaps it was miffed at me for failing to feed and exercise it. "Just shut up," I told it. "Go away and leave me alone." It continued to smirk at me, so I ignored it and stepped into the hall.

And I walked almost directly into Sergeant Doakes—or most of him, anyway.

Doakes had always hated me, even before a crazed doctor had cut away his hands, feet, and tongue when I had failed to rescue him. I mean, I had tried—really—but things had just not worked out, and as a direct consequence Doakes had lost a few overrated body parts. But even before that, he had hated me because, out of all the cops I had ever met, he was the only one who suspected what I was. I had given him no reason and no evidence, but somehow he just *knew*.

And now he stood there on his artificial feet, glaring at me with all the venom of a thousand cobras. For a moment I wished that the mad doctor had taken away his eyes, too, but I quickly realized that this was an unkind thought, unsuitable for the new and human me, so I put it out of my mind and instead gave him a friendly smile. "Sergeant Doakes," I said. "It's good to see you, and moving around so well, too."

Doakes did nothing at all, just kept looking at me, and I looked down at the silvery metallic claws that had replaced his hands. He was not carrying the small notebook-size speech box he used to talk—possibly he wanted both claws free to strangle me, or more likely, he planned to use the vending machines, too. And since he no longer had a tongue, his attempts at speech without the synthesizer were so embarrassing, filled with "ngah" sounds and so on, that he probably didn't want to risk looking silly. So he just stared at me for a moment, until finally the anticipation of a sprightly encounter withered away within me.

"Well," I said, "it's been very nice speaking with you. Have a lovely day." I walked away toward my lab, turning back to look only once. Doakes was still watching me with his poisonous stare.

I told you so, gloated the soft voice of the Passenger, but I just waved at Doakes and went back to the lab.

When Vince and the others got back around three, the taste of the crackers was still lingering unpleasantly in the back of my mouth.

"Wow," Vince said as he came in and dropped his bag on the floor. "I think I got a sunburn."

"What did you do about lunch?" I asked him.

He blinked as if I'd asked a crazy question, and maybe I had. "One of the cops drove back to a Burger King," he said. "Why?"

"You didn't lose your appetite thinking about that girl being roasted and eaten right there?"

Vince looked even more astonished. "No," he said, shaking his head slowly, "I had a double Whopper with cheese, and fries. Are you okay?"

"I'm just hungry," I said, and he looked at me a moment longer, so rather than sit through a staring contest, I turned away and went back to work.

SIXTEEN

THE TELEPHONE WOKE ME UP WHILE IT WAS STILL DARK, and I rolled over to look at the clock radio beside the bed. It said 4:47 in obnoxiously cheerful digits. I'd had just over twenty minutes of real sleep since the last time Lily Anne had cried, and I did not appreciate the wake-up call. But hoping against hope that the ringing would not reawaken her, I grabbed at the telephone. "Hello," I said.

"I need you here early," declared the voice of my sister. She did not sound at all tired, in spite of the hour, and I found that just as annoying as being wakened at this dreadful time of night.

"Deborah," I said, the hoarseness of sleep still in my throat, "it's another two and a half hours until early."

"We matched up your DNA sample," she said, ignoring what was really a pretty clever remark, considering the hour. "It's Tyler Spanos."

I blinked rapidly a few times, trying to bring my brain into some kind of state that approached wakefulness. "The girl in the Ever-glades?" I said. "That was Tyler Spanos? Not Samantha Aldovar?"

"Yeah," she said. "So this morning they're setting up a task force. Chambers is coordinating, but I got lead investigator." And I could hear the excitement in her voice as she said it.

"That's great," I said, "but why do you need me early?"

She dropped her voice as if she was afraid someone would hear her. "I need your help, Dex," she said. "This is turning into a huge thing and I can't fuck it up. And it's getting, you know. Political." She cleared her throat slightly, sounding a little bit like Captain Matthews. "So I got you down to lead Forensics on the task force."

"I have to take the kids to school," I protested, and beside me I heard a soft rustling.

Rita's hand came down on my arm, and she said, "I can take the kids."

"You shouldn't drive yet," I protested. "Lily Anne is too small."

"She'll be fine," Rita said. "And so will I. Dexter, I've done this before, and without help the first two times."

We never talked about Rita's ex, the bio dad of Cody and Astor, but I knew enough about him to know that he could not have been terribly helpful. Clearly, she really had done this before. And in truth, Rita looked fine, not at all unhealthy—but naturally enough, it was Lily Anne I was worried about. "But the car seat," I said.

"It's fine, Dexter, really," Rita said. "Go do your job."

I heard something that might have been a snort from Deborah. "Tell Rita I said thanks," Debs said. "See you soon." And she hung up.

"But," I said into the phone, even though the line was dead.

"Get dressed," Rita said, and she repeated, "Really, we'll be fine."

Our society has many laws and customs to protect women from the brute force of men, but when two women make up their minds about something and gang up on a man there is absolutely nothing he can do but go along. Perhaps someday we will elect a compassionate woman as president, and she will pass new laws on the subject; until then, I was a helpless victim. I got up and showered, and by the time I was dressed Rita had a fried-egg sandwich ready for me to eat in the car, and a cup of coffee in a shiny metal travel mug.

"Work hard," she said with a tired smile. "I hope you catch these people." I looked at her with surprise. "It was on the news," she said. "They said it was— That poor girl was *eaten*." She shuddered and took a sip of coffee. "In Miami. In this day and age. I don't— I mean, *cannibals*? A whole *group* of them? How can you . . ." She shook her head, took another sip of coffee, and put the cup down—and to my surprise I saw a tear form in one corner of her eye.

"Rita," I said.

"I know," she said, knuckling away the tear. "It's just hormones, I'm sure, because— And I don't really . . ." She sniffled. "It's just the baby," she said. "And now somebody else's little girl— Go on, Dexter. This is important."

I went. I was not really awake yet, and still suffering from psychological whiplash from my treatment at the hands of Rita and Debs, but I went. And oddly enough, I was surprised as much by what Rita had said as by her tears. *Cannibals*. It seems very stupid to say so, but I had not really thought of that word yet. I mean, Dexter is not dull: I knew the poor girl had been eaten by people, and I knew that people who ate other people were called cannibals. But to put those thoughts together and say cannibals had eaten Tyler Spanos—it brought the whole thing onto a level of everyday, toe-stubbing reality that was somehow a little bit strange and scary. I know that the world is full of bad people: After all, I am one of them. But a whole group of partygoers eating a young girl at an outdoor barbecue? That made them real cannibals—*contemporary*, modern-day, right-here-in-Miami cannibals—and it felt like the level of badness had just gone up a few notches.

And there was an additional tinge of quaintness to the whole thing, too, as if a book of frightening fairy tales had come to life: first vampires and now cannibals. What a very interesting place Miami had suddenly become. Perhaps next I would meet a centaur or a dragon, or even an honest man.

I drove to work in darkness and light traffic. A large chunk of moon hung in the sky, scolding me for my sloth. *Get to work, Dexter*, it whispered. *Slice something up*. I gave it the finger and drove on.

One of the conference rooms on the second floor had been set aside to make a command center for Deborah's task force, and it was already buzzing with activity when I strolled in. Chambers, the shaven-headed man from FDLE, sat at a large table that was already heaped with folders, lab reports, maps, and coffee cups. He had a pile of six or seven cell phones beside him, and he was talking into another one.

And, unfortunately for all concerned—except possibly the ghost of J. Edgar Hoover, who must have been hovering protectively in a spectral house frock—sitting next to Chambers was Special Agent Brenda Recht. She had a pair of very chic reading glasses on the end of her nose that she pushed down even farther in order to look at me with disapproval. I smiled back at her and looked to the far end of the room, where a man in a state trooper uniform was standing next to the giant black man I had seen at the crime scene. He turned to stare at me, so I just nodded and moved on.

Deborah was briefing two Miami-Dade detectives, with her partner, Deke, sitting beside her, flossing his teeth. She looked up at me and beckoned for me to join her. I pulled a chair over next to her group and sat as one of the detectives, a guy named Ray Alvarez, interrupted her.

"Yeah, hey, listen," he said. "I don't like it at all. I mean, the guy is fucking city hall—you been called off once already."

"It's different now," Deborah told him. "We got a murder like nobody's ever seen, and the press is going nuts."

"Yeah, sure," Alvarez said, "but you know fucking well Acosta is just waiting to bust somebody's balls."

"Don't worry about it," Deborah said.

"Easy for you," Alvarez said. "No balls to bust."

"That's what you think," said Hood, the other detective, a hulking brute I knew a little. "She got twice your balls, Ray."

"Fuck you," Alvarez said. Deke snorted, either a laugh, or perhaps some small particle of food had gotten flossed out and become lodged in his nose.

"You just find Bobby Acosta," Debs said sharply, "or you won't have any balls to worry about." She glared at him, and he shrugged, looking up at the ceiling as if to ask why God was picking on him. "Start with the motorcycle," she said. She glanced at a folder in her lap. "It's a red Suzuki Hayabusa, one year old."

Deke whistled and Alvarez said, "A what?"

"Hayabusa," Deke said, looking suitably impressed. "Very hot bike."

"Right, got it," Alvarez said, looking at Deke with weary resignation, and Debs turned to Hood.

"You get on Tyler Spanos's car," she said. "It's a 2009 Porsche, blue, convertible. It's gotta turn up somewhere."

"Probably Colombia," Hood said, and as Deborah opened her mouth to scold him he added, "Yeah, I know; I'll find it if it isn't gone already." He shrugged. "Not that it'll do any good."

"Hey," Deke said. "Gotta do the routine stuff, you know?"

Hood looked at him with amusement. "Yeah, Deke," he said. "I know."

"All right," Chambers said in a loud voice, and all eyes in the room clicked over to him as if they were on the same switch. "If I could have your attention over here for a minute."

Chambers stood up and backed to a spot where he could see everybody. "First, I want to thank Major Nelson"—he nodded at the man in the trooper uniform—"and Detective Weems from the Miccosukee Tribal Police." And the giant man raised a hand to wave and, oddly, smiled at everyone.

I nudged Deborah and whispered, "Watch and learn, Debs. Politics."

She elbowed me hard and whispered, "Shut up."

Chambers went on. "They're here because this thing is turning into an A-one, world-class, top-of-the-line screamer, and we might need their help. We got a possible connection into the Everglades," he said, nodding again to Weems, "and we're gonna need all the help we can get covering the roads statewide." Major Nelson didn't even blink at this.

"What about the Fibby?" Hood said, pointing at Special Agent Recht, and Chambers stared at him for a moment.

"The FBI is here," Chambers said carefully, "because this is a *group* we're looking for, and if it's at all organized, maybe national, they want to know about it. Besides, we still got one girl missing, and it may turn out to be kidnapping. And frankly, since this is such a freaking mess, you are damned lucky you don't have Treasury, ATF, and Naval Intelligence in here, too, so shut up and cowboy on."

"Yes, sir," Hood said with a sarcastic little salute. Chambers watched him just long enough to make Hood squirm, before he started talking again.

"All right," he said. "Sergeant Morgan has the lead here in the Miami area. Anything points somewhere else, bring it to me first." Deborah nodded.

"Questions," Chambers said, looking around the room. Nobody said anything. "Okay," he said. "Sergeant Morgan is going to give you a summary of what we know so far."

Deborah stood up and walked over to where Chambers stood, and he sat down, yielding the floor to her. Debs cleared her throat and started on her summary. It was painful to watch; she is not a good public speaker, and aside from that she is extremely self-conscious. It seems to me that she has always felt ill at ease in the body of a beautiful woman, since she has a personality more suited to Dirty Harry, and she hates to have people looking at her. So for anyone who really cared about her, which was probably limited to me at the moment, it was an uncomfortable experience to see her stumble over words, repeatedly clear her throat, and lunge at cop-talk clichés as if she were drowning.

Still, everything has to end sometime, no matter how unpleasant it is, and after a long and nerve-racking interlude Debs finished up and said, "Questions?" And then she blushed and looked at Chambers, as if he would be upset that she had used his line.

Detective Weems raised a finger. "What you want us to do in the Everglades?" he said in a remarkably soft and high-pitched voice.

Deborah cleared her throat. Again. "Just, you know," she said, "put the word out. If anybody sees something out there, if these guys try to throw, you know, another party. Or if there's an old one we don't know about yet, a place that maybe there's some evidence on the site we could find." And she cleared her throat. I wondered if I should offer her a cough drop.

Luckily for Deborah's image as a two-fisted investigator, Chambers decided that enough was enough. He stood up before Deborah actually melted, and said, "All right. You all know what to do. The only thing I want to add is, keep your mouth shut. The press is having too much fun with this already, and I don't want to give them anything else to kick around. Got it?"

Everybody nodded, even Deborah.

"All right," Chambers said. "Let's go get the bad guys."

The meeting broke up to the sound of squeaking chairs, shuffling feet, and cop chatter, as everyone sitting stood up and formed into little conversation groups with those already standing—except for Major Nelson of the Highway Patrol, who just jammed his hat onto his closely cropped head and marched out the door as if the "Colonel Bogey March" was playing. The huge man from the tribal police, Weems, sauntered over to talk to Chambers, and Special Agent Recht sat by herself and looked around the room, quietly disapproving. Hood caught her eye and shook his head.

"Shit," he said. "I fucking hate the Fibbies."

"I bet that worries them," Alvarez said.

"Hey, Morgan, seriously," Hood said. "Is there some way we can twist that federal bitch's tail?"

"Sure," said Debs, in a tone of voice so reasonable that it could only mean trouble for somebody. "You can find the fucking girl, catch the fucking killer, and do your fucking job so she doesn't have an excuse to do it for you." She showed him some teeth; it was not a smile, although possibly Bobby Acosta might have thought so. "Think you can do that, Richard?"

Hood looked at her for a moment and then just shook his head. "Shit," he said.

"Hey, how about that, you were right," Alvarez said. "And she got more balls than you, too."

"Shit," Hood said again, and, clearly looking for an easy target to win back a few points, he said, "What about you, Deke?"

"What's that?" Deke said.

"What are you doing?" Hood said.

Deke shrugged. "Oh, you know," he said. "Captain wants me to stick with, uh, Morgan here."

"Wow," Alvarez said. "Really dangerous."

"We're partners," Deke said, looking slightly hurt.

"You be careful, Deke," Hood said. "Morgan is pretty hard on her partners."

"Yeah, she kind of loses 'em now and then," Alvarez said.

"You two assholes want me to hold your hand all the way to the DMV database?" Deborah said. "Or can you get your head out of your ass long enough to find it by yourself?"

Hood stood up and said, "On my way, boss," and headed for the door, and Alvarez followed. "Watch your back, Deke," he said as he left.

Deke watched them go with a slight frown, and as the door closed behind them he said, "Why they gotta bust my chops? 'Cause I'm the new guy, or what?" Deborah ignored him, and he turned to me. "I mean, what? What'd I do? Huh?"

I had no answer for him other than the obvious, which was that cops are like all other pack animals—they pick on any member of the herd that seems different or shows weakness. With his absurd good looks and somewhat limited mental abilities, Deke was both, and therefore an obvious target. Still, it seemed like a tough idea to get across without a lot of unpleasantness and groping for small words, so I just gave Deke a reassuring smile. "I'm sure they'll ease up when they see what you can do," I told him.

He shook his head slowly. "How'm I supposed to do anything?" he said, leaning his head toward Debs. "I gotta stick with her like a fuckin' shadow."

He watched me as if I was supposed to supply an answer, so I said, "Well, I'm sure a chance will come up for you to show some initiative."

"Initiative," he said, and for a moment I thought I would have to tell him what that meant. But happily for me, he just shook his head sourly and said, "Shit," and before we could explore any of the subtleties of that thought, Chambers came over and put a hand on Deborah's shoulder.

"All right, Morgan," he said. "You know what you gotta do. Downstairs, ninety minutes."

Debs looked at him with an expression that was closer to terror than anything I had ever seen on her face before. "I can't," she said. "I mean, I thought you were going to— Can't you do it?"

Chambers shook his head with something like malicious glee in his smile. It made him look like a wicked and very deadly elf. "Can't," he said. "You're the lead here. I'm just the coordinator. Your captain wants *you* to do this." He patted her shoulder again and moved away.

"Shit," Deborah said, and for a moment I felt intense irritation that this was the only word anyone could come up with this morning; and then she ran a hand through her hair and I noticed that her hand was shaking.

"What is it, Debs?" I said, wondering what on earth could cause my fearless sister to tremble like a fragile leaf in a storm.

She took a deep breath and squared her shoulders. "Press conference," she said. "They want me to talk to the press." And she swallowed and then licked her lips as if everything inside her had just gone completely dry. "*Shit*," she said again.

SEVENTEEN

O NE OF THE THINGS I FIND MOST REWARDING ABOUT MY job is that there is always a certain amount of variety. Some days I get to use large and expensive machinery to run very modern scientific tests; some days I simply peer into a microscope. And if nothing else, the scenery changes when I go out to crime scenes. Of course, the crimes are all different, too, ranging from the common and vulgar wife slashing to some really quite interesting eviscerations from time to time.

But in all my vast and varied experience with the department, I had never before been asked to use my scientific training and acumen to prepare my terrified sister for a press conference, and I have to say this was a good thing, because if it had been a regular part of my job, I would have seriously considered quitting forensics and getting a job teaching middle school physical education.

Deborah dragged me off to her cubicle and immediately burst into a very unattractive cold sweat; she sat down, stood up, paced three steps in each direction, sat down again, and began to squeeze her hands together. And just to add to an already sky-high Irritant Quotient, she began to say, "Shit. Shit shit shit shit shit," over and over in various volumes and inflections, until I began to think she had lost the power of intelligent speech altogether.

"Debs," I said at last, "if that's your statement, Captain Matthews is going to be very unhappy."

"Shit," she said, and I wondered if I should slap her. "Dexter, Jesus, please, what am I supposed to say?"

"Anything but 'shit,' " I said.

She stood up again and walked to the window, still mangling her hands. Every little girl who has ever lived has grown up wanting to be an actress or dancer or some kind of performer—all of them except Deborah. All she ever wanted out of life, even at the tender age of five, was a badge and a gun. And through hard work, dogged intelligence, and really painful arm punches, she had achieved her goal—only to find that in order to keep it, she now had to be an actress. The word "irony" is terribly overused, but still, the situation seemed to call for a bit of wry amusement at the very least.

But it also called for a certain amount of Dexter's newfound Lily Anne–born compassion, since I could tell that without my help, my sister was going to prove once and for all that there really was something to the idea of spontaneous combustion. So when I decided that Debs had suffered enough, I got up from my rickety little chair and went to stand beside her. "Debs," I said. "This is something so easy that Captain Matthews is *good* at it."

I think she almost said "shit" again, but she caught herself and just bit her lip instead. "I can't do it," she said. "All those people— and reporters—cameras— I just can't, Dexter."

I was glad to see that she had recovered a little, enough to separate "people" from "reporters," but clearly I still had work to do. "You *can*, Deborah," I told her firmly. "And it will be a lot easier than you think. You may even get to like it."

She ground her teeth and I think she would have punched me if she hadn't been so distracted. "Don't hold your breath," she said.

"It's easy," I said again. "We're going to write out a few short paragraphs, and all you have to do is read them out loud. Just like giving a book report in sixth grade."

"I flunked book reports," she growled.

"You didn't have me to help," I said, with a great deal more confidence than I felt. "Now come on; let's sit down and write this thing."

She ground her teeth and squeezed her hands together some more for a few seconds, and she seemed to think about jumping out the window. But it was only the second floor, and the windows were sealed shut, so finally Debs turned away and slumped back into her chair. "All right," she said through clenched teeth. "Let's do it."

There are only a very few cop clichés that are necessary for saying almost anything to the press. That is one reason, of course, that a talking suit like Captain Matthews could become good enough at it to rise up to his lofty rank based solely on his ability to memorize them all and then put them in the right order when standing in front of a camera. It was really not even a skill, since it took a great deal less ability than the simplest card trick.

Still, it was a talent Deborah did not have, not even a little, and trying to explain it to her was like describing plaid to a blind person. Altogether it was a nasty and unpleasant interlude, and by the time we headed down to the press conference I was nearly as sweaty and frazzled as my sister. Neither of us felt any better when we saw the standing-room-only crowd of salivating predators waiting for us. For a moment Deborah froze in place, one foot raised in the air. But then, as if somebody had flipped a switch, the reporters turned on her and began their routine of shouting questions and taking pictures, and as I saw Deborah clamp her jaw and frown, I took a deep breath. *She's going to be all right*, I thought, and I watched her climb to the podium with something like pride in my creation.

Of course, that lasted only until she opened her mouth, and after that began one of the most miserable fifteen-minute spells I can remember. Deborah trying to speak to a roomful of cops was profoundly uncomfortable. Deborah trying to make a statement at a press conference was torture so intensely painful that I am quite sure that the men in black hoods who worked for the Inquisition would have shuddered and refused to participate. Deborah stammered, stuttered, stumbled, sweated, and lurched from phrase to carefully polished phrase in a tangled sweat so thorough she looked like she was confessing to child rape, and when she finally finished the prepared statement I had worked on so hard there was stunned silence in the room for several seconds. And then, alas, the reporters smelled blood in the water and leaped on Deborah with a savage frenzy. All that had come before was cupcakes and kitties by comparison, and I watched as Deborah slowly and carefully tied the rope around her own neck and hoisted herself into the air, where she twisted in the wind with agonizing completeness until finally, mercifully, Captain Matthews had suffered enough and stepped forward to say, "No more questions." He did not quite shove Deborah off the podium, but it was clear that he had to think about it.

The captain glared forcefully at the assembled lynch mob, as if he could beat them into submission with his manly stare, and they did actually quiet down just a bit. "All right," he said after a moment. "The, uh, family members." He put a fist to his mouth and cleared his throat and I wondered if Deborah was contagious. "Mr. and Mrs. Um Aldovar. Would like to make a brief statement." He nodded and then held out an arm in a half embrace.

A stunned-looking Mr. Aldovar led his wife up to the microphones. She looked exhausted and several years older, but as they stood there in front of the crowd she visibly gathered herself, pushed away from her husband, and fumbled out a sheet of paper. And the reporters, bizarrely enough, actually went silent for a moment.

"To the person or persons who took our little girl," she began, and then she had to stop for a moment and, just for consistency, clear her throat. "Our Samantha," she said. "We don't have a lot of money, but whatever we have or can get, it's yours. Just please don't hurt our little girl. . . . Just . . ." And that was as far as she could get. She covered her face with her hands and the paper fluttered to the ground. Mr. Aldovar stepped forward and took her into his arms and glared at the crowd as if they knew where Samantha was and refused to tell.

"She's a good kid," he said angrily. "There's no reason in the world to, to— Please," he said with a softer tone. "Please just let her go. Whatever it is you want, just please let her go. . . ." And then his face crumpled and he just turned away. Captain Matthews stepped forward and glared out at the room again.

"All right," the captain said. "You all have a picture of the girl. Samantha. We're asking that you help us get it out there, and, uh— if people see her, you know, citizens. You can call that special task force hotline, which—you have that number, too, in the media. And if we can, uh, circulate the number, and the picture, let's get this girl back. Alive." He gave the room his money shot, a determined and virile glare straight into the cameras, and held it for a beat before he said, "Thank you for your help." And he stood there for a moment longer with his manly jaw clenched, to give the photographers one last good shot of his commanding facial features, and then he said, "All right, that's it," and turned away.

Predictably enough, the room erupted into enormously loud chaos, but Matthews just waved an arm and turned away to say comforting things to the Aldovars, and that really was it. I pushed forward to get to Deborah, collecting and distributing several hard elbows to the ribs along the way. I found my sister standing off to the side, opening and closing her fists. A little bit of color had returned to her cheeks and she looked oddly rumpled, as if some-body had just woken her from a bad dream.

"If I ever have to do that again," she said through her teeth, "I'll turn in my goddamn badge."

"If you ever try to do it again," I said, "Captain Matthews will take it from you himself."

"Jesus fuck," she said. "Was it as bad as it felt?"

"Oh, no," I said. "Much worse."

I suppose my sour mood prevented me from seeing it coming, but Debs whacked me with an arm punch. On the one hand, it was nice to see her recovering from her ordeal. But on the other hand, it really hurt.

"Thanks for the support," she said. "Let's get out of here." She turned and began pushing angrily through the crowd, and I followed, rubbing my arm.

Reporters are odd creatures. They have to think very highly of themselves in order to do their job at all, and clearly some of them who had seen Deborah's pitiful performance must have been very good at that kind of self-delusion, because they apparently believed that if they only shoved a microphone at Debs and shouted a question, she would cave in under the pressure of their perfect hair and teeth and blurt out an answer. Unfortunately for their professional self-esteem, however, Deborah just kept moving forward, batting away anything they put in front of her, and pushing hard at anyone foolish enough to stand in her way. And even the reporters standing back toward the exit, who saw quite clearly what happened to their colleagues, thought so highly of themselves that they tried the exact same thing—and seemed surprised when they got the same result.

Because I was following Deborah, several of them eyed me speculatively, but after many years of diligent maintenance, my disguise was too good for them, and they all decided that I was exactly what I wanted to appear—an absolute nonentity with no answers to anything. And so, relatively unmolested, battered only on the upper arm from Deborah's arm punch, I made it out of the press conference and, with my sister, back to the task force command center on the second floor.

Somewhere along the way, Deke joined us, trickling in behind to lean against the wall. Somebody had set up a coffee machine and Deborah poured some into a Styrofoam cup. She sipped it and made a face. "This is worse than the coffee service stuff," she said.

"We could go for breakfast," I said hopefully.

Debs put down the cup and sat down. "We got too much to do," she said. "What time is it?"

"Eight forty-five," Deke said, and Deborah looked at him sourly, as if he had chosen an unpleasant time. "What," he said. "It is."

The door swung open and Detective Hood came in. "I am so fucking good I scare myself," he said as he swaggered over and slumped into a seat in front of Deborah.

"Scare me, too, Richard," Deborah said. "What have you got?"

Hood pulled a sheet of paper out of his pocket and unfolded it. "In record time," he said. "Tyler Spanos's 2009 blue convertible Porsche." He flicked a finger at the paper, making a popping sound.

"Guy runs a chop shop, he owed me a favor; I cut him a break last year." He shrugged. "It woulda been his third fall, so he called me with this." He flicked the paper again. "It's in a repaint place up at Opa-Locka," he said. "I got a squad car there now, holding the guys were painting it, a couple of Haitians." He tossed the paper on the desk in front of Deborah. "Who's your daddy?" he said.

"Get out there," Debs said. "I want to know who sold it to them, and I don't care how you find out."

Hood gave her a huge meat-eating smile. "Cool," he said. "Sometimes I love this job." He slid up and out of the chair with a surprising grace and was out the door and away, whistling "Here Comes the Sun."

Deborah watched him go and as the door swung closed she said, "Our first break, and that dickhead gets it for me."

"Hey, I dunno, break?" Deke said. "By the time they're painting it, won't be any prints or anything."

Debs looked at him with an expression that would have sent me scurrying under the furniture. "Somebody got stupid, Deke," she said, with a little extra emphasis on the word "stupid." "They should have put the car in a sinkhole, but somebody wanted to make a quick couple of grand, so they sold it. And if we find who sold it to them—"

"We find the girl," Deke said.

Deborah looked at him, and her face looked almost fond. "That's right, Deke," she said. "We find the girl."

"Okay, then," Deke said.

The door swung open again, and Detective Alvarez came in. "You're gonna love this," he said, and Deborah looked at him expectantly.

"You found Bobby Acosta?" she said.

Alvarez shook his head. "The Spanos family is here to see you," he said.

EIGHTEEN

IF THE MAN WHO CAME THROUGH THE DOOR FIRST WAS
Mr. Spanos, then Tyler's father was a twenty-eight-year-old
bodybuilder with a ponytail and a suspicious bulge under his
left arm. That would have meant he fathered Tyler at the age of ten,
which seemed to be pushing the envelope, even in Miami. But whoever this man was, he was very serious, and he looked the room
over carefully, which included glaring at me and Deke, before he
stuck his head back into the hall and nodded.

The next man into the room looked a little bit more like you
would hope a teenage girl's father might look. He was middle-aged,
relatively short, and a little chubby, with thinning hair and gold-
rimmed glasses. His face was sweaty and tired and his mouth hung
open as if he had to gasp for breath. He staggered into the room,
looked helplessly around for a moment, and then stood in front of
Deborah, blinking and breathing heavily.

A woman came hustling in behind him. She was younger and
several inches taller, with reddish blond hair and way too much
very good jewelry. She was followed by another young bodybuilder, this time with a buzz cut instead of a ponytail. He carried a

medium-size aluminum suitcase and he closed the door behind him and leaned against the doorframe. The woman marched over to where Deborah sat, pulled a chair out, and guided Mr. Spanos into it. "Sit down," she said to him. "And close your mouth." Mr. Spanos looked at her, blinked some more, and then let her lever him into the chair by his elbow, although he did not close his mouth.

The woman looked around and found another chair at the conference table, and pulled it over beside Mr. Spanos. She sat, looked at him, and then shook her head before turning her attention to Deborah.

"Sergeant—Morgan?" she said, as if unsure of the name.

"That's right," Deborah said.

The woman looked hard at Deborah for a moment, as if she was hoping my sister would morph into Clint Eastwood. She pursed her lips, took a breath, and said, "I'm Daphne Spanos. Tyler's mother."

Deborah nodded. "I'm very sorry for your loss," she said.

Mr. Spanos sobbed. It was a very wet sound, and it took Deborah by surprise, because she goggled at him as if he had started to sing.

"Stop it," Daphne Spanos said to him. "You have to pull yourself together."

"My little girl," he said, and it was very clear that he was not really pulling himself together quite yet.

"She's my little girl, too, goddamn it," Daphne hissed at him. "Now quit blubbering." Mr. Spanos looked down at his feet and shook his head, but at least he did not make any more wet noises. Instead he took a deep breath, closed his eyes, and then sat up as straight as he could and looked at Deborah.

"You're in charge of finding the animals that did this," he said to Debs. "That killed my little girl." And I thought he was going to snivel again, but he clamped his jaw shut tightly, and nothing more came out except a ragged breath.

"It's a task force, Mr. Spanos," she said. "We have a team made up of officers from all the different branches of—"

Mr. Spanos held up his hand and waved it to cut her off. "I don't care about the team," he said. "They said you're in charge. Are you?"

Deborah glanced at Alvarez, who looked away with a suddenly

very innocent face. She looked back at Spanos. "That's right," Deborah said.

He stared at her for a long moment. "Why not a man?" he said. "Is this a politically correct thing, they put a woman in charge?"

I could see Alvarez struggling to control himself; Deborah didn't need to struggle. She was used to this, which is not the same thing as saying she liked it. "I am in charge," she said, "because I am the best and I have earned it. If you have a problem with that, too bad."

Spanos looked at her, shook his head. "I don't like this," he said. "It should be a man."

"Mr. Spanos," Deborah said, "if you have something to say, spit it out. If not— I am trying to catch a killer here, and you are wasting my time." She glared at him, and he looked uncertain. He glanced at his wife, who compressed her lips and then nodded, and Spanos turned to Mr. Ponytail. "Clear the room," he said, and Ponytail took a step toward Deke.

"Back off," Deborah barked, and Ponytail froze. "We're not clearing the room," she said. "This is a police station."

"I have something for your ears only," Spanos said. "I want it confidential."

"I'm a cop," Debs said. "You want confidential, get a lawyer."

"No," Spanos said. "This is for you only, for the head of the investigation, not these other guys."

"It doesn't work that way," Debs said.

"Just this once," Spanos said urgently. "It's my little girl."

"Mr. Spanos," Deborah said.

Mrs. Spanos leaned forward. "Please," she said. "It will only take a minute." She reached over and grabbed Deborah's hand and gave it a squeeze. "It's important," she said. "For the investigation." She saw Deborah look uncertain, just for a second, and she squeezed the hand again. "It will help you find them," she said in a seductive whisper.

Deborah pulled her hand away and looked at the two of them. Then she glanced up at me for an opinion, and I admit I was curious, so I just shrugged.

"Your guys wait in the hall," Deborah said at last. "I'll send out two of my guys."

Spanos shook his head. "Just you and us," he said. "So it's family."

Deborah jerked her head in my direction. "My brother stays," she said, and Mr. and Mrs. Spanos looked at me.

"Your brother," he said, and looked at Mrs. Spanos; she nodded. "All right."

"Mackenzie," Mr. Spanos said, holding out his hand. The guy with the buzz cut came over and gave him the suitcase. "You and Harold wait outside," Spanos said, placing the suitcase on his lap, and the two bodybuilders marched to the door and went out. "Sergeant?" he said to Debs, and she waved at Deke.

"Deke, Alvarez," she said, "keep an eye on those two guys in the hall."

"I'm s'posa keep an eye on you," Deke said. "Captain said."

"Get out," Debs said. "Two minutes."

Deke stared at her stubbornly for a moment, and then Alvarez stepped over and put a hand on his back. "Come on, sport," he said. "Boss lady says go, we go."

Deke jutted out his dimpled chin at Deborah, and for just a second he looked every inch the manly Saturday-morning TV hero. "Two minutes," he said. He looked at her a little longer, as if he was going to say something else, but apparently he couldn't think of anything, so he merely turned away and went out. Alvarez gave Debs a mocking smile and followed.

The door closed behind them, and for a second nobody moved. Then Mr. Spanos made a grunting noise and plopped the aluminum suitcase into Deborah's lap. "Open it," he said.

Deborah stared at him. "Go on, open it," he said. "It won't explode."

She stared for just a second longer, and then she looked down at the suitcase. It had two locks holding it closed and she slowly undid them and then, with a last look at Spanos, she flipped the lid open.

Deborah looked inside and froze absolutely still, her hand motionless on the raised lid and her face caught between expressions—and then she looked up at Spanos with one of the coldest expressions I had ever seen. "What the fuck is this," she said through her teeth.

Having human feelings was new to me, but having curiosity was not, and I leaned forward for a look, and it did not take a great deal of scrutiny to see what the fuck it was.

It was money. Lots of it.

From the visible top layer it appeared to be bundles of hundred-dollar bills, all with the bank's tape around them. The suitcase was crammed full, so full that I didn't see how Spanos had gotten it closed, unless Mr. Ponytail had stood on top while Spanos locked it.

"Half a million dollars," Spanos said. "In cash. Untraceable. I deliver it anywhere you say. Cayman Islands bank, whatever."

"For what," Deborah said in a very flat voice, and, if he had known her as I did, Mr. Spanos should have gotten very nervous.

But Spanos did not know Deborah, and he seemed to gain confidence from the fact that she had asked what it was for. He smiled, not really a happy smile, more like he wanted to show his face could still do that. "For almost nothing," he said. "Just this." He held up his hand and wagged one finger in the air. "When you find the animals that killed my little girl . . ." His voice broke a little and he stopped, took his glasses off, and wiped them on his sleeve. He put the glasses back on, cleared his throat, and looked at Deborah again. "When you find them, you tell me first. That's all. Ten minutes before you do anything else. One phone call to me. And that money is all yours."

Deborah stared at him. He stared back, and for a few seconds he was no longer a sniveling, snuffling man, but instead a man who always knew exactly what he wanted, and exactly how to get it.

I looked at the money in the still-open suitcase. Half a million dollars. It seemed like an awful lot. I had never really been motivated by money—after all, I had not gone to law school. Money to me had always been merely something the sheep used to show each other how wonderful they were. But now, as I looked at the stacks of cash in the suitcase, it did not look like abstract markers for keeping score. It looked like ballet lessons for Lily Anne. An entire college education. Pony rides and new dresses and braces and finding shells on the beach in the Bahamas. And it was all right there in that one small suitcase, winking its sly greenbacked eyes and saying, *Why not? What could it hurt?*

And then I realized that the silence had gone on a little too long for comfort, and I tore my eyes away from Lily Anne's future happiness and looked up to Deborah's face. As far as I could tell neither she nor Spanos had changed expression. But at last Deborah took a deep breath and put the suitcase on the floor and looked back at Spanos.

"Pick it up," she said, and she nudged it toward him with her foot.

"It's yours," he told her, shaking his head.

"Mr. Spanos," she said, "it is a felony to bribe a police officer."

"What bribe?" he said. "It's a gift. Take it."

"Pick it up, and get it out of here," she said.

"It's one phone call," he said. "Is that such a crime?"

"I am very sorry for your loss," Deborah said very slowly. "And if you pick that up and get it out of here right now, I will forget this happened. But if it is still there when the other detectives come back in, you are going to jail."

"I understand," Spanos said. "You can't say anything right now; that's fine. But take my card, call me when you find them, the money's yours." He flipped a business card to her and Deborah stood up, letting the card fall to the floor.

"Go home, Mr. Spanos," she said. "Take that suitcase with you." And she walked past him to the door and opened it.

"Just call me," Spanos said to her back, but his wife was once again more practical.

"Don't be an idiot," she said. She leaned down and grabbed the suitcase and, with a mighty shove down on the top, just barely got it locked before Deke and Alvarez came back in with the two bodyguards. Mrs. Spanos handed the suitcase to the one with the buzz cut and stood up. "Come on," she said to her husband. He looked at her, and then he turned and looked at Deborah by the door.

"Call me," he said.

She held the door open. "Good-bye, Mr. Spanos," she said.

He looked at her for a few seconds more, and then Mrs. Spanos took him by the elbow and led him out.

Deborah closed the door and let out a loud breath, then turned around and went back to her chair. Alvarez watched her sit, grinning. She looked up at him before he could wipe the smile off.

"Very fucking funny, Alvarez," she snarled.

Deke came over and leaned in the same spot he'd been leaning before the interruption. "How much?" he asked her.

Deborah looked at him in surprise. "What?"

Deke shrugged. "I said, how much?" he said. "How much was in the suitcase?"

Deborah shook her head. "Half a million," she said.

Deke snorted. "Chump change," he said. "Guy in Syracuse tried to give my buddy Jerry Kozanski two mil, and it was only a rape."

"That's nothing," Alvarez said. "Few years ago one of the cocaine cowboys offered me *three* million for the junkie that stole his car."

"Three million and you didn't take it?" Deke said.

"Ah," Alvarez said, "I was holding out for four."

"All right," Deborah said. "We lost enough time with that shit. Let's get back to it." She pointed at Alvarez. "I got no time for your crap. I want Bobby Acosta. Go get him."

And as Alvarez sauntered out the door, I thought that suddenly half a million dollars didn't seem like that much money, not for an entire eaten daughter. And because it was such a small amount, it also seemed like it wouldn't be such a big deal to take it from Spanos for something so trivial as a simple phone call. Yet Deborah apparently felt absolutely no temptation, and even Deke acted like it was something funny and commonplace, nothing at all out of the ordinary.

Apparently Debs agreed. She straightened up and looked right at me. "Let's get this done," she said. "I want to know about that stuff—you called it punch. The stuff we found in the Everglades. It's part blood, but whatever else is in it might lead somewhere. Get on it."

"All right," I said. "What are you and Deke doing?"

She looked at me with a repeat of the bad-lemon glare she'd given Deke. "We," she said with a distaste that matched her expression, "are going to hit the last three names on the list from that dentist. The guys who had the vampire fangs put in." She glanced again at Deke and then away, clamping her jaw tight. "Somebody knows," she said. "Goddamn it, one of those boys knows something, and we're going to get it from him."

"All right," Deke said softly.

"Well, then," I said, "I'll toddle off to my lab and get busy."

"Yeah," Deborah said. "You do that."

I did that, leaving my sister with her unwanted partner.

NINETEEN

VINCE MASUOKA WAS ALREADY BUSTLING AROUND WHEN I got to the lab. "Hey," he said. "I ran my ecstasy test on that stuff from the Everglades?"

"Wonderful," I said. "Just what I was going to suggest."

"So it's positive," he said. "But there's something else in there, too, that's a big part of it." He shrugged and held up his hands helplessly. "It's organic, but that's about all I got."

"Persistence," I said. "We will find it, *mon frère.*"

"Is that French again?" he said. "How long are you going to keep doing French?"

"Until the doughnuts get here?" I said hopefully.

"Well, they're not coming, so *zoot alours* to you," he said, apparently unaware that he made no sense in any language, let alone French. But it was not really my place to educate him, so I let it go and we got busy with the sample from the cannibal party punch bowl.

By noon, we had run almost every test we could do in our own small lab, and found one or two useless things. First, the basic broth was made from one of the commercially popular high-octane energy drinks. Human blood had been added in and, although it was difficult to be absolutely certain using the small and badly degraded sample, I was reasonably sure it had come from several sources. But the last ingredient, the organic something, remained elusive.

"Okay," I said at last. "Let's go at this a different way."

"What," Vince said, "with a Ouija board?"

"Almost," I said. "How about we try inductive logic?"

"Okay, Sherlock," he said. "More fun than gas chromatography any day."

"Eating your fellow humans is not natural," I said, trying to put myself into the mind of someone at the party, but Vince interrupted my slow-forming trance.

"What," he said, "are you kidding? Didn't you read any history at all? Cannibalism is the most natural thing in the world."

"Not in twenty-first-century Miami," I said. "No matter what they say in the *Enquirer*."

"Still," he said, "it's just a cultural thing."

"Exactly," I said. "We have a huge cultural taboo against it that you would have to overcome somehow."

"Well, you got 'em drinking blood, so the next step isn't that big."

"You've got a crowd," I said, trying to shut out Vince and picture the scene. "And they're getting cranked up on the energy drink, drawn in with the ecstasy, and psyched up by watching, and you probably have some kind of hypnotic music playing—" I stopped for a second as I heard what I had said.

"What," Vince said.

"Hypnotic," I said. "What's missing is something to put the crowd into a receptive mental state, something that, you know, works with the music and everything else to make them suggestible in the right way."

"Marijuana," Vince said. "It always gives me the munchies."

"Shit," I said as a small memory popped into my head.

"No, shit wouldn't do it," Vince said. "And it tastes bad."

"I don't want to hear how you know what shit tastes like," I said. "Where's that book of DEA bulletins?"

I found the book, a large, three-ringed notebook into which we put all the interesting notices sent to us by the DEA. After leafing through it for just a few minutes I got to the page I remembered. "There," I said. "This is it."

Vince looked where I pointed. "Salvia divinorum," he said. "Hey, you think so?"

"I do," I said. "Speaking from a purely inductive-logic standpoint."

Vince nodded his head, slowly. "Maybe you should say, 'Elementary'?" he said.

"It's a relatively new thing," I told Deborah. She sat at the table in the task force room with me, Vince, and Deke standing behind her. I leaned over and tapped the page in the DEA book. "They just made salvia illegal in Dade County a couple of years ago."

"I know what the fuck salvia is," she snapped. "And I never heard of it doing anything but making people stupid for five minutes at a time."

I nodded. "Sure," I said. "But we don't know what it might do in incremental doses, especially combined with all this other stuff."

"And for all we know," Vince added, "it doesn't really do anything. Maybe somebody just thought it was cool to mix it in there."

Deborah looked at Vince for a long moment. "Do you have any idea how fucking lame that sounds?" she said.

"Guy in Syracuse smoked some," Deke said. "He tried to flush himself." He looked at the three of us staring at him and shrugged. "You know, in the toilet."

"If I lived in Syracuse, I'd flush myself, too," Deborah said. Deke held up both hands in an eloquent *whatever* gesture.

"Ahem," I said, in a valiant attempt to keep us on topic. "The real point here is not *why* they used it, but that they *did* use it. Considering the size of the crowd, they used a *lot* of it. Probably more than once. And if somebody is using it in quantities that large—"

"Hey, we should find the dealer easy," Deke said.

"I can do the fucking math," Deborah snapped. "Deke, get

over to Vice. Get a list of the biggest salvia dealers from Sergeant Fine."

"I'm on it," Deke said. He looked at me and winked. "Show a little initiative here, right?" he said. He cocked a finger-pistol at me and dropped the thumb. "Boom," he said, smiling as he turned away, and as he sauntered out the door he very nearly collided with Hood, who pushed past him and came over to our little group with a very large and unattractive smirk on his face.

"You are in the presence of greatness," he said to Debs.

"I am in the presence of two nerds and an asshole," Debs said.

"Hey," Vince objected. "We're not nerds; we're geeks."

"Wait'll you see," Hood said.

"See what, Richard?" Debs said sourly.

"I got these two Haitians," he said. "Guaranteed to fucking make your day."

"I hope so, Richard, because I really fucking need my day made," Deborah said. "Where are they?"

Hood went back and opened the door and waved at somebody out in the hall. "In here," he called, and a group of people began to file in past him as he held the door.

The first two were black and very thin. Their hands were fastened behind them with handcuffs, and a uniformed cop pushed them forward. The first prisoner was limping slightly, and the second was sporting an eye that was swollen almost shut. The cop gently pushed them over to stand in front of Deborah, and then Hood stuck his head back in the hall, looked both ways, apparently spotted something, and called, "Hey, Nick! Over here!" And a moment later, one last person came in.

"It's *Nichole*," she said to Hood. "Not Nick." Hood smirked at her, and she shook her head, swirling a shining mass of dark and curly hair. "In fact, for you, it's Ms. Rickman." She looked him in the eye, but Hood just kept smirking, and she gave up and came to the table. She was tall and fashionably dressed and she carried a large sketch pad in one hand and a handful of pencils in the other, and I recognized her as the department's forensic artist. Deborah nodded at her and said, "Nichole. How are you?"

"Sergeant Morgan," she said. "It's nice to be drawing somebody who's not dead." She arched an eyebrow at Debs. "He's not dead, is he?"

"I hope not," Deborah said. "He's my best hope to save this girl."

"Well, then," Nichole said, "let's give it a shot." She put her pad and pencils down on the table, slid into a chair, and began to arrange herself to work.

Meanwhile, Deborah was looking over the two men Hood had brought in. "What happened to these two?" she said to Hood.

He shrugged and looked preposterously innocent. "Whataya mean?" he said.

Debs stared at Hood a little longer. He shrugged and leaned against the wall, and she turned her attention back to the prisoners. "*Bonjour*," she said. Neither of them said anything; they just looked at their feet, until Hood cleared his throat. Then the one with the swollen eye jerked his head up and looked at Hood nervously. Hood nodded toward Deborah, and the prisoner turned to her and began to speak in rapid Creole.

For some quixotic reason, Deborah had studied French in high school, and for a few seconds she apparently thought it was going to help her understand the man. She watched him as he raced through several paragraphs, and then finally shook her head. "*Je nais comprend*— Goddamn it, I can't remember how to say it. Dexter, get somebody up here to translate."

The other man, the one with the sore leg, finally looked up. "There is no need," he said. His words were very heavily accented, but at least they were easier to understand than Deborah's attempts at French.

"Good," Deborah said. "What about your friend?" She nodded at the other man.

Sore Leg shrugged. "I will speak for my cousin," he said.

"All right," Debs said. "We're going to ask you to describe the man who sold you that Porsche—it was a man, wasn't it?"

He shrugged again. "A boy," he said.

"Okay, a boy," Debs said. "What did he look like?"

Another shrug. "A *blanc*," he said. "He was young—"

"How young?" Deborah interrupted.

"I could not say. Old enough to shave, because he did not—maybe three, four days."

"Okay," Deborah said, and frowned.

Nichole leaned forward. "Let me do this, Sergeant," she said. Deborah looked at her for a moment, then leaned back and nodded.

"All right," she said. "Go ahead."

Nichole smiled at the two Haitians. "Your English is very good," she said. "I just need to ask you a few simple questions, all right?"

Sore Leg looked at her suspiciously, but she kept smiling, and after a moment he shrugged. "All right," he said.

Nichole went into what seemed to me like a very vague series of questions. I watched with interest, since I had heard that she was supposed to be good at what she did. At first, I thought her reputation was inflated; she just asked things like, "What do you remember about this guy?" And as Sore Leg answered her she would just nod, scribble on her pad, and say, "Uh-huh, right." She led him through an entire description of someone coming into their garage with Tyler's Porsche, what they had said, and so on, all the boring details. I didn't see how it could possibly lead to a picture of anyone living or dead, and Deborah clearly thought the same thing. She began to fidget almost immediately, and then to clear her throat as if she were trying not to interrupt. Every time she did, the Haitians would glance at her nervously.

But Nichole ignored her and continued with her hopelessly general questions, and very slowly I began to realize that she was getting a pretty good description. And at just that point she shifted to more specific things, like, "What about the outside shape of his face?" she said.

The prisoner looked at her blankly. "Outside . . . ?" he said.

"Answer her," Hood said.

"I don't know," the man said, and Nichole glared at Hood. He smirked and leaned back against the wall, and she turned back to Sore Leg.

"I'd like to show you a few shapes," she said, and she took out a large sheet of paper with several roughly oval shapes on it.

"Does one of these remind you of the shape of his face?" she said, and the prisoner leaned forward and studied them. After a moment, his cousin leaned forward to look, and said something softly. The first man nodded and said, "That one, on the top."

"This one?" Nichole said, pointing at one with her pencil.

"Yes," he said. "That one."

She nodded and began to draw, using quick and very certain strokes, pausing only to ask questions and show more pictures: What about his mouth? His ears? One of these shapes? And so on, until a real face began to take form on the page. Deborah kept quiet and let Nichole lead the two men through it. At each of her questions they would lean together and confer in soft Creole, and then the one who spoke English would answer while his cousin nodded. Altogether, between the two handcuffed men doing their muted Creole patter and the nearly magical emergence of a face on the page, it was a riveting performance, and I was sorry to see it end.

But end it did, at last. Nichole held up the notebook for the two men to study, and the one who spoke no English looked hard and then began to nod. "*Oui*," he said.

"That is him," the other said, and he gave Nichole a sudden very large smile. "Like magic." He said *majeek*, but the meaning was clear.

Deborah had been leaning back in her chair and letting Nichole work. Now she stood and walked around the conference table, looking in over Nichole to look at the drawing. "Son of a bitch," she said. She looked up at Hood, who was still lounging around by the door with a faintly sleazy smirk still on his face. "Get that file over there," Debs said to him. "The one with the photos."

Hood stepped over to the far end of the table, where a stack of folders teetered beside the telephone. He flipped through the top five or six while Deborah fidgeted. "Come on, goddamn it," she said to him, and Hood nodded, held up one folder, and brought it over to her.

Deborah scattered a pile of photographs on the table, sorted through them quickly, and nudged one out and over to Nichole.

"Not bad," she said, as the artist picked up the photo and held it beside her sketch, and Nichole nodded.

"Yeah, not bad at all," Nichole said. She looked up at Deborah with a happy smile. "Damn, I *am* good." She flipped the photo back to Deborah, who grabbed it and held it up for the two Haitians to see.

"Is this the man who sold you the Porsche?" Deborah asked them.

The man with the swollen eye was already nodding and saying, "*Oui.*" His cousin made a great show of staring at the picture, leaning forward to study it carefully, before finally saying with complete authority, "Yes. Absolutely. That is him."

Deborah looked at the two of them and said, "You are positive? Both of you?" And both of them nodded vigorously.

"*Bon,*" Debs said. "*Très beaucoup bon.*" The two Haitians smiled, and the one with the swollen eye said something in Creole.

Deborah looked at the cousin for a translation.

"He says, will you please speak English, so he can understand you," the man said with an even bigger smile, and Vince and Hood both snickered.

But Deborah was far too happy with the picture to let a minor jab bother her. "It's Bobby Acosta," she said, and she looked at me. "We got the little bastard."

TWENTY

THE UNIFORMED COP LED THE TWO PRISONERS AWAY TO A holding cell. Nichole gathered her things and left, and Deborah sat back down and stared at the picture of Bobby Acosta. Vince looked at me with a shrug and an expression of, *Now what?* and Deborah looked up at him. "Are you still here?" she said.

"No, I left ten minutes ago," Vince said.

"Beat it," Deborah said.

"I wouldn't have to beat it if you'd just hold it for a minute," Vince said.

"Go shit in your ear," Debs said, and Vince walked out with one of his horrible artificial laughs trailing behind him. Deborah watched him go and, since I know her very well, I knew what was coming, so I was not surprised when it came. "All right," she said to me when Vince had been gone for about thirty seconds. "Let's go."

"Oh," I said, trying very hard to look like I had not expected this, "do you mean you're not going to wait for your partner, as department policy and a specific order from Captain Matthews have suggested?"

"Just get your ass out the door," she said.

"What about my ass?" Hood said.

"Go boil it," Deborah said, snapping up out of her chair toward the door.

"What do I tell your partner?" Hood said.

"Tell him to check the salvia dealers," she said. "Come on, Dex."

It occurred to me that I spent far too much of my time obediently following my sister around. But it did not occur to me how I could avoid doing so again, so I followed.

In the car, Deborah drove us up onto the Dolphin Expressway and then north on 95. She did not volunteer any information, but it was not terribly hard to figure out where we were going, so just for the sake of small talk, I said, "Have you somehow figured out a way to find Bobby Acosta, just by staring at his picture?"

"Yeah," she snapped, very grumpy again. Deborah had never been very good with sarcasm. "As a matter of fact, I have."

"Wow," I said, and I thought about it for a moment. "The list from the dentist? The guys who got the vampire fangs?"

Deborah nodded, steering around a battered pickup hauling a trailer. "That's right," she said.

"And you didn't check all of them with Deke?"

She looked at me, which I thought was a bad idea, since we were going ninety miles an hour. "One left," she said. "But this is the one; I *know* it."

"Look out," I said, and Debs glanced at the road just in time to steer us around a large gasoline tanker that had decided to switch lanes for no apparent reason.

"So you think this last name on the list can tell us how to find Bobby Acosta?" I said, and Deborah nodded vigorously.

"I had a gut feeling about this one, right from the start," she said, steering into the far right lane with one finger.

"And so you saved it for last? Deborah!" I said as a pair of motorcycles cut in front of us and began to brake for the exit.

"Yeah," she said, gliding back into the middle lane.

"Because you wanted to build the suspense?"

"It's Deke," Deborah said, and I was thrilled to see that she was watching the road now. "He's just . . ." She hesitated for a moment, and then blurted out, "He's bad luck."

I have spent my life around cops so far, and I expect that the rest of my life I'll do the same, especially if I get caught someday. So I know that superstitions can pop up at some odd times and places. Even so, I was surprised to hear them from my sister. "Bad luck?" I said. "Debs, do you want me to call a *santero*? Maybe he can kill a chicken, and—"

"I know how it sounds, goddamn it," she said. "But what the hell else can it be?"

I could think of a lot of other things it could be, but it didn't seem politic to say so, and after a moment Deborah went on.

"All right, maybe I'm full of shit," she said. "But I need some luck on this thing. There's a clock ticking here, and that girl . . ." She paused almost as if she were feeling strong emotion, and I looked at her with surprise. Emotion? Sergeant Iron Heart?

Deborah didn't look back at me. She just shook her head. "Yeah, I know," she said. "I shouldn't let it get to me. It's just . . ." She shrugged and looked grumpy again, which was a bit of a relief. "I guess I've been a little . . . I dunno. Weird lately."

I thought about the last few days, and realized that it was true: My sister had been uncharacteristically vulnerable and emotional. "Yes, you have," I said. "Why do you think that is?"

Deborah sighed heavily, another action that was very unlike her. "I think . . . I dunno," she said. "Chutsky says it's the knife wound." She shook her head. "He says it's like postpartum depression, that you always feel bad for a while after a major injury."

I nodded. It made a certain amount of sense. Deborah had recently been stabbed, and had come so close to death from blood loss that the difference was a matter of a few seconds in the ambulance. And certainly Chutsky, her boyfriend, would know about that—he had been some kind of intelligence operative before being disabled, and his body was a raised-relief road map of scar tissue.

"Even so," I said, "you can't let this case get under your skin." As soon as I said it I braced myself, since it was a surefire setup line for an arm punch, but once again Debs surprised me.

"I know," she said softly, "but I can't help it. She's just a girl. A kid. Good grades, nice family, and these guys—cannibals . . ." She trickled off into a moody and reflective silence, which was a really striking contrast to the fact that we were speeding through heavy traffic. "It's complicated, Dexter," she said at last.

"I guess so," I said.

"I think I empathize with the kid," she said. "Maybe because she's so vulnerable at the same time I am." She stared straight ahead at the road, but didn't really seem to see it, which was a little bit alarming. "And all this other stuff. I dunno."

It might have been because I was hanging on for dear life in a vehicle that was careening through traffic at breakneck speed, but I didn't quite get her point. "What other stuff?" I said.

"Ah, you know," she said, even though I had said quite clearly that I did not know. "The family shit. I mean . . ." She scowled suddenly and looked at me again. "If you say one fucking word to Vince or anybody else about my bio clock ticking, I swear I'll kill you."

"But it is ticking?" I said, feeling mildly astonished.

Deborah glared at me for a moment and then, happily for life and limb, looked back at the road again. "Yeah," she said. "I think it is. I really want a family, Dex."

I suppose I could have told her something comforting based on my experience: perhaps that families were overrated and kids were really just a sinister device to make us all prematurely old and crazy. But instead, I thought of Lily Anne, and I suddenly wanted my sister to have her family so she could feel all the things I was learning to feel. "Well," I said.

"Shit, that's the exit," Deborah said, swerving hard for the off-ramp and effectively killing the mood, as well as guaranteeing that I lost all sense of what I had been about to say. The sign that flashed by, seemingly just a few inches from my head, told me we were heading for North Miami Beach, into an area of modest houses and shops that had changed very little in the last twenty years. It seemed like a very odd neighborhood for a cannibal.

Deborah slowed down and nosed into traffic at the end of the off-ramp, still moving too fast. She took us several blocks east, then

a few more north, and then steered into six or seven blocks of
houses where the residents had planted rows of hedges to seal off all
the roads leading in, except one main entry street. It was a practice
that had become common in this part of town, and was supposed to
cut down crime. Nobody had told me whether it worked.

We went through the entrance to the minicommunity and two
blocks over, and then Debs pulled up onto the grass in front of a
modest, pastel yellow house and the car rocked to a stop. "That's it,"
Deborah said, glancing at the paper on the seat beside her. "Guy's
name is Victor Chapin. He's twenty-two. House is owned by Mrs.
Arthur Chapin, age sixty-three. She works downtown."

I looked at the little house. It was slightly faded and very ordinary. There were no skulls stacked outside, no hex signs painted on
the yellow walls, nothing at all to say that evil lived here. A ten-year-
old Mustang squatted in the driveway, and everything about the
place was still and suburban.

"He lives with his mom?" I said. "Are cannibals allowed to do
that?"

She shook her head. "This one does," she said, opening her
door. "Let's go."

Deborah got out of the car and marched briskly toward the front
door, and I could not help remembering that I had been sitting in the
car and watching when she had gone alone to another door and
been stabbed—so I got out quickly and joined her just as she pushed
the doorbell. From inside the house we heard an elaborate chime
playing, something that sounded very dramatic, although I couldn't
quite place it. "Very nice," I said. "I think it's Wagner."

Deborah just shook her head and tapped her foot impatiently on
the cement stoop.

"Maybe they're both at work," I suggested.

"Can't be. Victor works at a late-night club," Debs said. "Place
on South Beach called Fang. They don't even open until eleven."

For a moment I felt a small twitch somewhere on the ground
floor of my deepest and darkest dungeon. *Fang*. I had heard of that
before, but where? In the *New Times*? In one of Vince Masuoka's
tales of late-night clubbing? I couldn't quite remember, and it went

out of my head when Deborah snarled and slapped the doorbell again.

Inside, the music swelled up a second time, but this time, over the top of the most dazzling chord, we heard somebody shout, "Fuck! All right!" and a few seconds later the door swung open. A person who was presumably Victor Chapin stood there holding the door and glaring out at us. He was thin, about five inches short of six feet tall, with dark hair and several days of stubble on his cheeks, and he was wearing a pair of pajama bottoms and a wife-beater undershirt. "Yeah, what!" he said belligerently. "I'm tryna sleep!"

"Victor Chapin?" Deborah asked, and the official cop tone of her voice must have penetrated his sulkiness, because he stiffened suddenly and looked at us a bit more warily. His tongue darted out and moistened his lips, and I could see one of his Dr. Lonoff–capped fangs for a second as his eyes moved from Debs to me and back again.

"Whuddya— Why?" he said.

"Are you Victor Chapin?" Deborah repeated.

"Who are you?" he demanded.

Deborah reached for her badge. As soon as it was obvious that it was, in fact, a badge, and even before she flipped it open, Chapin said, "Fuck!" and tried to slam the door. Purely out of reflex, I got my foot in the way, and as the door bounced back open and swung toward Chapin, he turned and ran for the rear of the house.

"Back door!" Deborah said, already running for the corner of the house. "Stay here!" And then she was gone around the side. In the distance I heard a door slam, and then Deborah yelling at Chapin to stop, and then nothing. I started thinking again of the time so recently when my sister had been stabbed, and the bleak helplessness I had felt watching her life drain out onto the sidewalk. Debs had no way of knowing Chapin had actually run for a back door— he could just as easily have gone for a flamethrower. He could be attacking her right now. I peeked into the dimness of the house, but there was nothing to see, and no sound of any kind except for the rush of a central air conditioner.

I stepped back outside and waited. Then I waited a little bit more. Still nothing happened, and I heard nothing new. In the distance a siren warbled. A plane flew overhead. Somewhere nearby somebody strummed a guitar and began to sing "Abraham, Martin, and John."

Just when I had decided that I couldn't stand it any longer and I had to go take a look, I heard a petulant voice rising up in the side yard, and Victor Chapin came into view, his hands cuffed behind him and Deborah right behind, frog-marching him toward the car. There were grass stains on the knees of his pajamas, and one side of his face looked red.

"You can't—fuck—lawyer—shit!" Chapin said. Possibly it was some kind of verbal shorthand used by cannibals, but it made no apparent impression on Debs. She simply pushed him forward and, as I hurried over to join her, she gave me a look that was as close to happy as I had seen from her in quite some time.

"What the fuck!" Chapin said, turning his eloquence on me.

"Yes, it is, isn't it?" I said agreeably.

"This is fucked!" he yelled.

"Get in the car, Victor," Deborah said.

"You can't— What!" he said. "Where are you taking me?!"

"We're going to take you to the detention center," she said.

"You can't just fucking take me," he said.

Deborah smiled at him. I hadn't met very many vampires, but I thought her smile was probably scarier than anything the blood-suckers could come up with. "Victor, you refused a lawful order and ran away from me. That means I *can* just fucking take you," she said. "And I'm *going to* just fucking take you, and you are going to answer some fucking questions for me, or you are not going to see the outside for a long time."

He opened his mouth and just breathed for a moment. His nice shiny fangs didn't look so intimidating all of a sudden. "What kind of questions?" he said.

"Been to any good parties lately?" I asked him.

I have often heard or read of all the blood draining from some-body's face, but this was the first time I had ever seen it—except, of course, in the very literal sense, in connection with my playtime activities. Victor turned paler than his shirt, and before Deborah could even glare at me for talking out of turn, he blurted out, "I swear to Christ I didn't eat any of it!"

"Any of what, Victor?" Deborah said pleasantly.

He was trembling now, and shaking his head back and forth. "They'll kill me," he said. "Jesus fuck, they'll fucking kill me."

Deborah gave me one quick glance of absolute triumph and joy. Then she stuck her hand on Victor's shoulder and pushed him gently toward the car. "Get in the car, Victor," she said.

TWENTY-ONE

EBORAH HAD VERY LITTLE TO SAY ON THE WAY TO THE detention center. She tried to call Deke to have him meet us there, but for some reason he wasn't answering, neither his radio nor his cell phone. Debs left word with the dispatcher for him to join us, and other than that we rode in silence—if that's the right word for it when you are forced to listen to a ten-minute disjointed monologue consisting mostly of the word "fuck." Chapin was secured in the backseat—the motor-pool cars had rings bolted to the floor for just that reason—and he sat in his durance vile mumbling, ranting, threatening, and overusing the same naughty word. For my part, I was thrilled when we reached our destination, but Debs seemed quite happy to have it go on forever. She had a look on her face that was very nearly a smile every time she glanced at Chapin in the mirror, and she was downright cheerful when she parked the car and pulled him out.

By the time we had the paperwork done, Victor was comfortably locked up in an interrogation room, and Chambers of the FDLE had arrived to see our prize. He stood with us as we looked in at Chapin, who had placed his forearms on the table and slumped forward over them, head hanging just a few inches over his cuffs.

"All right," Chambers said. "I know I don't have to remind you that this goes absolutely by the book." Deborah gave him a startled glance, and he went on without even looking at her. "You did good work, Morgan; you got a really good suspect here, and we pay attention to the rules, with just a little bit of luck we're gonna stick this guy with a couple of felonies."

"I don't give a shit about a conviction," Deborah said. "I want to get the girl back."

"We all want that," Chambers said. "But it would be really nice to put this guy away, too."

"Listen," Deborah said. "This isn't about politics or public relations."

"I know that," Chambers said, but Debs rode right over him.

"I got a guy in there who knows something," she said. "And I got him feeling all alone and naked and scared to death and ready to break, and I'm going to fucking break him."

"Morgan, you've got to do your job *right* and—"

Deborah turned on Chambers as if he were personally hiding Samantha Aldovar. "My job is to find this girl," she said, poking Chambers in the chest with her index finger. "And that little asshole in there is going to tell me how."

Chambers very calmly grabbed Deborah's finger and pushed it down to her side, slowly and deliberately. He put his hand on her shoulder and moved his face closer to hers, and said, "I hope he will tell us what we need to know. But if he does or if he doesn't, you are going to play by the rules and not let your feelings take over and fly you into the hillside. All right?"

Deborah glared at him, and he looked back; neither one of them blinked, breathed, or said a word, and for several long seconds it was her anger versus his gunfighter's cool—fire against ice. It was an absolutely fascinating face-off, and under other circumstances I could have watched it all day just to see who would win. But things being what they were, I thought it had gone on quite long enough, and I cleared my throat in a deliberately artificial way.

"Ahem," I said, and they both glanced at me. "I really hate to interrupt," I said, and nodded through the glass at Chapin. "But *tempus* is kind of *fugit*ing, isn't it?"

They both stared at me and I felt as if one side of my face was melting and the other freezing. Then Chambers looked at Debs with one eyebrow raised, she looked back at him and finally nodded, and the spell was broken.

"Where's your partner?" Chambers said. "He should be here for this."

Deborah shook her head. "He's not answering," she said, "and I can't wait."

"All right," Chambers said. "I'll do this with you." He turned to look at me and the impact of his cold blue eyes almost hurt. "You stay here," he said, and I felt absolutely no impulse to argue.

I watched through the glass as the two of them went into the room with Chapin. I could hear through the speaker everything that went on, but based on what was said, it was hardly worth the expense of miking the room. Deborah said; "You're in a ton of fucking trouble, Chapin," and he didn't even look up. So she stood about three feet behind him, crossed her arms, and said, "What did you mean when you told me you didn't eat any of it?"

"I want a lawyer," Chapin said.

"Kidnapping, murder, and cannibalism," Deborah said.

"It's Vlad; it's all Vlad," he said.

"Vlad made you do it? You mean Bobby Acosta?"

Chapin looked up at Deborah, mouth hanging open, and then put his head back down. "I want a lawyer," he said.

"You give us Bobby, they'll go easy on you. Otherwise . . . that's about five hundred years in prison," Debs said. "If they let you live."

"I want a lawyer," Chapin said. And he looked up again, and focused past Debs to where Chambers stood, across the table from him. "I want a lawyer," he repeated, and then he jumped to his feet and yelled it. "I want a fucking lawyer!"

For the next two minutes there was more, but nothing really instructive. Chapin yelled louder and louder that he wanted a lawyer and, aside from a few tediously repeated naughty words, that was all he had to say. Chambers tried to calm him down and get him back into his chair and Deborah stood with her arms folded and glared. When Chambers finally got Chapin seated again, he took Debs by the arm and led her from the room.

I joined them in the hallway just in time to hear Chambers say, "... and you know damned well we have to get him one now."

"Fuck it, Chambers!" Deborah said. "I can bend the paperwork and hold him twenty-four hours!"

"He has asked for a lawyer," Chambers said, as if he were telling a child she can't have a cookie before dinner.

"You're killing me," Deborah said. "And you're killing that girl."

For the first time I saw a little flash of heat run across Chambers's face, and he took a short step in to stand right in Deborah's face. I thought I was about to witness another attempt on my sister's life and I tensed, ready to leap in and separate them. But Chambers took a deep breath, clamped both his hands on Deborah's upper arms, and said very carefully, "Your suspect has asked to see an attorney, and we are required by law to provide one for him. Now." He stared at her, she stared back, and then Chambers let go of her arms and turned away. "I'll go get a public defender," he said, and disappeared down the hall.

Deborah watched him go, a series of unpleasant thoughts obviously running through her head. She looked back through the window in the door to the interrogation room. Chapin was seated again, in his opening pose, leaning over the table. "Fuck," Debs said. "Fucking Chambers." She shook her head. "This wouldn't have happened if that asshole Deke was here."

"He'd be here if you hadn't ditched him," I said.

"Go fuck yourself, Dexter," she said, and she turned away and followed after Chambers.

Miami is a city with an overcrowded court system, and the public defender's office may well be stretched thinner than all the rest of it. This is one of the very good reasons why Dexter has been careful to save his money over the years. Of course, the capital cases get priority, but then, there are so many of those that someone facing a mere murder charge had better be able to afford his own attorney, because the public defender's office, once a nest of hardworking liberal idealists, has become a small and temporary burnout stop for young lawyers hoping to make a splash. It takes a really special case to get anything more than their flustered, part-time attention.

So it was a pretty good indication of how high the profile of our case was when, less than an hour later, a smart young woman fresh out of Stetson Law School showed up to represent Victor Chapin. She wore a very nice business pantsuit, the latest Hillary Clinton model. She walked with a swagger that said she was the Avatar of American Justice, and she carried a briefcase that probably cost more than my car. She took it and her attitude into the interrogation room and sat down across from Chapin and, laying the briefcase on the table, she said crisply to the guard, "I want all the microphones and recording devices turned off, and I mean *now*."

The guard, an elderly guy who looked like he hadn't cared about anything since Nixon resigned, just shrugged and said, "Yeah, sure, okay," and walked out into the hall and flipped the switch, and the speaker went silent.

Behind me somebody said, "*Fuck!*" and I realized that my sister had returned. I glanced over my shoulder, and sure enough, Deborah was glaring into the now-silent room. I wasn't sure if we were speaking to each other, since I had disobeyed her direct order and failed to go fuck myself, so I just turned back around and watched the peep show. There was really very little to see: Chapin's brand-new attorney leaned in toward him and spoke rapidly for a few minutes. He looked up at her with growing interest, and eventually he talked back. She pulled out a legal pad and took a few notes, and then asked him a few questions, which he answered with increasing animation.

After only ten or fifteen minutes the attorney stood up and went to the door, and Deborah went to meet her as she stepped into the hall. She looked Deborah over from head to toe with something that was not really approval. "You are Sergeant Morgan?" she asked, with icicles forming in the air as she spoke.

"Yes," Deborah said grimly.

"You are the arresting officer?" the attorney said, as though that was another term for "baby rapist."

"Yes," Deborah said. "And you are?"

"DeWanda Hoople, public defender's office," she said, like everybody would know that name. "I think we're going to have to let Mr. Chapin go."

Deborah shook her head. "I don't think so," she said.

Ms. Hoople revealed a world-class set of front teeth, though it would be an exaggeration to call it a smile. "It doesn't matter what you think, Sergeant Morgan," she said. "Plain and simple, in one-syllable words, You Don't Have a Case."

"That little shit is a cannibal," Deborah snarled, "and he knows where I can find a missing girl."

"Oh, my," Ms. Hoople said. "I assume you have some proof of that?"

"He ran from me," Deborah said, a little sulky, "and then he said he didn't eat any of it."

Hoople raised her eyebrows. "Did he say any of *what*?" she said with sweet reason dripping from her tongue.

"The context was clear," Debs said.

"I'm sorry," said Hoople. "I'm not familiar with the statutes concerning context."

Knowing my sister as well as I did, I could see that she was about to explode, and if I had been Ms. Hoople I would be backing away with my hands held out in front of me. Deborah took a very deep breath and said through her teeth, "Ms. Hoople. Your client knows where Samantha Aldovar is. Saving her life is the important thing here."

But Ms. Hoople just smiled wider. "Not more important than the Bill of Rights," she said. "You're going to have to let him go."

Deborah looked at her and I saw that she was almost trembling as she fought to control herself. If ever there was a situation that clearly called for a strong right fist to the nose, this was it, and it was not normally my sister's way to ignore that call. But she struggled, and she won. "Ms. Hoople," she said at last.

"Yes, Sergeant?"

"When we have to tell Samantha Aldovar's parents their daughter is dead and this guy could have saved her but we had to let him go," Deborah said, "I want you to come with me."

"That's not my job," Ms. Hoople said.

"It shouldn't be mine, either," Deborah told her. "But you just made sure it is." Ms. Hoople had nothing to say to that, and Deborah turned and walked away.

TWENTY-TWO

I DROVE HOME THROUGH THE RUSH-HOUR TRAFFIC AT THE usual snail's pace, and I will admit that I was pondering. So many strange and baffling things going on at once; Samantha Aldovar and cannibalism in Miami and Deborah's strange emotional meltdown and the troubling reappearance of my brother, Brian. And perhaps strangest of all was the New Dexter who stood facing all these challenges. No longer the Sly Master of Dark Delights, now amazingly transformed into Daddyman, Champion of Children and the Family Way.

. . . And yet here I was spending all my time away from my family, in a pointless chase after bad people and a girl I didn't even know. I mean, a job is one thing, but could I really excuse neglecting my new child for all these extra hours just to support Deborah's Freudian search for a missing family? Wasn't it just a little bit of a contradiction?

And now, even more bizarre and unsettling, as I pondered these things, I began to feel bad. Me, Dark Dead Dexter, not merely feeling but feeling *bad*; it really boggled the imagination. I had been patting myself on the back for my amazing transformation, and yet in reality I had turned from the Happy Slasher into just another absentee parent, which was no more than a different kind of abuse. Aside from the fact that I hadn't actually killed anybody lately, what was there to be proud of?

Feelings of guilt and shame washed over me. So this was what it was like to be a real human parent. I had three wonderful kids, and all they had was me. They deserved so much more. They needed a father who was there to guide their steps and teach them about life, and they were stuck with someone who apparently cared more about finding somebody else's girl than playing with his own. It was horrible, inhuman. I had not really reformed at all—I had just changed into a different kind of monster.

And the older two, Cody and Astor—they still lived willingly in a desire for darkness. They looked to me to teach them to chase through the shadows. I had not only neglected to do that, but far worse, I had never even begun to steer them away from wanting to do it. Guilt upon guilt: I knew that I had to spend real quality time with them, bring them back to the light, show them that life held joys deeper than any knife could go. And to do all this, I had to be there, do things with them, and I had failed.

But maybe it wasn't too late. Maybe I could still make my mark with them. After all, I could not change completely just by wanting to, bursting from my wicked cocoon and emerging as a totally new human father. It took time to learn how to be a human, let alone to be a parent, and I was very new at this. I had to give me a little bit of credit—I had much to learn, but I was trying. And kids are very forgiving. If I could really start now and do something rare and special, as a way to show them that things had changed and that their Real Father had arrived, surely they would respond with gladness and respect.

And with that resolved I felt instantly better—Dex-Daddy was back on track. As if to prove that things were falling into place just the way a wise and compassionate Universe wanted them, I saw a giant toy store in a strip mall on my left, and without hesitation I pulled into the lot, parked, and went in.

I looked around the store and what I saw was not encouraging. There were rows and rows of violent toys, almost as if I had wandered into a store designed for the children of the old Dexter. There were swords, knives, light sabers, machine guns, bombs, pistols and rifles that shot plastic bullets and paintballs and Nerfs, rockets that blew up your friends or your friends' whole city—aisle after aisle of training devices for recreational slaughter. No wonder our world was such a mean and violent place—and no wonder there were people like I had been. If we teach children that killing is fun, can we really be surprised if now and then someone is smart enough to learn?

I wandered through the havoc factory until I finally found a small corner of the store labeled EDUCATIONAL. There were several shelves of crafts, some science kits, some board games. I looked it all over carefully, searching for something that hit just the right tone. It had to be educational, yes, but not dull or geeky, and not something that you did by yourself, like the kits. I needed something that was inspiring, but fun for us all.

I finally settled on a quiz game called Head of the Class. One person asked questions and everyone else took turns answering— perfect. It would bring us all together as a family, and we would all learn so much—and enjoy doing it. Cody would even have to speak in full sentences. Yes, this was it.

As I headed for the register I passed a shelf stacked with talking books, the kind with the row of buttons you push to make sound effects. There were several with fairy tales, and I immediately thought of Lily Anne. What a great way to hook her into a lifetime of reading enjoyment—I could read her the stories while she pushed the appropriate button on cue, and all while reading classic fairy tales. It was much too good to pass by, and I picked three of the most promising fairy tales.

I took the box and the books to the register and paid. The game was almost twenty dollars with tax, but I truly felt it was worth it, money well spent, and I did not regret the expense.

It was already dark by the time I turned my car down the street where I lived. Three-quarters of a lonely moon guttered low on the horizon and called to me in a voice of longing, making plaintive and playful suggestions about what Dexter could do with a knife and a night like this. *We know where Chapin lives*, it whispered. *We could cut him to the canines and make him tell us many useful things, and everybody would be happy. . . .*

For a moment I rolled with that seductive tug, the intoxicating whirl of the dark tide as it flowed around me and pulled at my feet. But then I felt the weight of the game and the books I had bought, and it pulled me out of the rising surge of moonlight and back to the dry land of New Dexter. No more; I would not give in to that moon-voiced urge. With a few harsh words I pushed the Passenger back in its place, deep in cold storage. *Go away*, I told it, and with a reptilian sniff it coiled itself away. It had to understand that I was not that man anymore. I was Dex-Daddy, the man who comes home filled with longing for Lily Anne and all the clean and common comforts of domestic life. I was the breadwinner, the pathfinder for small feet, the shield against all harm. I was Dex-Daddy, the rock upon which Lily Anne's future would be built, and I had Head of the Class to prove it.

And as I slowed to a stop in front of my house and saw Brian's car already parked there, I realized that apparently I was also Dex-Dopey, because I had no idea what my brother was doing here again but I did not like it, whatever it was. He stood for all I had been and did not want to be anymore, and I did not want any of that anywhere near Lily Anne.

I got out of the car and circled slowly around Brian's little red car and I caught myself looking at it as if it were the real danger. That was stupid, of course. Brian's style did not run to car bombs, but to the quick slice with the sly knife, just like the old me. I was not like that anymore, no matter how much I felt it pulling at me as I approached the front door and heard squeals of childish glee from inside the house. Of all the mounting absurdities this was the worst; that I should feel resentment, suspicion, even so-very-human anger, because the kids were clearly having a good time without me.

And so it was a very confused Dex-Daddy who pushed open the front door to see his little family-plus-brother gathered in front of the television. Rita sat at one end of the couch holding Lily Anne, Brian sat at the other end, with Astor between them, all with large smiles stretched across their faces. Cody stood between them and the TV holding some kind of grayish plastic thing, which he was waving at the TV as he jumped up and down and the others cheered him on.

As I came in all eyes but Cody's swung to me and then back to the TV without any real recognition of what I was—all eyes but Brian's, which stayed fastened on me, his large and phony smile growing larger as he watched me trying, and failing, to figure out what was happening in the living room of my very own hearth and home.

And then a great burst of cheering from the crowd ended in a prolonged, "Aawwwwwww . . ." and a suddenly frowning Cody jerked himself away from the screen.

"Great try, Cody," Brian said without taking his eyes off me. "Really, really great."

"I got high score," Cody said, an astonishingly long speech for him.

"Yes, you did," Brian said. "Let's see if your sister can beat that."

"Course I can!" Astor shouted, leaping into the air and waving another of the plastic things. "You're *toast*, Cody!"

"Would somebody tell me what on earth is going on here?" I said, and even to me it sounded forlorn.

"Oh, Dexter," Rita said, looking at me as if I were something very common and she was seeing me ground into her carpet for the first time. "Brian is just— Your brother bought the children a Wii, and it's very— But he can't just," she went on, turning back away from me to look at the TV. "I mean, it's way too expensive, and— Can you ask him? Because— Oh! Good shot, Astor!" Rita actually bounced a little bit with excitement, causing Lily Anne's head to roll slightly, and it was clear that I could take off my clothes and set myself on fire and no one but Brian would even notice.

"It's really quite good for them," Brian said to me with his Cheshire Cat smile. "Very good exercise, and they develop their motor skills. And," he added with a shrug, "it's an awful lot of fun. You should try it, brother."

I looked at my brother with his huge, phony, mocking smile, and I heard the moon call from the street, promising clean and happy fulfillment, so I turned away from him and saw the children and Rita all wrapped in the joy of this wonderful new experience, and suddenly the box under my arm—Head of the Class, almost twenty dollars with tax—felt as heavy and useless as an old oil drum filled with fish heads. I let it drop to the floor, and into my head popped a brief cartoon picture of Dexter running from the room in tears to flop facedown on the bed and cry away his tattered heart.

And happily for the worldwide image of tough-but-caring fatherhood, the mental picture was so ridiculous that all I did was take a deep breath, say, "Oops," and bend to pick up the package.

There was no room for me on the couch, so I walked past the cozy group sitting there, watching them twist to see around me so they would not miss a single riveting second of Astor's epic television battle. I put my game on the floor and sat, uneasy in the easy chair. I could feel Brian's eyes on me but I did not look back; I simply concentrated on forming and maintaining a facade of polite excitement, and after a few seconds he looked away, back at the TV, and as far as the rest of the room was concerned, I had disappeared as completely as if I had never been.

I watched Cody and Astor take turns with their expensive new game system. Somehow, no matter how animated they got, I could not feel any real enthusiasm. They switched to a different game that involved killing things with a sword instead of a gun, and even the use of a blade sparked absolutely no fire in my breast. And of course, they were so thoroughly happy that only a true curmudgeon could possibly object—which merely meant that I could now add "curmudgeon" to my résumé. *Dexter Morgan, BS. Blood-spatter Analyst, Reformed Slasher; Currently employed as killjoy.* I almost wished Debs could have been here—in the first place, because Brian would leave, but more important, so I could say, "See what you're missing? Kids, family— Ha!" And I would give a bitter chuckle that underlined the ultimate fickleness of all family.

Astor said, "Ooooooooohhh," in a very loud and high voice, and Cody jumped up to play. It was clear to me that it wouldn't matter what I did—they would never truly appreciate me or learn what I had to offer. They were far beyond fickle—they were insensible, like kittens, predatory little things, distracted by the first bit of string or shiny bauble that rolled across the floor, and nothing I could ever say or do could possibly make any kind of dent in their willful ignorance.

And then they grew up—into what? Into murderous dead-eyed pretenders like Brian and me, ready at the drop of a hat to stab each other in the back, literally or figuratively. Where was the point? Because they would clatter through childhood leaving a wake of random chaos and by the time they were old enough to understand what I had to say they would be too old to change. It was enough to make me renounce my new humanity and simply slip outside into the liquid moonlight and find somebody to take apart—no finesse, no careful selection, just sudden and cleansing savagery and release, exactly like Brian did it.

I looked at my brother where he sat—on my couch, with my wife, making my children happier than I seemed able to do. Is that what he wanted to do? Become me, but a better me than I had ever managed to be? Something rose up in me at the thought, something in between bile and anger, and I made up my mind that I would confront him tonight, demand to know what he thought he was doing, and make him stop. And if he would not listen to me—well, there was always Deborah.

So I sat grimly with a polite and completely fake half smile stitched onto my face for another half hour of dragons and magic fists and happy yelling. Even Lily Anne seemed content, which felt like an ultimate betrayal. She blinked and waved her fists in the air when Astor yelled and then snuggled back down onto Rita's chest, more enthusiasm than I had seen her show before for anything except feeding. And finally, when I didn't think I could maintain my artificial composure for even a second longer, I cleared my throat and said, "Hey, Rita? Did you have any plans for dinner?"

"What?" she said, without looking at me, still totally engrossed in the game. "Did you have a— Oh, Cody! I'm sorry, Dexter, what did you say?"

"I said," I said in overdistinct syllables, "Did You Have Any Plans for Dinner?"

"Yes, of course," she said, still without looking away from the TV. "I just have to— Oh!" she said with real alarm, and this time it was not from something in the game but because she glanced up and saw the clock. "Oh, my God, it's after eight! I didn't even— Astor, set the table! Oh, my God, and it's a school night!"

I watched with mild satisfaction as Rita leaped up off the couch at last and, thrusting Lily Anne at me, ran into the kitchen still talking. "For the love of— Oh, I know it's burned, what was I— Cody, get the silverware out! I've never been such a— Astor, don't forget to set a place for Uncle Brian!" And then a nonstop clatter for several minutes as she opened the oven, slammed pots and pans around, and set normal life back on the tracks.

Cody and Astor glanced at each other, clearly reluctant to leave their new TV world even to eat, and then, still wordless, they looked in unison at Uncle Brian. "Well, come on," he said with his awful fake cheeriness, "you have to do what your mother says."

"I wanna play some more," Cody said, which was several more syllables than I had heard him say together in a very long time.

"Of course you do," Brian said. "But right now you can't." He gave them his big smile, and I could see that he was trying very hard to look sympathetic, but it was truly not all that convincing, nowhere near as good as I did it. But Cody and Astor apparently accepted it at face value; they just looked at each other, nodded, and trundled off to the kitchen to help get ready for dinner.

Brian watched them go and then turned to look at me, his eyebrows raised in artificially polite anticipation. Naturally enough, he could not hope to anticipate any of the things I wanted to say to him, but as I took a deep breath to start, it occurred to me that I really couldn't, either. I felt that I had to accuse him of something—but of what? Buying an expensive toy when I had bought one so much cheaper? Of taking the kids for Chinese food and probably something slightly more sinister? Of trying to be me when I was too busy to play the part? I suppose the old, dead-inside Dexter would simply say, "Whatever you're doing, stop." But the new me simply could not wrap his tongue around all the many complicated things—*feelings*—that swirled through me. And to make matters even worse, as I sat there with my brain idling and my mouth open, Lily Anne made a burbling noise and my shirt was suddenly covered with a sour milk pudding of baby blarp.

"Oh, my," Brian said with a sympathy that was every bit as real as all his other emotions.

I got to my feet and went down the hall, holding Lily Anne at a kind of port-arms position. In the bedroom there was a changing table that had a stack of towels for the purpose stored on a shelf underneath. I grabbed two of them—one to mop up the mess, and the second to place under the baby to preserve whatever might remain of my shirt.

I went back to the easy chair and sat, draping the second towel over my shoulder and arranging Lily Anne facedown on top of it, gently patting her on the back. Brian looked at me again, and I opened my mouth to speak.

"Dinner," Rita said, roaring into the room with a platter held between two large oven mitts. "I'm afraid it's not— I mean, it isn't actually burned, but I didn't— It's just a little too dry and, Astor, get the rice into the blue bowl. Sit down, Cody."

Dinner was a cheerful affair, at least as far as the video warriors were concerned. Rita kept apologizing for the Orange Juice Chicken—which indeed, she really should have. It was one of her signature dishes, and she had let it overcook to the point of dryness. But Cody and Astor found it very funny that she was embarrassed, and began to play her with just a touch of cruelty. "It's dry," Cody said after Rita's third apology. "Not like usual." And he smirked at Brian.

"Yes, I know, but— I really am sorry, Brian," Rita said.

"Oh, it's delicious; think nothing of it, dear lady," Brian said.

"Think nothing at all, dear Mom," Astor echoed loftily, and she and Brian laughed. And so it went until dinner was over and the kids jumped up to clear the table, goaded on by the promise of fifteen more minutes of Wii before bed. Rita took Lily Anne down the hall for a diaper change, and for just a moment, Brian and I faced each other across the table. This was the moment to speak, to bring things out in the open between us, and I leaned forward to seize it.

"Brian," I said.

"Yes?" he said, raising his eyebrows expectantly.

"Why have you come back?" I said, trying very hard not to sound like I was accusing him of something.

He gave me a look of cartoon astonishment. "Why, to be with my family, of course," he said. "Why else?"

"I don't know why else," I said, irritated even more. "But there must be something."

He shook his head. "Why would you think that, brother?" he said.

"Because I know you," I said.

"Not really," he told me, locking his eyes onto mine. "You only know one small part of me. And I thought— Oh, damn," he said, as the tinny notes of "Ride of the Valkyries" swelled up from somewhere in his pocket. He pulled out his cell phone, glanced at the screen, and said, "Oh, my. I'm afraid I have to eat and run. As much as I've enjoyed talking with you. I'd better make my apologies to your lady wife." And he got quickly to his feet and swept into the kitchen, where I could hear him flinging his flowery compliments and apologies.

The entire family followed him to the front door, but I managed to cut them off by stepping outside with Brian and firmly closing the door between them and my brother and me. "Brian," I said, "we need to talk a little more."

He paused and turned to face me. "Yes, brother, let's," he said. "A good old-fashioned chin-wag. Catch up with each other and all that. Tell me, how are you coming along with finding that missing girl?"

I shook my head. "That's not what I mean," I said, determined to see this through to the end and drag things into the light. But once again his phone began its frantic Wagnerian chorus and he glanced at it and shut it off.

"Another time, Dexter," he said. "I really do have to go now." And before I could protest, he patted me awkwardly on the shoulder and then hurried away to his car.

I watched him drive away, and my only consolation was that the shoulder he had patted was still slightly damp from Lily Anne's blarp.

TWENTY-THREE

I STOOD AND WATCHED THE TAILLIGHTS OF BRIAN'S CAR UNTIL they were gone in the distance. But my unhappiness did not leave with my brother. It swirled around me and rose higher as the moonlight poured in and mixed with the irritation and once more the serpent voice began to wheedle and coax and make its sly suggestions. *Come with us,* it whispered in honeyed tones of pure and perfect reason. *Come away into the night; come and play and you will feel much better. . . .*

And I pushed it away, standing firm on the shores of my new land, human fatherhood—but the moonlight flowed back and tugged harder and I closed my eyes for just a moment to shut it out. I thought of Lily Anne. I thought of Cody and Astor, and the fawning pleasure they showed with Brian, and another small rivulet of irritation surged up. I pushed it down, and thought of Deborah and her deep unhappiness. She had been so pleased with catching Victor Chapin, and so miserable when she'd had to let him go. I wanted her to be happy. I wanted the kids to be happy, too—and the wicked little voice trickled back in and said, *I know how to make them happy, and you, too.*

For just a moment I listened, and everything clicked together with perfect sharpness and clarity and I saw myself slipping away into the night with my duct tape and a knife—

And I pushed back one more time, hard, and the picture shattered. I took a deep breath and opened my eyes. The moon was still there, beaming at me expectantly, but I shook my head firmly. I would be strong, and I would prevail. I turned away from the night with brittle resolve and marched briskly back into the house.

Inside, Rita was in the kitchen cleaning up. Lily Anne burbled in the bassinet, and Cody and Astor were already back on the couch in front of the TV, playing with the Wii. Now was the time to start, to set things straight between us, to stamp out the embers of Brian's influence and get these children moving out of the darkness; it could be done. I would do it. I went straight to Cody and Astor and stood between them and the TV screen. They looked up at me and seemed to see me for the first time tonight.

"What," Astor said. "You're in the way."

"We need to talk," I said.

"We need to play Dragon Blade," Cody said, and I did not like what I heard in his voice. I looked at him, and I looked at Astor, and the two of them looked back at me with smug and self-righteous irritation, and it was too much. I leaned over to the Wii's control box and pulled its plug out of the wall socket.

"Hey!" Astor said. "You lost the game! Now we gotta start over on level one!"

"The game is going in the trash," I said, and their mouths dropped open in unison.

"Not fair," Cody said.

"Fair has nothing to do with this," I said. "This is about what's right."

"That doesn't make any sense," Astor said. "If it's right then it's fair, too, and you said . . ." And she was going to go on, but she saw my face and trickled to a stop. "What?" she said.

"You don't even like Chinese food," I said sternly. Two small and blank faces looked at me, and then at each other, and I heard the echo of what I had just said. It didn't even make sense to me. "What

I mean is," I said, and their eyes swung back to me, "when you went out with Brian. My brother. Uncle Brian."

"We know who you mean," Astor said.

"You told your mother you went for Chinese food," I said. "And that was a lie."

Cody shook his head, and Astor said, "*He* told her that. We would have said pizza."

"And that would have been a lie, too," I said.

"But Dexter, you told us already," she said, and Cody nodded. "Mom isn't supposed to know about, you know. All that other stuff. So we *have* to lie to her."

"No, you don't," I said. "What you have to do is not do it anymore."

I watched astonishment blossom on their faces. Cody shook his head with bewilderment and Astor blurted, "But that's not—I mean, you can't really— What do you mean?" And for the first time in her life she sounded just like her mother.

I sat down on the couch between them. "What did you do with Uncle Brian that night?" I said. "When he said you went for Chinese food?"

They looked at each other, and an entire conversation went on between them with no audible words. Then Cody looked back at me. "Stray dog," he said.

I nodded, and anger surged through me. Brian had taken them out and found them a stray dog to learn and experiment with. I had known it was something like that, of course, but to hear it confirmed fed my sense of moral outrage—with my brother and with the children. And oddly enough, even as I drew myself up into a lofty tower of righteous indignation, a small and mean voice whispered that it should have been me who did this with them. It should have been my hand guiding their fledgling knife strokes, my wise and patient voice steering and explaining and teaching them how to catch and cut and then how to clean up when playtime was over.

But that was absurd; I was here to lead them away from darkness, not to teach them how to enjoy it. I shook my head and let sanity flow back in. "What you did was wrong," I said, and once more they both looked blank.

"What do you mean?" Astor said.

"I mean," I said, "that you have to stop—"

"Oh, Dexter," Rita said, bursting into the room wiping her hands on a dish towel. "You can't let them play anymore; it's a school night. Look at the time, for goodness' sake, and you haven't even— Come on, you two; get ready for bed." She hustled them up and out of the room before I could do more than blink. Cody turned back to look at me just before his mother pushed him into the hallway, and his face was a jumble of confusion, hurt, and irritation.

And as the three of them clattered into the bathroom and the sounds of running water and toothbrushing came back to me, I felt myself grinding my teeth in frustration. Nothing was going right. I had tried to bring my little family together, and found my brother there before me. When I tried to confront him, he had fled with the words still forming on my tongue. And I had finally begun my important job of shepherding the kids away from wickedness, only to be interrupted at the crucial point. Now the kids were mad at me, Rita ignored me, and my sister was jealous of me—and I still didn't know what Brian was up to.

I had worked just as hard as I knew how to be the new and squeaky-clean straight-arrow family man I was supposed to be, and at each attempt I had been slapped down, sneered at, and utterly crushed. Irritation grew inside me and morphed into anger, and then that started to change, too, as I felt a cold and acid bath of contempt burble up inside: contempt for Brian, and Rita, and Deborah, and Cody and Astor, for all the dribbling idiots in the whole stumble-footed world—

—and most of all, contempt for me, Dexter the Dummkopf, who wanted to walk in the sunlight, smelling the flowers and watching rainbows curl across the rose-tinted sky. But I had forgotten that the sun is nearly always hidden by clouds, flowers have thorns, and rainbows are always out of reach. You could dream the impossible dream all you wanted to, but it was always gone when you woke up. I was finding that out the hard way, each new reminder grinding my nose further and further into the dirt, and now all I really wanted was to grab something by the throat and squeeze—

The monotonous drone of Rita and the kids saying their prayers came down the hall at me. I still didn't know the words, and it was just one more annoying reminder that I was not really Dex-Daddy and probably never would be. I thought I could be the first leopard in history to change his spots, but in reality I was just another alley cat forced to dine on garbage.

I stood up. I just needed to move around, try to calm down, collect my thoughts, tame these weird and wild and brand-new emotions, before they carried me away on a flood tide of stupidity. I walked into the kitchen, where the dishwasher was already whirring away at the dinner dishes. Past the refrigerator, its ice-maker clicking. I walked into the back hall by the washer and dryer. All around me, through the whole house, everything was clean and functional, all the machinery of domestic bliss, in its place and ready to do exactly what it was supposed to do—all of it but me. I was not made to fit under the counter of this or any other house. I was made for moonlight gleaming off a very sharp knife and the soothing ratchet of duct tape purring off the roll and the muffled horror of the wicked in their neat and careful bonds as they met their unmaker—

But I had turned my back on that, turned away from all I really was, tried to fit myself into a picture of something that did not even exist, like squeezing a demon onto a *Saturday Evening Post* cover, and I had done nothing but make myself look like a complete idiot. No wonder Brian could so easily take away my kids. I would never bring them away from the dark side if I couldn't even give them a convincing performance of virtuous normality.

And with such a vast amount of wickedness in the world, how could I beat my bright blade into a dull and functional plowshare? There was so much yet to do, so many playground bullies who needed to learn the new rules to the game, Dexter's rules—there were even cannibals abroad in my very own city. Could I really just sit on the couch and knit while they worked their horrible will on the Samantha Aldovars of the world? After all, she was somebody's daughter, and someone felt about her just the way I felt about Lily Anne.

And as that thought hit home a red-hot surge of anger roared up inside me, burning away all my careful control. *It could have been Lily Anne.* Someday it still could be, and I was doing nothing to protect her. I was a self-deluded fool. I was being attacked from all sides, and I was simply letting it happen. I was allowing the predators to stalk and slay, and if someday they came for Lily Anne—or Cody and Astor—it would be my fault. It was in my power to protect my family from a very nasty world, and instead I was pretending that kind thoughts would keep the dragon away, while in fact it was roaring at my very own door.

I stood at the back door and looked out the window into the darkness of the yard. The clouds had rolled in up above, covering over the moon and bringing complete darkness. That was it, a perfect picture of all that was real; just darkness, hiding a few patches of brown grass and dirt. Nothing worked. Nothing ever worked, not for anyone anywhere. It was all just darkness, decay, and dirt, and trying to pretend there was anything else got you nothing but grief, and there was not a thing I could do about it. Nothing.

. . . And the clouds rolled open to let one small moonbeam trickle through to light up the darkness, and the sibilant whisper tickled and teased once more and said, *There is one thing. . . .*

And that one simple thought made all the sense in the world.

"I'll be right back," we said to Rita as she sat on the couch with the baby held close. "I left some things at work."

"Back?" she warbled in confusion. "You mean you're going to— But it's night!"

"Yes, it is," we said, and we let a cold gleam of teeth show in our face at the thought of that welcoming velvet darkness just outside the door.

"Well, but don't you— Can't it wait until morning?" she said.

"No," we said, and the happy madness of it echoed in our voice. "It can't wait. It's something I need to do tonight."

The truth of it clearly showed on our face. Rita frowned but said no more than, "Well, I hope you— Oh! But I emptied the diaper pail, and it's really— Could you take the bag and—" She jumped up and went into the hall and the cold acid roiled through me at the interruption, but she was back in mere seconds, clutching a garbage bag. She thrust it at me and said, "On your way out, if you— You really have to go in? I mean, it won't take too long? Because, I mean, drive carefully, but—"

"It won't take long," we said, and then impatience flooded in and we were out the door into the welcoming night with its thin fingers of moonlight trickling through the clouds and promising that one wonderful thing that could wash away all the cramped misery of trying to be something we were not and never would be. In a hurry now, we flung the garbage bag onto the floor of the backseat with our playtime toys and got into the car.

We drove north through thin traffic, north to work, just as we had said we would, but not the daytime work of office and disorder; we went to a much happier task, beyond the dull and into delight, north past the airport, onto the off-ramp that led to North Miami Beach, and slower now, carefully nosing down the trail in our memory, to a certain small pastel yellow house in a modest neighborhood.

The club doesn't even open until eleven, Deborah had said. We drove past with care and saw the lights on, inside and out, and a car in the driveway that had not been there before. The mother's car, of course, and it made perfect sense—she took it to work during the day. Closer to the house, half into the shadows, was the Mustang. He was still here. It was not yet ten o'clock and the drive to South Beach was not a long one. He would be inside, enjoying his unjust freedom and thinking that all was once more right with his little world, and that was just the way we wanted it. We had made it with plenty of time and we felt a cold and pleasing certainty that we would not be disappointed.

We went one time around the block and watched for any sign that things were not what they should be and we found nothing. All was quiet and safe and all the little houses were clean and lighted and buttoned up against the razor-sharp fangs of the night.

We drive on. Four blocks away there is a house with a Dumpster squatting in its overgrown yard and this was just what we wanted. The houses nearby are dark, too, one light showing in a place two doors away, but otherwise it is all a quiet part of our night, and the house with the Dumpster is perfect. Foreclosed, empty, waiting for somebody to come in with a new dream, and very soon somebody will, but it will not be a pretty dream. We find a broken streetlight a block away and park there, beside a hedge. We get out slowly, enjoying the anticipation, enjoying as always the happy task of preparation, making things just right for all that had to happen and now would happen once more and oh so soon.

The back door of the foreclosed house is hidden from any possible prying eyes and it opens silently, quickly. Inside, the house is all empty darkness—except for the kitchen, where a skylight spills moonbeams across a butcher-block countertop, and as we see it the inner whisper rises into a chorus of delight. Here was a sign that this night was meant to be and it had been made just for us; this room was the perfect place for what we must do, and as if to underline the fact that all was right with the wicked world, there is even half a box of garbage bags on the counter.

Quickly now; time is pressing, but neatness counts. Slit the seams of the garbage bags and turn them into flat plastic sheets. Spread them carefully across the butcher block, the floor around it, the nearby walls, anyplace a random dreadful red splat might fall unobserved in the lighthearted rush of playtime, and soon it is ready.

We take a breath. We are ready, too.

It is a quick walk back to the small yellow house. Hands empty now, nothing needed, except the one small loop of nylon. Fifty-pound-test fishing line, perfect for making a leader, even better for making a follower out of some naughty playmate who would hear the light and powerful noose whistle through the air and settle on his throat and he would feel it speak into his surprise and say, *Come with us now. Come and learn your limit.* And he would follow, because he had to, as the world grew dark and dim and even his last few breaths would be given to him in pain and only when we wished it.

And if he squirmed or fought more than what was right we would pull just a little bit more until the breath no longer came and he heard nothing but the frantic growing thunder of his heartbeat in his ears and the whisper of the nylon saying, *See? We have taken away your voice and your breath, and soon we will take away more, much more, take away everything, and then we will tumble you back into dust and darkness and a few neat bundles of garbage—*

And the thought comes in on a slightly ragged breath and we paused to be calm, to let the icy fingers soothe away jangled nerves and rub them toward the first careful trickle of pleasure.

Steady now: Another breath until we become cool and certain and knew that all was bright and wary readiness and we let the clean steely awareness grow into the one true fact of the night: *This will happen now. Tonight.*

Now.

Our eyes snap open to a landscape of shadows and all our cool awareness slithered out and stretched into every dim hint of darkness, searching for movement, seeking any small trace of a watcher. There was nothing, no one, not human, animal, or Other like me. Nothing stirred or lurked; we were the only hunter on the trail tonight and all was what it should be. We were ready.

One careful foot in front of the other, a perfect imitation of casual walking, back around the block to the modest yellow house. Oh so carefully we slip past the house and into the shadow of a hedge next door and then we wait. No sound comes to challenge us; nothing moves or waits with us. We are alone and unseen and ready and we slide closer, careful and quiet, until we are there at the faded yellow corner of the house and we breathe deeply, quietly, and become a small and silent part of the shadows.

Closer, still careful and quiet, and all is exactly what it should be and then we are at the door of the Mustang.

Unlocked—the contemptible little beast has made it far too easy for us and we slide into the backseat so careful-quiet and melt into the unseen darkness on the car's floor—and then we wait.

Seconds, minutes—time passes and we wait. Waiting is easy, natural, part of the hunt. Our soft and steady breath comes in and out and everything about us is cool and coiled and waiting for the moment that must come.

And it does.

A distant yell; the front door opens and the tail end of the very last argument comes out to us.

"—lawyer said to do!" he says in his mean little tantrum voice. "I gotta go to work now, all right?" And he slams the door shut and storms over to the Mustang. His small and nasty voice mutters on as he opens the door and jerks himself into the car behind the wheel and as he puts the key into the ignition and starts the engine the shadows on the floor behind him spit out a shape and up we come with all our hushed and silent speed and the whistle of a nylon noose that whips around his throat and closes off all thought and air.

"Not a sound, not a move," we say in our terrible cold Other Voice, and he jerks to rigid stillness. "Listen carefully and do exactly what we say and you will live a little longer. Do you understand?"

He nods stiffly, bug-eyed with terror, face slowly growing dark from the lack of air, and we let him feel it, feel what it is to stop breathing, just a taste of what will come, a sample of his approaching forever, the endless darkness when all breathing is ended.

And we pull just a little, just enough to let him know that we could pull so very much harder, pull until it all stops right now, and his face gets even darker while his eyes begin to push out of his face and grow bright with blood—

—and we give him a breath, letting slackness run down our arm and into the nylon loop, just a little, just enough for one dry and tattered gasp of air, and then we tighten it once more before he can cough or speak.

"You belong to me," we tell him, and the cold truth of it is in our voice and for just a moment he forgets that he cannot breathe as the true shape of his future fills his mind and he flails his arms for just one second before we pull again, a little harder now.

"Enough," we say, and the frigid hiss of our command voice stops him immediately. We let his nasty little world grow dark again, not as much now, just enough so that when we loosen again he will have a very small hope—a frail hope, a hope made of moonbeams, a hope that will live just long enough to keep him docile and quiet until that quietness, too, becomes forever. "Drive," we tell him, with a very slight twitch of the noose, and we let him rasp in a breath.

For a moment he does not move and we jerk the noose. "Now," we say, and with a spasm of movement to tell us he is eager to please, he pushes the car into gear and we roll slowly out of the driveway and away from the pastel yellow house, away from his small and dirty life on earth and into the dark and joyous future of this wonderful moonlit night.

We take him to the empty house with the nylon tight around his throat, quickly and carefully marching him through the darkness and into the room we have readied, into the plastic-wrapped room where golden shafts of moonlight stab through the skylight and light up the butcher block as if it were the altar in a cathedral of pain. And it is: a true temple of suffering, and tonight we are its priest, master of the rites, and we will lead him through our ritual and into the last epiphany, to the final release into grace.

We hold him there by the butcher block and let him breathe, just for a moment, just long enough to let him see what is waiting, and his fear grows once more as he understands that this is all just for him, and he twists around to look at us and see if maybe this is some rough joke—

"Hey," he says in a voice already half-ruined. Recognition trickles into his face and he shakes his head slightly, as much as the noose will let him. "You're that cop," he says, and now there is new hope in his eyes and it blossoms into boldness as he ratchets on in his newly raspy voice. "You're the fucking *cop* that was with that crazy bitch cop! Motherfucker, you are in so much fucking trouble! I am fucking well going to have your ass in jail for this, you piece of shit—"

And we pull on the noose, very hard now, and the sound of his filthy crow-sounding words stops as though it had been cut off by a knife, and once more his world grows dark, and he scrabbles feebly at the nylon on his throat until he forgets what his fingers are for and his hands fall away as he drops to his knees and sways there for just a moment while I pull it tighter, tighter, until at last his eyes roll up into his head and he goes slack, flopping bonelessly to the floor.

We work quickly now, heaving him onto the butcher block, cutting away the clothing, taping him down into unmoving readiness before he wakes—which he quickly does, eyes fluttering open, arms twitching slightly against the tape as he explores his new and final position. The eyes go wider and he tries so very hard to move away but he cannot. And we watch him for just a moment, letting the fear grow, and with it grows the joy. This is who we are. This is what we are for, the conductor of the dark ballet, and this night is our concert.

And the music rises and we take him away to where the dance begins, the lovely choreography of The End, with its same sharp steps and familiar movements and its smells of fear amid the soft sounds of tape and terror, and the knife is sharp and swift and certain tonight as it races to the well-known rhythm of the slowly swelling music of the moon that rises and grows into the final chorus of fulfillment until joy, joy, joy is in the world.

Just before the end we pause. A very small and awful lizard of doubt has scuttled into our pleasure and squatted on the halo of our happiness and we look down at him, still writhing in eye-popping horror at what has happened to him and the certainty that even more will come.

It is nearly done, comes the whisper. *Don't stop now. . . .*

And we do not—could not stop; but we pause. We look at the thing that squirms beneath our knife. He is nearly done and his breath comes slower now, but he is still moving against his bonds with one last bubble of hope forming and fighting to rise up behind the terror and pain. And there is one little thing we must know before we pop that bubble, one tiny detail we need to hear to make this complete, to blow down the floodgates and let our pleasure pour out across the land.

"Well, Victor," we say in our frosty happy hiss, "how did Tyler Spanos taste?" And we pull the duct tape from his lips; he is too far gone into true pain to notice the rip of the sticky tape coming off, but he breathes in deep and slow and his eyes find mine. "How did she taste?" we say again, and he nods with that final acceptance of what must be.

"She tasted great," he says in a raspy voice that knows there is no time left for anything but very final truth. "Better than the others. It was . . . fun. . . ." He closes his eyes for a moment and when he opens them again that small hope still floats in his eyes. "Are you going to let me go now?" he says in a raspy, lost-little-boy voice, although he knows what the answer must be.

The whir of wings surrounds us and we do not even hear our voice as we answer, "Yes, you can go," we say, and very soon after, he does.

We left Chapin's Mustang behind a Lucky 7 convenience mart three-quarters of a mile from the house, the key still in it. It was far too tempting to last all night in Miami; by morning it would be repainted and on a boat for South America. We'd had to rush things with Victor just a little more than we wanted to, things being what they were, but we felt a great deal better now, as always, and I was very nearly humming when I climbed out of my trusty little car and trudged into the house.

I washed myself carefully, feeling the glow begin to fade. Debs would be a little happier—not that I would tell her, of course. But Chapin had earned his leading role in the night's little drama, and the world was a tiny bit better for it.

And so was I—much calmer, drained of tension, far readier to face the rush and tumble of recent events. It was true that I had tried to put this kind of thing behind me, and true that I had failed—but it was one small and necessary slip, and I would be very careful to see that it was the last. One little step backward, one time, no big deal—after all, nobody quits smoking right away, do they? I was much more collected and composed now, and this would not happen again. End of incident, back to my sheep's clothing—permanently this time.

Even as this thought tried to plant itself in the sunlight of my new persona, I felt a smug twitch of claws from the Passenger, and the almost-voiced thought, *Of course . . . until next time . . .*

The sudden sharpness of my reaction surprised us both: a quick flash of anger and my unspoken shout of, *No! No next time—go away!* And clearly I really meant it this time, so clearly that there was a stunned silence, followed by a sense of great and leathery dignity receding up the staircase until it was gone. I took a deep breath and let it out slowly. Chapin was the last time, one minor setback on my new and sparkling path to Lily Anne's future. It would not happen again. And just to be sure, I added, *And stay away!*

There was no answer, only the distant slamming of a door in one lofty tower of Castle Dexter. I looked into the mirror over the sink as I scrubbed my hands. That was the face of a new man looking back at me. It was over now, really and truly over, and I would not go into that dark place ever again.

I dried off, put my clothes in the hamper, and tiptoed into the bedroom. The bedside clock said 2:59 as I slid quietly into bed.

The dreams came right away, immediately after my nearly instant slide into darkness. I am standing over Chapin once again, raising the knife for a perfect slice—but it is no longer Chapin on the table; it is Brian now, Brian lying taped below me. He gives me a smile so large and fake I can see it through the duct tape across his mouth, and I lift the knife higher—and then Cody and Astor are there beside me. They raise up their plastic Wii controllers and point them at me, clicking furiously, and I find myself moving to their control, lowering the knife, turning away from Brian and pointing the knife at myself until the blade is at my own throat and a terrible wailing cry comes from the table behind me and I turn to see Lily Anne taped in place and reaching up for me with her tiny perfect fingers—

—and Rita is thumping me with her elbow and saying, "Dexter, please, come on, wake up," and at last I do. The bedside clock says 3:28 and Lily Anne is crying.

Rita groaned beside me and said, "It's your turn," before rolling over and dragging a pillow over her head. I got up, feeling like my limbs were made of lead, and staggered to the crib. Lily Anne was waving her feet and hands in the air and for one dark and dreadful moment I couldn't tell it from the dream I'd just had and I stood there, wavering and stupid as I waited for things to make sense. But then the expression on Lily Anne's small and lovely face began to change and I could see that she was about to launch herself into all-out, full-volume wailing, and I shook my head to clear away the fumes of sleep. Stupid dream—all dreams are stupid.

I picked up Lily Anne and placed her gently on the changing table, mumbling soothing nothings to her that sounded strange and far from comforting as they came from my sleep-raspy throat. But she got quieter as I changed her diaper, and when I settled with her into the rocking chair beside the changing table she twitched a few times and went right back to sleep. The sense of dread that lingered from my idiotic dream began to fade, and I rocked and hummed softly for a few more minutes, enjoying it far more than seemed right, and when I was sure that Lily Anne was sound asleep I got up and placed her carefully into the crib, tucking the blanket around her into a snug little nest.

I had just settled myself back into my own little nest when the phone rang. Instantly, Lily Anne began to cry, and Rita said, "Oh, Jesus," which was quite shocking coming from her.

There was never any real doubt who it would be, calling at this hour. Of course it was Deborah, calling to tell me of some hideous new emergency and make me feel guilty if I didn't instantly leap out of bed and run to her side. For a moment I considered not answering—after all, she was a grown woman, and it was time she learned to stand on her own two feet. But duty and habit kicked into gear, combined with an elbow from Rita. "Answer it, Dexter, for God's sake," she said, and at last I did.

"Yes?" I said, letting the grumpiness show in my voice.

"I need you here, Dex," she said. There was real fatigue in her voice, and something else as well, some trace of the pain she had been showing lately, but it was still an old refrain, and I was tired of the song. "I'm coming to pick you up now."

"I'm sorry, Deborah," I said with real firmness. "Work hours are over and I need to be here with my family."

"They found Deke," she said, and from the way she said that I knew I didn't want to hear the rest, but she went on anyway. "He's dead, Dexter," she said. "Dead, and partly eaten."

TWENTY-FOUR

I T IS A WELL-WORN TRUTH THAT COPS GROW CALLOUS, A cliché so tattered that it is even common on television. All cops face things every day that are so gruesome, brutal, and bizarre that no normal human being could deal with them on a daily basis and stay sane. And so they learn not to feel, to grow and maintain a poker-faced whimsy toward all the surprising things their fellow humans find to do to each other. All cops practice not-feeling, and it may be that Miami cops are better at it than others, since they have so many opportunities to learn.

So it is always a little unsettling to arrive at a crime scene and see grave and shocked faces on the uniforms holding the perimeter; even worse to slide under the tape and see ace forensic geeks Vince Masuoka and Angel Batista-No-Relation standing pale and mute to one side. These are people who find the sight of an exposed human liver a rare opportunity for wit, and yet whatever they had seen here was apparently so horrific that it had failed to tickle their funny bones.

All cops grow a layer of unfeeling in the presence of death—but for some reason, if the victim is another cop the layer of callus splits and the emotions run out like sap from a tree. Even if it's a cop that nobody cared for, like Deke Slater.

His body had been dumped behind a small theater on Lincoln Road, beside a pile of old lumber and canvas and a barrel overflowing with plastic trash bags. And it lay on its back, rather theatrically, shirtless, with hands folded over chest and clutching the shaft of what looked to be a plain wooden stake, pounded into the approximate area of his heart.

His face was set in a tight mask of agony, presumably caused by the stake slamming through living skin and bone, but it was quite clearly Deke, even with the chunks of flesh gouged out from his face and arms, the teeth marks visible from ten feet away. And even I felt a small twinge of pity for the man as I stood and looked down on all that was left of my sister's annoying and ridiculously handsome ex-partner.

"We found this," Debs said, standing at my shoulder and holding up a plastic evidence bag with a sheet of plain white paper in it. There was a red-brown stain of dried blood on one corner, but I took the bag from her and looked: On the paper was written a short message, in a large and ornate font that could have come from any computer printer in the world. It said, *He disagreed with someone who ate him.*

"I didn't realize cannibals were so clever," I said. Deborah stared at me, and all the soft despair she had been fighting with lately seemed to settle on her face and begin to smolder.

"Yeah," she said. "It's pretty funny. Especially to somebody like you who enjoys this kind of thing."

"Debs," I said, looking around me to see if anybody might have overheard. There was no one in immediate earshot, but judging by her face, I doubt she would have cared.

"Which is why I need you here now, Dexter," she went on, and now there was definitely fire in her voice as it rose higher and louder. "Because I have run out of patience with this shit, and I have run out of partners—and Samantha Aldovar has run out of time and I need to fucking understand this shit—" She paused and took a deep, ragged breath before going on in a quieter tone. "So I can find these assholes and put them away." She poked me in the chest with her finger and got even quieter, without losing any intensity. "And that is where *you* come in. *You*"—poke, poke—"put yourself into your trance, or talk to your spirit guide, or get your Ouija board, whatever it is you do"—and she poked me with each syllable—"and—you—do—it—now."

"Deborah, really," I said. "It isn't that simple." My sister was the only living person I had tried to talk to about my Dark Passenger, and I think she deliberately misunderstood my clumsy description of the whispered not-quite-voice that lurked in the basement just under consciousness. Of course, it had helped me in the past with some good guesses, but Debs apparently pictured it as some kind of dark Sherlock I could summon up at will.

"Make it that simple," she said, and she turned away and walked back toward the yellow-tape perimeter.

Not terribly long ago I had thought of myself as lucky to have family. Now, in one night, I had been ignored by my wife and children, replaced by my brother, and shoved into a late-night session of impossible expectation by my sister. My loving family—I would have traded them all for one decent jelly doughnut.

Still, I really was on the spot, and I had to try. So I took a deep breath and tried to put away all my brand-new emotions. I laid down my kit and knelt beside the ravaged body of Deke Slater, looking carefully at the wounds on the face and arms, almost certainly caused by human teeth and showing some dried blood— which meant the wounds had been made while his heart was still pumping. Eaten alive.

There were traces of blood starting where the stake punctured the chest and running all over the exposed torso, indicating that he had also been alive briefly after they had pounded it in. Probably the blood had soaked his shirt, which was why they removed it. Or maybe they just liked his abs. That would explain why several mouthfuls of them were missing.

Around the teeth marks on the stomach wounds there was a faint brown stain: I didn't think it was blood, and after a moment

I remembered the stuff we had found in the Everglades. The party drink, made of ecstasy and salvia. I reached behind me and got some collection tools out of my kit, swabbing carefully at the brown spots and then placing the swab in an evidence bag.

I looked higher, up by the chest wound, and then to the hands gripping tightly around the wooden stake: not a lot to see there. A plain piece of wood that could have come from anywhere. Under several of the visible fingernails I could see something dark, possibly collected in a struggle—and as I looked and tried to analyze it by sight, I realized I was behaving exactly like Dark Sherlock, and it was a waste of time. The rest of the forensics team would swoop in and do all this better than I could hope to do with the naked eye. What I needed and what Deborah expected from me was one of my special insights into the twisted and wicked minds that had come up with this particular way to kill Deke. Always before I had been able to see these things a little clearer than the others in forensics, because I was twisted and wicked myself.

But now? Now that I had reformed, changed into Dex-Daddy? Ignored and even snubbed the Passenger? Could I still do it?

I didn't know if I could, and I didn't really want to find out, but it seemed like my sister had left me no choice—just like in every other situation involving family, my options were limited to either impossible or unpleasant.

So I closed my eyes and listened, waited for the sly whispered hint.

Nothing. Not a leathery rustle of wings, not a suggestion of offended disregard, not even an almost-syllable of huffish dismissal. The Passenger was as silent as if it had never been there at all.

Oh, come on, I said silently to the place where it lived. *You're just sulking.*

There was at last a ruffle of aloof disregard, as if I were not worth answering.

Please . . . ? I thought at it.

For a moment there was no response, and then I quite clearly almost heard a kind of reptilian *Hmmph*, a reordering of wings, and then a snide echo of my own voice right back at me—*And stay away*—and then silence, as if it had hung up on me.

I opened my eyes. Deke was still dead, and I had no more idea about how and why than I'd had before my mini-séance. And quite clearly, if I was going to come up with any kind of idea, I was going to have to do it alone.

I looked around. Deborah was standing behind me about thirty feet away and she stared back at me with angry expectation. I had nothing to tell her, and although I did not know what she might do when I told her that, I had a feeling that we were beyond arm-punch territory into something new and potentially much more painful.

All right, then: Scientific forensics was for the others, there was no time for diligence, and the Passenger was on huffy hiatus— that left dumb luck. I looked around the body. There were no tell-tale footprints from tailor-made left-handed shoes, nobody had dropped a one-of-a-kind matchbook or a business card, and Deke had apparently not scrawled the name of his killer in blood. I looked further around, and at last something caught my eye. In the heap of plastic trash bags overflowing the garbage can by the door, all of the bags were semitransparent yellowish brown industrial garbage bags. But one of them, shoved into the pile halfway down, was white.

It almost certainly meant nothing: Probably the cleaning service had run out of the other bags, or somebody brought their garbage from home. Still, if I was really relying on luck, I might as well roll the dice. I stood up, trying to remember the name of the old Roman goddess of chance—Fortuna? It didn't matter. I was quite sure she only spoke Latin, and I didn't.

I approached the garbage pile carefully, not wanting to disturb any potential evidence that might be lying on the ground, and I crouched again, putting my face a few inches from the white bag. It was smaller than the others, too, a standard kitchen trash bag that anybody might use at home. Even more interesting, it was much less than half-full. Why would anybody throw away a bag of trash that close to empty? At the end of a business day, maybe—but this one was shoved in under three or four others; it had either come out at the same time only part-full . . . or somebody had shoved it into the pile later. And why not just drop it on top of the heap? Because somebody in a hurry wanted to hide this bag, and had done a half-assed rush job.

I took a ballpoint pen from my pocket and poked at the bag with the blunt end. Whatever was inside was soft, yielding—fabric? I pushed a little harder and the inside of the plastic bag came up against something, close enough so that I could just see dark red blotches on whatever was inside, and I shuddered involuntarily. It was blood; I was certain. And even though it was not really one of my Passenger-driven hunches, I was reasonably sure the blood had not come from someone inside the theater cutting their finger on the popcorn machine.

I stood up and looked for my sister. She was in the same place, still glaring at me. "Deborah?" I called. "Come look at this."

She crossed the space between us quickly, and as I squatted down again, she did, too.

"Look," I said. "This bag is different from all the others."

"Big fucking deal," she said. "That's the best you got?"

"No," I said. "This is." Once more I poked at the bag with my pen, and once more the awful red stains swam into view pressed against the white plastic. "It's probably a coincidence," I said.

"Shit," she said with quiet violence. Then she rose up and looked over at the barricade. "Masuoka! Get over here!" Vince looked at her like a deer caught in the headlights, and she yelled, "Move it!" He clumped into motion and hustled over.

Standard procedure is only one step away from ritual, and so I have always found it kind of comforting. I really like doing things that have definite rules and a well-established order, because that means I don't have to worry about how to fake something appropriate for the occasion. I can just relax and follow the correct steps. But this time, the routine seemed dull, pointless, and frustrating. I wanted to rip open that bag, and I found that I was fretting with impatience as Vince slowly and methodically dusted for finger-prints; all over the garbage can, the wall behind it, and then each individual garbage bag on top of the white one. We had to lift each bag up in careful gloved hands, dust it, examine it under regular and then UV light, and then cautiously open it, removing and examining each item inside. Junk, garbage, waste, crap. By the time we finally got to the white bag I was ready to scream and fling the garbage at Vince's head.

But we did get to it at last, and the difference was obvious immediately, even to Vince, the moment he dusted.

"Clean," he said, goggling up at me with surprise. The other bags had been like mosaics of smudged and greasy fingerprints. This one was as pristine as if it had just come out of the box.

"Rubber gloves," I said, and my impatience burst. "Come on, open it up." He looked at me as if I had suggested doing something indecent. "Open it!" I said.

Vince shrugged and began to carefully undo the plastic tie. "So impatient," he said. "You must learn to wait, Grasshopper. All things come to those who—"

"Just open the goddamn bag," I said, which startled me a great deal more than it did Vince. He just shrugged again and removed the tie, placing it carefully into an evidence bag. I realized I was leaning in a little too close, and I straightened up—and bumped into Deborah, who had been leaning over me. She didn't even blink, just hunkered down into the position I had left.

"Come on, goddamn it," she said.

"You guys must be related or something," Vince said. But before I could kick him, he opened the top of the bag and began to peel it slowly back. He reached into it cautiously and, with a truly irritating lack of speed, began to pull out—

"Deke's shirt," Deborah said. "He was wearing that this afternoon." She looked at me and I nodded: I remembered the shirt, a beige guayabera sprinkled with light green palm trees. But it had a new pattern on it now, an awful wet soaked-in swirl of blood, kept damp inside the sealed bag.

Slowly and carefully Vince pulled the bloody shirt out of the bag, and as it came all the way out at last, something else clattered onto the ground and rolled away toward the building's back door. Deborah said, "Shit," and jumped up to follow the thing as it wobbled to a stop a few feet away. I came right behind her and, since I was wearing gloves, I bent and picked it up.

"Let me see," Deborah demanded, and I held it out on the palm of my hand.

There was not really much to see. The thing looked like a poker chip, perfectly round, the edges grooved like a gear. But it was jet black, and on one face there was a gold symbol embossed onto it. It looked something like a 7, except it had a line drawn through the vertical leg.

"The fuck is that?" Debs said, staring at the symbol.

"Maybe a European seven?" I said. "That's how they make 'em sometimes, with the line through it."

"Okay," she said, "and so what the fuck does a European seven mean?"

"That's not a seven," Vince said. He had crowded in behind us and was peering over Deborah's shoulder. We both looked at him. "It's a cursive 'F,' " he said, as if that were an obvious truth.

"How do you know?" Debs demanded.

"I've seen it before," he said. "You know, out clubbing."

"What do you mean, clubbing?" Debs said, and Vince shrugged.

"Hey, you know," he said. "Nightlife out on South Beach. I've seen those things." And he looked back down at the black token and reached in between us, poking the thing with his gloved fingertip. " 'F,' " he said.

"Vince," I said, very politely refraining from putting my hands around his throat and squeezing until his eyes popped out. "If you know what this thing is, please tell us before Deborah shoots you."

He frowned and raised both hands, palms up. "Hey, take it easy. Jeez." He poked it again. "It's an entrance token. 'F,' for Fang." He looked up at us and smiled. "You know, Fang? The club?" Something tickled at the back of my brain as he said that, but before I could scratch it, Vince poked the token again and went on talking. "You can't get in without one of these things, and they're really hard to get. I tried. 'Cuz it's a private club—they're open like all night, after all the other clubs close, and I heard it gets like totally wild in there."

Deborah stared at the token as if she were waiting for it to speak. "What's Deke doing with one of these?" she said.

"Maybe he likes to party," Vince said.

Deborah looked at Vince, and then over to Deke's body. "Yeah," she said. "Looks like he had a real rave." Then she turned to Vince. "How late does this place stay open?"

Vince shrugged. "Pretty much all night, you know," he said. "It's like vampire theme, I mean, 'Fang'? So all night. And it's private, members only. So they can do that."

Deborah nodded and grabbed my arm. "Come on," she said.

"Come on where?"

"Where do you think?" she snarled.

"No, wait a second," I said. This wasn't making any sense. "How did the token get in there with Deke's shirt?" I said.

"What do you mean?" Debs said.

"There's no pocket in the shirt," I said. "And it's not the kind of thing you hold in your hand while you get rid of a body. So somebody put the token in there. On purpose."

Deborah stood absolutely still for a moment, not even breathing. "It could have fallen in, and . . ." She stopped, hopefully realizing how stupid that sounded.

"It couldn't have," I said. "You don't believe that for a second. Somebody wants us to go into that club."

"All right," she said, "then let's go."

I shook my head. "Debs, that's crazy. This has got to be a trap."

She set her jaw and looked stubborn. "Samantha Aldovar is in that club," she said. "I'm going to get her out."

"You don't know where she is," I said.

"She's in there," Debs said through her teeth. "I know she is."

"Deborah—"

"Fuck it, Dexter," she said. "It's the only lead we've got."

Once again I seemed to be the only one who could see the runaway locomotive hurtling down at us. "For God's sake, Debs, it's way too dangerous. Somebody put that thing in there to get us into the club. It's either a trap or a red herring."

But Deborah just shook her head and pulled on my arm, leading me away toward the perimeter. "I don't give a shit if it's a red herring," she said. "It's the only fish we got."

TWENTY-FIVE

THE CLUB WAS ON OCEAN DRIVE IN SOUTH BEACH, ON the edge of the area that TV programs always show when they want to portray the glittering superhip world of Miami nightlife. Every night of the week, the sidewalks were crowded with people wearing minimal clothing and showing off bodies that made that seem like a good idea. They strolled and rolled past the Deco hotels lit up from the inside with neon, loud music, and throngs of even more people who looked just like them, spilling in and out of the buildings in a kind of ultra-chic Brownian motion. A few years ago those same buildings were all cheap retirement hotels, filled with old people who could barely walk and had come south to die in the sun. Now a room that used to cost fifty dollars a night went for ten times that, and the only difference was that the tenants were prettier and the buildings had been on television.

Even at this hour of the night there were people on the sidewalk, but these were the leftovers, the ones who had partied too hard and couldn't remember how to get home, or those who just didn't want to call it a night and lose the glow, even after all the clubs had closed.

All but one: Fang was at the end of the block in a building that was not as dark and quiet as the others, although the front side was subdued for South Beach. But down the alley on the far end there was a glow of black light and a relatively small sign that said FANG in a sort of nouveau Gothic script, and sure enough, the initial "F" matched the one on the black token we had found with Deke's shirt. The sign hung over a dim door that appeared to be painted black and studded with silver metallic brads, like a teenager's idea of what an old dungeon door should look like.

Deborah didn't bother trying to find a parking spot. She just jammed her car up onto the sidewalk and jumped out into the thinning crowd. I got out quickly, but she was already halfway down the alley before I caught up with her. As we got closer to the door I began to feel a rhythmic thumping deep in the folds of my brain. It was an annoying and insistent sound that seemed to come from inside me and demand that I *do something, now*, without making any concrete suggestions about what. It pounded relentlessly, at twice the speed of a healthy heartbeat, and turned into actual sound only when we were finally standing in front of the glossy black door.

There was small sign with raised gold letters in the same script as the token and the sign above the door. It said, PRIVATE CLUB. MEMBERS ONLY. Deborah didn't seem impressed. She grabbed at the doorknob and turned; the door stayed closed. She thumped her shoulder into it, but it didn't budge.

I leaned past her. "Excuse me," I said, and I pushed the small button set into the doorframe below the sign. She twitched her lips angrily, but didn't say anything.

After only a few seconds the door opened, and I had a very unsettling moment of disorientation. The man who opened the door and stood looking down at us was very nearly a dead ringer for Lurch, the butler on the old *Addams Family* TV show. He was close to seven feet tall and wore a classic butler's outfit, complete with morning coat. But happily for my sense of unreality, when he spoke to us it was in a high voice with a thick Cuban accent. "Joo rang?" he said.

Deborah held up her badge; she had to hold it straight up in the air, as high as her arm could reach, to get it anywhere close to Lurch's face. "Police," she said. "Let us in."

Lurch put a long knobby finger on the sign that said PRIVATE CLUB. "Hee's a pribait clope," he said.

Deborah looked up at him, and in spite of the fact that he was almost two feet taller and had a cooler costume, he took a half step backward. "Let me in," she said, "or I will come back with a warrant, and *la migra*, and you will wish you had never been born." And whether it was the threat of INS or just the magic of Deborah's glare, he stepped to the side and held the door open for us. Debs put away her badge and stormed in past the man, and I followed.

Inside the club, the thumping sound that had been annoying outside turned into a pure agony of overwhelming noise. Riding over the top of the torturous beat was a reedy electronic sound, two notes played together that did not quite harmonize but went through a ten-second pattern that repeated over and over. Every two or three times the pattern repeated, a deep electronically distorted voice would whisper something over the music, low and wicked and suggestive and sounding far too much like the nearly heard voice of the Passenger.

We went down a short hallway toward the place where the hideous din was coming from, and as we got closer I could see the reflected fluttering of what appeared to be a strobe light, except that it was black light. Somebody shouted, "Whoo!" and the lights went wine red, flickered rapidly, and then, as a new and more horrible "song" started up, the light turned bright white and then back to ultraviolet. The beat never stopped and never changed, but the two reedy notes went into a new pattern, accompanied now by a shattering screech that might have been a distorted and badly tuned electric guitar. And then the voice again, this time audible—"Just drink it," it said, and it was answered by several voices calling "Whoo!" and other syllables of modern encouragement, and then as we got to the doorway, the deep malignant voice gave a kind of old-movie evil chuckle, "Moo-hahahaha," and then we were looking into the main room of the club.

Dexter has never been a real partygoer: Large gatherings of

people generally make me feel quite grateful that I am not ruled by human impulse. But never before had I seen a more compelling example of all that is wrong with trying to have fun with others, and even Deborah stopped dead for a moment in a vain attempt to take it all in.

Through a thick haze of incense we could see that the room was packed with people, almost all apparently under the age of thirty, and all dressed in black. They were writhing back and forth across the floor to the beat of the horrible noise, their faces twisted into expressions of glazed delirium, and, as the black light strobed, it lit up the sharpened fangs that many of them had so that their teeth glowed weirdly.

Off to my right was a raised platform, and standing in the middle of it, rotating slowly on two facing turntables, were two women. They both had long dark hair and very pale skin that turned almost greenish in the flickering lights that played over them. They wore sleek black dresses that looked painted on, with high collars that completely covered their necks and a front that opened up in a diamond-shaped cutout to show the area between their breasts. They stood very close together, and as they turned around past each other their faces would touch gently, and they would brush their fingertips lightly over each other.

Along the side of the room three thick velvet curtains hung down and as I looked, one of them slid open to reveal an alcove containing an older man dressed all in black. He held a young woman by the arm and wiped at his mouth with his other hand. For a moment a flash of the lights glistened off something on the woman's bared shoulder and a small voice whispered to me that this was blood—but the woman smiled at the man and leaned her head on his arm, and he led her out of the alcove and back onto the dance floor. They vanished into the crowd.

At the far end of the room was a giant fountain. A darkish liquid burbled up from it, lit from underneath with a colored light that pulsed and faded from one color to the next in time to the relentless drumbeat. And standing behind the fountain and lit from below with a terribly theatrical blue light was none other than Bobby

Acosta. He held up a huge, two-handed golden goblet with an enormous red gem on the front, and he poured from it into every cup raised up by the passing dancers. He was smiling a little too hard, obviously showing off his expensive pointed crowns from Dr. Lonoff, and as he raised the goblet high above his head and looked happily around the room, his eyes fell on Deborah and he froze, which unfortunately made whatever was in the goblet slop out onto his head and roll down into his eyes. Several of the partiers held their cups up imperiously and bounced in place, but Bobby just stared at Deborah, and then dropped the goblet and ran into a back hallway. Deborah said, "Motherfucker!" and lurched forward onto the crowded dance floor and I had no choice but to follow into the madly twisting herd.

The dancers were moving in one direction in a tightly packed mass, and Deborah was trying to cut straight across them to get to the hallway where Bobby Acosta had disappeared. Hands clutched at us, and one slender hand with black-painted fingernails held a cup up to my face and sloshed something onto my shirtfront. I looked down the arm and saw it belonged to a svelte young woman wearing a T-shirt that said TEAM EDWARD. She licked her black-painted lips at me, and then I was bumped hard from behind, and I turned toward my sister. A large and vacuous-looking guy wearing a cape and no shirt grabbed at Debs and tried to pull her shirt open. She slowed down just long enough to plant her feet and throw a perfect right cross at the guy's jaw and he went down. Several people nearby shouted happily and began to push harder, and the rest of the crowd heard them and turned, and in just an eyeblink they were all pushing toward us and chanting rhythmically, "Hai! Hai! Hai!" or words to that effect, and we were slowly forced backward, back toward the door guarded by Lurch where we had come in.

Deborah struggled, and I could see her lips moving in the right shape for some of her favorite X-rated syllables, but it was no good. We were slowly and inevitably pushed off the dance floor, and as we got close to our original entrance, very strong hands clamped onto our shoulders from behind and pulled us up and out of the room as if we were small children, and set us down in the hallway.

I turned to face our rescuers and saw two exceptionally large guys, one white and one black, both with enormous sculpted muscles bulging out of their sleeveless tuxedo shirts. The black man had a long and gleaming ponytail tied back with what looked like a string of human teeth. The white one had a shaved head and a very large golden skull in one ear, and they both looked like they were perfectly ready to pull off our heads if anybody wanted to see them do it.

And in between them, as they stood at a kind of bored attention, stepped someone who seemed like he might suggest exactly that. If the doorman was Lurch, here was Gomez Addams himself: forty-ish, dark-haired, with the pin-striped suit, blood-red rose pinned to the lapel, and a pencil-thin mustache. But this was a very angry Gomez, and he jabbed a finger at Deborah as he spoke over the din of the music. "You got no right coming in here!" he said. "This is harassment and I will sue your ass!"

He glanced at me and away, and then he looked back again and our eyes locked for just a moment, and suddenly there was a chill in the stale fug of the club's air and a faint leathery huff rattled through me as the Passenger sat up and whispered a warning, and something black and reptilian formed in the air between us and a small piece of a neglected puzzle fluttered up into my brain. I remembered where I had heard of Fang before; it had been in my recently shredded file of potential playmates. And now I knew who this other predator was. "George Kukarov, I presume?" I could see Deborah look at me, startled, but that did not matter; all that mattered was that two Dark Passengers were meeting and exchanging sibilant warnings.

"Who the fuck are you?" Kukarov said.

"I'm with her," I said, and though it sounded mild there was a message in it that only another predator would hear, and the message was, *Leave her alone or you will deal with me.*

Kukarov stared back and there was a distant, just-below-sound roaring of hidden monsters, and then Deborah said, "Tell this asshole to get his hands off me. I am a police officer!" And the spell was broken as Kukarov jerked his eyes away and back to Debs.

"You've got no fucking right to be here," he hissed, and then he yelled again, just for the effect. "This is a private club and you are *not* invited!"

Deborah matched his volume and raised his venom. "I have reason to believe a felony was committed on these premises—" she said, but Kukarov cut her off.

"You got due cause?" he snarled. "You got no due cause." And Deborah bit her lip. "I got lawyers who will eat you alive!" he said. The white bouncer thought that was pretty funny, but Kukarov glared at him and he wiped the smirk off his face and went back to staring straight ahead. "Now you get the fuck outta my club!" he said, and he pointed at the door. The two bouncers stepped forward and grabbed Deborah and me by the elbows and half carried us down the short hallway. Lurch held the door open and they threw us out onto the sidewalk. We both managed to avoid falling onto our heads, but it was a near thing.

"Stay the fuck outta my club!" Kukarov shouted, and I turned to look just in time to see Lurch smile brightly and slam the door shut.

"Huh," said my sister, "looks like you were wrong." And she spoke so calmly that I looked at her with very real concern, thinking that she must have hit her head in all the scuffle—because the two things she cared about most in the entire world were the authority of her badge, and not letting anybody push her around, and both of those had just been trampled. And yet here she was standing on the sidewalk and dusting herself off as if nothing at all had happened, and I was so astonished that her words didn't really register for a moment. When they did, they seemed like the wrong words.

"Wrong?" I said, and I felt like I was in the wrong conversation. "What do you mean, I was wrong?"

"Who gets thrown out of a trap?" she said; it took me a second to realize what she meant, and by then she had gone right on. "What kind of red herring has bouncers that toss us onto the sidewalk after two minutes?"

"Well," I said.

"God*damn* it, Dexter!" she said. "Something is going on in there!"

"Quite a lot, actually," I admitted, and she punched my arm, hard. It was nice to see her recovering her spirits, but on the other hand, it really hurt.

"I mean it!" she said. "Either somebody goofed and that token fell in by accident—which is stupid—or else . . ." She paused, and I understood what she meant. There was definitely an "or else" here—but what was it? I waited politely for her to supply it, and when she didn't, I finally said it.

"Or else . . . somebody connected with this wants us to take a look at what's going on without anybody else knowing it."

"Right," she said, and she turned back to glare at the glossy black door. The door didn't even flinch. "Which means," she said thoughtfully, "that you are going back in there."

I opened my mouth, but nothing came out except air, and after a moment I had to believe I hadn't really heard her. "I'm sorry?" I said, and I admit it was a bit squeaky.

Debs grabbed both of my arms and shook me. "You are going to go back inside that club," she said, "and find out what they're hiding."

I pulled my arms out of her grasp. "Debs, those two bouncers will kill me. To be honest, it would probably only take one of them."

"That's why you're going in later," she said, almost like she was suggesting something reasonable. "When the club is closed."

"Oh, good," I said. "So I won't just be trespassing and get beaten. I'll be breaking and entering, too, so they can shoot me. Great idea, Deborah."

"Dexter," she said, and she looked at me with more intensity than I could remember seeing from her in quite some time. "Samantha Aldovar is in there. I *know* it."

"You can't know that."

"But I do," she said. "I can feel it. Goddamn it, you think you're the only one with a voice inside? Samantha Aldovar is in there, and she is out of time. If we back off, they kill her and eat her. And if we take the time to go through channels and go in with SRT and all that, she disappears and she's dead. I *know* it. She's in there now, Dex. I got such a strong feeling; I've never been more sure about something."

It was all very compelling, but aside from one or two minor problems with her argument—like how she *knew* it—there was one overwhelming flaw with the whole thing. "Debs," I said. "If you're so sure—why not do it right, get a warrant? Why does it have to be me?"

"No way I get a warrant in time. No probable cause," she said, and I was glad to hear that, since it might mean she wasn't completely insane. "But I can trust you," she said. She patted my chest, and it felt wet. I looked down, and saw that there was a large brownish stain across the front of my shirt, and I remembered the girl who had spilled her drink on me on the dance floor.

"Look," I said, pointing at the stain. "This is that same stuff we found in the Everglades—salvia and ecstasy." And just to show her that two could play, I said, "I *know* it's the same stuff. And it's illegal—with this sample, you have probable cause, Debs."

But she was already shaking her head. "Illegally obtained," she said. "And by the time we got it argued in front of a judge it'll be too late for Samantha. This is the only way, Dexter."

"Then *you* do it."

"I can't," she said. "I'd lose my job if I got caught, maybe even do jail time. You'll just get a fine—and I'll pay it."

"No, Debs," I said. "I'm not going to do it."

"You have to, Dex," she said.

"No," I said. "Absolutely not."

TWENTY-SIX

ND THAT IS HOW I FOUND MYSELF SITTING IN DEBORAH'S car a few hours later and watching the doorway at Club Fang. There wasn't a whole lot to see at first. People trickled out a few at a time and either wandered away down the street or climbed into a car and drove off. As far as I could tell, nobody turned into a bat, or flew off on a broom. Nobody noticed us, but Deborah had reparked the car in a dark spot across the street, in the shadow of a delivery van nosed up onto the sidewalk. She didn't have much to say, and I was still too peeved for light conversation.

This was Deborah's case, and this was Deborah's hunch, and yet here I was getting ready to take on the stupid part. I didn't even agree with her that it had to be done, but merely because I was her brother—and adopted, at that—I had to do it. I don't ask for fair; I know better than that. But shouldn't things at least make sense? I go through life and work hard to blend in, follow the rules, and be a good sport—and yet when it comes time for the cigar to explode, somehow it's always me puffing on it.

But there was no point in arguing anymore. If I refused to break into the club, Deborah would do it, and she was right; as a sworn

officer of the law, she could go to prison if they caught her, while
I would probably just get community service, picking up trash at a
park, or teaching inner-city kids to knit. And Deb's stay in the ICU
with the knife wound was far too recent for me to let her take any
kind of risk—which I'm quite sure was part of her calculations. So it
was Dexter through the window, and that was that.

Just before dawn, the sign above the club's door switched off
and a lot of people came out at the same time, and then nothing at
all happened for half an hour. Out over the far end of the ocean the
sky got lighter and somewhere a bird began to sing, which showed
how little he knew. The first jogger went by on Ocean Drive, and a
delivery truck rumbled past. And finally, the black door swung
open and Lurch came out, followed by the two bouncers, then
Bobby Acosta, and a couple of other drudges I hadn't seen before. A
few minutes later, Kukarov himself came out, locked the door, and
got into a Jaguar parked half a block away. The car started right up,
which contradicted all I had ever heard about Jaguars, and Kukarov
drove away, off into the dawn to Morticia and a peaceful day of rest
in his crypt.

I looked at Deborah, but she just shook her head, so I waited
some more. A bright orange finger of light poked up out over the
ocean, and then suddenly it was a new day. Three young men in
tiny swimsuits walked by speaking German and headed for the
beach. I pondered the rising sun and, in a rush of dawn-inspired
optimism, decided there was a one-in-three chance that this was not
my last day on earth.

"Okay," Deborah said at last, and I looked at her. "It's time," she
said.

I looked at the club. It didn't feel to me like it was time—time for
bed, maybe, but not time for sneaking into the dragon's den, not in
all this daylight. Dexter needs shadows, darkness, guttering moonlight. Not bright morning in the Twinkie Capital of the Western
World. But as usual, I was not being offered a choice.

"There might be somebody in there. A guard or whatever," she
said. "So be careful."

I really didn't feel like dignifying that kind of remark with a response, so I simply took a deep breath and tried to bring up the darkness to prepare myself.

"You got your phone, right?" she went on. "If there's trouble, or if you see her and she's, like, got a guard, just call nine-one-one and get out of there. It should be simple."

"Not as simple as sitting in the car," I said, and I admit I was irritated. On top of everything else, Debs had suddenly developed motormouth. How can a guy call his Passenger when everyone else wants to chat?

"Fine," she said. "Just be careful, that's all I'm saying, all right?"

It was quite clear to me that the small talk was not going to stop, so I put a hand on the door and said, "I'm sure I'll be fine. What could possibly go wrong, breaking into a nest of vampires and cannibals who have already kidnapped and murdered several people?"

"Jesus, Dexter," Deborah said, but I felt no mercy.

"After all, I have a cell phone," I said. "If they catch me, I'll threaten to text."

"All right, shit," she said. I pushed the car door open.

"Pop the trunk," I said to her.

She blinked. "What?"

"Open up the trunk of the car," I repeated. She opened her mouth to say something or other, but I was already out of the car and around to the trunk. The release thumped and I opened it, found the tire iron, and slid it into my pocket, pulling my shirt over the protruding handle to hide it. I closed the trunk and stepped around to Deborah's window. She rolled it down.

"Farewell, sis," I said. "Tell Mother I died game."

"For Christ's sake, Dexter," she said, and I crossed the street, leaving her muttering a few syllables of worried profanity.

In truth, I was hoping that it was going to be as simple as Deborah wanted to believe it would be. Getting in would certainly be easy enough for someone of my modest abilities—I had broken into many places, in the pursuit of my innocent hobby, that seemed a great deal more formidable than this one, and most of those were inhabited by real monsters, not these playtime Halloween freaks, with their opera capes and fake teeth. In the light of the morning sun that now poured onto South Beach, it seemed very hard to take their adolescent party games at all seriously.

It was also surprisingly hard to bring the Dark Passenger online. I really needed the soft voice of guidance, the invisible cloak of interior darkness, that only the Passenger could provide, but in spite of the brief flutter of alarm in the club, apparently the snit was not over. I paused on the far side of the street and closed my eyes, placing my hand on a telephone pole and thinking, *Hello? Anybody home?* Somebody was home, but they still didn't feel like visiting: I felt a slow and silken rustle of wings, as if it were merely recrossing its legs and waiting for something good to happen. *Come on,* I thought. Still nothing.

I opened my eyes. A truck went by on Ocean Drive, its radio playing salsa music much too loud. But it was the only music I heard. Apparently, I was going to have to do this alone.

All right, then: When the going gets tough and so on. I put my hands in my pockets and started to amble around the building as if I didn't really have anyplace to go and was just gawking. Gee whiz, look at the palm trees. Nothin' like that back in Iowa. Golly.

I strolled around the building one time, looking it over without really seeming to do anything but walk and gawk. As far as I could tell, nobody cared enough to be impressed by my wonderful Innocent Act, but it never hurts to be thorough, so I played tourist for five minutes. The building took up the entire block, and I walked along past all four sides. The vulnerable spot was obvious: In a short and narrow alleyway on the far side of the club's door there was a Dumpster. It stood beside a doorway that obviously led into the club's kitchen. The door was protected from view unless someone stood right in the mouth of the alley.

I pulled my right hand out of my pocket and "accidentally" scattered half a handful of coins onto the sidewalk and, stooping to pick them up, I looked around me in all directions. Unless there was somebody on a rooftop with binoculars, I was not being watched. I left thirty-seven cents on the sidewalk and slid quickly into the alley.

It was much darker in the narrow alley, but that did not encourage the Passenger to start a conversation, and I hurried to the Dumpster all alone. I reached the back door quickly and examined it. It had two dead-bolt locks on it, which was discouraging. I could have opened them both easily enough given a little time and my own set of very special tools, but I had neither, and the tire iron would just not do: The door was out of the question. I would have to get inside by some other, less genteel entryway.

I looked up at the building: Directly above the doorway was a row of windows, one every five or six feet, that went along the side of the building to the street. The second one to my left was in easy reach from the top of the Dumpster, and an agile person could pull himself up and through the window without too much trouble. No problem: Dexter is deft, and assuming I could slide open the window it would be simple.

The Dumpster had two lids, side by side, and one of them was open. I put both hands on the closed side—and something bolted up and out of the opening with a horrible screech and flew past my ear and I was absolutely paralyzed by sheer terror before I recognized it as a cat. It was tattered and filthy and beat-up, but it landed a few feet away and arched its back and spit at me in the full Halloween pose. I just looked back and for a second I thought the music had started up again in the club, until I realized the thumping was only my heartbeat. The cat turned and stalked away out of the alley, I leaned on the Dumpster and took a deep breath, and the Passenger stirred itself just enough to give me a serves-you-right chuckle.

I took a moment to recover, and then, just to be safe, I looked inside the Dumpster. There didn't seem to be anything else inside except garbage, which I thought was a very positive development. I hoisted myself up onto the closed side and, looking once more toward the mouth of the alley to make sure nobody was watching, I reached up and touched the window. I pushed at it and it rattled ever so slightly. Good news: That meant it was not nailed shut, or sealed by too many years of sloppy paint jobs.

I could not see the very top of the window frame, but as far as I could tell there was no alarm sensor anywhere on the frame, which was also good news but not too surprising. Most places save a little money by pretending that any break-in will take place on the ground floor. It was nice to know that even vampires can be thrifty.

I reached for the tire iron and almost dropped it as it cleared my pocket. It would have hit the Dumpster's lid with enough of a clatter to wake up the whole neighborhood, and I realized my hands were slick with sweat. This was a new experience; always before I had been icy cold and calm, but between the Passenger's sulking and the feral cat's levitation I seemed to be in something of a stew. Certainly sweat was understandable—this was Miami. But fear sweat? On Dexter the Dark and Dashing, the King of Cool? This was not a good sign, and I paused one more time for a deep breath before I reached up and slid the tire iron between the window and the bottom of the frame.

I pulled down on the tire iron's handle, gently at first, and then with increasing force as the window refused to budge. I didn't want to pull too hard, since the frame might well give way, which would shatter the glass and make so much noise that I might as well bounce a dozen tire irons off the Dumpster's lid. I pulled for about ten seconds, slowly increasing the pressure, and just when I thought I would have to try something else there was a *pop!* and the window slid upward. I held very still for a moment, listening for any movement or shouting or alarms going off. Nothing: I pulled myself up, slid through the window, and pulled it closed behind me.

I stood up and looked around me. I was in a hallway that dead-ended at the street to my left and led to a corner down to the right. There was one door along the hall, and I went quietly over to it. There was a dead-bolt lock on the door, but no doorknob. I pushed gently and the door opened. The room was completely dark, but there was a faint smell of Lysol and urine, and I suspected it was a restroom. I stepped inside, closed the door, and found a light switch by feeling along the wall. I flipped it on; it was, in fact, a small restroom, with a sink, one toilet, and a cupboard built into the wall. Just to be thorough I opened the cupboard and found nothing more sinister than toilet paper. There was nothing else in the room, no place they could have hidden a body, alive or dead, so I switched off the light and stepped back out into the hallway.

I cat-footed down the hall to the corner, where I paused, and then slowly and carefully peeked around. The hallway was empty, lit by a single security lamp that hung above a door halfway down. There were two other doors along the hall, and what looked like the top of a staircase at the far end.

I stepped around the corner and went to the first door on my left. I turned the knob slowly and carefully, and it gave way. I pushed the door open and went in, once again closing the door behind me and feeling for the light switch on the wall. I found it, flipped it on. The light was dimmer than even that from the security light in the hall, but it was enough to show a private party room. There was a flat-screen TV on the left wall, and a long, low couch along the right with a coffee table in front of it. Behind the couch was a bar topped with greenish marble, with a small refrigerator underneath. Along the back wall, a thick red velvet curtain hung down.

I went to the bar. There were a few bottles, but instead of glasses there was a rack of what looked like laboratory beakers. I picked one up; it was, indeed, a Pyrex beaker. The side was stamped FIRST NATIONAL BLOOD BANK in gold letters.

I pulled the velvet curtain away from the wall. There was a door behind it, and I pulled it open, holding the curtain up and away so I could see inside. It was nothing more than a small closet, empty except for cleaning supplies: broom, mop, and bucket, a bag of rags. I closed the door and dropped the curtain.

The next door along the hall was on the right, underneath the security light. It was locked, and I procrastinated by moving along the hall to the last door down on my left. It was unlocked; I slipped inside and found another private party room, a virtual duplicate of the first one.

That left the locked door. Reason told me that anything worth seeing would be locked away, but it also told me that the lock would be a good one, and I would not get it open without leaving some very obvious hints that I had been there, and possibly even setting off an alarm. Did I want to stay invisible, or just assume that if I found Samantha Aldovar it didn't matter who knew I had been there? I hadn't talked about it with Deborah, and it had just become an important question. I thought about it, and after only a moment of really high-order thinking, I decided that I was here to find Samantha, and I had to look everywhere—especially places that they didn't want anyone to see, like behind this locked door.

And so, with my courage screwed to the sticking place, I went to work on the locked door with the tire iron. I tried to be quiet and leave the fewest possible marks, but I was a little better controlling the noise than the damage to the wooden doorframe, and by the time I had the door pried open it looked like it had been attacked by rabid beavers. Still, the door was open, and I went through it.

As far as carefully hidden secrets went, the room would have been a major disappointment to anyone but an accountant. It was clearly the club's office, with a large wooden desk, a computer, and a four-drawer filing cabinet. The computer had been left on, and I sat at the desk and quickly scanned the hard drive. There were some Quicken files showing that the club was making a nice profit, some Word documents, standard letters to club members and prospective members. There was a rather large file named Coven.wpd that was password-encrypted with a security program so old I could have broken it in two minutes. But I didn't have two minutes, so I merely admired their naïveté and moved on.

There was nothing else remotely interesting, no file labeled Samantha.jpg or anything similar that might have told me where she was. I went quickly through the drawers of the desk and the filing cabinet, and again found nothing.

All right—I had trashed the doorframe for no reason. I did not feel any real guilt about that, which was a relief, but I had wasted quite a lot of time, and I had to start thinking about finishing my mission and getting out of here; there could well be a cleaning crew coming in, or Kukarov returning to admire his office doorframe.

I left the office and pushed the door closed, and then I headed for the stairs. I was reasonably sure that I didn't need to look through the main public areas of the club. It was just plain impossible that everybody who came in was in on the cannibalism—there was no way that hundreds of people could keep a secret like that. So if Samantha really was here somewhere, it would be in an area that most people didn't see.

And so I went down the stairs and across the dance floor without pausing to look around. At the back, behind the raised area that Bobby had stood on with his goblet, there was a short hallway, and I went down it. It led to the kitchen area and the back door I had admired from the outside. It was not an elaborate kitchen, just a small stove, microwave, sink, with a metallic hanging rack holding pots and several very nice-looking knives. At the far side of the room was a large metal door that looked like it led to a walk-in refrigerator. Nothing else, not even a locked pantry.

Out of a compulsion to be thorough more than anything else I went over to the refrigerator. There was a small window at eye level, made of thick plate glass, and to my surprise, it revealed that there was a light on inside the walk-in. Since I had always believed that the light goes out when you close the door, I stuck my nose to the glass and peeked in.

The refrigerator was about six feet wide and stretched back a good eight feet. There were rows of shelves on each side, most of them loaded with a series of large, gallon-size jars, and stuck up against the back wall was something you don't usually see in a refrigerator: an old folding cot.

And stranger than that, the cot was occupied. Sitting there quietly, huddled up inside a blanket, was a bundle that appeared to be a young human female. Her head was down and she was not moving, but as I watched she raised her head slowly, as if she was exhausted or drugged, and her eyes met mine.

It was Samantha Aldovar.

Without a moment's thought I grabbed for the handle of the door and pulled. It was not locked from the outside, although I could see that it could not be opened from the inside. "Samantha," I called to her. "Are you all right?"

She gave me a weary smile. "Really great," she said. "Is it time?"

I had no idea what that meant, so I just shook it off. "I'm here to rescue you," I said. "Take you home to your parents."

"Why?" she said, and I decided that she was indeed doped. It made sense; drugs would keep her calm and reduce the amount of work it took to watch her. But it also meant I would have to carry her out of here.

"All right," I said. "Just a second." I looked around me for something to prop the door open, and settled on a large five-gallon cooking pot that hung from the rack above the stove. I grabbed it, stuck it between the refrigerator door and the frame, and went into the refrigerator.

I got just two steps in when I realized what was in all the jars that filled the shelves in the big refrigerator.

Blood.

Jar after jar, gallon after gallon, they were filled with blood, and for a very long moment I looked at the blood and it looked back and I could not move. But I took a deep breath, let it out, and reality slid back into focus. It was just a fluid, nicely locked away where it couldn't hurt anybody, and the important thing was to get Samantha and get out of here. So I took the last few steps to the cot and looked down at her.

"Come on," I said. "You're going home."

"Don't want to," she said.

"I know," I said soothingly, thinking that this was a clear example of Stockholm syndrome. "Let's go." I put an arm around her and lifted her off the cot and she came up without resistance. I slung her arm around my shoulder and walked her toward the door and freedom.

"Wait a sec," she said, and the words were a little slurred. "Need my purse. On the bed," she said, nodding toward the cot, and she took her arm off me and held on to the shelf.

"Okay," I said, and I returned to the cot and looked down. I didn't see a purse—but I did hear a clatter, and I turned around to see that Samantha had kicked the five-gallon pot out of the way and, as I watched, was pulling the refrigerator door closed.

"Stop!" I said, which felt even stupider than it sounds, and I guess Samantha thought so, too, because she didn't stop, and before I could get to her she had slammed the door shut and turned to look at me with an expression of half-glazed triumph on her face.

"Told you," she said. "I don't want to go home."

TWENTY-SEVEN

I T WAS COLD INSIDE THE REFRIGERATOR. YOU MIGHT THINK that would be obvious, but obviousness doesn't provide any warmth, and I had been shivering since the shock of Samantha's betrayal wore off. It was cold, and the small room was filled with jars of blood, and there was no way out, not even with the help of my tire iron. I had tried to shatter the small glass window in the refrigerator's door, which shows how low I had descended into panicked unreason. The glass was an inch thick and reinforced with wire, and even if I had managed to break it, the opening was barely big enough for one of my legs.

Naturally enough, I had tried to call Deborah on my cell phone, and of course, more naturally, there was no reception at all inside an insulated box with thick metal walls. I knew they were thick, because after I gave up trying to break the window and then bent the tire iron trying to pry open the door, I had hammered on the walls for a few minutes, which was almost as effective as twiddling my thumbs would have been. The tire iron bent a little more, the rows and rows of blood seemed to close in on me, and I started to breathe hard—and Samantha just sat and smiled.

And Samantha herself—why did she sit there with that Mona Lisa smile of perfect contentment? She had to know that at some point in the not-too-distant future, she would become an entrée. And yet when I had arrived on my white horse in perfectly service-able armor, she had kicked the door shut and trapped us both. Was it the drugs they had obviously fed her? Or was she so delusional that she believed they wouldn't really do to her what they had already done to her best friend, Tyler Spanos?

Gradually, as the impulse to hammer at the walls faded and the shivering took over, I began to wonder about her more and more. She paid no attention at all to my feeble and comical efforts to break out of a giant steel box with a cheesy piece of iron—it should have been called a "tire tin" in this case—and she just smiled, eyes half-closed, even when I gave up and sat beside her and let the cold get at me and take over.

It really started to annoy me, that smile. It was the kind of expression you might see on someone who had taken too many recreational downers after making a killing in real estate; filled with a relaxed sense of complete satisfaction with herself, all she had done, and the world as she had shaped it, and I began to wish they had eaten her first.

So I sat beside her and shivered and alternated anxiety with thinking terrible thoughts about Samantha. As if she hadn't behaved badly enough already, she didn't even offer to share her blanket with me. I tried to shut her out—difficult to do in a small and very cold room when you are sitting right next to the thing you want to forget, but I tried.

I looked at the jars of blood. They still made me faintly queasy, but at least they took my mind off Samantha's treachery. So much of the awful sticky stuff—I looked away, and finally found a patch of metal wall to stare at that was not filled with either blood or Samantha.

I wondered what Deborah was going to do. It was selfish of me, I know, but I hoped she was starting to get very worried about me. I had been gone just a little bit too long by now, and she would be sitting in the car and grinding her teeth together, tapping her fingers on the steering wheel, glaring at her watch, wondering if it was too soon to do something and, if not, what that something ought to be. It cheered me up a little—not just the thought that she was certainly going to do something, but that she was fretting about it, too. It served her right. I hoped she would grind her teeth so hard she needed dental work. Maybe she could see Dr. Lonoff.

For no other reason than because I was anxious and bored, I took out my cell phone and tried to call her again. It still didn't work.

"That won't work in here," Samantha said in her slow and happy voice.

"Yes, I know," I said.

"Then you should stop trying," she said.

I know I was new to having human feelings, but I was pretty certain that the one she was inspiring in me was annoyance verging on loathing. "Is that what you've done?" I said. "Given up?"

She shook her head slowly with a kind of low-pitched two-syllable chuckle. "No way," she said. "Not me."

"Then for God's sake, why are you doing this? Why did you trap me in here and now you just sit there and smirk?"

She turned her head toward me and I got the feeling that she actually focused on me for the first time. "What's your name?" she asked.

I saw no reason not to tell her—of course, I also saw no reason not to slap her, but that could wait. "Dexter," I said. "Dexter Morgan."

"Whoa," she said, with another syllable of that annoying laugh. "Weird name."

"Yes, completely bizarre," I said.

"Anyway," she said. "Dexter. Do you have anything in your life that you really, really want?"

"I'd like to get out of here," I said.

She shook her head. "But something that's, you know. Like, totally, totally, ahh . . . forbidden? Like, really wrong? But you want it anyway, so much it's like— I mean, you can't even talk about it to anybody, but it's all you can think about sometimes?"

I thought about the Dark Passenger, and it stirred slightly as

I did, as if to remind me that none of this had to happen if only I'd listened. "No, not a thing," I said.

She looked at me for a long moment, her lips parted but still smiling. "Okay," she said, as if she knew I was lying but it didn't really matter. "But I have. I mean, there is something. For me."

"It's wonderful to have a dream," I said. "But wouldn't it be a lot easier to make it come true if we got out of here?"

She shook her head. "Um, no," she said. "That's just it. I have to be in here. Or, you know. I don't get to—" And she bit her lip in a kind of funny way and shook her head again.

"What?" I said, and her coy act was nudging me even closer to an uncontrollable urge to rattle her teeth. "You don't get to what?"

"It's really hard to say, even now," she said. "It's kind of like . . ." She frowned, which was a pleasant change. "Don't you have some kind of secret that, you know . . . you can't help it, but it makes you kind of, like, ashamed?"

"Sure," I said. "I watched a whole season of *American Idol*."

"But that's everybody," she said, waving a hand dismissively and making a sour-lemon face. "Everybody does that. I mean something that . . . You know, people want to fit in, be like everybody else. And if there's something inside you that makes you . . . You know it's totally wrong, weird; you'll never be like everybody else—but you still really want it. And that hurts, and it also makes you maybe more careful? About trying to fit in. Which is maybe more important when you're my age."

I looked at her with a little bit of surprise. I had forgotten that she was eighteen, and rumored to be bright. Perhaps whatever drugs they had given her were wearing off, and maybe she was just glad to have somebody to talk to for the first time in quite a while. Whatever the case, she was finally showing a little bit of depth, which at least removed one small layer of torture from durance vile.

"It's not," I said. "It stays important your whole life."

"But it *feels* so much more hurtful," she said. "When you're young, and it's like there's a party going on all around you, but you weren't invited." She looked away, not at the blood, but at the bare steel wall.

"All right," I said. "I do know what you mean." She looked at me encouragingly. "When I was your age, I was different, too. I had to work very hard to pretend to be like everyone else."

"You're just saying that," she said.

"No," I said. "It's true. I had to learn to act like the cool kids, and how to pretend I was tough, and even how to laugh."

"What," she said with another of her two-syllable chuckles. "You don't know how to laugh?"

"I do now," I said.

"Let's see."

I made one of my perfect happy faces, and gave her a very realistic that's-a-good-one chuckle.

"Hey, pretty good," she said.

"Years of practice," I said modestly. "It sounded pretty horrible at first."

"Uh-huh, well," she said, "I'm still practicing. And for me it's a whole lot harder than just learning to laugh."

"That's just teenaged self-involvement," I told her. "You think everything is harder for you, because it's *you*. But the fact is, being a human being is very hard work and it always has been. Especially if you feel like you're not one."

"I think I am," she said softly. "Just a really, really different kind."

"Okay," I said, and I admit that I was starting to feel a little bit intrigued. Who knew she would turn out to be such a *person*? "But that's not a bad thing. And if you can just give it some time, it might actually turn out to be a *good* thing."

"Yeah, right," she said.

"And you can't do that if you don't get out of here—staying here is a permanent solution to a temporary problem."

"That's cute," she said.

She was back to being flippant again, which frayed at my new human temper. She had begun to seem interesting, and I had opened up, started to like her, even felt real, actual empathy for her—and now she was slipping back into her aloof, teenage, you-can't-know disguise, and it made me just a little bit cranky and filled me with the urge to shake her up. "For God's sake," I said. "Don't you understand why you're in here? These people are going to cook you and eat you!"

She looked away again. "Yeah, I know," she said. "That's what I want." She looked back at me, her eyes large and moist. "That's my big secret," she said.

TWENTY-EIGHT

I T'S FUNNY HOW MANY LITTLE SOUNDS YOU CAN HEAR when you think you're sitting in absolute silence. For example, I could hear my heartbeat lub-dubbing away in my ears, and right next to me Samantha took a long, slow breath—and beyond that there was a metallic whirring sound as the little fan ticked on and blew more cold air across the length of the walk-in refrigerator, and I even heard something scuttling in a piece of paper under the cot I sat on, probably a palmetto bug or cockroach.

Even with all this thunderous noise, the most overwhelming sound was the all-enveloping white noise of Samantha's last words as they crashed and echoed around the little room, and after a while they stopped making sense to me, even the individual syllables, and I turned my head to look at her.

Samantha sat unmoving, the annoying smile once again in place on her face. Her shoulders were hunched and she looked straight ahead, not really avoiding eye contact so much as just waiting to see what might happen next, and at last it was more than I could stand.

"I'm sorry," I said. "When I said they're going to eat you, and you said that's what you want—what the hell do you mean?"

She was silent for several seconds, but at least her smile faded and her face settled into a look of dreamy thoughtfulness. "When I was really little," she said at last, "my father was always away somewhere, at a conference or whatever. So when he finally came home he would read these stories to me to make up. You know, fairy tales. And he would come to the part where the ogre or the witch eats somebody, and he would, you know. Make these eating noises and pretend to eat my arm, or my leg. And, you know, I mean, I'm just a kid, and I love it, and I'm like, 'Do it again, do it again.' And he'd go, 'Gobble gobble,' and I'd be laughing like crazy, and . . ."

Samantha paused and pushed a tuft of hair off her forehead. "After a while," she went on, quieter now, "I started to get older. And . . ." She shook her head, which made the hair fall back down onto her forehead, and she pushed it away again. "I realized it wasn't the stories I loved so much. It was . . . my dad gobbling on my arm. And the more I thought about it, the more it was just the idea of somebody eating me. Of having some witch or, you know, just somebody slowly, slowly roasting my body, and cutting off little slices, and eating me, and really . . . *liking* it. Liking *me*, and liking the way I tasted and . . :"

She took a deep breath and shuddered, but not from fear. "And I get, you know, puberty and all that. And all the other girls are talking about, 'Ooh, this boy, that one, I'd like to do whatever with him, and I'd let him do anything to me'—and I can't really get into that at all, all the squealing and comparing boys and— Because all I can think about, all I really want is, *I want to be eaten*." She began nodding her head rhythmically and speaking in a low husky voice. "I want to be slow-roasted while I'm still alive and can still watch these people chew me up and go, 'Yum, yum,' and come back for more until . . ."

She shivered again and pulled the blanket tighter around her shoulders, hugging herself tightly, and I tried to think of something to say, something better than asking if she'd thought of trying counseling. But nothing came to me, except a favorite remark of Deborah's.

"Holy shit," I said to Samantha.

She nodded. "Yeah, I know," she said.

Beyond that there did not seem to be very much to say, but after a moment I remembered that I was paid by the City of Miami to investigate things, so I asked her, "Tyler Spanos?"

"What?" she said.

"You two were friends," I said. "But you seemed to have nothing in common."

She nodded, and the half-dreamy smile slid back onto her face. "Yeah. Nothing except this," she said.

"This was her idea?"

"Oh, no," she said. "These people have been here for, you know, years." She nodded at the jars filled with blood and smiled. "But Tyler, she's a little wild?" She shrugged and her smile got bigger. "*Was* a little wild. She met this guy at a dark rave."

"Bobby Acosta?"

"Bobby, Vlad, whatever," she said. "So he's trying to impress her, you know, to hook up? And he says, 'I'm in this group; you wouldn't believe what we do. We *eat* people.' And she says, 'You can eat me,' and he thinks she doesn't get it and says, 'No, I mean really *eat* them.' And Tyler says, 'Yeah, well, I mean really, too, me *and* my friend.'"

Samantha shivered again and hugged herself tightly, rocking back and forth very slightly. "We had talked about finding somebody like this. I mean, we did the Yahoo chat groups and all, but it's mostly bullshit and porn, and anyway, how can you trust somebody you meet online? And now this guy comes right out with it and says, 'We eat people.'" She shivered more, really big this time. "Tyler comes to me and says, 'You won't believe what happened last night.' Which she says a lot, and I'm like, 'Okay, again?' And she says, 'No, really,' and she tells me about Vlad and his group. . . ."

Samantha closed her eyes and licked her lips before going on. "It's like a dream come true," she said. "I mean, it's *too* good. I don't believe her at first. Because Tyler is—was—kind of flaky, and guys could see that and they would say stuff to her just, you know, to have sex with her? And I'm sure she'd taken X or something anyway, so how can I be sure this guy is for real? But she takes me to meet Vlad, and he shows us some pictures and things, and I think, 'This is it.' "

Samantha looked straight at me and brushed the hair from her forehead. It was nice hair, a mousy brown color, but clean and shiny, and she looked for all the world like a normal teenage girl telling a sympathetic adult about something interesting that happened in French class—until she started talking again.

"I always knew I would do this someday," she said. "Find somebody who would eat me. It's what I wanted most. But I thought it would be later, you know, after college or—" She shrugged and shook her head. "But here he was, and Tyler and me are like, 'Why wait?' Why should I spend my parents' money on college, when I can have what I want without it, right now? So we told Vlad, 'Okay, totally, we're in,' and he takes us to meet the head of the group, and . . ." She smiled. "Here I am."

"And Tyler isn't," I said.

Samantha nodded. "She was always lucky. She got to go first." The smile got bigger. "But I'm next. Soon."

And her apparent eagerness to follow Tyler into the cauldron dried up all my professional zeal, and I had nothing more to say. Samantha just watched me to see what I would do—and for the first time in my life, I had absolutely no idea what that would be. What is the correct facial expression to put on when someone tells you their lifelong fantasy is to be eaten? Should I go for shock? Disbelief? What about moral outrage? I was quite sure the subject had never come up in any of the movies or TV shows I had studied, and even though I am considered a clever and creative person in some circles, I could not imagine anything at all that might be appropriate.

So I stared, and Samantha looked back at me, and there we were: a perfectly normal married man with three kids and a promising career who just happened to enjoy killing people, staring at a perfectly normal eighteen-year-old girl who went to a good school and liked *Twilight* and who wanted to be eaten, sitting next to each other in a walk-in refrigerator at a vampire club in South Beach. I had been trying so hard lately to achieve some close approximation of normal life, but if this was it, I thought I would prefer something else. Outside of Salvador Dalí I really can't believe the human mind could handle anything more extreme.

And at last even the mutual staring began to seem too strange, even for two dedicated non-humans like us, and we both blinked and looked away.

"Anyway," she said. "It doesn't matter."

"What doesn't matter?" I said. "Wanting to be eaten?"

She shrugged, an oddly genuine teen gesture. "Whatever," she said. "I mean, they'll be here soon."

I felt like someone was tickling my spine with an icicle. "Who will?" I said.

"Somebody from the coven," she said, and she glanced back at me. "That's what they call it. The, you know. The group that, um, eats people."

I thought of the file I had seen on the computer. Coven. I wished I had copied it and run for home. "How do you know they're coming?" I said.

She shrugged again. "They have to feed me. Like, three times a day, you know."

"Why should they?" I said. "If they're just going to kill you, why do they have to take care of you?"

She gave me a you-are-so-dumb look, combined with a head shake. "They're going to *eat* me, not kill me," she said. "They don't want me to get all sick and skinny. I gotta be, you know. Chubbed up. Marbled. For flavor."

Between my job and my hobby I have to say without bragging that I have a pretty strong stomach, but this was putting it to a real test. The idea that she would cheerfully eat three healthy meals a day so her flesh would taste better was just a little too much before breakfast, and I turned away again. But happily for my appetite, a practical thought nudged its way in. "How many of them will come?" I asked.

She looked at me, then looked away. "I don't know," she said. "It's usually just two guys. In case, you know, I decide to change my mind and run. But . . ." She looked at me. And then down at her feet.

"I think Vlad is coming with them this time," she said at last, and it did not sound like a happy thought.

"Why do you think that?" I said.

She shook her head but did not look up. "When it was going to be Tyler," she said, "he started to come with them. And he would, you know . . . *do* things to her." She licked her lips but still did not look up. "Not just, you know . . . Not sex. I mean, not *normal* sex. He, um. He really, really hurt her. Like that was how he got off, and . . ." She shuddered, and at last she looked up. "I think that's why they put stuff in my food, some kind of tranquilizer?" she said. "So it keeps me, you know, kind of calm and quiet? Because otherwise . . ." She looked away again. "Maybe he won't come," she said.

"But at least two guys *will* come?" I said.

She nodded. "Yeah."

"Are they armed?" I said, and she looked up at me, blank. "You know, knives, guns, bazookas? Are they carrying any weapons?"

"I don't know," she said. "I mean, I would."

I thought that I would, too, and although it might have been uncharitable, I also thought that I would have noticed what weapons my captors were carrying. Of course, I didn't think of myself as a banquet, and that would almost certainly affect my powers of observation.

So there would be two of them, probably armed, which probably meant guns, since this was Miami. And it might mean Bobby Acosta, too, who would have some kind of weapon, since he was a wealthy fugitive. And I was in a small room with no place to hide, and I was burdened with Samantha, who would probably yell, "Watch out!" at them if I tried to surprise them. On the plus side, my heart was pure and I had a bent tire iron.

It wasn't much, but I have learned that if you examine the situation carefully, you can almost always find a way to improve your odds. I stood up and looked around the room, thinking that someone might have left an assault rifle lying on a shelf; I even made myself touch the jars and look behind them, but no such luck. "Hey," Samantha said. "If you're thinking, like, you know— I mean, I don't want to be rescued or anything."

"I think that's wonderful," I said. "But I do." I looked at her, sitting there hunched up in her blanket. "I don't want to be eaten. I have a life, and a family. I have a new baby," I said, "and I want to see her again. I want to watch her grow up, and read her fairy stories."

She flinched a little bit and looked uncertain. "What's her name?" she said.

"Lily Anne."

Samantha looked off to the side again, and I could see her trying to swim through the doubt, so I pushed a little. "Samantha," I said. "Whatever it is you want, you don't have the right to force it on me." I felt remarkably hypocritical preaching to her, but after all, there was an awful lot at stake, and in any case I had been practicing hypocrisy all my adult life.

"But—I want this," she said. "I mean, my whole life . . ."

"Do you want it enough to kill me?" I said. "Because that's what you're doing."

She looked at me and then looked away again quickly. "No," she said. "But . . ."

"Yes, but," I said. "But if I don't get past the guys who feed you, I am going to be dead, and you know that."

"I can't just give this up," she said.

"You don't have to," I told her, and she looked at me attentively. "All you have to do is let me escape, and you can stay here."

She chewed on her lower lip for a few seconds. "I don't know," she said. "I mean, how can I trust you not to, you know. Call the cops and come storming back here to get me?"

"By the time I could get back here with the cops," I said, "they will have moved you someplace else."

"Yeah," she said, nodding slowly. "But how do I know you won't, like, drag me out of here and, you know. Save me from myself?"

I went down on one knee in front of her. It was melodramatic, I know, but she was a teenager, and I thought she would probably buy it. "Samantha," I said. "All you have to do is just let me try. Do nothing, and I won't try to get you out of here against your will. You have my solemn word of honor." There was no crash of thunder, not even the sound of distant laughter, and in spite of my recent epidemic of unpleasant emotions, I felt no shame. And I believe I did it very convincingly. In fact, I think it was the performance of a lifetime—I didn't mean a word of it, of course, but under the circumstances I would gladly have promised her a ride on my flying saucer if it would get me out of here.

And Samantha began to look more than half-convinced. "So—I don't know. I mean, what. I just sit here and like don't say anything? That's all?"

"That's all," I said. I took her hand and looked deep into her eyes. "Please, Samantha," I said. "For Lily Anne." Totally shameless, I know, but to my surprise, I found I actually meant it—and even worse, I felt moisture collecting in the corners of my eyes. Perhaps it was just a Method actor moment, but it interfered with my vision and was extremely disconcerting.

And, apparently, extremely effective. "All right," she said, and she actually squeezed my hand. "I won't say anything."

I squeezed back. "Thank you," I said. "Lily Anne thanks you." Again, maybe a bit over-the-top, but there were so few guidelines for this situation. I stood and picked up my tire iron. It wasn't much, but it was better than nothing. I went to the door and tried to wedge myself in beside the frame, where I would be invisible if they looked through the small window first. I chose the side closest to the handle; the door opened outward, and it would be much easier for them to see into the other corner. I had to hope that they would not notice anything and, after glancing in and seeing Samantha in her place on the cot, they would simply walk in unsuspecting. Then with any luck at all it would be one-two, *snicker-snak*, and Dexter would go galumphing back.

I had been scrunched into my place for about five minutes when I heard voices coming faintly through the thick door. I took a deep breath, let it out slowly, and tried to make myself even smaller in my corner. I looked at Samantha, and she licked her lips, but nodded at me. I nodded back, and then I heard someone pulling on the door's handle and the big door swung open.

"Sooo-wee, piggy," somebody said, with a very mean-sounding chuckle. "Oink, oink."

A man stepped through carrying a red nylon insulated bag. I brought the tire iron down on his head, hard, and he pitched forward without another sound. Like greased lightning, I stepped around his body and into the doorway, holding my tire iron up, ready for anything—

—except for the huge arm that was already swinging at my face and sweeping me back against the wall, and I had time for only one quick glimpse of the massive bouncer with the shaved head, as he pinned me with a forearm across my throat, and Bobby Acosta standing behind him yelling, "Kill the fucker!"

And then the bouncer swung a fist the size of a grand piano at my chin and I was gone into darkness.

TWENTY-NINE

I WAS FAR AWAY IN A PLACE WHERE TINY SPARKS OF LIGHT flittered through a great sea of darkness and Dexter swam through it with legs made of lead and arms that did not move at all with a very unpleasant buoyancy that seemed to float up from a queasiness in my center and there was no other thought or feeling of any kind except for mere *being* for a very long time until finally, from far away, an urgent sound came in to me and carried on its back a very strong idea that tumbled into focus in one crystal-clear syllable: *Ow!* And I became aware that "ow" was not a mystic word for use in meditation, nor a lost land of the Bible, but, in fact, the only way I could succinctly sum up the State of Dexter, from shoulders upward. *Ow* . . .

"Come on, wake up, Dexter," a soft female voice said, and I felt a cool hand on my forehead. I had no idea whose hand, nor whose voice, and in truth it really did not seem nearly as important as the fact that my head was an endless ocean of pain and I could not move my neck.

"Dexter, please," the voice insisted, and the cool hand patted my cheek a great deal harder than seemed to be polite, strictly speaking, and each little pat-pat sent an echoing wave of *ow* rolling through my head, and at last I found the controls for my arms and moved one up to brush away the hammering hand.

"Ow," I said out loud, and it sounded like the distant cry of a large and weary bird.

"You're alive," the voice said, and then that damned hand came back and patted my cheek again. "I was really worried." I thought I might have heard that voice before, but I couldn't say where, and it wasn't a high priority at the moment, considering that my head was filled with flaming oatmeal.

"Owww," I said again, with a little more force. It was really all I could think of to say, but that didn't matter, since it summed things up so nicely.

"Come on now," the voice said. "Open up your eyes, Dexter. Come on."

I thought about that word: "eyes." I was pretty sure I knew that one. Something to do with, um—seeing? Located somewhere in or near the face? That sounded right, and I felt a dull and dim glow of pleasure; I got one right. Good boy.

"Dexter, please," the female voice said again. "Open up, come on." I felt her hand move again, as if to pat my cheek, and the sheer annoyance of that idea sparked a memory—I could open my eyes like *this*. I tried it. The right one popped open while the left fluttered a few times before finally coming open to a blurry world. I blinked them both several times and the picture settled into focus, but it did not make any sense.

I was looking straight up at a face only a little more than a foot away from my own. It was not a bad face, and I was pretty sure I had seen it before. It was young, female, and creased with concern at the moment, but as I blinked at it and tried to remember where I had seen it, it broke into a smile. "Hey, there you are," she said. "You had me so totally worried." I blinked again; it was an awful lot of work, and it was just about all I could manage. Trying to think at the same time was just too hard, so I stopped blinking.

"Samantha," I croaked, and I was very pleased with myself.

That was the name that went with that face. And her face was so close to mine because my head was resting in her lap.

"The one and only," she said. "Nice to have you back with us."

Things were slowly filtering into my throbbing brain: Samantha, cannibals, refrigerator, giant fist. . . . It took some work, but I began to connect the separate thoughts and the picture came slowly together into a memory of what had happened—and it was far more painful than my head and I closed my eyes again. "Owww . . ." I said.

"Yeah, you said that already," Samantha said. "I don't have any aspirin or anything, but this might help—here." I felt her turn a bit under me and I opened my eyes. She held a large plastic water bottle up and twisted the top off. "Take a sip," she said. "Slow. Not too much, you might hurl."

I sipped. The water was cool, with a very faint taste I couldn't identify, and as I swallowed I realized how parched and sore my throat was. "More," I said.

"A little bit at a time," Samantha said, and she let me take another small sip.

"Good," I said. "I was thirsty."

"Wow," she said. "Three whole words together. You're really coming around." She took a sip, too, and then put the water bottle down.

"Could I have a little more?" I said, and added, "That's six words."

"It sure is," she said, and she sounded happy with my wonderful new talent for using multiple words. She held the bottle to my lips and I took another sip. It seemed to ease the muscles in my throat and brought a slight relief to my headache, as well as a growing awareness that things were not entirely as they should be.

I turned my head to look around, and was rewarded with an electrifying stab of pain running from my neck right up through the top of my head. But I could also see a little bit more of the world than Samantha's face and shirt, and the picture was not encouraging. There was a fluorescent strip light overhead, and it lit up a light green wall. In the place where reason said a window might have been, there was a plain, unpainted piece of plywood. And I could see nothing else without moving my head some more, which I very definitely did not want to do, considering the searing pain I had just experienced moving it this far.

I slowly rolled my head back to where it had been and tried to think. I did not recognize my surroundings, but I was no longer in the refrigerator, at least. I could hear a mechanical rattle nearby, and I knew it, as any Floridian would, as the sound of a window air conditioner. But neither that nor the plywood told me anything important.

"Where are we?" I asked Samantha.

She swallowed a sip of water. "In a trailer," she said. "Way out in the Everglades somewhere, I don't know. One of the guys in the coven has like fifty acres out here with this thing on it, trailer, for hunting. And they brought us here, like, totally isolated. Nobody will ever find us out here." She sounded happy about that, but at least she remembered to look a little guilty about it and tried to cover it with a sip of water.

"How?" I said, and it sounded croakish again, and I reached for the water bottle. I took another swig, a bigger one this time. "How did they get us out of the club?" I said. "With nobody seeing us?"

She waved a hand, and the movement jolted my head—a slight jolt, but a much larger pain. "They rolled us up in rugs," she said. "These two guys in overalls come in and carry out the rugs, with us inside, and dump 'em into a van, and just drive us out here. 'Gonzalez Carpet Cleaners,' it said. Easy." She gave a half smile, half shrug, and took a sip of water.

I thought about it. If Deborah had still been watching, seeing two large bundles carried out would certainly have made her suspicious—and, being Debs, if she got suspicious she would have jumped out with her gun drawn and stopped them right then and there. So she had not been watching—but why not? Would she really abandon me, her own dear brother? Leave me to a fate worse than death, although certainly including it? I didn't think she would, not willingly. I took a sip of water and tried to think it through.

She would not willingly leave me. On the other hand, she couldn't really call in backup—her partner was dead, and she was technically doing something just a little bit outside department regulations and, for that matter, the Florida Penal Code. So what would she do?

I took another sip of water. The bottle was more than half-empty now, but it did seem to ease the pain in my head a bit—not that the pain went away, but hey—it wasn't really so bad. I mean, pain meant I was alive, and who was it who said, "Where there's life there's hope"? Maybe Samantha knew—but as I opened my mouth to ask her she took the water bottle back and took a big sip and I remembered I was trying to think about what my sister would have done, and why that led to my being here.

I took the bottle back from Samantha and sipped the water. Deborah wouldn't leave me like that. Of course not. Deborah loved me. And the realization flooded into me—I loved her, too. I took another swig of water. It's a funny thing, love. I mean, to realize this at my age was weird, but I was actually surrounded by so much love—my whole life, from my adoptive parents, Harry and Doris; they didn't have to love me—I wasn't really their kid—but they did. They did love me, like so many others, all the way up to now, with Debs—and Rita, Cody, Astor, and Lily Anne. Beautiful, wonderful, miraculous Lily Anne, the ultimate bringer of love. But all those others, too, they all loved me in their own way—

Samantha took the water bottle and sipped, and it hit me with a tremendous rush of insight: Even Samantha had shown me so much love. She had proved it by risking everything that meant anything to her, everything she had always wanted, just to give me a chance to escape! Wasn't that an act of pure love?

I took another sip of water and felt myself completely surrounded by all these wonderful people, people who loved me even though I had done some very bad things—but what the hell, I had stopped, hadn't I? Wasn't I now trying to live a life of love and responsibility, in a world that had suddenly blossomed into a place of wonder and joy?

Samantha grabbed the bottle and took a big swig. She handed it back and I finished it eagerly—delicious, the best water I'd ever tasted. Or maybe I was just appreciating things more. Yes. The world was really an amazing place after all, and I fit in perfectly. And so did Samantha. What a wonderful person she was. She had taken care of me, too, and she didn't have to. And she was taking care of me now! Nurturing me and stroking my face with what could only be called love—what a wonderful girl she was! And if she wanted to be eaten—wow: I had an epiphany. Food is love—so wanting to be eaten was just another way to share love! And that was the way Samantha had chosen because she was so filled with love she couldn't possibly hope to express it except in some ultimate form like this! Amazing!

I looked up at her face with a new appreciation. This was a wonderful, giving person. And even though it hurt my neck, I had to show her that I understood what she was doing and truly appreciated what a wonderful, beautiful person she was—so I raised my arm up and put my hand on her face. The skin felt soft, warm, vibrantly alive, and I rubbed the palm of my hand softly across her cheek for a moment. She looked back at me, smiling, and put her hand back on my face.

"You are so beautiful," I said. "I mean, just saying the word, 'beautiful'—that doesn't really sum it up, except in a kind of superficial way that only talks about the outside and doesn't really get at the true, absolute *depths* of what I mean by beautiful—especially in your case, because I think I just understood what it is you're doing with this whole 'eat me' business—I mean, you're beautiful on the outside, too; that's not what I mean, not to take any of that away from you, because I know it's important to a girl. A woman. You're eighteen; you're a *woman*, I know, because you've made a very adult choice with what to do with your life, and there's no turning back from it, which makes it a *really* adult choice, and I'm sure you understand the consequences of your decision, and there can't be a better definition of adulthood than that, to make a decision with ultimate consequences and know you can't turn back from it, and I really admire you for that. And also because like I said you are really, really beautiful."

Her hand rubbed my face and then slid down across my neck and through the collar of my shirt and she rubbed my chest. It felt good. "I know what you're saying *exactly* and you are the first person who I think really understood what it means for me to go through all this—" She took her hand away from my chest to wave it in the air, indicating everything all around us, and I reached up and pulled it back down onto my chest because it felt really good and I wanted to keep touching her. She smiled and rubbed softly across my chest again. "Because it isn't something that's easy to understand, I *know* that, and that's one reason why I never thought I could ever talk about it to anybody and why, you know, I've been so completely alone for most of my life, all of it really, because who could ever understand something like this? I mean, if I just say it to somebody, 'I want to be eaten,' then it's gotta be like this whole, 'Oh, my God, we're getting you to a shrink' thing and nobody ever looking at you like you're normal ever again and I *feel* like this is totally normal, a totally normal expression of—"

"Love," I said.

"You *do* understand!" she said, and she slid her hand lower, across my stomach, and then back up onto my chest again. "Oh, God, I *knew* you would get it, because even when we were in that refrigerator there was just something about you that was different from everybody else I have ever met in my whole life and I thought maybe just once before it happens I can talk to somebody who really *gets* it and they won't look at me like I'm some kind of perverted sick twisted freak monster!"

"No, no, you're just so *beautiful*," I said. "Nobody could ever think that about you, just even your face is so amazing—"

"No, but that's not it—"

"No, I know that, that's not what I mean," I said. "But it's *part* of what makes you who you are, and to see that part really leads to understanding about the rest—I mean, if you're not a total idiot, you can't look at your face and not think, Wow, what an incredible person, and then to see that the insides are even more beautiful is just amazing." And because mere words could not really express it completely and I really wanted her to understand what I meant, I pulled her face down to mine and kissed her. "You are beautiful inside and out," I said.

She smiled with an incredible warmth and appreciation that just made me feel like everything would always be all right. "You are, too," she said, and she lowered her face and kissed me again and this time the kiss was longer and it led into another kind of feeling that was new for me and I could tell that it was new for her, too, but neither one of us wanted to stop until she stretched out beside me on the floor as we kissed and after a long time of that she did stop, just for a second, and said, "I think they put something in the water."

"I don't think that matters," I said. "Because what we have started to understand doesn't really come from anything you can put in water because it comes from inside us, the *real* inside, and it is really true, which I know you can feel as well as I can." I kissed her and she kissed back for a minute before she stopped and put both hands on my cheeks.

"In any case," she said, "even if it is just something in the water it doesn't matter because I always kind of thought that this is just so important—I mean *love*, and you know, I mean, not just the kind that you feel but the kind you *do* and I thought, I'm eighteen; I should do it at least once before I check out, don't you think?"

"At least once," I said, and she smiled and closed her eyes and brought her face back to mine and we did.

More than once.

THIRTY

"I'M THIRSTY," SAMANTHA SAID. THERE WAS A WHINING NOTE in her voice. I found it irritating but I didn't say anything. I was thirsty, too. What was the point to saying it again? We were both thirsty. We had been thirsty for some time. The water was all gone. There wasn't any more. That was the least of my problems: My head hurt, and I was trapped in a trailer in the Everglades, and I had just done something I couldn't begin to understand. Oh, and somebody was coming to kill me, too.

"I feel sooooo stupid," Samantha said. And again, there was very little to say in response. We both felt stupid, now that whatever was in the water had worn off, but she seemed to have more trouble accepting that we had acted under the influence of the drugs. As we had come back to our senses Samantha had gradually looked uncomfortable, then nervous, and then downright alarmed, scrabbling around the trailer for articles of clothing that had been enthusiastically misplaced. In spite of how awkward she made it look, I decided it was the right idea. I found and put on all my clothing, too.

And a small touch of intelligence returned to me with my pants. I got up and looked over the trailer from one end to the other. It didn't take long. It was only around thirty feet long. All the windows were securely boarded with three-quarter-inch marine plywood. I thumped on them. I threw my full weight against them. They didn't budge. They were reinforced from the outside.

There was only one door. Same story: Even when I ran my shoulder against it, I got nothing except more pain in my head. Now I had a matching pain in my shoulder. I sat down to nurse it for a few minutes. That was when Samantha had started whining. Apparently putting her clothes on made her feel she could complain about almost anything, because it didn't end with the water. And through some mean-spirited trick of acoustics or plain bad luck, the pitch of her voice was in perfect resonance with the throbbing of my head. Every time she complained it sent an extra pulse of dull pain deep into the battered gray tissue in my cranium.

"It smells . . . *funky* in here," she said.

It did actually smell funky, a combination of very old sweat, wet dog, and mold. But it was far beyond pointless to mention something when there was nothing we could do about it. "I'll get my herbal sachet," I said. "It's out in the car."

She looked away. "You don't have to get sarcastic," she said.

"No," I said. "But I do have to get out of here."

She didn't look at me, and she didn't have any response, which seemed like a small blessing. I closed my eyes and tried to will away the thumping anguish. It didn't work, and after a minute Samantha interrupted again.

"I wish we hadn't done that," she said. I opened my eyes. She still looked away, over to a plain corner of the trailer. It was completely barren and blank, but apparently better to look at than me.

"Sorry," I said.

She shrugged, still looking away. "It's not your fault," she said, which I thought very generous, though accurate. "I knew there was probably something in the water. They always put something in." She shrugged again. "I never had ecstasy before, though."

It took me a moment to realize she meant the drug. "Me either," I said. "Is that what it was?"

"I'm pretty sure," she said. "I mean, from what I heard. Tyler said—she takes it a lot—*took* it a lot." She shook her head and then she actually started to blush. "Anyway. She said it makes you want to . . . I mean, touch everybody and . . . you know. Be touched."

If that had indeed been ecstasy, I would have to agree. I would also have to say that either we had taken far too much, or it was a very powerful drug. I could nearly blush myself when I remembered what I had said and done. Trying to become a little more human was one thing—but this had been far over the edge into the sludge of dumb, yammer-headed personhood. Perhaps the stuff should be called excess-tasy. In retrospect, I was very glad there was a drug to blame. I did not like to think of myself as behaving like a cartoon.

"Anyway, I got to do it," Samantha said, still blushing. "I won't miss it much." Another shrug. "It wasn't that great."

I don't know an awful lot about what is popularly called "pillow talk," but I rather thought that this kind of honesty was not considered proper form. From the little I did know, I was pretty sure you were supposed to make flattering remarks, even if you thought it was a mistake. You said things like, "It was wonderful—let's not soil the memory by trying to equal that magic." Or, "We'll always have Paris." In this case, "We'll always have that horrible smelly trailer in the Everglades," didn't have quite the same ring, but at least she could have tried. Maybe Samantha was getting revenge for the massive discomfort she was feeling, or maybe it was true and she, as a callow youth, didn't know she wasn't supposed to say such things.

In any case, it combined with my headache and activated a mean streak I didn't know I had. "No, it wasn't that great," I said. She looked at me now, with an expression that actually approached anger, but she didn't say anything, and after a moment she looked away again, and I took a last stretch and rub at my neck muscles and stood up.

"There has to be a way out of here," I said, more to myself than her, but of course she answered anyway.

"No, there doesn't," she said. "It's secure. They keep people here all the time, and nobody ever gets out."

"If they're always drugged, did anyone ever try?"

She half closed her eyes and slowly shook her head to indicate that I was stupid, and looked away. And maybe I was stupid, but not enough to sit and wait for them to come and eat me—not without trying my best to get away.

I went once more through the trailer. There was nothing new to see, but I looked at everything a little more carefully. There was no furniture at all, but down at the far end there was one built-in bench that had obviously served as a bed. It had a thin strip of foam rubber on it, covered by a ratty gray sheet. I lifted the mattress onto the floor. Under it there was a square of plywood fitted into an opening. I pulled up the plywood. Underneath was something that was clearly a locker. There was a very flat pillow inside, covered with a case that matched the sheet. The locker seemed to run the whole width of the trailer, although I could not see into the darkness on either side.

I pulled out the pillow. There was nothing else inside except a short length of an old two-by-four, maybe a foot and a half long. One end of it was cut to a very dull, flat point and there was dirt all over the tapered part. At the other end there were notches cut into each side, and a groove worn into the wood, possibly by rope. The wood had been used as a stake for whatever arcane reason, hammered into the ground to hold something or other with rope tied to it. There was even an old and bent nail stuck in the top to tie off the rope. I took the stake out and laid it beside the pillow. I stuck my head into the locker as far as I could, but there was nothing else to see. I pushed on the bottom and felt a little bit of give, so I pushed harder and was rewarded with a *whump-ah* of flimsy metal bending.

Bingo. I pushed harder, and the metal visibly bent. I pulled my head out and stood up, stepping into the locker with both feet. I just barely fit into the opening, but it was enough, and I started to jump as hard as I could. It made a very loud booming sound, and after about the seventh *boom!* Samantha came to see what all the noise was.

"What are you doing?" she said, which struck me as silly as well as annoying.

"Escaping," I said, and gave an extra hard jump. *Boom!*

She watched as I jumped several more times, and then shook her head and raised her voice, very thoughtfully, so I could hear her negativity over the noise. "I don't think you can get out like that," she said.

"The metal is thin here," I said. "Not like the floor."

"It's the tensile strength," she said in her loud voice. "Like surface cohesion in a cup of water. We did this in physics."

I took a second to marvel at the kind of physics class that taught its students about the tensile strength of a trailer's floor when one is escaping from a cannibal coven, and then I paused in midjump. Perhaps she was right—after all, Ransom Everglades was a very good school and they probably taught things that never made it into the public school curriculum. I stepped out of the locker and looked at what I had accomplished so far. It wasn't much. There was a noticeable dent, but nothing that could really inspire hope.

"They'll be here way before you get out like that," she said, and somebody who lacked charity might have said she was gloating.

"Maybe so," I said, and my eye fell on the two-by-four. I did not actually say, "Aha!" but I certainly had one of those moments when the lightbulb goes on. I picked up the chunk of wood and worried out the old nail. I wedged the head of it into a crack on the point of the stake, and placed the point in the center of the dent I had already made. Then, with a significant glance at Samantha, I pounded on the top of the stake as hard as I could.

It hurt. I counted three splinters in my hand.

"Ha," Samantha said.

It has been said that behind every successful man there is a woman, and by extension we can say that behind every escaping Dexter is a really annoying Samantha, because her happiness at seeing me fail spurred me to new heights of inspiration. I took off my shoe and fitted it over the top of the stake and smacked it experimentally. It didn't hurt nearly as much, and I was sure I could hammer it hard enough to make a hole in the locker's floor.

"Ha yourself," I said to Samantha.

"Whatever," she said, and walked back to where she had been sitting in the middle section of the trailer.

I went right back to work, pounding on the sole of my shoe with all my strength. I paused after a couple of minutes and looked; the dent had gotten much deeper, and there were signs of stress at the edges. The point of the nail had gone into the metal, and a few more minutes could very well see a small hole; I went back at it with a will. After two more minutes, the tone of the thumping seemed to change, and I pulled out the stake and had another look.

There was a small hole all the way through, just large enough to see daylight under the trailer. With a little more time and effort, I was sure I could punch through, enlarge the hole, and be on my way.

I wiggled the point of the stake back into the opening as far as I could and pounded even harder. I could feel it sinking slowly through, and then suddenly I pounded and the stake dropped several inches. I stopped pounding and began to work the wood back and forth, stretching the metal back, making the hole as big as possible. I worked it and worried it and jammed the stake sideways and even put my shoe back on and kicked at it, and for twenty minutes the metal of the trailer fought back, but at last I had a way out.

I paused for a moment, looking at the hole I had made. I was exhausted and sore and soaked with sweat, but I was one step away from freedom.

"I'm outta here," I called to Samantha. "This is your last chance to get away."

"Bye-bye," she called back. "Have a nice trip." It seemed a little bit callous after all we had gone through together, but it was probably all I would get from her.

"Okay," I said, and I climbed into the locker, pushing my legs down into the hole I had made. My feet touched ground and I wiggled the rest of me downward. It was a very tight fit, and I felt first my pants and then my shirt catch on the metal edges and tear. I held my arms up above my head and kept wiggling and in just a moment I was through, sitting on the warm and wet dirt of the Everglades. I could feel it soak through my pants, but it felt wonderful, much better than the floor of the trailer.

I took a deep breath; I was free. Around me was the trailer's concrete-block foundation, holding it several feet off the ground. There were two gaps in it, one of them close by and opposite the trailer's door. I rolled onto my stomach and crawled toward it. And just as my head poked out into the light of day and I began to think I was going to get away, a massive hand came down and grabbed me by the hair. "That's far enough, asshole," a voice snarled at me, and I felt myself lifted almost straight up with only a short pause to bang my head against the trailer. Through the bright lights bursting in my already painful head I could see my old friend, the bouncer with the shaved head. He threw me up against the side of the trailer and, as he had when he knocked me out in the refrigerator, he pinned me with a forearm across my throat.

Behind him I could see that the trailer sat in a small clearing, surrounded by the lush vegetation of the Everglades. A canal ran along one side, and mosquitoes hummed and homed in on us happily. Somewhere a bird called. And from a path at the near end of the clearing came Kukarov, the club manager, followed by two other nasty-looking men, one of them carrying the insulated lunch bucket and the other a leather tool pouch.

"Well, piggy," Kukarov said with a truly awful smile. "Where do you think you're going?"

"I have a dentist's appointment," I said. "I really can't miss it."

"Yes, you can," Kukarov said, and the bouncer slapped me, hard. On top of the growing collection of head pains I already had, it hurt far more than it should have.

People who know me well will tell you that Dexter never loses his temper, but enough was enough. I swung my foot up, fast and hard, and kicked the bouncer in the crotch with enough force to make him let go of me and bend over, and he began to make small retching noises. And since that had been so easy and rewarding I turned to face Kukarov with my hands raised to fighting position.

But he was holding a pistol, and pointing it directly between my eyes. It was a very large and expensive pistol, a .357 Magnum by the look of it. The hammer was pulled back, and the only thing darker than the hole at the end of the barrel was the expression in his eyes.

"Go ahead," he said. "Try it."

It was an interesting suggestion, but I decided against it, and raised my hands up high. He watched me for a moment and then, backing away a few steps without taking his eyes off me, he called to the others. "Tie him up," he said. "Smack him around a little, but don't damage the meat. We can use a male piggy."

One of them grabbed me and pulled my arms behind me, hard enough to hurt, and the other one started pulling duct tape off a roll. He had just gotten a few loops around my wrists when I heard what might be the most beautiful sound I had ever heard in my life—the squeal of a bullhorn, followed by Deborah's voice coming through it.

"This is the police," she said. "You are surrounded. Drop your weapons and lie facedown on the ground."

The two helpers flinched away from me and looked at Kukarov with their mouths hanging open. The bouncer was still leaning on his knees and retching. Kukarov snarled. "I'll kill this asshole!" he shouted, and I could see his finger tighten on the trigger as he raised the pistol.

A single shot split the air and the front half of Kukarov's head disappeared. He whipped away sideways as if pulled by a rope and fell in a heap on the ground.

The two other cannibals dove to the ground in unison, and even the bouncer flopped over onto his face, and I watched as Deborah charged out of the vegetation at the edge of the clearing and ran toward me, followed by at least a dozen police officers, including a bunch of heavily armed and armored guys from SRT, the Special Response Team, and Detective Weems, the ebony giant from the Miccosukee Tribal Police.

"Dexter," Deborah called. She grabbed me by the arms and looked into my face for a moment. "Dex," she said again, and it was gratifying to see a little anxiety on her face. She patted my arms and almost smiled, a very rare display for her. Of course, since it was Debs, she had to spoil the effect immediately. "Where's Samantha?" she said.

I looked at my sister. My head was pounding, my pants were torn, my throat and my face hurt from the bouncer's rough treatment, I was embarrassed by what I had recently done, my hands were still taped behind me—and I was thirsty. I had been beaten, kidnapped, drugged, beaten again, and threatened with a very large revolver, all without a single complaint—but Debs could only think about Samantha, who was well fed and sitting inside in air-conditioned comfort—sitting there willingly, even eagerly, whining about minor discomforts while I tried and failed to dodge all the slings and arrows and, I could not fail to notice, an increasing number of mosquitoes that I could not swat with my hands taped behind me.

But of course, Deborah was family, and anyway I couldn't use my hands, so slapping her was out of the question. "I'm fine, sis," I said. "Thank you for asking."

As always, it was wasted on Deborah. She grabbed my arms and shook me. "Where is she?" she said. "Where is Samantha?"

I sighed and gave it up. "Inside the trailer," I said. "She's fine." Deborah looked at me for a second and then whirled away around the trailer to the door. Weems followed her and I heard a loud crunching noise as he apparently pulled the door off its hinges. A moment later he wandered past, the door dangling by its knob from one enormous hand. Debs came right after him with an arm around Samantha, leading her away to the car and murmuring, "I've got you, you're all right now," to a plainly pissed-off Samantha, who was hunched over and muttering, "Leave me alone."

I looked around the little clearing. A handful of cops in SRT outfits were cuffing Kukarov's guys, none too gently. Things were definitely winding down—except for a new and frantic burst of activity from the nine million mosquitoes that had found my unprotected head. I tried to swat them away—impossible, of course, with my hands taped behind me. I shook my head to scare them away, but it didn't work, and it hurt so much that it wasn't worth it even if it did. I tried to wave my elbows at them—also impossible, and I thought I heard the mosquitoes laughing at me and licking their chops as they called all their friends to the feast.

"Could somebody please undo my hands?" I said.

THIRTY-ONE

I DID EVENTUALLY GET THE DUCT TAPE OFF MY WRISTS. AFTER all, I was surrounded by cops, and it would have been terribly wrong for so many sworn officers of the law to keep me tied up as if I was some kind of—well, to be honest, I actually was some kind of, but I was trying really hard not to be one anymore. And since they did not know what I had been, it made sense that sooner or later one of them would take pity on me and cut me loose. And one of them finally did: It was Weems, the gigantic man from the tribal police. He came over and looked at me, a very large smile growing on his very large face, and shook his head. "Why you standing there with your hands all taped up?" he said. "Nobody love you no more?"

"I guess I'm just a low priority," I said. "Except to the mosquitoes."

He laughed, a high-pitched and overly joyful sound that went on for several seconds—much too long, in my still-taped opinion, and just when I was thinking of saying something rather sharp he pulled out a huge pocketknife and flipped the blade open. "Let's get you slapping flies again," he said, and motioned with the blade for me to turn around.

I was happy to oblige, and very quickly he laid the edge of the knife onto the tape binding my wrists. The knife was apparently very sharp; there was almost no pressure at all, and the tape burst open. I brought my hands in front of me and peeled off the tape. It also peeled off most of the hair on my wrists, but since my first swat at the back of my neck squashed at least six mosquitoes, it seemed like a good trade-off.

"Thank you very much," I said.

"No problem," he told me in that soft, high voice. "Nobody oughta be all bound up like that." He laughed at his own great wit and I, thinking it was the least I could do in return for his kindness, gave him a small sample of my very best fake smile.

"Bound up," I said. "That's very good." I might have been lay-ing it on a bit thick, but I was grateful, and in any case my head still hurt too much for any really good comeback to blossom in it.

It wouldn't have mattered in any case, because Weems was no longer paying attention. He had gone very still, tilted his nose up into the air, and half closed his eyes as if he were hearing something calling his name in the far distance.

"What is it?" I said.

He didn't say anything for a moment. Then he shook his head. "Smoke," he said. "Somebody got an illegal fire going out there." He jerked his chin in the direction of the heart of the Everglades. "This time of year, that's not good."

I didn't smell anything except the standard loamy Everglades aroma, plus sweat and a faint trace of gunpowder that still hung in the air, but I was certainly not going to argue with my rescuer. Besides, I would have been arguing with his back, since he had already spun away and headed off toward the edge of the clearing. I watched him go, rubbing my wrists and taking my terrible vengeance on the mosquitoes.

There was really not a great deal more to see around the trailer. The regular cops were frog-marching the cannibals away to durance vile, and the viler the better, as far as I was concerned. The SRT guys were standing around one of their own, probably the one who had made the shot that took off Kukarov's face; his expression was a combination of ebbing adrenaline and shock, and his fellow shoot-ers watched him protectively.

Altogether, the excitement was fading and it was clearly time for Dexter's Departure. The only problem, of course, was that I had no transportation, and depending on the kindness of strangers is always an iffy thing. Depending on the kindness of family is often much worse, of course, but it still seemed like the best bet, so I went to look for Deborah.

My sister was sitting in the front seat of her car trying to be sen-sitive, nurturing, and supportive of Samantha Aldovar. These were not things that came naturally to her, and it would have been tough sledding even if Samantha were willing to play along. She was not, of course, and the two of them were rapidly approaching an emo-tional impasse when I slid into the backseat.

"I'm *not* going to be all right," Samantha was saying. "Why do you keep saying that like I'm some kind of *ree*-tard?"

"You've had a really big shock, Samantha," Debs said, and in spite of the fact that she clearly meant to be soothing, I could almost hear quotation marks around her words, as if she was reading from *The Rescued Hostage Handbook*. "But it's over now."

"I don't *want* it over, goddamn it," she said. She looked back at me as I closed the car door. "You bastard," she said to me.

"I didn't do anything," I said.

"You brought them here," she said. "This was all a setup."

I shook my head. "Nope," I said. "I have no idea how they found us."

"Riiiiight," she sneered.

"Really," I said, and I turned to Debs. "How did you find us?"

Deborah shrugged. "Chutsky came out to wait with me. When the carpet van came, he slapped a tracer on it." It made sense: Her boyfriend, Chutsky, a semiretired intelligence operative, would certainly have the right sort of toys for that. "So they carried you out and drove away; we stayed back and followed. When we all got out here in the swamp, I called in for SRT. I really hoped we'd get Bobby Acosta, too, but we couldn't wait." She looked back at

Samantha. "Saving you was the highest priority we had, Samantha."

"For fuck's sake, I didn't want to be saved," Samantha said.
"When are you going to get that?" Deborah opened her mouth, and
Samantha rode right over her with, "And if you say I'm going to be
all right again, I swear to God I'll scream."

To be honest, it would have been a relief if she had screamed.
I was so tired of Samantha's carping that I was ready to scream
myself, and I could see that my sister was not far behind me. But
apparently Debs still nurtured the delusion that she had rescued an
unwilling victim from a terrible experience, and so even though
I could see her knuckles turn white with the effort of refraining from
strangling Samantha, Deborah kept her cool.

"Samantha," she said very deliberately. "It's perfectly natural
for you to be a little confused right now about what you're feeling."

"I am so totally *not* confused," Samantha said. "I'm feeling
pissed off, and I wish you hadn't found me. Is that perfectly natural,
too?"

"Yes," Deborah said, although I could see a little doubt creeping
into her face. "In a hostage situation, the victim often starts to feel an
emotional bond with her captors."

"You sound like you're reading that," Samantha said, and I had
to admire her insight, even though her tone still set my teeth on edge.

"I'm going to recommend that your parents get you some
counseling—" Deborah said.

"Oh, great, a shrink," Samantha said. "That's all I need."

"It will help you if you can talk to somebody about all that's
happened to you," Deborah said.

"Sure, I can't wait to talk about *all* that's happened to me,"
Samantha said, and she turned and looked right at me. "I want to
talk about *all* of it, because some stuff happened that was, you know,
totally against my will, and *everybody* is really going to want to hear
about that."

I felt a sharp and very unwelcome shock—not so much at what
she said, but at the fact that she was saying it to me. There was no

way to mistake what she meant; but would she really tell everyone about our little ecstasy-inspired interlude, and claim it was against her will? It hadn't occurred to me that she would—after all, it was kind of a private thing, and it hadn't actually been *my* will, either. I hadn't put the drugs into the water bottle, and it certainly wasn't something I would ever brag about.

But an awful sinking feeling began to bloom in my stomach as her threat began to hit home. If she claimed it had been against her will—technically speaking, the word for that was "rape," and although it was really quite far outside my normal area of interest, I was pretty sure the law frowned on it, nearly as much as some other things I had done. If that word came up, I knew that none of my clever and wonderful excuses would count for anything. And I could not really blame anyone for believing it; older man about to die, penned up with young woman, no one would ever know—it was a picture that wrote its own caption. Perfectly believable—and totally unforgivable, even if I thought I'd been about to die. I had never heard a rape defense based on extenuating circumstances, and I was pretty sure it wouldn't work.

And no matter what I said, even if Dexter's eloquence over-flowed the bounds of human speech and moved the marble statue of justice to tears—the very best outcome would be he-said/she-said, and I would still be a guy who'd taken advantage of a helpless captive girl, and I knew very well what everyone would think of me. After all, I had cheered aloud every time I heard about older married men losing their jobs and their families for having sex with younger women—and that was exactly what I had done. Even if I convinced everyone that the drugs made me do it and it really wasn't my fault, I would be finished. Drug-induced teen sex party sounded more like a tabloid headline than an explanation.

And not even the greatest lawyer who had ever lived could get me off the hook with Rita. There was still a lot I did not understand about human beings, but I had seen enough daytime drama to fig-ure this one out. Rita might not believe I had committed rape, but that wouldn't matter. She would not care if I had been bound hand

and foot, drugged, and then forced to have sex at gunpoint. She would divorce me when she found out, and she would raise Lily Anne without me. I would be all alone, out in the cold without roast pork, with no Cody and Astor, and no Lily Anne to brighten my days; Dex-Daddy Dumped.

No family, no job—nothing. She would probably even take custody of my fillet knives. It was terrible, hideous, unthinkable; everything I cared about yanked away, my entire life flung into the Dumpster—and all because I'd been drugged? It was far beyond unfair. And some of this must have shown on my face, because Samantha kept looking at me, and she began to nod her head.

"That's right," she said. "You just think about that."

I looked back at Samantha and I did think about it. And I wondered if just this once I could dispose of somebody because of something they hadn't done yet; proactive playtime.

But luckily for Samantha, before I could even reach for the duct tape Deborah decided to impose herself again in the role of compassionate rescuer. "All right," she said. "This can all wait. Let's just get you home to your parents now." And she put her hand on Samantha's shoulder.

Naturally enough, Samantha pushed the hand off as if it were a loathsome insect. "Great," she said. "I can't fucking wait."

"Put your seat belt on," Deborah told her, and, completely as an afterthought, she turned to me and said, "I guess you can ride along."

I almost told her, *No, don't bother, I will stay here and feed mosquitoes*, but at the last second I remembered that Deborah's record with sarcasm was not good, so I just nodded and buckled up.

Deborah called the dispatcher and said, "I've got the Aldovar girl. I'm taking her home," and Samantha muttered, "Big whoopee-shit." Deborah just glanced at her with something that looked like a rictus but was probably supposed to be a reassuring smile, and then she put the car in gear, and I had a little over half an hour to sit in the backseat and picture my life splintering into a million decorative shards. It was a terribly depressing picture—Dexter

Disenfranchised, tossed on the scrap heap, stripped of his carefully built costume and all its comfy props—flung naked and unloved into the cold and lonely world, and I could see no way to avoid it. I'd had to go down on my knees and beg just to get Samantha to do nothing while I tried to escape—and she had been neutral then. Now that she was peeved with me, there was nothing I could possibly do to stop her from telling, short of actual vivisection. I couldn't even give her back to the cannibals; with Kukarov dead and the rest of the group either captured or on the run, there would be no one left to eat her. The picture was grim and very clear: Samantha's fantasy was over, she blamed me, and she would take her terrible revenge—and there was nothing I could do about it.

I have never really had an appetite for irony, but I couldn't help but see more than a little of it here: After all I had done, willingly and joyfully, and now I would be brought down by a sulking young woman and a bottle of water? It was so subtly ludicrous that only the French could truly appreciate it.

Just to underline my predicament and her own determination, Samantha turned and glared at me every few miles as we drove the long, depressing way to her home, back along Route 41 and then over LeJeune and into the Grove to the Aldovars' house. And just to remind me that even the worst joke has a punch line, when we turned down Samantha's street and approached her house, Deborah muttered, "Shit," and I hunched forward and looked through the windshield at what appeared to be a carnival in front of the house.

"That goddamned son of a bitch," she said, and she smacked the steering wheel with the palm of her hand.

"Who?" I said, and I admit I was eager to see somebody else take a little heat.

"Captain Matthews," she snarled. "When I called it in, he got the whole fucking press corps here so he can hug Samantha and jut his fucking chin at the cameras."

And sure enough, as Deborah brought the car to a stop in front of the Aldovars' house, Captain Matthews appeared at the passenger door as if by magic, and reached in to help a still-sullen Samantha out of the car as flashbulbs popped and even the horde of savage reporters murmured, "Awwww." The captain flung a protective arm around her shoulders and then waved commandingly at the crowd to move aside and let them through—a truly great moment in the history of irony, since Matthews had summoned them all here to watch this exact moment, and now he was pretending he wanted them to leave him alone while he comforted Samantha. I admired the performance so much that for a full minute I only worried about my future two or three times.

Deborah did not seem quite as impressed as I was. She trailed along behind Matthews with a wicked scowl on her face, shoving at any reporter foolish enough to get in her way, and generally acting like she had just been indicted for waterboarding. I followed the happy little group through the crowd until Matthews reached the front door, where Mr. and Mrs. Aldovar were waiting to smother their wayward daughter with hugs and kisses and tears. It was an extremely touching scene, and Captain Matthews played it perfectly, as if he had been rehearsing for months. He stood beside the family group and beamed at them as the parents snuffled and Samantha scowled and finally, when he could sense that the reporters were reaching the end of their attention span, he stepped in front of them and held up a hand.

Just before he spoke to the crowd, he leaned over to Deborah and said, "Don't worry, Morgan; I won't make you say anything this time."

"Yes, sir," she said through her teeth.

"Just try to look proud and humble," he told her, and he patted her shoulder and smiled at her as the cameras rolled. Deborah showed him her teeth, and he turned back to the crowd.

"I told you we would find her," Matthews told the crowd in a manly growl, "and we found her!" He turned around and looked at the Aldovar trio so the reporters would get a shot of him gloating protectively at them. Then he turned back around and gave a short speech of praise for himself. Of course there was no word about Dexter's terrible sacrifice, nor even Deborah's diligence, but perhaps that would have been too much to expect. It went on predictably enough for a little longer, but finally the Aldovars went in their house, the reporters got tired of the captain's chin, and Deborah grabbed my arm, pulled me through the crowd to her car, and took me home.

THIRTY-TWO

DEBORAH DROVE UP TO DIXIE HIGHWAY AND TURNED SOUTH toward my house without speaking, but after a few minutes the angry glare faded from her face, and her hands on the wheel lost their white-knuckled grip. "Anyway," she said at last, "the important thing is that we got Samantha."

I admired my sister's ability to identify the "important thing," but I really felt I should point out that it was the wrong one, because it did not include me. "Samantha didn't want to be got," I said. "She wants to be eaten."

Deborah shook her head. "Nobody wants that," she said. "She said that because she's maybe a little fucked-up, and she started to identify with the assholes that grabbed her. But wants to be? I mean, *eaten*?" She made the sour-lemon face again and shook her head. "Come on, Dex."

I could have told her that I was quite convinced, and that she would be, too, if she talked to Samantha for five minutes. But when Deborah makes up her mind, it takes a written order from the police commissioner to change it, and I didn't think there was one in the works.

"And besides," she said, "she's back with her family now, and they can get her a shrink or whatever. The more important thing for us is to wrap this thing up, round up Bobby Acosta and the last of the group."

"The coven," I told her, and maybe I was being pedantic. "Samantha says it's called a coven."

Deborah frowned. "I thought that was witches," she said.

"It's apparently cannibals, too," I said.

"I don't think you can call a group of guys a coven," she said stubbornly. "I think it has to be witches. You know, women."

It seemed like such a small point, especially after all I had just been through, and I was far too tired to argue it. Happily, my time with Samantha had prepared me to give exactly the right response. "Whatever," I said. Deborah seemed satisfied with that, and after a few more empty remarks we were at my street. Deborah let me out in front of my house and drove off, and I thought no more about it in the pleasure of being home.

Home was waiting for me, and for some reason I found that surprising and touching. Deborah had called Rita and told her I would be late, not to worry, everything was fine, which seemed very close to callous overconfidence on her part. Rita had seen the news, though, which had made the capture into the evening's lead story—and really, how could they possibly resist? Cannibals, missing teen, Everglades shootout—it was a perfect story. There had already been a phone call from a premium cable network, trying to get the rights to the story.

In spite of Deborah's reassurance, Rita had known somehow that I was right in the middle of things and in grave danger, and she responded like a true champion. She was waiting for me at the door in a state of ditherhood that was unmatched in my experience. "Oh, Dexter," she sniffled as she half-drowned me in hugs and kisses. "We were so— It was on the news, and I saw you there, but even after Deborah called," she said, and kissed me again. "The children were watching TV, and Cody said, 'It's Dexter,' and I looked— It was a newsbreak," she said, I suppose reassuring me that I had not made a surprise guest appearance on *SpongeBob*. "Oh, my God," she went on, pausing to shudder and then hug me, burying her head up to the shoulders in my neck. "You shouldn't have to do those things," she said, with a great deal of justice. "You're supposed to do forensics and— You don't even have a gun, and it isn't— How can they— But your sister said, and on TV they said it was the cannibals and they had you, and at least you found that girl, which I know was very important, but oh, my God, cannibals, I can't even think how— And they *had* you, and they could have—" And she finally broke off, possibly from oxygen deprivation, and concentrated on snuffling into my shirt for a minute.

I took advantage of the break to look around with satisfaction at my modest kingdom. Cody and Astor were sitting on the couch watching us with matching expressions of disgust at the emotional exhibition, and right next to them sat my brother, Brian, beaming a huge and dreadful smile at one and all. Lily Anne was in her basket beside the couch, and she waved her toes at me in a warm and heartfelt greeting. It was a perfect family picture, suitable for framing; The Hero Returns to His Home. And although I was not completely pleased to see Brian here I could think of no reason to wish him gone, either. Besides, all the good will was infectious, even the artificial stuff coming from my brother, and the air was filled with a wonderful, saliva-inducing aroma that I recognized as one of the great miracles of the modern world: Rita's roast pork.

Dorothy was right. There's no place like home.

It would have been terribly rude to tell Rita she had snuffled long enough, but I had been through an awful lot, including starvation, and the smell that filled the house was setting off a frenzy in my guts that made the overdose of ecstasy look tame. Rita's roast pork was a great work of art that could have made a statue lunge off its pedestal and cry, "Yummy!" So after I managed to disengage myself and dry my shoulder, I thanked her profusely and headed straight for the table, with only a brief pause to see Lily Anne and count her fingers and toes, just to make sure they were all still there.

And so we sat around the table, looking like a perfect family portrait, and it occurred to me how deceptive pictures can be. At the head of the table, of course, sat Dex-Daddy, a true monster trying to be a little more human. At his left was Brother Brian, a far worse monster and still completely unrepentant; and across from him sat two fresh-faced, innocent-seeming children, who wanted nothing more than to be just like their wicked uncle. And all of them wearing totally fake expressions of the deepest, most mundane humanity possible. It would have made a wonderful subject for Norman Rockwell, especially if he was feeling particularly sardonic.

Dinner went its tasty way, the silence broken mostly by lip smacking, moans of pleasure, and Lily Anne demanding to be fed, probably overcome by the smell and sound of the pork roast. Rita would occasionally shatter the silence with small non sequiturs of concern, rambling on until someone held out their plate for more—which we all did several times, except Lily Anne. And as the meal meandered on to its end and we proved again that "leftover roast pork" was an oxymoron in our house, I was very glad indeed to have returned in one piece to my little nest.

The feeling of bloated satisfaction continued, even after dinner, when Cody and Astor stampeded for the Wii and a game that involved killing awful-looking monsters, and I sat on the couch burping Lily Anne while Rita cleaned up. Brian sat next to me, and we watched the kids absentmindedly for a while before Brian finally spoke.

"Well," he said at last. "So you survived your run-in with the coven."

"Apparently," I said.

He nodded and, as Cody obliterated a very nasty-looking creature, Brian called out, "Good one, Cody!" After a moment he turned back to me and said, "And have they caught the head witch yet?"

"George Kukarov," I said. "He was shot and killed on the scene."

"The man who ran that club, Fang?" he said, with surprise in his voice.

"That's right," I said. "And I have to say it was a very good shot, and just in time."

Brian was silent for a minute, and then said, "I always thought the head of a coven had to be a woman."

This was the second time tonight someone had argued with me about this, and I was a little tired of hearing about it. "It really isn't my problem," I said. "Deborah and her task force will round up the rest of them."

"Not if she thinks that Kukarov guy is the leader," he said.

Lily Anne erupted with a small but explosive belch, and I felt it soak slowly through the towel and into my shirt as she settled her head down and nodded off to sleep. "Brian," I said. "I have spent a very bad day with these people, and I'm all done. I don't care if the real leader of the coven is a man, or a woman, or a two-headed lizard from the Planet Nardone. It's Deborah's problem, and I'm all done with it—and why do you care, anyway?"

"Oh, I don't care," he said. "But you're my little brother. Naturally I'm interested."

And I might have said something else, something really cutting, but Astor overwhelmed any possible response with an anguished wail of "Nooooooo!" and we both jerked around to look at the TV screen, just in time to see the little golden-haired figure that represented her on-screen being eaten by a monster. Cody said, "Ha," quietly but triumphantly, and raised his controller; the game went on, and I thought no more about witches, covens, and my brother's interest in them.

The evening wound relentlessly on to its conclusion. I found myself yawning, hugely and loudly, and even though it was a little bit embarrassing, I could not stop myself. Of course, the dreadful ordeal I had been through was taking its toll on my poor battered system, and I am sure that roast pork is loaded with tryptophan or something like it. Perhaps it was the combination, but whatever the case it soon became plain to all that Dex-Daddy was on the ropes and about to join Lily Anne in Dreamland.

And just as I was about to excuse myself from the delightful company—several of whom would not have noticed, judging from their concentration on the video game—the swelling notes of "Ride of the Valkyries" began to pour out of Brian's cell phone. He pulled it from its holster and glanced at it, frowning, and almost immediately stood up and said, "Oh, darn. I'm afraid I have to leave at once, as delightful as the company may be."

"It *may* be," Astor muttered, watching Cody rack up points on the screen, "but it isn't yet."

Brian gave her his large and phony smile. "It is for me, Astor," he said. "It's family. But," he said, and the smile got wider, "duty calls, and I have to go to work."

"It's *night*," Cody said without looking up.

"Yes, it is," Brian said. "But sometimes I have to work at night." And he looked at me happily, almost as if he was about to wink at me, and my curiosity overcame my sleepiness.

"What kind of work are you doing right now?" I asked him.

"Service industry," he said. "And I really do have to go." He patted me on the shoulder, the one that Lily Anne wasn't using, and said, "And I'm sure you need your sleep after all you've been through."

I yawned again, which made it pointless to deny that I really did need sleep. "I think you're right," I said, and I stood up. "I'll walk you out."

"No need," Brian said, and headed for the kitchen. "Rita? I thank you again for another wonderful meal and a delightful evening."

"Oh," Rita said, and she came out of the kitchen, wiping her hands on a dish towel. "But it's still early, and— Did you want some coffee? Or maybe—"

"Alas," Brian said, "I really do have to leave posthaste."

"What does *that* mean?" Astor said. " 'Posthaste'?"

Brian winked at her. "It means, quick as a mailman," he said, and he turned back to Rita and gave her a clumsy hug. "Many thanks, dear lady, and good night."

"I'm just so sorry that— I mean, it is getting a bit late for work, and you— Maybe a new job? Because this isn't really—"

"I know," Brian said. "But this job actually matches my skill set perfectly." He looked at me, and I felt a cold nausea burble up in the pit of my stomach. He had only one skill that I knew of, and as far as

I knew, nobody would pay him for it. "And," he went on to Rita, "it does have its compensations, and at the moment I do need to do it. And so, a fond farewell to one and all," he said, and he raised his hand, presumably in fond farewell, and headed for the door.

"Brian," I said to his back, and I had to stop as another real jaw-creaker of a yawn took control of my entire body.

Brian turned back with a raised eyebrow. "Dexter?" he said.

I tried to remember what I had been about to say, but another yawn hammered it out of my head. "Nothing," I said. "Good night."

Once again his terrible fake smile stretched across his face. "Good night, brother," he said. "Get some sleep." And he opened the front door and was gone into the night.

"Well," Rita said. "Brian really is getting to be one of the family."

I nodded, and I could feel myself sway slightly, as if nodding my head might overcome my balance and pitch me face-forward onto the floor. "Yes, he is," I said, and of course I punctuated it with a yawn.

"Oh, Dexter, you poor— You need to get to bed right now; you must be— Here, give me the baby," Rita said. She threw the dish towel into the kitchen and rushed over to grab Lily Anne. In my sadly depleted state it seemed barely short of amazing that she could move so fast. But in no time at all she had Lily Anne tucked into her basket and was propelling me down the hall to the bedroom. "Now," she said, "you take a nice hot shower and get into bed, and I think you should sleep late in the morning. They can't really expect— I mean, after all you've been through?"

I was far too tired to respond. I did manage to stumble through a shower before falling into bed, but even though I could feel the accumulated slime and grime of the dreadful day all over me, it was hard work to stay awake under the stream of hot water long enough to get thoroughly clean, and it was with a feeling of almost supernatural bliss that I finally collapsed onto the pillow, closed my eyes, and pulled the sheet up to my chin. . . .

And naturally enough, once I was actually in bed, I couldn't sleep at all. I lay there with my eyes closed, and I could feel a deep sleep welling up just on the other side of the pillow, but it would not come to me. I listened to Cody and Astor down the hall, still playing the Wii, now a little more hushed at Rita's insistence, since I was, as she told them, trying to sleep—and I was trying, really I was, but I was having no success.

Thoughts trudged through my brain like a slow-motion parade. I thought about the four of them just down the hall: my little family. It still seemed faintly bizarre. Dex-Daddy, protector and provider, family man. Even more bizarre was that I liked it.

I thought about my brother. I still didn't know what he was up to, why he kept coming around. Was it really possible that he simply wanted to feel some kind of family connection? It was very hard to believe—but then, it would have been just as hard to believe it about me before Lily Anne, and here I was, forswearing all Dark Delights and wallowing in the bosom of a real family. Maybe Brian wanted the same simple, human connection. Maybe he wanted to change, too.

And maybe I could clap my hands three times and bring Tinker-bell back to life, too. It was just as likely; Brian had lived his whole life on the Dark Path and he couldn't possibly change, not that much. He had to have some other reason for shoehorning into my nest, and sooner or later it would come out. I didn't think he would hurt my family—but I would watch him until I knew for certain what he was doing.

And of course, I thought about Samantha and her threat to tell all. Was it just a threat, an acting out of her large frustration at being alive and well and uneaten? Or would she really talk, tell everyone a vindictive version of what had happened? The moment that awful word "rape" was out, everything changed forever, and not for the better. It would be Dexter in the Docket, ground to a pulp beneath the wheels of the injustice system. It was horrible beyond measure, and completely unfair. No one who knew me could possibly think of me as a leering sex-mad ogre. I had always been a very different kind of ogre. But people believe clichés, even when they're untrue, and the older man with the teen girl qualified as one. It truly wasn't my fault—but who would hear that without a wink and a smirk? I hadn't willingly taken the drugs—would she really punish me for a situation in which I had been the real victim? It was hard to say for sure, but I thought she might. And that would destroy every piece of my carefully constructed life.

But what could I do? I could not avoid the idea that killing her would solve everything—and I could even get her to cooperate by promising to nibble a few small pieces before I finished her off. I wouldn't, of course—yuck—but if a small lie makes somebody happy, where's the harm?

It would never come to that, anyway. It seemed like another great irony, but I couldn't kill Samantha, as much as we both wanted it. Not that I had grown a conscience yet; it was just that it would be totally contrary to the Harry Code, and far too dangerous, too, since she was very much in the spotlight right now, much too closely watched for me to get close. No, it was too risky. I would have to think of some other way to save my life.

But what? The solution would not come to me, and neither would slumber, and the thoughts kept up their leaden tumbling across the soggy floor of my sleep-starved brain. Covens—who cared if it was led by a woman or a man? Kukarov was dead, and the coven was over.

Except for Bobby Acosta. Maybe I could find him and feed him Samantha. And then give him to Deborah. It would cheer them both up.

Debs really needed cheering: She had been acting very weird lately. Did it mean something? Or was it just the emotional hangover from her knife wound?

Knives—could I really give up my Dark Delights forever? For Lily Anne?

Lily Anne: I thought about her for what seemed like a long time, and then suddenly it was morning.

THIRTY-THREE

I TOOK RITA'S ADVICE AND SLEPT LATE THE NEXT MORNING. I woke up to the sounds of an empty house; a distant drip in the shower, the air conditioner coming on, and the tick of the dishwasher switching gears down the hall in the kitchen. I lay there for a few minutes enjoying the relative quiet and the feeling of dopey fatigue that ran through me from my toes to my tongue. Yesterday had been quite a day and, on the whole, I thought it was a very good thing that I had survived it. My neck was still a little stiff, but the headache was gone and I felt a lot better than I should have—until I remembered Samantha.

So I lay there awhile longer wondering if there was anything at all I could do to persuade her not to talk. There was a very small chance that I could reason with her, I suppose. I had managed it once, in Club Fang's refrigerator, and reached soaring heights of emotive rhetoric I had never touched before. Could I do it again, and would it work on her a second time? I was not sure—and as I mulled my chances that moth-eaten line about "the tongues of men and of angels" popped into my head. I couldn't remember how it ended, but I didn't think it was happy. I wished I'd never read Shakespeare.

I heard the front door open and Rita hustled into the house, home from dropping the children at school. She went through the living room and into the kitchen making all the loud and distinct sounds of someone trying to be quiet. I heard her talking softly to Lily Anne as she changed a diaper, and then she went back into the kitchen and a moment later I heard the coffee machine clear its throat and begin to brew. Soon the smell of fresh coffee drifted into the bedroom, and I began to feel a little bit better. I was home, with Lily Anne, and all was well, at least for now. It was not really a rational feeling, but then, as I was learning, feelings never are, and you might as well enjoy the good ones while you can. There aren't very many of them, and they don't last long.

I sat up on the side of the bed at last, slowly rotating my neck to get the last of the soreness out of it. It didn't work, but it wasn't too bad. I stood up, which was a little harder than it should have been. My legs were stiff and a bit sore, too, and so I tottered into the shower and ran hot water all over myself for ten long and luxurious minutes, and it was a renewed and nearly normal Dexter who finally made his way into his clothes and all the way to the kitchen, where a medley of heavenly smells and sounds told me that Rita was hard at work.

"Oh, Dexter," she said, and she put down the spatula and gave me a kiss on the cheek. "I heard you in the shower, and so I thought—would you like some blueberry pancakes? I had to use the frozen berries, which aren't really as— But how are you feeling? Because it isn't— I could make you eggs instead and freeze the pancakes for— Oh, honey, sit down; you look exhausted."

I made it into a chair with Rita's help and said, "Pancakes would be wonderful," which they were. I ate far too many of them, telling myself that I had earned it, and trying not to listen to the wicked whisper in my inner ear saying that after all, this could be the last time, unless I did something final about Samantha.

After breakfast I sat in the chair and sipped several cups of coffee, in the vain hope that it would live up to the advertisement and fill me with energy. It was very good coffee, but it didn't quite wash away the fatigue, and so I dawdled around the house a bit longer. I sat and held Lily Anne for a while. She threw up on me once, and I thought how strange it was that it didn't bother me. And then she fell asleep in my arms and I just sat for a while longer and enjoyed that, too.

But finally the small and unwelcome voice of duty began to nag at me, and so I put Lily Anne in her basket, gave Rita a kiss, and headed out the door.

Traffic was light, and I let my mind wander a little bit as I headed up Dixie Highway, but as I nosed onto the Palmetto Expressway I began to get a very uneasy feeling that things were not what they should be and I brought Dexter's mighty brain back online and searched for what was wrong. It was a very quick search, not because of the power of my logic, but because of the power of the smell, which was coming from behind me, somewhere in the backseat of my car. It was a terrible smell, an odor of old and unnameable things decomposing and fermenting and growing deader and deader, and I could not say what it might be except that it was awful and getting worse.

I couldn't see anything behind me while driving, even when I tipped the mirror down, and as I drove north to work I pondered, until a school bus wandering across the road brought my attention back to driving. Even in light traffic it does not do to turn your thoughts away from the road, not in Miami, so I rolled down the window and concentrated on getting to work alive.

And as I pulled into the lot at work and slowed to nose into my parking spot, the smell built up again and I thought about it. The last time I had driven my car had been right before the whole mess with Samantha that started at Fang, and before that—

Chapin.

I had taken the car to my playdate with Victor Chapin, and I had carried away the leftovers in garbage bags when I was done—was it possible that some small piece had fallen out and was still there, slowly rotting in the heat of a car closed up all day, and now making this hideous smell? Unthinkable, I was always so careful—but what else could it be? The odor was far beyond dreadful, and now it seemed to get worse, fumes fanned by my near-panic. I stepped on the brake and turned all the way around to look—

A garbage bag. I had missed one somehow—but that was impossible, I could never be so stupid, so careless—

Except I had hurried that night, rushed through the whole thing to get it done and get back to bed. Laziness—stupid, selfish sloth, and now here I was at police headquarters with a bag of body parts in my car. I shoved the gear lever into park and climbed out, and the panic sweat was already soaking my back and rolling off my face as I opened the back door and knelt down to look.

Yes, a garbage bag. But how? How did it get here, on the floor in the backseat, when all the others had gone carefully into the trunk, and then—

And then a car pulled into the slot next to mine and after a bright stab of total panic I took a deep and calming breath. This was not a problem, not for me. Whoever it was, I would simply give them a cheerful hello and they would be off and into the building, and I would drive this bag of Chapin away. No big deal, I was just good old Dexter, the blood-spatter guy, and there was no one on the entire force who had any reason to think otherwise.

No one, except for the man who climbed out of the car and glared down at me. Or to be precise, the two-thirds of a man. His hands and feet were gone, of course, as well as his tongue, and he carried a small notebook computer to help him speak, and as I struggled for breath, he flipped it open and, without taking his eyes off me, he punched buttons to make an electronic sentence.

"What—is—in—bag?" Sergeant Doakes said through his computer.

"Bag?" I said, and I admit it was not my very best moment.

Doakes glared at me, and whether it was just the fact that he hated me and suspected me of being what I really was, or whether I actually looked guilty squatting there and fingering a bag of leftovers, I don't know. Whatever the case, I saw a bright gleam of something horrible flash into his eyes and before I could do anything except gape, Doakes jerked forward, whipped his metallic claw of a hand down, and grabbed the bag out of my car.

And as I watched with horror and dread and a growing sense of my own very imminent mortality, he placed his artificial voice box on the roof of the car, opened the bag, reached inside with a triumphant show of teeth at me—and pulled out a truly filthy, rotting, and horrible diaper.

And as I watched Doakes's face run the entire spectrum from victory to utter disgust, I remembered. As I had left for my impromptu session with Chapin, Rita had thrust the bag of dirty diapers at me. In my haste, I had left it for later. Then the whole business of Deke's death, my abduction, the dreadful episode with Samantha—it had all driven that tiny unimportant diaper bag out of my mind. But as the memory flooded back, I felt a rising happiness wash back in with it, made even tastier by the realization that Lily Anne, that wonderful, magical child—Lily Anne, the diaper queen, the paragon of poop—my own sweet Lily Anne had saved me with her dirty diapers. And even better, she had humiliated Doakes at the same time.

Life was good; fatherhood was once more a wonderful adventure.

I stood up and faced Doakes with great good cheer. "I know it's toxic," I said. "And it probably breaks several city ordinances, too." I held out my hand for the bag. "But I beg you, Sergeant, don't arrest me. I promise to throw it away properly."

Doakes turned his eyes away from the diaper and onto me, and he looked at me with an expression of loathing and rage so powerful that for just a moment it overpowered the open diaper bag. Then he very carefully said, "Nguggermukker," and opened the claw holding the bag. It dropped to the pavement, and a moment later the diaper he held in the other claw flopped down beside it.

"Nguggermukker?" I said brightly. "Is that Dutch?" But Doakes just grabbed his silver voice box from the roof of the car, turned away from me and the dirty diapers, and stomped away across the parking lot on his two artificial feet.

I felt utter and complete relief as I watched him go, and when he vanished at the far end of the parking lot I took a deep, relaxing breath—which was a very big mistake, considering what lay at my feet. Coughing slightly, and blinking away the tears, I bent down and pushed the diaper back into the bag, twisted the bag closed, and carried it to the Dumpster.

It was one-thirty in the afternoon by the time I finally got to my desk. I fiddled with a few lab reports, ran a routine test on the spectrometer, and suffered through a cup of truly despicable coffee while the hands on the clock trudged 'round the dial to four-thirty. And just when I thought I had made it safely all the way through my first day back from bondage, Deborah walked in with a horrible expression on her face. I could not read it, but I knew that something had gone terribly wrong, and it seemed to be something she was taking rather personally. And because I have known Deborah my whole life and I knew how her mind worked, I assumed it meant trouble for Dexter.

"Good afternoon," I said brightly, in the hope that if I was cheerful enough the problem would go away, whatever it was. It didn't, of course.

"Samantha Aldovar," my sister said, looking straight through me, and all my anxiety from the night before washed over me, and I knew that Samantha had talked already and Deborah was here to arrest me. My irritation with the girl went up several notches; she couldn't even wait a decent interval for me to come up with some kind of airtight excuse. It was as if her tongue was spring-loaded and had to burst out into furious activity the moment she took her first free breath. She had probably been babbling about me before the front door of her house even swung shut, and now it was all over for me. I was finished, washed up, completely—and with no pun intended—*screwed*. I was immediately filled with apprehension, alarm, and bitterness. Whatever happened to good old-fashioned discretion?

Still, it was done, and there was nothing left for Dexter except to face the music and pay the piper. So taking a deep breath, I looked it square in the face and did so. "It wasn't my fault," I said to Deborah, and I began to gather my soggy wits for Stage One of Dexter's Defense.

But Deborah blinked, and a small frown of confusion crept into the bleakness on her face. "What the fuck do you mean, it's not your fault?" she said. "Who said anything about— How could it possibly be your fault?"

Once again, I had the sensation that everyone else was working off a fully rehearsed script, and I was being asked to improvise. "I just meant—nothing," I said, hoping for a clue on what my line was supposed to be.

"Jesus fuck," she said. "Why is everything always about you?"

I suppose I could have said, *Because somehow I am always in the middle of it, usually unwilling, and usually because you have pushed me there,* but cooler heads prevailed. "I'm sorry," I said. "What's wrong, Debs?"

She stared at me a little longer, and then shook her head and slumped down in the chair beside my desk. "Samantha Aldovar," she repeated. "She's gone again."

Sometimes I think it is a very good thing that I have had so many years of practice at showing only what I want to show on my face, and this was absolutely one of those times, because my first impulse was to shout, *Whoopee! Good girl!* and burst into light-hearted song. And so it was quite possibly one of the greatest demonstrations of acting skill our age has yet seen when I managed instead to look shocked and concerned. "You're kidding," I said, thinking, *I really hope you're not kidding.*

"She stayed home from school today, resting," Deborah said. "I mean, she went through an awful lot." It apparently didn't occur to my sister that I had gone through even more, but nobody's perfect. "So around two o'clock, her mother went out to the store," she said. "And she comes back a little while ago, and Samantha was gone." Deborah shook her head. "She left a note: 'Don't look for me; I'm not coming back.' She ran, Dex. She took off and ran."

I was feeling so much better that I actually managed to fight down the impulse to say, *I told you so*. After all, Debs had refused to believe me when I told her Samantha had gone into cannibal captivity willingly, even eagerly, the first time. And since I was right about that, it made perfect sense that she would take off again at the first opportunity. It was not a terribly noble thought, but I hoped she found a good hiding place.

Deborah sighed heavily and shook her head again. "I never heard of Stockholm syndrome so strong the victim ran back to the bad guys," she said.

"Debs," I said, and now I really couldn't help it, "I told you. It's not Stockholm. Samantha *wants* to be eaten. It was her fantasy."

"That's bullshit," she said angrily. "Nobody wants that."

"Then why did she run away again?" I said, and she just shook her head and looked down at her hands.

"I don't know," she said. She stared at her hands where they lay in her lap, as if the answer might be written on her knuckles, and then she straightened up. "It doesn't matter," she said. "What matters is *where* she went." She looked up at me. "So where would she go, Dex?"

To be honest, I didn't really care where Samantha went, as long as she stayed there. Still, I had to say something.

"What about Bobby Acosta?" I said, and it made sense. "Did you find him yet?"

"No," she said, very grumpy, and she shrugged. "He can't stay lost forever," she said. "We're bringing way too much heat. Besides," she said, and she raised both palms, "his family has money, and political clout, and they're gonna figure they can get him off."

"Can they?" I asked.

Deborah looked at her knuckles "Maybe," she said. "Fuck. Yeah, probably. We got witnesses who can connect him to Tyler Spanos's car—but a good lawyer could chop up those two Haitians in two seconds on the stand. And he ran from me—but that's not much, either. The rest is guesswork and hearsay so far, and— Shit, yeah, I guess he could walk." She nodded to herself and looked at her hands again. "Yeah, sure, Bobby Acosta will walk," she said softly.

"Again. And then nobody goes down for this. . . ." She studied her knuckles again, and then looked up at me, and her face was wearing an expression unlike anything I had ever seen before.

"What is it?" I said.

Deborah bit her lip. "Maybe," she said. She looked away. "I don't know." She looked back at me and took a deep breath. "Maybe there's something, you know," she said. "Something you could do about it."

I blinked several times, and I just barely managed to stop myself from looking down to see if there was still a floor underneath our feet. It was impossible to misunderstand what she was suggesting. As far as Debs was concerned I only did two things, and my sister was not talking about using my forensic skills on Bobby Acosta.

Deborah was the one person on earth who knew about my hobby. I thought she had come to accept it, however reluctantly—but to have her suggest that I should actually *use* it on somebody was so completely outside the limits of what I thought Deborah would ever approve of that the idea never occurred to me, and I was truly stunned. "Deborah," I said, and the shock had to be showing in my voice. But she leaned as far forward as she could without tipping out of her chair and lowered her voice.

"Bobby Acosta is a killer," she said with savage intensity. "And he's going to walk—*again*—just because he's got money and clout. It's not right, and you know it—and that has to be the kind of thing that Dad wanted you to take care of."

"Listen," I said, but she wasn't quite done.

"God*damn* it, Dexter," she said, "I tried like hell to understand you, and what Daddy wanted with you, and I finally do—I get it, okay? I know exactly what Daddy was thinking. Because I'm a cop like he was, and every cop comes up against a Bobby Acosta some-day, somebody who does murder and walks, even if you do every-thing right. And you can't sleep and you grind your teeth and you want to scream and strangle somebody but it's your job to eat the shit and like it and there's nothing you can do about it." She actually stood up, and she leaned her fist on my desk and put her face about six inches away from mine. "Until now," she said. "Until finally

Daddy solved this whole thing, the whole fucked-up mess." She poked me in the chest. "With *you*," she said. "And now I need you to be what Daddy wanted you to be, Dexter. I need you to take care of Bobby Acosta."

Debs glared at me for several seconds as I scrambled for something to say. And in spite of my well-deserved reputation for a glib tongue and a ready wit, there were absolutely no words there for me to grab on to and speak. I mean, really; I had been trying so hard to reform, to live a normal life, and because of that I had been drugged, forced into an orgy, taunted and beaten by cannibals—and now my sister, a sworn officer of the law and a lifelong opponent of everything I held dear, was actually asking me to kill someone. I began to wonder if perhaps I was still lying somewhere, tied up and drugged, and hallucinating all this. The idea was very comforting— but my stomach was growling, and my chest hurt where Debs had poked me, and I realized that something so unpleasant was probably true, and that meant I had to deal with it.

"Deborah," I said carefully. "I think you're a little bit upset—"

"You're goddamned right I'm upset," she said. "I bust my ass to get Samantha Aldovar back, and now she's gone again—and I'm betting Bobby Acosta has her, and he's going to get away with it."

Of course, it would have been more accurate for Debs to say she had busted *my* ass getting Samantha back—but now was not the best time to correct her, and anyway I suspected she was right about Bobby Acosta. Samantha had gotten into this because of him, and he was one of the last people left who could still help her fulfill her dream. But at least it offered a way out of the awkward moment—if I could steer the conversation on to where Acosta was, rather than what to do with him.

"I think you're right," I said. "Acosta got her started on all this. Samantha would go to him now."

Deborah still didn't sit back down, and she was still looking at me with red spots on her cheeks and fire in her eyes. "All right," she said. "I'm going to find the little bastard. And then . . ."

Sometimes a short reprieve and a change of subject is the very best you can hope for, and clearly I was there now. I could only hope that in the time it took to find Acosta, Debs would calm down a little bit and decide that feeding her felon to Dexter was not the wisest course. Maybe she would shoot him herself. In any case, I was off the hook—temporarily, at least.

"Okay," I said. "How are you going to find him?"

Deborah straightened up and ran a hand through her hair. "I'll talk to his old man," she said. "He's got to know Bobby's best chance is to walk in here with a lawyer."

That was almost certainly true—but then, Joe Acosta was a rich and powerful man, and my sister was a tough and stubborn woman, and a meeting of two such people would probably go a lot smoother if at least one person present had just a tiny smidgen of tact. Deborah had never had any; she probably couldn't even spell it. And judging from his reputation, Joe Acosta was the kind of man who would buy tact if he ever needed any. So that left me.

I stood up. "I'll come with you," I said.

She studied me for a moment, and I thought perhaps she was going to tell me "no" out of sheer perverseness. But then she nodded. "Okay," she said, and she headed out the door.

THIRTY-FOUR

L
IKE MOST PEOPLE WHO LIVE IN MIAMI, I KNEW A GOOD deal about Joe Acosta from what I'd read in the newspapers. It seemed like he had been a county commissioner forever, and even before that little chunks of his life story had slipped into the media from time to time. It was the kind of story that makes for wonderful, heartwarming reading, a real boy-makes-good tale. Or in Acosta's case, perhaps it should be *chico* makes *bueno*.

Joe Acosta had come to Miami from Havana on one of the first Pedro Pan Freedom Flights. He had been young enough at the time to make an easy transition to America, but he stayed *gusano* enough over the years to keep a high standing in the Cuban community, and he had done very well for himself. He had gone into real estate in the boom time of the eighties and put all his profits into one of the first big developments south of South Miami. It had sold out in six months. And now Acosta's construction and development business was one of the largest in South Florida, and driving around town you saw a sign with his name on it at nearly every construction site. He was so successful that even the current financial meltdown apparently hadn't hurt him too badly. Of course, he didn't need to rely solely on his construction business. He could always fall back on the salary of six thousand dollars a year he made as a county commissioner.

Joe was about ten years into a second marriage, and it seemed like even the divorce had not wiped him out, because he still lived very well and publicly. He was often in the celebrity gossip section of the papers, pictured with his new wife. She was a British beauty who had been responsible for a number of truly terrible techno-pop dance hits in the nineties and then, when the public realized how awful her music was, she came to Miami, found Joe, and settled into a comfortable life as a trophy wife.

Acosta kept a business office on Brickell Avenue, and that's where we found him. He had the entire top floor of one of the newer skyscrapers that were remaking the Miami skyline into something that looked like a giant mirror had fallen from outer space and shattered into tall and jagged shards that were now jammed into the ground at random intervals. We got past the guard in the lobby and rode up to the top in a sleek elevator. Even Acosta's ultrachic steel-and-leather waiting room had a wonderful view of Biscayne Bay, though, and that turned out to be a good thing. We had plenty of opportunity to enjoy it, because Acosta kept us waiting for forty-five minutes; after all, there is no real point in having clout if you don't use it to make the police uncomfortable.

And it worked wonderfully well, at least on Deborah. I sat and flipped through a couple of very high-end sports-fishing magazines, but Deborah fidgeted, clenching and unclenching her hands and her jaw, crossing and recrossing her legs, and drumming her fingers on the arm of her chair. She looked like someone waiting for the methadone clinic to open.

After a while, I couldn't even concentrate on all the glossy pictures of ridiculously rich men with one arm around a bikinied model and the other around a big fish, and I put down the magazine. "Debs, for God's sake, stop fidgeting. You'll wear out the chair."

"That son of a bitch is keeping me waiting because he's up to something," she hissed.

"That son of a bitch is a busy man," I said. "As well as being rich and powerful. Besides, he knows you're after his son. And that means he can keep us waiting as long as he wants. So relax and enjoy the view." I picked up a magazine and offered it to her. "Have you seen this issue of *Cigar Aficionado*?"

Debs slapped the magazine away, making a *thwack* noise that sounded unnaturally loud in the hushed and clinical elegance of the waiting area. "I'm giving him five more minutes," she snarled.

"And then what?" I said. She didn't have an answer for that, at least not in words, but the look she gave me would almost certainly have curdled milk if I'd been holding any.

I never got to find out what she might have done after five minutes, because after only three and a half minutes more of watching my sister grind her teeth and jangle her legs like a teenager, the elevator door opened and an elegant woman strolled past us. She was tall, even without the spike heels, and her platinum-colored hair was short, possibly to keep it from hiding the gigantic diamond that hung around her neck on a thick gold chain. The jewel was set in the eye of what looked to be an ankh, but with a sharp, daggerlike point to it. The woman gave us one snooty glance and went right to the receptionist.

"Muriel," she said in an icy British accent. "Send in some coffee, won't you." And without pausing she went by the receptionist, opened the door to Acosta's office, and sauntered in, closing the door behind her.

"That's Alana Acosta," I whispered to Debs. "Joe's wife."

"I know who it is, goddamn it," she said, and went back to grinding her teeth.

It was clear that Deborah was beyond any of my paltry efforts at bringing her comfort and joy, so I grabbed another magazine. This one was devoted to showing the kind of clothing you have to wear on boats that cost enough to buy a small country. But I had not even looked at it long enough to discover why twelve-hundred-dollar shorts were better than the kind that cost fifteen dollars at Walmart when the receptionist called to us.

"Sergeant Morgan?" she said, and Deborah shot up out of her chair as if she were sitting on a big steel spring. "Mr. Acosta will see you now," the receptionist said, and waved us at the office door.

"About fucking time," Debs muttered under her breath, but I think Muriel heard her, because she gave us a superior smile as my sister stormed by her with me in her wake.

Joe Acosta's office was big enough to host a convention. One whole wall was taken up by the largest flat-screen TV I had ever seen. Covering the entire wall opposite was a painting that really belonged in a museum under armed guard. There was a bar, complete with a kitchenette, a conversation area with a couple of couches, and a handful of chairs that looked like they had come from an old British Empire men's club and cost more than my house. Alana Acosta lounged in one of the chairs, sipping from a bone china coffee cup. She didn't offer us any.

Joe Acosta sat at a massive glass-and-steel-frame desk in front of a tinted glass wall that framed Biscayne Bay as if it was a photo of Joe's personal cottage in the woods. In spite of the tint, the late-afternoon light came up off the water and filled the room with a supernatural glow.

Acosta stood up as we entered, and the light from the window behind him surrounded him in a bright aura, making it hard to look at him without squinting. But I looked at him anyway, and even without the halo he was impressive.

Not physically; Acosta was a thin and aristocratic-looking man with dark hair and eyes, and he wore what looked like a very expensive suit. He was not tall, and I was sure his wife would tower over him in her spike heels. But perhaps he felt that the power of his personality was strong enough to overcome a little thing like being a foot shorter than her. Or maybe it was the power of his money. Whatever it was, he had it. He looked at us from behind his desk, and I felt a sudden urge to kneel, or at least knuckle my forehead.

"Sorry to keep you waiting, Sergeant," he said. "My wife wanted to be here for this." He waved an arm at the conversation area. "Let's sit where we can talk," he said, and he walked around the desk and sat down in the big club chair opposite Alana.

Deborah hesitated for a moment, and I saw that she looked a little bit uncertain, as if it had really hit her for the first time that she was confronting somebody who was only a few steps down the chain of command from God. But she took a breath, squared her shoulders, and marched over to the couch. She sat down, and I sat beside her.

The couch was apparently built on the same principle as a Venus flytrap, because when I sat I was immediately sucked down into a deep plush cushion, and as I struggled to remain upright it occurred to me that this was on purpose, another silly little trick Acosta used to dominate people, like putting his desk in front of the bright window. Deborah apparently came to the same conclusion, because I saw her tighten her jaw, and pull herself forward with a jerk to perch awkwardly on the edge of the couch.

"Mr. Acosta," she said. "I need to talk to your son."

"What about?" Acosta said. He sat comfortably in his chair, his legs crossed, and an expression of polite interest on his face.

"Samantha Aldovar," Debs said. "And Tyler Spanos."

Acosta smiled. "Roberto has a lot of girlfriends," he said. "I don't even try to keep up."

Deborah looked angry, but happily for us all she managed to control herself. "As I am sure you are aware, Tyler Spanos was murdered, and Samantha Aldovar is missing. And I think your son knows something about both of them."

"Why do you think that?" Alana said from her chair opposite Joe. Another trick: We had to whip our heads back and forth to keep up, like watching a Ping-Pong match.

But Deborah looked at her anyway. "He knows Samantha," she said. "And I have witnesses that say he sold them Tyler's car. That's felony car theft and accessory to murder, and that's just the beginning."

"I am not aware that any charges have been filed," Acosta said, and we both swung our heads back to face him.

"Not yet," Deborah said. "But they will be."

"Then perhaps we should have a lawyer here," Alana said.

Deborah looked at her briefly, then back to Acosta. "I wanted to talk to you first," she said. "Before the lawyers get into it."

Acosta nodded, as if he expected a police officer to show that kind of consideration for his money. "Why?" he said.

"Bobby is in trouble," she said. "I think he knows that. But his best chance at this point is to walk into my office, with a lawyer, and surrender himself."

"That would save you some work, wouldn't it?" Alana said with a superior smile.

Deborah stared at her. "I don't mind the work," she said. "And I'll find him anyway. And when I do it's going to go very hard on him. If he resists arrest, he might even get hurt." She looked back at Acosta. "It's going to be a whole lot better for him if he comes in on his own."

"Why do you think I know where he is?" Acosta said.

Deborah stared at him, then looked away for a moment, out the bright window at the bay. "If it was my son," she said, "I would know where he was. Or how to find out."

"You have no children, do you?" Alana said.

"No," Debs said. She looked at Alana for a long and awkward moment, and then swung her head back to face Acosta. "He's your son, Mr. Acosta. If you know where he is and don't tell when I file charges, that's concealing a fugitive."

"You think I should turn in my own son?" he demanded. "You think that looks good?"

"Yeah, I do," she said.

" 'Commissioner upholds law, even when it hurts,' " I said in my best headline-news voice. He looked at me with an anger that was almost physical, and I shrugged. "You can come up with something better if you want," I said.

He didn't even try. He just stared at me for another long moment. There was nothing to hide under, so I just looked back, and finally he turned back to Deborah. "I won't rat out my own son,

Sergeant," he said, in a voice that was almost a hiss. "No matter what you think he's done."

"What I *think* is that he's involved in drugs, murder, and worse," Deborah said. "And it's not the first time."

"That's all over," he said. "In the past. Alana straightened him out."

Debs glanced at Alana, who just gave her another superior smile. "It's not over," Deborah said. "It's getting worse."

"He's my *son*," Acosta said. "He's just a kid."

"He's a bug," Deborah said. "Not a kid. He kills people and he eats them." Alana snorted, but Acosta turned pale and tried to say something. Debs didn't let him. "He needs *help*, Mr. Acosta. Shrinks, counseling, all of that stuff. He needs *you*."

"Goddamn you," Acosta said.

"If you let this play out, he's going to get hurt," she said. "If he comes in on his own—"

"I won't turn in my own son," Acosta said again. He was clearly fighting for control, but he seemed to be winning.

"Why not?" Deborah said. "You know damned well you can get him off; you have before." She sounded very hard now, and it seemed to surprise Acosta. He looked back at her and moved his jaw, but no sound came out, and Debs went on in a deadly, factual voice. "With your connections, and your money, you can get the best lawyers in the state," she went on. "Bobby will walk away from this with a slap on the wrist. It's not right, but it's a fact, and we both know it. Your son will walk, just like the other times. But not unless he comes in voluntarily."

"So you say," Acosta said. "But life is uncertain. And however it goes, I have still sold out my son." And he glared at me again. "For a sound bite." He looked back at Deborah. "I won't do it."

"Mr. Acosta—" she said, but he raised a hand and cut her off.

"In any case," he said, "I don't know where he is."

They looked at each other for a moment, and it was plain to me that neither of them knew how to give in, and it quickly became obvious to them, too; Deborah just looked at him, and then shook her head slowly and struggled up out of the couch. She stood for a second looking down at Acosta, and then she just nodded.

"All right," she said. "If that's how you want to play it. Thank you for your time." She turned and headed for the door, and before I could break the grip of the carnivorous couch she had a hand on the doorknob. As I lurched up and onto my feet, Alana Acosta unfolded her long legs and rose up from her chair. The movement was so sudden and dramatic that I paused only halfway up and watched as she slid up to her great height and sauntered past me to Acosta.

"That was rather boring," she said.

"You're going home?" Acosta asked her.

She bent and pecked at his cheek. The huge diamond ankh swung forward and bumped his cheek, too. It didn't open a cut, and he didn't seem to mind. "Yes," she said. "I'll see you tonight." She sauntered for the door, and after a moment, realizing I was still staring, I shook myself and followed.

Deborah was standing by the elevator, arms crossed, tapping her foot impatiently. And evidently unaware that there was any awkwardness in the situation at all, Alana strolled right up and stood next to her. Deborah looked at her; she had to crane her neck to see all the way up to Alana's face, but she did. Alana looked back with no expression, and then looked away as a chime sounded and the elevator doors slid open. Alana went right in and Deborah, gritting her teeth, marched in after, leaving me no choice at all but to jump in between them and hope I could stop the knife fight.

But there was no fight. The doors slid shut, the elevator lurched downward, and before Deborah could even recross her arms, Alana looked down at her and said, "I know where Bobby is."

THIRTY-FIVE

NOBODY SAID ANYTHING AT FIRST. IT WAS ONE OF THOSE moments when the words were hanging in the air, and everybody knew what the individual words meant, but we couldn't quite get them mentally strung together to mean what we thought they meant. The elevator hurtled downward. I looked up at Alana. My eyes were just about at her chin, and I had a very good view of her necklace. The pendant actually was an ankh, as I had guessed. It was slightly elongated and came to a point that was sharp enough to puncture skin. I wondered if she had any scars from it. And although I really don't know a lot about diamonds, even up this close it looked real, and it was very large.

Of course, Deborah didn't have my view of the jewelry, so she recovered first. "What the hell does that mean?" she said.

Alana looked down her nose at Deborah. Naturally, from her great height she would have to, but there was more to it than that. She gave Debs that look of condescending amusement that only the Brits can really master, and said, "What would you like it to mean, Sergeant?" And she made "sergeant" sound like some kind of funny insect, which was not lost on my sister. She blushed.

"I mean, is that supposed to be some kind of tease, to watch us little people squirm, like some kind of game?" Deborah said. "Why the fuck would you say you know where he is, when we both know you won't tell me?"

Alana looked even more amused. "Who says I won't tell you?" she said.

Deborah stepped to the side and slapped at the big red button on the elevator's control panel. The elevator jerked to a stop and outside the car a bell began to ring.

"Listen," Deborah said, stepping right up into Alana's face—or her neck, anyway. "I don't have time for bullshit games. I got a girl out there whose life is in danger, and I think Bobby Acosta has her, or at least knows where she is, and I need to find her before she gets killed. If you know where Bobby is, tell me. Now. Or you're coming to the detention center with me on a charge of withholding evidence of a murder."

It didn't seem to impress Alana. She smiled, shook her head, and leaned past Debs and pushed the button. The elevator lurched into motion again. "Really, Sergeant," Alana said. "You needn't threaten me with your whips and chains. I'm happy to tell you."

"Then quit jerking me around and tell me," Deborah said.

"Joe has a property that Bobby's quite fond of," she said. "It's rather large, over a hundred acres, and completely deserted."

"Where?" Deborah said through her teeth.

"Did you ever hear of Buccaneer Land?" Alana said.

Deborah nodded. "I know it," she said. So did I. Buccaneer Land used to be the greatest amusement park in South Florida, and we had both been there many times as young children, and loved it. Of course, we were yokels back then who didn't know any better, and when an overaggressive mouse opened a place north of us, we realized how hokey Buccaneer Land was. So did everyone else in South Florida, and Buccaneer Land closed shortly afterward. But I still had a few memories of the place.

"That closed years ago," I said, and Alana looked at me.

"Yes," she said. "It went bankrupt and sat there for ages, and finally Joe bought it up for pennies. It's a very good piece of commercial property. But he hasn't done anything with it. Bobby likes to go there. Sometimes he turns on the rides for his friends."

"Why do you think he's there?" Debs said.

Alana shrugged, an elegant gesture that was somehow another put-down. "It makes sense," she said, sounding like she hoped Deborah knew that word. "It's empty, completely isolated. He likes it there. And there's an old caretaker's cottage on the property he's kept fixed up." She smiled. "I believe he takes girls there from time to time."

The elevator thumped to a stop. The doors slid open and a dozen people began to stampede inside. "Walk me to my car," Alana said above the crowd, and she moved forward through the pedestrians with absolute confidence that they would melt away at her approach. Somehow, they all did.

Deborah and I followed her, not quite so easily, and I took an elbow to the ribs from a large middle-aged woman, and then had to stop the closing door with my hand before I managed to get off the car and into the building's lobby. Debs and Alana were already at the far side of the lobby, walking briskly toward the door to the parking garage, so I had to hurry to catch up.

I caught them just as they were pushing through the door to the garage and heard the tail end of what sounded like a rather queru-lous question from Deborah. ". . . supposed to believe you?" she was saying.

Alana moved briskly through the door and into the parking area. "Because, ducks," she said, "Bobby is jeopardizing everything I have worked for."

"*Worked?*" Deborah said scornfully. "Isn't that kind of a strong word for what you do?"

"Oh, I assure you, it's work," Alana said. "Starting at the begin-ning, with My Recording Career." She said the words like they were the title of a foolish and boring book. "But believe me, a musical career is very hard work, especially if you have no talent, like me." She smiled fondly at Debs. "A great deal of it involves fucking terribly unpleasant people, of course. I'm sure you'll grant me that that isn't easy."

"A lot harder than turning in your own son, I guess," Debs said.

"Stepson, actually," Alana said, totally unfazed. She shrugged and stopped beside a bright orange Ferrari convertible parked by a No Parking sign. "Bobby and I never really got on, no matter what Joe thinks. And in any case, as you so cleverly pointed out, with Joe's money and influence intact, Bobby will certainly walk away from this. But if this situation is allowed to escalate, we could lose all that. And then Bobby will serve hard time, Joe will neglect business and go broke trying to get him out, and I will have to try to find a new way to make a living, which would be much harder now, as I'm afraid I'm a few years past my prime."

Deborah looked at me with a frown, and I frowned back. What Alana said made sense, of course, especially to someone untroubled by human feelings, like I used to be. It was clinically cold reasoning, serpentine but clear, and that certainly fit what we were coming to know about Alana. And yet—something was wrong with it, whether it was the way she said it or something else, I couldn't say; it didn't quite add up for me.

"What will you do if Joe finds out you've told us?" I asked Alana.

She looked at me, and then I knew what was wrong, because I saw something very dark and leather-winged at the back of her eyes, just for a moment, before the cover of icy amusement slid back into place on her face. "I shall make him forgive me," she said, and her lips turned up higher in a wonderful fake smile. "Besides, he won't find out, will he?" And she turned to Deborah. "This will be our little secret, all right?" she said.

"I can't keep this a secret," Deborah said. "If I take the task force into Buccaneer Land, people are going to know."

"Then you must go alone," Alana said. " 'Acting on an anonymous tip'—isn't that how they say it? You go alone, without telling anyone. And when you show up with Bobby, who will care how you knew where he was?"

Deborah stared at Alana, and I was quite sure she would tell her

the idea was ridiculous, out of the question, an unacceptable devia-
tion from police procedure, and far too dangerous. But Alana
curved her lips and raised an eyebrow, and there was no question
now that it was a challenge. And just to be sure a dullard like Debs
couldn't miss that, Alana said, "Surely you can't be afraid of one
young man? You have a lovely pistol, after all, and he's quite alone
and unarmed."

"That's not the point," Debs said.

All the amusement left Alana's face. "No, it's not," she said.
"The point is that you must go alone or there will be a huge fuss and
Joe will find out I told you, and in truth I really don't wish to risk
that. And if you insist on taking a team out there and making a great
bloody riot of it, I shall go warn Bobby that you're coming and he'll
be in Costa Rica before you can do a thing about it." The dark wings
fluttered in her eyes one more brief time, and then she forced a smile
back onto her face, but it still wasn't very pleasant. "What's the
expression? 'My way or the highway.' All right?"

I could see a lot of other options besides taking the on-ramp to
Alana's particular road, and I certainly didn't like the idea of going
into a deserted and hostile environment and trying to catch Bobby
Acosta without considerable backup, merely because Alana said he
was alone and unarmed. But apparently Deborah was made of
sterner stuff, because she just looked back, and after a moment she
nodded.

"All right," Debs said. "I'll do it your way. And if Bobby's there,
I don't have to let Joe know how we found out."

"Brilliant," Alana said. She opened the Ferrari's door, slid onto
the seat, and fired up the engine. She revved it twice for effect, and
the thick concrete walls of the parking garage trembled. She gave us
one last cold and terrible smile—and once again, just for a second, I
saw the shadow flutter behind her eyes. Then she closed the door,
put the car in gear, and was gone in a wail of rubber.

Deborah watched her go, which gave me a little time to recover
from my encounter with the inner Alana. It surprised me that I was
shocked to find a predator in such a cool and beautiful package.
After all, it made a great deal of sense. From what I knew about

Alana, her biography told a ruthless story, and as I knew very well, it takes a special kind of person to slip the knife in so many times, and apparently so well.

And at least it made sense of her betrayal of Bobby Acosta. It was precisely the right sort of move for a dragon trying to protect her hard-won golden nest; in one clever stroke she safeguarded the treasure and eliminated a rival. Very sound gamesmanship, and the dark part of me admired her thinking.

Debs abruptly turned away from the sound of the vanishing Ferrari and headed for the door back into the lobby. "Let's get it done," she said over her shoulder.

We hurried back through the building and out the front door to Brickell Avenue without conversation. Deborah had angled her car in at an illegal spot by the curb in a perfect job of Cop Parking, and we climbed in. But in spite of her haste coming to the car, she didn't start the engine right away. Instead, she put her forearms on the steering wheel and leaned forward with a frown.

"What?" I said at last.

She shook her head. "Something just isn't right here," she said.

"You don't think Bobby is there?" I said.

She made a face and didn't look at me. "I just don't trust that bitch," she said.

I thought that was very sensible. I knew quite well from my glimpse into Alana's real self that she could only be trusted to do what was best for Alana, no matter what the consequences might be for everyone else. But secretly helping us put Bobby in jail seemed to fit her agenda nicely. "You don't need to trust her," I said. "But she is acting in her own self-interest."

"Shut up, okay?" she said, and I shut. I watched Deborah drum her fingers on the wheel, purse her lips, rub her forehead. I wished I could find some similar twitch to fill the time, but nothing occurred to me. I did not like the whole idea of the two of us trying to corner Bobby Acosta. He didn't seem particularly dangerous—but of course, most people thought the same thing about me, and look where that got them.

Bobby might not be deadly—but there was too much about the

situation that was unknown and gravely random. And to be perfectly honest, which is sometimes necessary, I thought that any small chance of Samantha remaining silent would be gone forever if I showed up again with another rescue party.

On the other hand, I knew very well that I could not let Deborah go alone. That would break every rule I had carefully learned over the course of a studiously wicked life. And to my surprise, I found that New Dexter, Lily Anne's dad, who was working so hard to be human, actually had a *feeling* on the subject. I *felt* protective of Deborah, unwilling to see harm come to her, and if she was going to put herself in harm's way I wanted to be there to keep her safe.

It was a very strange sensation, to be torn by the conflicting emotions of concern for Deborah and at the same time a very real desire to see Samantha out of the way somehow—polar opposites, both pulling at me strongly. I wondered if that meant that I was exactly halfway on my journey between Dark Dexter and Dex-Daddy. Dark-Daddy? It had possibilities.

Deborah snapped me out of my pathetic fugue by slapping her hands on the steering wheel. "Goddamn it," she said. "I just don't fucking trust her."

I felt better: Common sense was winning. "So you're not going?" I said.

Deborah shook her head and started the engine. "No," she said. "Of course I'm going." And she put it in gear and pulled out into traffic. "But I don't have to go alone."

I suppose I should have pointed out that since I was right there beside her, she was not technically alone. But she was already accelerating to a speed at which I began to fear for my life, so I simply grabbed for my seat belt and buckled it on extra tight.

THIRTY-SIX

I HAVE ALWAYS REGARDED IT AS AN ACUTE MENTAL DEFECT that some people think it's perfectly safe to drive at high speeds while talking on a cell phone. But Deborah was one of those people, and family is family, so I didn't say anything to her when she pulled out her phone. As we roared up onto I-95 she had one hand on the wheel while she dialed a number with the other. It was only one digit, which meant it was speed dial, and I had a pretty good idea who it would be, which was confirmed when she spoke.

"It's me," she said. "Can you find Buccaneer Land? Yeah, north. Okay, meet me outside the main gate, ASAP. Bring some hardware. Love you," she said, and hung up.

There were very few living people Debs loved, and even fewer she would admit it to, so I was sure I knew who she had called.

"Chutsky's meeting us there?" I said.

She nodded, sliding the phone back into its holster. "Backup," she said, and then happily for my peace of mind she put both hands on the wheel and concentrated on weaving through the traffic. It was about a twenty-minute drive north up the highway to the spot where Buccaneer Land lay moldering, and Deborah made it in twelve minutes, flying down the off-ramp and onto the back road that leads up to the main gate at a rate of speed that seemed to me to be several very big steps beyond reckless. And since Chutsky was not there yet, we could have gone at a more reasonable pace and still had plenty of time to hang around waiting for him. But Debs kept her foot down until the gate was in sight, and then she finally slowed and pulled off the road beside what used to be the main gate to Buccaneer Land.

My first reaction was relief. Not just because Debs hadn't killed us, but because Roger, the twenty-five-foot-tall pirate I remembered so well from my childhood, was still there guarding the place. Most of his bright paint job had worn off. Time and weather had removed the parrot from his shoulder, and his raised sword was half-gone, but he still had his eye patch, and there was still a bright and wicked gleam in his remaining eye. I climbed out of the car and looked up at my old friend. As a child I had always felt a special kinship with Roger. After all, he was a pirate, and that meant he was allowed to sail around on a big sailboat and chop up anybody he wanted, which seemed like an ideal life to me back then.

Still, it was very strange to stand in his shadow again and remember what this place had been like once upon a time, and what Roger the Pirate had meant to me. I felt I owed him some kind of homage, even in his dilapidated state. So I stared up at him for a moment, and then said, "Aaarrhhh." He didn't answer, but Debs looked at me strangely.

I stepped away from Roger and looked through the chain-link fence that surrounded the park. The sun was setting, and in the last light of the day there wasn't much to see from here; the same clutter of gaudy signs and rides I remembered, now battered and greatly faded after so many years of neglect in the cruel Florida sunlight. Looming over everything was the tall and extremely unpiratical tower they had named the Mainmast. It had a half dozen metal arms hanging off it, each with a caged car dangling from the end. I had never understood what it had to do with buccaneers, no matter how many signs and flags they'd draped on it, but Harry had just patted my head when I asked him and said they got a deal on it, and anyway it had been fun to ride up to the top. There was a great view from up there, and if you closed one eye and muttered, "Yo, ho, ho," you could almost forget that the thing was so modern-looking.

Now the whole tower seemed to lean slightly to one side, and all the cars but one were either missing or shattered. Still, I wasn't planning on riding to the top today, so it didn't seem important.

From the fence where I stood I couldn't see much more of the park, but since there was nothing else to do but wait for Chutsky, I let the nostalgia in. I wondered if there was still water in the artificial river that wound through the park. There had been a pirate ship ride on that river: Roger the Pirate's pride and joy, the wicked ship *Vengeance*. It had cannons that really fired sticking out of each side. And on one bank of the river, they had one of those rides where you sit inside a fake log and ride down a waterfall. Beyond it, on the far side of the park, there was the Steeplechase. Just like with the tower, the connection between a Steeplechase and pirates had always escaped me, but the ride had been Debs's favorite. I wondered if she was thinking about it.

I looked at my sister. She was pacing back and forth in front of the gate, glancing up the road and then into the park, then standing still and folding her arms, and then snapping back into a walk, back and forth again. She was clearly about to pop from the nervous anticipation, and I thought this might be a good time to calm her down a little and share a family memory, so as she paced by me I spoke to her back.

"Deborah," I said, and she whipped around to look at me.

"What?" she said.

"Remember the Steeplechase?" I asked her. "You used to love that ride."

She stared at me as if I had asked her to jump off the tower. "Jesus Christ," she said. "We're not here to walk down memory fucking lane." And she spun back around and stalked away to the far side of the gate.

Obviously, my sister was not quite as overwhelmed by fond recollection as I was. I wondered if she was becoming less human while I became more so. But of course, there was the strange and very human moodiness that had been afflicting her lately, so it didn't seem likely.

In any case, Debs clearly thought that pacing and grinding her teeth was more fun than sharing happy memories of our youthful frolics in Buccaneer Land. So I let her stomp around while I looked through the fence for five more long minutes until Chutsky arrived.

And he finally did arrive, steering his car up behind Deborah's and climbing out holding a metallic briefcase, which he put down on the hood of his car. Deborah stormed over and gave him a typically warm and loving greeting.

"Where the fuck have you been?" she said.

"Hey," Chutsky said. He reached to give her a kiss, but she pushed past him and grabbed for the briefcase. He shrugged and nodded at me. "Hey, buddy," he said.

"What have you got?" she said, and he took the case from her and popped it open.

"You said hardware," he said. "I didn't know what you were expecting, so I brought a selection." He lifted out a small assault rifle with a folding stock. "Heckler and Koch's finest," he said, holding it up, then laid it on the hood and reached back into the case and came out with a pair of much smaller weapons. "Nice little Uzi here," he said. He patted one affectionately with the steel hook he had nowadays instead of a left hand, and then put it down and took out two automatic pistols. "Couple of standard service models, nine-millimeter, nineteen shots in the mag." He looked at Deborah fondly. "Any one of 'em a whole lot better than that piece of shit you carry around," he said.

"It was Daddy's," Deborah said, lifting up one of the pistols.

Chutsky shrugged. "It's a forty-year-old wheel gun," he said. "Almost as old as me, and that ain't good."

Deborah dropped the magazine out of the pistol, worked the

action, and looked in the chamber. "This isn't the siege of Khe fucking Sanh," she said, and she slammed the magazine back into the pistol. "I'll take this one."

Chutsky nodded. "Uh-huh, good," he said. He reached past her into the case. "Extra magazine," he said, but she shook her head.

"If I need more than one, I'm dead and fucked," she said.

"Maybe," Chutsky said. "What are we expecting in there, anyway?"

Debs shoved the pistol into the waistband of her pants. "I don't know," she said. "We were told he's in there alone." Chutsky raised an eyebrow at her. "Twenty-two-year-old white male," she explained. "Five-foot-ten, a hundred fifty pounds, dark hair—but honest to God, Chutsky, we don't have a clue if he's really there, or if he's alone, and I sure as shit don't trust the bitch that gave us the tip."

"Okay, good, I'm glad you called me," he said, nodding happily. "Old days, you would have gone in there alone with your daddy's popgun." He looked over at me. "Dex?" he said. "I know you don't like guns and violence." He smiled and shrugged. "But hey—you don't wanna go in there naked, buddy." He tilted his head at his little armory, spread out on the hood of the car. "How 'bout joo say hello to my little fren?" It was the worst Scarface impression I'd ever heard, but I stepped forward for a look anyway. I really don't like guns—they're so loud and messy, and they take all the skill and pleasure out of things. Still, I was not here for the fun of it.

"If it's okay with you," I said, "I'll take the other pistol. And the extra magazine." After all, if I needed the thing at all, I would probably *really* need it, and nineteen extra bullets don't weigh that much.

"Yeah, great," he said happily. "You sure you know how to use it?"

It was a small joke between us—small mostly because only Chutsky thought it was funny. He knew very well I could handle a pistol. But I played along anyway and held it up by the barrel. "I think I hold this end and point it like that," I said.

"Perfect," Chutsky said. "Don't shoot off your balls, okay?" He picked up the assault rifle. It had a strap that he slid over his shoulder. "I'll take this little beauty. And if it turns into Khe Sanh after all, I'm ready for Charlie." He looked at the weapon for a moment with the same fondness as I had looked at Roger the Pirate—clearly there were some happy memories there.

"Chutsky," Deborah said.

He jerked his head up to Debs as if he had been caught looking at porn. "Okay," he said. "So how you wanna do this?"

"Through the gate," she said. "Fan out and head for the far side of the park. That's where the employees' area used to be." She looked at me, and I nodded.

"I remember," I said.

"So that's where the caretaker's place is," she said. "Where Bobby Acosta ought to be." She pointed at Chutsky. "You come in from the right and cover me. Dexter from the left."

"What," Chutsky said. "You're not gonna just kick down the door and charge in there. That's nuts."

"I'm going to tell him to come out," Deborah said. "I want him to think I'm alone. Then we see what happens. If it's some kind of trap, you guys got my back."

"Sure," Chutsky said dubiously. "But you're still out there in the open."

She shook it off, irritated. "I'll be fine," she said. "I think the girl is in there, too, Samantha Aldovar," she said. "So be careful. None of your Rambo shit."

"Uh-huh," he said. "But this kid, Bobby, you want him alive, right?"

Deborah looked at him for just a moment too long. "Of course," she said at last. It wasn't very convincing. "Let's go." She turned away and marched for the gate. Chutsky watched her for a second, then took two extra clips from the case and slipped them into his pocket. He closed the case and tossed it into the car.

"Okay, buddy," he said. And then he turned and looked at me, a long and surprisingly damp look. "Don't let anything happen to her," he said, and for the first time since I had known him, I saw what seemed like real emotion on his face.

"I won't," I said, slightly embarrassed.

He squeezed my shoulder. "Good," he said. He looked at

me a moment longer, and then turned away and lurched after Deborah.

She was at the chain-link gate, reaching through the mesh for a padlock. "Shouldn't somebody point out that you're about to illegally enter the property?" I said. And even though that was true, I was really more worried about finding Samantha again and turning her loose on a world that was far too eager to listen to her lurid tales.

But Debs pulled at the lock, and it fell open in her hand. She looked at me. "This lock has been opened," she said in a voice meant for the witness stand. "Somebody has gone into the park, possibly illegally, and possibly to commit a felony. It is my clear duty to investigate."

"Yeah, hey, just a second," Chutsky said. "If this kid is hiding out in there, why would it be unlocked?"

I managed to stop myself from hugging him and instead merely added, "He's right, Debs. It's a setup."

She shook her head impatiently. "We knew it might be," she said. "That's why I brought you two."

Chutsky frowned, but he didn't move forward. "I don't like this," he said.

"You don't have to like it," Deborah said. "You don't even have to do it."

"I'm not letting you go in there alone," he said. "Dexter won't, either."

Normally I suppose I would have felt like kicking Chutsky for offering up Dexter's tender skin on the altar of unnecessary danger. But as it happened, I agreed—just this once. It was clear to me that someone with a little bit of common sense should tag along, and looking around our gathering, counting everyone, that left me. "That's right," I said. "Besides, we can always call in for backup if it gets sticky."

Apparently, that was exactly the wrong thing to say. Deborah glared at me, and then marched over to me and stood one quarter of an inch away from my face. "Give me your phone," she said.

"What?"

"Now!" she barked, and she held out her hand.

"It's a brand-new BlackBerry," I protested, but it was very clear that I was either going to hand it over or lose the use of my arms under a barrage of her arm punches, so I gave it to her.

"Yours, too, Chutsky," she said, stepping over to him. He just shrugged and handed over his phone.

"Bad idea, babe," he said.

"I'm not having one of you clowns panic and fuck it up," she said. She trotted back to her car and threw the phones into the front seat—hers, too—and came back to us.

"Listen, Debbie, about the phones—" Chutsky said, but she cut him off immediately.

"Goddamn it, Chutsky, I have to do this, and I have to do this now, my way, without worrying about Miranda or any of that shit, and if you don't like it shut up and go home." She yanked at the chain and it fell open. "But I'm going in and I'm going to find Samantha, and I'm going to take down Bobby Acosta," she said, and she yanked the lock off its chain and kicked at the gate. It bounced open with a tortured squeal and my sister glared at Chutsky and then at me. "See you later," she said, and she whipped away through the gate.

"Debs. Hey, Debbie, come on," Chutsky said. She ignored him and marched on into the park. Chutsky sighed and looked at me. "Okay, buddy," he said. "I got the right flank; you got the left. Let's move out." And he followed Deborah through the gate.

Have you ever noticed that no matter how often we all talk about freedom we never seem to have any? There were few things in the world I wanted to do less than follow my sister into the park, where a very obvious trap was set for us and, if everything went really well, the best I could hope for was having Samantha Aldovar ruin my life. If I truly had any freedom at all I would have taken Deborah's car and gone down to Calle Ocho for a palomilla steak and an Ironbeer.

But like everything else in the world that sounds good, freedom is an illusion. And in this case, I had no more choice than a man strapped into Old Sparky who is told he's free to stay alive as long as he can when they throw the switch.

I looked up at Roger the Pirate. His smile looked kind of mean all of a sudden. "Quit smirking," I told him. He didn't answer.

I followed my sister and Chutsky into the park.

THIRTY-SEVEN

I AM SURE WE HAVE ALL SEEN ENOUGH OLD MOVIES TO KNOW that sensible people avoid abandoned amusement parks, especially when the sun is going down, which it was. Terrible things lurk in these places, and anyone who wanders in is only setting himself up for some kind of dreadful end. And perhaps I was being oversensitive, but Buccaneer Land really did seem spookier than anything I had ever seen outside of a bad movie. There was an almost audible echo of distant laughter hanging over the dark and moldering rides and buildings, and it had a mocking edge to it, as if the long years of neglect had turned the whole place mean and it just couldn't wait to see something bad happen to me.

But apparently Deborah had not done her due diligence in the old-movie department. She seemed quite undisturbed as she drew her weapon and strode into the park, looking for all the world as if she were headed into the corner store to shoot some bacon rinds. Chutsky and I caught up with her about a hundred feet inside the gate, and she barely glanced at us. "Spread out," she said.

"Take it easy, Debs," Chutsky said. "Give us time to work the flanks." He looked at me and nodded to the left. "Go nice and slow around the rides, buddy. Go back behind the booths, sheds, any-place somebody could be hiding. Sneak and peek, buddy. Keep your eyes and ears open, keep one eye on Debbie, and be careful." He turned back to Deborah and said, "Debs, listen . . ." But she waved her gun at him to cut him off.

"Just do it, Chutsky, for God's sake."

He looked at her for a moment. "Just be careful," he said, and then he turned away and moved out to the right. He was a very large man, and he had one artificial foot, but as he glided off into the dusk the years and injuries seemed to melt away and he looked like a well-oiled shadow, his weapon moving from side to side automatically, and I was very glad that he was here with his assault rifle and his long years of practice.

But before I could begin to sing "Halls of Montezuma" Deborah nudged me hard and glared at me. "What the fuck are you waiting for?" she said. And so even though I would much rather have shot myself in the foot and gone home, I moved out to the left through the growing darkness.

We stalked carefully through the park in best paramilitary fash-ion, the lost patrol on its mission into the land of the B movie. To Deborah's credit, she was very careful. She moved stealthily from one piece of cover to the next, frequently looking right to Chutsky and then left at me. It was getting harder to see her, since the sun had now definitely set, but at least that meant it was harder for *them* to see *us*, too—whoever *them* might turn out to be.

We leapfrogged through the first part of the park like this, past the ancient souvenir stand, and then I came up to the first of the rides, an old merry-go-round. It had fallen off its spindle and lay there leaning to one side. It was battered and faded and somebody had chopped the heads off the horses and spray-painted the whole thing in Day-Glo green and orange, and it was one of the saddest things I had ever seen. I circled around it carefully, holding my gun ready, and peering behind everything large enough to hide a cannibal.

At the far side of the merry-go-round I looked to my right. In the growing darkness I could barely make out Debs. She had moved up into the shadow of one of the large posts that held up the cable car line that ran from one side of the park to the other. I couldn't see Chutsky at all; where he should have been there was a row of crumbling playhouses that fringed a go-kart track. I hoped he was there, being watchful and dangerous. If anything did jump out and yell *boo* at us, I wanted him ready with his assault rifle.

But there was no sign of him, and even as I watched, Deborah began to move forward again, deeper into the dark park. A warm, light wind blew over me and I smelled the Miami night: a distant tang of salt on the edge of rotting vegetation and automobile exhaust. But even as I inhaled the familiar smell, I felt the hairs go up on the back of my neck and a soft whisper came up at me from the lowest dungeon of Castle Dexter, and a rustle of leather wings rattled softly on the ramparts. It was a very clear notice that something was not right here and this would be a great time to be somewhere else; I froze there by the headless horses, looking for whatever had set off the Passenger's alarm.

I saw and heard nothing. Deborah had vanished into the darkness and nothing moved anywhere, except a plastic shopping bag blowing by in the gentle wind. My stomach turned over, and for once it was not from hunger.

My pistol suddenly looked very small and inadequate and I wanted to run out of the park more than I wanted my next breath. The Passenger might be peeved with me, but it would not let me walk into danger, and it was never wrong, not when it spoke this clearly. I absolutely had to grab Deborah and get us out of here before whatever it was hit us.

But how could I persuade her? She was so determined to free Samantha and collar Bobby that she would never listen, even if I could think of a way to explain how I knew that things were about to go terribly wrong. And as I clutched my pistol and dithered, the decision was taken out of my hands. There was a kind of giant *thunk* sound, and lights began to come on all over the park, and then the ground trembled, there was a terrible screech of rusty metal, and I heard a raspy groan—

And overhead, the cable cars lurched into motion.

I spent one long and precious second gaping upward and pic-
turing all the awful things that might rain down on me from someone riding past over my head. Then I had another truly horrible
moment in which vile altruism took over, and I looked to my right
to see if Deborah was okay; there was no sign of her. And then from
one of the cable cars swinging by overhead I heard a gunshot and a
savage and happy screeching sound, the cry of a hunter who has
spotted its prey, and I recovered my precious self-interest and dived
for cover into the darkness under the canopy of the merry-go-
round. In my haste to bury myself under one of the horses I banged
my nose into a large and hard lump that turned out to be one of the
severed fiberglass horse heads. By the time I scrabbled my way past
it and shoved it uphill toward the outer rim of the merry-go-round,
the screeching from above had stopped.

I waited; nothing happened. There were no more gunshots. No
one opened fire with a howitzer. No napalm bombs whistled down
from the cable cars. There was no sound at all except the dysfunc-
tional thumping of the old and rusty cable running through its stan-
chions. I waited a little longer. Something tickled at my nose and
I rubbed it; my hand came away with blood on it and for a very long
and frozen second I stared at it, unable to think or move or see anything except that awful red smear of precious Dexter fluid. But happily for me, my brain came back online and I wiped my hand on my
pants leg and put it out of my mind. Clearly, it had happened when
I dived for cover and bumped my nose. No big deal. We all have
blood in us. The trick is to keep it inside.

I wiggled carefully around into a position where I was still
safe but I could see out, and I pushed the big horse head farther up
the slope in front of me for cover and rested my pistol on top of it.
Off to my right, above the last place I had seen Deborah, a shattered
cable car went by on the wire. There was nothing left of it except the
piece that attached to the cable and one small chunk of metal tubing
that had been part of the seat, and it bobbed and wobbled crazily
past. The next car lurched into view, and although there was more of
it, the side panels were gone and it, too, was empty.

I watched several more of the broken cars go by. Only one of them seemed to be in good enough condition to hold a passenger, but it bounced past with no sign that it ever had, and I began to feel a little bit silly, huddling underneath a gilded, crumbling, Day-Glo merry-go-round pony and pointing my pistol at a series of broken-down and very empty cable cars. Another deserted and beat-up car went by—nothing. Still, I had certainly heard somebody pass by overhead, and the warning from the Passenger had been quite clear. There was danger out there in the park, lurking among the carefree memories of Buccaneer Land. And it knew I was here.

I took a deep breath. Clearly, Bobby was here, too, and it sounded like he was not alone. But there could not be more than two or three people total in one of those rickety old cable cars. So if we continued with the original plan and moved on through the park, the three of us should still be able to round up a few loopy kids. Nothing to worry about: Keep breathing, follow the plan, home in time for Letterman. I wriggled back out toward the rim of the merry-go-round, and I had one leg out and on the ground when I heard once again a kind of primitive, fraternity-house whooping sound—from behind me, in the direction of the front gate—and I slid back down the tilted spindle and into the cover of my headless horse.

A few seconds later, I heard happy voices, the shuffle of many feet, and I peeked out as a crowd of eight or ten people began to troop past me. They were mostly Bobby Acosta's age, the sort of bright-faced young monsters we had seen in Fang, possibly the exact same ones, and they were dressed in stylish buccaneer cos-tumes, which I am sure would have pleased Roger the Pirate. They hurried past, excited and happy and clearly on their way to a party, and leading the way, with a rather lethal-looking sword raised high, was the ponytailed bouncer from Fang.

I watched from behind my decapitated pony until they were gone and the sound of their passing had faded away and I thought about it, and they were not terribly happy thoughts. The odds had changed, and the whole situation was different now. I am not a very sociable person by nature, but this seemed like a really good time to seek out my companions for some quality survival time together.

So I waited another minute to be sure there were no stragglers, and then I left my horse head behind and wormed my way slowly out to the rim of the merry-go-round. As far as I could see, they were gone and the park might as well be completely deserted. There was a building ahead and slightly to the left that I recognized from my childhood. I had spent several dull and puzzled hours wandering through it back then, completely unable to understand why it was supposed to be fun. But if it would provide cover for me, I would forgive it for its misleading name. And so, with a last glance at the still-vacant cable car, I rolled off the merry-go-round and ran for the funhouse.

The outside of the building was in very bad shape, and only a few vague shadows remained of the mural that had once decorated it. I could just barely make out the painted scene of cheerful pirates looting and raping a small town. Its loss was a great blow to the art world, but that was not my main concern at the moment. There was one dim light shining in front of the funhouse, so I circled around to the back at a half crouch, trying to stay in the shadows. It took me in the opposite direction from the last place I had seen Deborah, but I had to find new cover. Whoever was in the cable car had certainly seen me wallowing on the merry-go-round and I needed to get away from it.

I moved carefully around the back of the funhouse. The back door was hanging limply open on one hinge, with half a sign still visible on it. The faded red letters spelled out GENCY EX quite clearly. I paused at the side of the doorway, pistol ready. I didn't really think anyone would be hiding inside among the old mirrors. It was too much of a cliché, and surely even cannibals have some pride. And in any case, the mirrors had not really fooled anyone when they were in good condition. After so many years of neglect they were almost certainly no more reflective than the bottom of my shoe. But I took no chances; I moved past the door in a crouch with my pistol ready and aimed at the inside of the funhouse. Nothing lurked, nothing moved. I went on by to the next puddle of shadow.

At the far corner of the building I paused again, and peeked carefully around—still nothing. Was it possible that no one was actively looking for me? I remembered something my adoptive mother, Doris, had often said: *The wicked flee where none pursueth.* It was certainly true in my case. I spent far too much time fleeing, and so far no one had pursuethed me. But I knew with absolute certainty that they were in the park, and the only sensible move was to run for my life—but I knew just as certainly that my sister would never leave the park without Samantha Aldovar and Bobby Acosta, and I could not leave her to do it alone.

I heard unhappy muttering from the Passenger, and I felt the cold wind from his wings blowing through me, and every small voice of reason and common sense raised up on its toes and screamed at me to run for the exits—and I could not. Not without Deborah.

And so I took a breath, wondering how many more times I might be able to do so, and I scuttled for the next small and crumbling chunk of shelter. It had once been a ride for very young children, the kind with the large enclosed cars that go slowly around in a circle while you turn a big wheel in the center. Only two of the cars remained, and both were in very bad shape. I scuttled into the shade of the blue one and crouched there for a moment. The entire group of partying pirates had vanished and there was no sight or sound of anyone or anything paying attention to my hermit-crab progress. I could have been marching through the park leading a brass band and juggling live armadillos for all the attention they were paying me.

But sooner or later we would meet, and things being what they were, I wanted to see them first. So I got down on my hands and knees and peeked around the kiddie car.

I had come to the end of the area with the rides for small kids and was now in sight of the artificial river that had once held the pirate ship ride. It still had plenty of water in it, although it was not the most attractive tint I had ever seen. Even from here I could see that the water was a dull and vile green from years of neglect. Between me and the river there were three of the poles that supported the cable car. Each one of them had lamps hanging down from them, but only one of the lights actually worked. It was to my right, in the direction I had last seen Deborah. Straight ahead there was a dark open area about a hundred feet long that ended at the next chunk of cover, a grove of palm trees on a bluff above the water. The grove was not terribly large, barely big enough to hide a few small squads of Taliban waiting to ambush me. But there was no other cover in sight, so I eased out from behind the car and scuttled into the open at a running crouch.

It was an awful feeling to be unprotected, and it seemed to take several hours to cross the open and unshadowed ground until I came up next to the little grove. I paused beside the first palm tree. Now that I had the small security of its trunk, I worried again about what might be hiding on the other side. I hugged the tree and peered around it, in among the trees. A great deal of scrub and underbrush had grown up between them, and since a lot of it had sharp and pointy branches, it really did not look like a very attractive place to hide. I could see enough to be reasonably sure that nothing was lurking among the saw palmettos and thorny bushes, and I did not want to risk losing any flesh by lurking there either. I started to ease away from my tree trunk to look for better cover.

And then from up the river to my left I heard the unmistakable sound of fake cannon fire. I looked toward the sound and, in a clatter of torn cloth and half-shattered spars, the pirate ship came sailing around the bend.

It was only a decomposing husk of what it had once been. Chunks of wood dangled from the hull. The ratty remnants of its sails fluttered sadly, and less than half of the faded Jolly Roger still waved at the top of the mast, but still the ship came proudly on, just the way I remembered it. Another feeble broadside puffed out from the three cannons facing me and I took the hint and dove into the tangled scrub between the palm trees.

What had seemed like something to be avoided moments ago now seemed like precious security, and I wormed my way into the deepest clump of brush. Almost instantly, I was tangled in greenery and torn by thorns. I tried to pull away from a plant that had attacked me and I backed painfully into a small and well-named saw palmetto. By the time I had pulled myself free, I was bleeding from several deep cuts on my arms and my shirt was torn. But complaining never does any good, and I was sure no one had thought to bring Band-Aids, so I kept crawling.

I inched forward through the underbrush, leaving several more small and valuable pieces of my flesh behind on the carnivorous bushes, until I got to the far edge of the little forest, where I hunkered down behind a fan of palmetto fronds and peeked out at the river. The water roiled as if a giant hand just under the surface had begun to swirl it into motion, and then it settled into a slow and steady stream, as if it were a real river instead of a circular pond.

And as I watched, the pride of Buccaneer Land, the terror of the seven seas, the wicked ship *Vengeance* floated into view and came to a stop at the ancient and rotting pier that jutted into the river on the bank, just below me and to my right. The water roiled again, settled down into a slow flow, and the *Vengeance* rocked ever so slightly but stayed in place at the dock. And although there was no sign of the ship's roguish crew, there was at least one passenger on board.

Tied securely to the mainmast was Samantha Aldovar.

THIRTY-EIGHT

S AMANTHA DID NOT LOOK LIKE THE KIND OF PASSENGER I had seen on board the *Vengeance* in my youth. Aside from having no cotton candy or souvenir pirate hat, she was slumped over, perhaps unconscious, maybe even dead, her weight hanging against the ropes. From my hiding spot on the small bluff, I had a decent view of most of the things on the deck. Next to Samantha stood a large black barbecue grill, with a thin column of smoke wafting up from under the cover. Beside it was a big five-gallon cooking pot on a stand, and a small table where several indistinct but familiar-looking objects gleamed sharply as they caught the light.

For a moment, nothing moved but the shredded half of the Jolly Roger flag on top of the mast. The deck was deserted, except for Samantha. But someone else had to be on board. In spite of a large fake wheel at the stern, I knew the boat was controlled from inside the cabin. There had also been a lounge in there, with a refreshment stand. Somebody must be down there, working the controls. But how many? Just Bobby Acosta? Or enough of his fellow cannibals to make things dicey for the good guys, who oddly enough included me tonight?

The flag flopped. A jet flew overhead, wheels down, coming in to land at Fort Lauderdale Airport. The boat rocked gently. And then Samantha rolled her head to one side, another anemic broadside puffed out from the cannons, and the cabin door thumped open. Bobby Acosta came out on deck with a scarf tied around his head and a very unpirate-ish Glock pistol held up high. "Whoohoo!" he yelled, and he fired two shots into the air as a small gaggle of happy-looking partygoers about his age, male and female, followed him out on deck. They were all dressed in pirate gear, and they all headed directly to the big cooking pot beside Samantha and began filling cups from it and chugging the contents.

And as they settled into their lighthearted and carefree amusement, I actually felt a tiny glimmer of hope blossom in my heart. There were five of them and only three of us, true, but they were clearly lightweights, and they were guzzling something I was quite sure was the intoxicating punch they liked so much. In a few moments they would be high, goofy, and no threat at all. Wherever the rest of the party might have gone, this bunch would be easy. The three of us could step out of cover and round them up. Deborah would have what she came for, we could sneak away and call for help, and Dexter could get back to reinventing normal life.

And then the cabin door opened again, and Alana Acosta slithered out on deck.

She was followed by the ponytailed bouncer from Fang, and three nasty-looking men carrying shotguns, and the world turned dim and dangerous once more.

I had known Alana was a predator from what the Dark Passenger had whispered as we stood beside her Ferrari. And now, seeing her here so clearly in command, I knew that my brother, Brian, had been right: The head of the coven was a woman, and it was Alana Acosta. And this was not merely her trap; it was also her invitation to dinner. And if I could not come up with something really clever, I was going to be on the menu.

Alana strode right to the rail, looked out into the park more or less between me and where I thought Deborah should be, and she called out, "Olly olly oxen free!" She turned and nodded at her posse, and they obligingly put the shotguns to Samantha's head. "Or else!" Alana yelled happily.

Clearly her bizarre yodel about oxen was some sort of British children's ritual, meant to summon everyone to come in: Game over, come to home base. But she must have thought we actually were children, and very dull children at that, if she supposed we would come obediently out of our hard-earned cover and trudge into her clutches. Only the rankest ninny would fall into that kind of stupidity.

And as I hunkered down for what I assumed would be a long game of cat and mouse, I heard a shout to my right, and a moment later, to my very great horror, Deborah came into view. She was apparently so obsessed with saving Samantha—again!—that she had not even spent two seconds thinking about the consequences of what she was doing. She simply sprang out of hiding, ran over to the ship, and raced up beside the pier to surrender. She stood there below me looking defiant, and then very deliberately she drew her pistol and dropped it to the ground.

Alana clearly enjoyed the performance. She went to stand closer, where she could gloat at Debs properly, and then turned and said something to the bouncer. A moment later he wrestled the decrepit boarding ramp over the side and thumped it down onto the dock.

"Come on up, dearie," Alana said to Deborah. "Use the ramp."

Deborah stood still and looked up at Alana. "Don't hurt that girl," she said.

Alana's smile grew huge. "But she *wants* us to hurt her; don't you see?" she said.

Deborah shook her head. "Don't hurt her," she repeated.

"Let's talk about that, shall we?" Alana said. "Come on aboard."

Deborah looked up at her and saw nothing but happy reptile. She dropped her head and trudged up the ramp, and a moment later two of the shotgun-toting lackeys grabbed her, jerked her arms behind her, and duct-taped them in place. A mean little voice in the back of my head suggested that this was only fair, since very recently she'd merely watched them as they did the same thing to me. But kinder thoughts emerged and shouted that one down, and I began to fret and scheme on how to get my sister loose.

Alana, of course, had no intention of allowing any such thing. She waited for a moment, looking out across the park, and then cupped her hands to her mouth and yelled, "I'm quite sure your charming companion is out there somewhere!" She looked at Deborah, who stood with her head down, saying nothing. "We saw him at the carousel, dearie. Where is the bugger?" she said. Deborah didn't move. Alana waited for a moment with a smile of pleasant anticipation on her face, and then called out loudly, "Don't be bashful! We can't start without you!" I stayed where I was, frozen motionless among the thorns.

"Well, then," she called out cheerily. She turned and held out a hand, and one of the lackeys put a shotgun into it. For a moment I was torn by anxiety, and it was worse than the thorns. If she threatened to shoot Debs . . . But she was going to kill her anyway . . . and why should I let her kill me, too? But I couldn't let her hurt Debs—

Unconsciously I raised up my pistol. It was a very good pistol, extremely accurate, and from this distance I had about a twenty percent chance of hitting Alana. The odds of hitting Debs were just as good—or hitting Samantha, and as I thought that the pistol rose higher, all by itself.

Of course, such things would never happen in a just world, but we don't live in one, and this small movement must have caught a glimmer from one of the few battered lights still working in the park, and it gleamed just enough to attract Alana's eye. She pumped the shotgun, briskly enough to leave no doubt about whether she knew how to use it, and she raised it to her shoulder, pointed it almost directly at me, and fired.

I had only a second to react, and I just barely managed to dive down behind the nearest palm tree. Even so, I felt the wind from the pellets as they slashed into the foliage where I had so recently been hiding.

"That's better!" Alana said, and there was another blast from the shotgun. A chunk of my protective tree trunk vanished. "Peekaboo!"

A moment ago I had been unable to choose between leaving my

sister in danger and placing my own head into the noose. Suddenly my decision was a whole lot easier. If Alana was going to stand there and remove the trees one shot at a time, my future was bleak either way, and since the more immediate danger was from buck-shot, it seemed like a much better idea to give myself up and count on my superior intellect to find a way out of captivity again. Besides, Chutsky was still out there with his assault rifle, more than a match for a couple of amateurs with shotguns.

All things considered, it was not much of a choice, but it was all I had. So I stood up, staying behind the tree, and called out, "Don't shoot!"

"And spoil the meat?" Alana called. "Of course not. But let's see your smiling face, with hands in the air." And she waved her shot-gun, just in case I was a little slow in getting her point.

As I've said, freedom is really an illusion. Anytime we think we have a real choice, it just means we haven't seen the shotgun aimed at our navel.

I put down my pistol, raised my hands as high as dignity would permit, and stepped out from behind the tree.

"Lovely!" Alana called. "Now over the river and through the woods, little piglet."

It stung a little more than it should have; I mean, on top of everything else, being called "piglet" was not much. It was just a minor indignity tossed lightly on top of some rather major calami-ties, and it may be that my new-grown semihuman sensibilities encouraged me to take it harder than necessary, but really: piglet? I, Dexter? Clean-limbed, physically fit, and tempered to a fine edge in the furnace of life's many fires? I resented it, and I beamed a men-tal message to Chutsky to shoot Alana carefully, so she would linger and suffer a little.

But of course, I also moved slowly down to the bank of the river with my hands in the air.

On the bank, I stood for a moment, looking up at Alana and her shotgun. She waved it encouragingly. "Come along, then," she said. "Walk the plank, old sod."

There was no arguing with the weapon, not at this range.

I stepped onto the ramp. My brain whirled with impossible ideas: Dive under the boat, away from the aim of Alana's weapon, and then—what? Hold my breath for a few hours? Swim downstream and get help? Send more mental messages and hope for rescue by a gang of paramilitary telepaths? There was really nothing else to do except climb up the ramp to the deck of the *Vengeance*. And so I did. It was old and wobbly aluminum, and I had to hold on to the frayed guide rope that ran up the left side. I slipped once, and held tightly to the rope as the whole rickety thing pitched and yawed. But in far too short a time I was on the deck, looking at three shotguns pointed my way—and even darker and deader than the weapons' barrels, Alana Acosta's blue and empty eyes. She stood much too close, as the others duct-taped my hands behind me, looking at me with an affection I found very unsettling.

"Brilliant," she said. "This is going to be fun. I can't wait to get started." She turned away and looked off toward the park's gate. "Where *is* that man?"

"He'll be here," Bobby said. "I got his money."

"He'd better be here," Alana said, and looked back at me. "I don't like to be kept waiting."

"I don't mind," I said.

"I really would like to get started," Alana said. "There's rather a press of time this evening."

"Don't hurt that girl," Deborah said again, through her teeth this time.

Alana turned her gaze on Debs, which was nice for me, but I had the feeling that it was going to prove very unpleasant for my sister. "We really are rather mother hen–ish about this little girl piglet, aren't we?" Alana said, stepping toward Deborah. "Why is that, Sergeant?"

"She's just a girl," Debs said. "A child."

Alana smiled, a wide smile filled with hundreds of perfect white teeth. "She seems to know what she wants," she said. "And since it's the same thing we want—where's the harm?"

"She can't possibly want that," Deborah hissed.

"But she does, dear," Alana said. "Some of them do. They want to be eaten—just as much as I want to eat them." Her smile was very large, and almost real this time. "Almost makes one believe in a benevolent God, doesn't it?" she said.

"She's just a fucked-up kid," Deborah said. "She'll get over this—she has a family that loves her, and she has a life ahead of her."

"And so, overcome by remorse and the beauty of all that, I should let her go," Alana purred. "Family and church and puppies and flowers—how lovely your world must be, Sergeant. But it's somewhat darker than that for the rest of us." She looked at Samantha. "Of course, it does have its moments."

"Please," Deborah said, and she looked both desperate and vulnerable in a way I had never seen before, "just let her go."

"I don't think so," Alana said crisply. "In fact, with all this excitement, I find that I'm getting a bit peckish." She picked up a very sharp knife from the table.

"No!" Deborah said in a violent, hissing voice. "Goddamn you, no!"

"Yes, I'm afraid," Alana said, looking at her with cold amusement. Two of the guards held Debs in place and Alana watched them struggle, clearly enjoying it. And with one eye still on Deborah, Alana stepped over to Samantha and held the knife up indecisively.

"I could never really do the butchering part properly," she said. Bobby and his posse gathered around, jiggling with barely suppressed excitement like kids sneaking into a movie. "This is the whole reason I put up with tardiness from that saucy bastard," Alana said. "He's very, very good at this. Wake up, piggy." She slapped Samantha's face, and Samantha rolled her head upright and opened her eyes.

" 'S it time?" she said dopily.

"Just a snack," Alana told her, but Samantha smiled. It was very clear from her drowsy happiness that she had been drugged again, but at least it wasn't ecstasy this time.

"Great, okay," she said. Alana looked at her, and then at us.

"Come on, go for it," Bobby said.

Alana smiled at him, and then snaked out her hand and

grabbed at Samantha's arm so quickly I saw almost nothing but a blurred gleam from the blade, and before I could blink she had sliced off most of the girl's triceps.

Samantha made a sound that was somewhere between a moan and a grunt, and it was neither pleasure nor pain but somewhere in between, a cry of agonized fulfillment. It set my teeth on edge and made all the hair on my neck rise straight up and then Deborah exploded into an insane fury that sent one of her guards spinning to the deck, and the other one dropped his shotgun and held on until the huge ponytailed bouncer stepped in and clubbed Debs to the floor with one gigantic hand. She went down like a rag doll and lay there unmoving.

"Take the good sergeant below," Alana said. "Make sure she's very well secured." The two lackeys grabbed Deborah and dragged her into the cabin. I did not at all like the way she hung between them, so completely limp and lifeless, and without thinking I took a step toward her. But before I could do much more than wiggle my toes in her direction, the enormous bouncer picked up the dropped shotgun and pushed it into my chest, and I was forced to do no more than watch helplessly as they took my sister through the doorway and into the cabin.

And as the bouncer prodded me back around to face Alana, she lifted the lid from the barbecue and placed the slice of Samantha-flesh on the grill. It hissed, and a tendril of steam rose up from it.

"Oh," Samantha said in a muted, faraway voice. "Oh. Oh." She rocked slowly against her bonds.

"Turn it in two minutes," Alana said to Bobby, and then she came back to me. "Well, piglet," she said to me, and she reached over and pinched my cheek; not as a doting grandmother might, but more like a shrewd shopper checking the cutlets. I tried to pull away, but it wasn't quite as easy as it sounds, with a very large man pushing a shotgun into my back.

"Why do you keep calling me that?" I said. It sounded more petulant than it should have, but I really didn't have a terribly strong position at the moment, unless you count the moral high ground.

My question seemed to amuse Alana. She reached forward again, both hands this time, and she grabbed my cheeks and shook my head fondly from side to side. "Because you are my *piglet*!" she said. "And I am going to absolutely *devour* you, darling!" And a small and very real gleam showed in her eyes this time, and the Passenger rattled its wings in alarm.

I would like to say that I had been in much tighter spots, and I had always found a way out. But the truth was that I could not think of any time I had ever felt quite so uncomfortably vulnerable. I was once again taped and helpless, with a gun in my back and an even more lethal predator in front. As for my companions, Deborah was unconscious or worse, and Samantha was truly being put over the coals. Still, I had one small hole card left: I knew that Chutsky was out there, armed and dangerous, and as long as he was alive he would never let any harm come to Debs or, by extension, to me. If I could keep Alana talking long enough, Chutsky would be here to save us.

"You have Samantha," I said as reasonably as I could. "There's more than enough of her to go around."

"Yes, but she *wants* to be eaten," Alana said. "The meat always tastes better if it's reluctant." She glanced at Samantha, who said, "Oh," again. Her eyes were wide now, wild with something I could not name, and focused on the grill.

Alana smiled and patted my cheek. "You *owe* us, darling. For escaping and causing all this trouble. And in any case, we need a male piggy." She frowned at me. "You look a bit stringy. We really should marinate you for a few days. Still, there's no time left, and I do love a nice man chop."

I will admit that it was a strange time and place for curiosity, but after all, I was trying to stall. "What do you mean, there's no time left?" I said.

She looked at me without expression, and somehow, the complete absence of emotion was more unsettling than her fake smile. "One last party," she said. "Then I'm afraid I must *flee* once again. Just as I had to flee England when the authorities decided that too many undocumented immigrants had gone missing there, as they now have here." She shook her head sadly. "I was just getting to like the taste of migrant worker, too."

Samantha grunted, and I looked. Bobby stood in front of her, slowly working the point of a knife across her partially exposed chest, as if he were carving his initials on a tree. His face was very close to hers, and he wore a smile that would wilt roses.

Alana sighed and shook her head fondly. "Don't play with your food, Bobby," she said. "You're supposed to be cooking. Turn it now, dear," she said, and he looked at Alana. Then he reluctantly put down the knife and reached onto the grill with a long-handled fork and flipped the flesh. Samantha moaned again. "And put something under that cut," Alana said, nodding at the growing pool of dreadful red blood dripping from Samantha's arm and spreading across the deck. "She's turning the deck into an abattoir."

"I'm not fucking Cinderella," Bobby said happily. "Stop the wicked-stepmother shit."

"Yes, but let's try to keep things a bit neater, shall we?" she said. He shrugged, and it was very clear that they were as fond of each other as two monsters could ever be. Bobby took a pot from the rack under the grill and placed it underneath Samantha's arm.

"I actually *did* straighten Bobby out," Alana said with just a trace of something that might have been pride. "He hadn't a clue how to do anything, and it was costing his father a small fortune to cover things up. Joe just couldn't understand, poor lamb. He thought he had given Bobby everything—but he hadn't given him the one thing he really wanted." She looked right at me with all her very bright teeth showing. "This," she said, waving at Samantha, the knives, the blood on the deck. "Once he had a small taste of long pig, and the power that goes with it, he learned to be careful. That dreary little club, Fang, that was Bobby's idea, actually. A lovely way to recruit for the coven, separating cannibals from vampires. And the kitchen help provided a wonderful source of meat."

She frowned. "We really should have stayed with eating immigrants," Alana said. "But I've grown so fond of Bobby, and he begged so prettily. Both girls did, too, actually." She shook her head. "Stupid of me. I do know better." She turned back to me, her bright smile back in place. "*But*, on the positive side, I have a good deal more cash this time for a new start, and a smattering of Spanish, too, which I shan't waste. Costa Rica? Uruguay? Someplace where all questions can be answered with dollars."

Alana's cell phone chirped, and it startled her for just a second. "Listen to me prattling on," she said, looking at the phone's screen. "Ah. About fucking time." She turned away and spoke a few words into the phone, listened for a moment, spoke again, and put the phone away. "Cesar, Antoine," she said, beckoning to two of the shotgun flunkies. They hurried over to her and she said, "He's here. But . . ." And she bent her head down next to theirs and added something I could not hear. Whatever it was, Cesar smiled and nodded and Alana looked up at the revelers by the grill. "Bobby," she said. "Go with Cesar and lend him a hand."

Bobby smirked and lifted up Samantha's hand. He took a knife from the table and raised it up, looking expectantly at Alana. Samantha moaned.

"Don't be a buffoon, love," Alana said to Bobby. "Run along and help Cesar."

Bobby dropped Samantha's arm, and she grunted, and then said, "Oh," several times as Cesar and Antoine led Bobby and his friends down the wobbly ramp and away into the park.

Alana watched them go. "We shall be getting started with you shortly," she said, and she turned away from me and walked over to Samantha. "How are *we* doing, little piggy?" she said.

"Please," Samantha said weakly, "oh, please . . ."

"Please?" Alana said. "Please what? You want me to let you go? Hm?"

"No," Samantha said, "oh, no."

"Not let you go, all right. Then what, dear?" Alana said. "I just can't think what." She picked up one of the oh-so-very-sharp-looking knives. "Perhaps I can help you speak up a bit, little piglet," she said, and she jabbed the point into Samantha's midsection, not terribly deep, but repeatedly, deliberately, which seemed more terrible, and Samantha cried out and tried to squirm away—quite impossible, of course, lashed to the mast as she was.

"Nothing at all to tell me, darling? Really?" she said, as Samantha at last collapsed, with terrible red blood seeping out in far too many places. "Very well, then, we'll give you some time to think." And she put the knife down on the table, and lifted the lid of the barbecue. "Oh, bother, I'm afraid this has burned," she said, and with a quick glance to be sure that Samantha was watching, she took the long-handled fork and flipped the piece of flesh over the rail and into the water.

Samantha gave a weak wail of despair and slumped over; Alana watched her happily, and then looked at me with her serpent's smile and said, "Your turn next, old boy," and went to the rail.

In truth, I was quite happy to see her go, as I had found her performance very hard to watch. Aside from the fact that I did not actually enjoy watching other people inflict pain and suffering on the innocent, I knew full well that it was at least partially intended for my benefit. I did not want to be next, and I did not want to be food—which I would be, apparently, if Chutsky didn't get here soon. I was sure he was out there in the dark, circling around to come at us at an unexpected angle, trying to find some way to improve his odds, performing some strange and deadly maneuver known only to hardened warriors, before he burst upon us with gun blazing. Still, I really wished he would hurry up.

Alana kept looking off toward the gate. She seemed to be a bit distracted, which was fine with me. It gave me a chance to reflect on my misspent life. It seemed terribly sad that it was ending now, so soon, long before I did anything really important, like taking Lily Anne to ballet lessons. How would she manage in life without me there to guide her? Who would teach her to ride a bicycle; who would read her fairy tales?

Samantha moaned weakly again, and I looked at her. She was rolling against her bonds in a kind of slow and spastic rhythm, as if her batteries were slowly running down. Her father had read to her, too. Read her fairy tales, she had said. Perhaps I shouldn't read Lily Anne fairy tales—it hadn't worked out very well for Samantha. Of course, as things stood now, I wouldn't be reading anything to anyone. I hoped Deborah was all right. In spite of her odd moodiness lately, she was tough—but she had taken a hard shot to the head, and she had looked very limp when they dragged her below.

And then I heard Alana say, "Aha," and I turned to look.

A group of figures was just now stepping into one of the pools of light cast from a working lamp. This new clump of young partiers in pirate costumes had come into the park and joined up with Bobby, and I had time to wonder: How many cannibals could there be in Miami? The group circled excitedly like a flock of gulls, waving pistols, machetes, and knives. At the center of their circle, five more figures came on. One of them was Cesar, the man Alana had sent off into the park. With him was Antoine, the other guard, as well as Bobby. Between them they were dragging another man. He was slumped over, apparently unconscious. Behind them stalked a man dressed in a black, hooded robe that hid his face.

And as the partiers circled and cawed, the unconscious man in the middle rolled back his head and the light caught his face so I could see his features.

It was Chutsky.

THIRTY-NINE

INSTEIN TELLS US THAT OUR NOTION OF TIME IS REALLY nothing more than a convenient fiction. I have never pretended to be the kind of genius who actually understands that sort of thing, but for the first time in my life I began to get a glimmer of what it meant. Because when I saw Chutsky's face, everything stopped. Time no longer existed. It was as if I was trapped in a single moment that went on forever, or a still-life painting. Alana was etched against the dim lights at the railing of the old fake pirate ship, face frozen into an expression of carnivorous amusement. Beyond her in the park were the five unmoving figures in their pool of light, Chutsky with his head rolled limply back, the guards and Bobby pulling him along by his arms, the strange black-robed figure stalking behind them, holding Cesar's shotgun. The group of pirates held comic-menacing poses around them, all in life-like postures without motion. I no longer heard any sound. The world had shrunk down to that one still picture of all hope ending.

And then in the near distance, in the direction of the Steeplechase, the horrible migraine-inducing beat of the music from Club Fang started up; somebody shouted, and normal time began to return. Alana started to turn from the rail, slowly at first, and then back up to regular speed, and once again I heard Samantha moaning, the Jolly Roger flopping at the masthead, and the remarkably loud pounding of my heart.

"Were you expecting someone?" Alana asked me pleasantly, as things came back to very horrible normal. "I'm afraid he's not going to be much help."

That thought had occurred to me, along with several others, but none of them offered me anything more than a semihysterical commentary on the rising sense of hopelessness that was now flooding the basements of Castle Dexter. I could still smell the lingering aroma of flesh toasting on the grill, and it did not take a great stretch of the imagination to picture that precious, irreplaceable Dexter would be sizzling there soon, one slice at a time. In a really good story with a perfect Hollywood structure, this would be the moment when a fantastically clever idea would pop into my head, and I would somehow cut my bonds, grab a shotgun, and blast my way to freedom.

But apparently, I was not in that kind of story, because nothing at all popped into my head except the forlorn and unshakable idea that I was about to be killed and eaten. I saw no way out, and I could not still the pointless yammering in my brain long enough to think of anything but that one central thing: This was *It*. End of game, all over, fade to black—Dexter into darkness. No more wonderful me, not ever again. Nothing left but a pile of gnawed bones and abandoned guts, and somewhere one or two people would have a few vague memories of the person I had pretended to be—not even the real me, which seemed deeply tragic, and not for very long. Life would go on without fabulous, inimitable *me*, and although it was not right, it was unavoidable. The end, finish, *finito*.

I suppose I should have died right then from pure misery and self-pity, but if those things were fatal, no one would ever make it past thirteen years old. I lived, and I watched as they dragged Chutsky up the wobbly ramp and dumped him on the deck with his hands taped behind him. The black-robed figure with Cesar's shotgun moved over to the grill where he could cover me and Chutsky, and Bobby and Cesar dragged Chutsky to Alana's feet and let him flop facedown into a limp and quivering heap. He had two darts sticking out of his back, which explained the quivering. They had somehow sneaked up behind Chutsky and Tasered him, and then knocked him out somehow while he shivered helplessly. So much for big-time professional rescue.

"He's rather a large brute," Alana said, nudging him with a toe. She glanced at me. "Friend of yours, is he?"

"Define *friend*," I said. After all, I had really been counting on him, and he was supposed to be good at this sort of thing.

"Yes," she said, looking back at Chutsky. "Well, he's no bloody use to us. Nothing but gristle and scar tissue."

"Actually, I'm told he's very tender underneath," I said hopefully. "I mean, much more than me."

"Ohhhh," Chutsky said. "Ohhh, *shit . . .*"

"Hey, looka that; he got a good jaw," Cesar said, nodding with approval. "I hit him good; he should still be out."

"Where is she?" Chutsky said, trembling. "Is she all right?"

"I did, I hit him good. I used to fight," Cesar said to no one in particular.

"She's here," I said to him. "She's unconscious."

Chutsky made a huge and apparently very painful effort and rolled his body so he could see me. His eyes were red and filled with anguish. "We fucked up, buddy," he said. "Fucked up bad."

It seemed a bit too obvious to call for comment, so I said nothing, and Chutsky collapsed back into his original shivering position with a weary, "Fuck."

"Take him down with Sergeant Morgan," Alana said, and Cesar and Bobby grabbed Chutsky again and dragged him to his feet and then through the door and into the cabin. "The rest of you, run along to the Steeplechase and make sure the fire is going. Enjoy yourselves," she said to the flock of pirates crowding the gangway, with a nod to Antoine. "Take along the punch bowl." Someone let out a whoop, and two of them grabbed the five-gallon pot by its handles. The figure in the black robe stepped carefully around them, keeping the shotgun pointed toward me while pirates trooped off down the gangway and away into the park. Then they were gone and Alana turned her frosty attention to me once again.

"Well, then," she said, and although I knew that she could not feel any emotions, there was certainly a dark and awful amusement shining out from the scaly thing that lived inside her as she looked at me. "And now we come to my man-piggy." She nodded at the bouncer and he backed away from me to the rail, gun still pointed at me, and Alana stepped forward.

It was a spring night in Miami and the temperature was in the upper seventies—and yet as she approached I felt an icy wind blow over me and through me and whip up from the darkest corners of the deepest parts of me, and the Passenger rose up on its many legs and cried out in helpless fury, and I felt my bones crumble and my veins turn to dust and the world shrank down to the steady and happy madness of Alana's eyes.

"Do you know about cats, love?" she said to me, and she was almost purring herself. It seemed rhetorical; in any case, my mouth was suddenly very dry and I didn't feel like answering. "They do love to play with their food, don't they?" She patted my cheek lovingly and then slapped it, very hard, with no change of expression. "I used to watch for hours. They torture their little mousie, don't they? Do you know why, dearie?" she asked me. She ran a long and very red fingernail down my chest and onto my arm, where she found one of the cuts there, made by the saw palmetto thorns. She frowned at it. "It's not mere cruelty, which seems a shame. Although I'm sure there's some of that, too." She put her fingernail into the cut. "But the torture releases the adrenaline in the little mousie."

Alana dug her fingernail into the tender open flesh of my wounded arm and I jumped as the pain needled in and the blood began to flow. She nodded thoughtfully. "Or in this case, the adrenaline in the piggy. The adrenaline flows out into the wee cowering timorous beastie's whole body. And guess what, love? Adrenaline is a marvelous natural meat tenderizer!" She jabbed her nail into the cut in rhythm with her words, deeper and deeper, twisting the nail to open the wound more, and although it did hurt, the sight of it was worse and I could not take my eyes off the terrible red of the precious Dexter blood running out in ever-increasing gouts as she poked harder and deeper.

"So *first* we *play* with our *food*, and *then* it *actually* tastes *better*! Some *terrific, relaxing fun*, and it *pays off* at *table. Isn't nature wonderful?*"

She held her long sharp nail deep in my arm and looked at me for a very long moment with her awful frozen smile. I heard a few of the revelers laughing madly somewhere in the distance, and Samantha moaned again, much softer now, and I turned my head toward her. She had lost a great deal of blood, and the pot Bobby had put under her arm had overflowed so that it was slopping onto the deck, and as I saw it I got a little bit dizzy and I pictured the blood from my cut pouring out to join it until the two of us covered the deck with a flood of terrible vile red sticky mess like that long-ago mommy time with my brother Biney in the cold box and my head began to spin and I felt myself whirl away from the pain and off into the red darkness—

And a new and deeper stab of pain brought me back to the deck of the wretched old pretend pirate ship, with the very real and elegant cannibal woman trying to push her fingernail all the way through my arm. I was sure she would soon open an artery, and then my blood would be everywhere. I hoped it would at least ruin Alana's shoes—not much as final curses go, but really just about all I had left.

I felt Alana's grip on my arm tighten, driving her fingernail even deeper into my arm, and for a moment the pain was so bad I thought I would have to yell, and then the cabin door banged open and Bobby and Cesar came back out onto the deck.

"Couple of lovebirds," Bobby sneered. "He's like, 'Debbie, oh, Debbie,' and she's like, nothing, still out cold, and he's like, 'Oh, God, oh, God, Debbie, Debbie.'"

"All very amusing," Alana said, "but is he tucked away safely, dear?"

Cesar nodded. "He's not going nowhere," he said.

"Brilliant," Alana said. "Then why don't you two totter away to the party?" She looked at me through hooded eyes. "I'm going to stay here and unwind for a few more minutes."

I am sure that Bobby answered with something he thought of as clever, and I am equally certain that he and Cesar clattered off down the rickety gangway and into the park to join the other revelers, but in truth none of that registered; my world had shrunk down to the horrible pictures forming in the air between Alana and me. She stood there looking at me, unblinking, with such a clear intensity of purpose that I began to think the force of her stare might actually open a wound on my face.

Unfortunately, she decided not to rely on the power of her eyes to tenderize me. She turned slowly, tauntingly, away from me, and stepped over to the table where the row of gleaming blades lay waiting for her. The black-hooded man stood there near the knives, and the muzzle of his shotgun never wavered from me. Alana looked down at the knives and put a finger to her chin as she regarded them thoughtfully. "So many really *good* choices," she said. "I do wish there was a little more time to do this properly. Really get to know you." She shook her head sadly. "I didn't have any time at all with that marvelous-looking policeman you sent me. I barely got a taste of him before I had to put him down. Rush, rush, rush. Takes all the joy out, doesn't it?" she said. So she had killed Deke. And I could not help hearing a slight echo of my own familiar playtime musings in her words, which did not seem fair at a time like this.

"*But*," Alana said, "I think you and I shall get on properly, any road. This one." She lifted up a large and very sharp-looking blade something like a bread knife that would almost certainly provide her with some quality amusement. She turned to me and raised the knife slightly and took one step back toward me and then stopped.

Alana looked at me, her eyes flicking over me as she rehearsed the things she was going to do, and it may be that I have an overactive imagination, or it may be that I recognized her intentions from my own modest experience, but I could feel every move she was thinking of making, every slice and cut she planned to try on me, and the sweat began to soak my shirt and pour off my forehead and

I could feel my heart hammering at my ribs as if it was trying to punch through the bones and escape, and we stood there, ten feet apart, sharing a mental pas de deux from the classical ballet of blood. Alana let her moment of enjoyment stretch out for a very long time, until I felt like my sweat glands had run dry and my tongue had swollen to the roof of my mouth. And then she said, "Right," in a soft and throaty voice and took a step forward.

I suppose there may be something to this New Age notion after all, that everything balances out eventually—I mean, aside from the fact that I was now getting a taste of my own medicine, which is really beside the point. What I mean is that this evening I had already lived through a period when time slowed and stopped, and now, just to even things out, as Alana turned toward me and raised her knife, everything seemed to kick into high gear and happen all at once in a kind of jerky high-speed dance.

First, there was a shattering bang and the enormous, ponytailed bouncer exploded; his midsection quite literally vanished in a horrifying red spray and the rest of him went flying away over the railing of the boat with an expression of numb resentment on his face, and he was gone so fast it was as if he had been clipped out of the scene by an omnipotent film editor.

Second, and so quickly it seemed to be almost simultaneous with the bouncer flying over the rail, Alana whipped around with the knife raised and her mouth wide open and she jumped at the man in the black robe, who pumped the shotgun and fired, taking off Alana's upraised arm with the knife. And then he pumped again and swiveled, faster than seemed possible, and shot the last of the guards, who was just bringing his weapon up. And then Alana slid down at Samantha's feet, the guard slammed into the rail and went over, and suddenly it was very still on the deck of the wicked ship *Vengeance*.

And then that melodramatic, ominous, black-robed figure racked the shotgun one more time and turned until the smoking barrel was pointed directly at me. For just a moment, everything froze again; I looked at that dark mask and the darker gun barrel pointed, naturally enough, right at my midsection—and I wondered: Had

I pissed off Somebody Up There? I mean, what had I done to be condemned to this endless smorgasbord of death? Seriously; how many
different and equally horrible ends can one relatively innocent man
face in one night? Is there no justice in this world? Other than the sort
I specialize in, I mean?

It just went on and on—I'd been beaten and slapped and poked
and tortured and menaced with knives and threatened with being
eaten and stabbed and shot—and I'd had it. Enough was enough.
I couldn't even get upset about this ultimate indignity. I was all out
of adrenaline; my flesh was as tenderized as it was going to get, and
it would almost be a relief to have it all over with. Every worm must
turn at last, and Dexter had reached the point where he could take
no more.

And so I drew myself up to my full height and I stood there,
filled with noble readiness to step up to the plate and meet my final
destiny with true courage and manly resolve—and once again life
threw me a knuckleball.

"Well," the hooded figure said, "it looks like I'm going to have
to pull your fat out of the fire one more time."

And as he raised the gun I thought, *I know that voice.* I knew it,
and I didn't know whether to cheer, cry, or throw up. Before I could
do any of those things, he turned around and fired at Alana, who
had crawled slowly and painfully toward him, leaving a thick trail
of blood. At close range the shot bounced her up off the deck and
nearly cut her in half before dropping the two elegant pieces back
down in a sadly untidy heap.

"Nasty bitch," he said as he lowered the shotgun, pulled back
the hood, and took off his mask. "Still, the pay was excellent, and
the work suited me—I'm very good with knives." And I was right. I
did know that voice. "And really, anyone would think you would
have figured it out," my brother, Brian, said. "I gave you enough
hints—the black token in the bag, everything."

"Brian," I said, and even though it was one of the stupidest
things I had ever said, I couldn't help adding, "You're here."

"Of course I'm here," he said, with his awful fake smile, and somehow it didn't seem quite so phony right now. "What's family for?"

I thought about the last few days: first Deborah getting me from the trailer in the Everglades, and now this, and I shook my head. "Apparently," I said, "family is for rescuing you from cannibals."

"Well, then," Brian said. "Here I am."

And for once his awful fake smile seemed very real and welcome.

FORTY

AS EVERY CLICHÉ-LOVING HUMAN BEING KNOWS, NO cloud dumps its load upon us unless it is hiding its very own silver lining. In this case, the one small perk of being held captive by cannibals is that there are always plenty of nice sharp knives lying around, and Brian had me cut free very quickly. Pulling the duct tape off my wrists didn't hurt quite as much the second time either, since there wasn't much arm hair left to rip out by the roots, but it still wasn't a great deal of fun, and I took a moment to rub my wrists. Apparently it was a moment too long.

"Perhaps you could massage yourself later, brother?" Brian said. "We really can't linger." He nodded at the gangway.

"I need to get Deborah," I said.

He sighed theatrically. "What is it with you and that girl?" he said.

"She's my sister."

Brian shook his head. "I suppose," he said. "But do let's hurry, all right? The place is crawling with these people, and we would really rather avoid them, I think."

We had to pass the mainmast to get to the cabin door and, in spite of Brian's urgency, I paused by Samantha, taking very great care to avoid the puddle of blood that spread out to her right. I stood on her left side and looked at her carefully. Her face was incredibly pale and she was no longer swaying or moaning and for a moment I thought she was already dead. I put a hand on her neck to feel for a pulse; it was there, but very faint, and as I touched her neck her eyes fluttered open. The eyeballs themselves twitched and did not quite focus and she clearly didn't recognize me. She half closed her eyes again and said something I could not hear and I leaned closer. "What did you say?" I said.

"Was I . . . good . . . ?" she whispered hoarsely. It took me a moment, but I finally did realize what she meant.

They like to tell us that it is important to speak the truth, but it has been my experience that real happiness lies in having people tell you what you want to believe, usually not the same thing at all, and if you have to stub your toe on the truth later, so be it. For Samantha, there was not going to be any later, and that being the case, I could not really find it in myself to hold a grudge and be mean enough to speak the truth now.

So I leaned down close to her ear and told her what she wanted to hear.

"You were delicious," I said.

She smiled and closed her eyes.

"I really don't think we have time for sentimental scenes," Brian said. "Not if you want to save that darn sister of yours."

"Right," I said. "Sorry." I left Samantha with no real reluctance, pausing only to pick up one of Alana's very nice knives from the table beside the barbecue.

We found Deborah behind the counter in what had once been the concession stand down in the main cabin of the old pirate ship. She and Chutsky had both been tied to a couple of large pipes that ran from a missing sink into the deck. Their hands and feet were duct-taped. Chutsky, to his credit, had almost freed one hand—his only hand, of course, but give kudos where it's due.

"Dexter!" he said. "Christ, I'm glad to see you. She's still breathing; we gotta get her outta here." He saw Brian lurking behind me for the first time and frowned. "Hey—that's the guy with the Taser."

"It's all right," I said unconvincingly. "Um, actually, he's—"

"It was an accident," Brian said quickly, as if afraid I would actually introduce him by name. He had flipped the hood back up to mask his face. "Anyway, I rescued you, so let's just get out of here quickly, before anybody else shows up, all right?"

Chutsky shrugged. "Yeah, sure, okay, you got a knife?"

"Of course," I said. I leaned over him, and he shook his head impatiently.

"No, fuck, come on, Dex, get Deborah first," he said.

It seemed to me that a man with only one hand and one foot who is bound hand and foot, as well as tied to a pipe, is in no place to give orders in a cranky tone of voice. But I let it pass, and I knelt beside Deborah. I cut the tape off her wrists and picked up one hand. The pulse felt strong and regular. I hoped that meant she was just unconscious; she was very healthy, and very tough, and unless she had caught a really bad break I thought she would probably be all right, but I did wish she would wake up and tell me so in person.

"Come on, quit fucking around, buddy," Chutsky said in the same petulant tone, and I cut the rope that secured Deborah to the pipe, and the tape that held her ankles together.

"We do need to hurry," Brian said softly. "Do we have to bring him?"

"Very fucking funny," Chutsky said, but I knew that my brother was serious.

"I'm afraid so," I said. "Deborah would be upset if we left him behind."

"Then for goodness' sake, cut him loose and let's go," Brian said, and he went to the door of the cabin and looked out, holding the shotgun at the ready. I cut Chutsky loose and he lurched to his feet—or to be accurate, to his foot, since one of them was a prosthetic replacement, like his hand. He looked down at Deborah for a second and Brian cleared his throat impatiently.

"All right," Chutsky said. "I'll carry her. Help me out, Dex."

And he nodded at Debs. Together we lifted her up and got her onto Chutsky's shoulder. He didn't seem to mind the weight; he shifted once to get her settled more comfortably, and then he moved toward the door as if he were off on a hike with a small day pack.

On deck, Chutsky paused briefly by Samantha, which made Brian hiss with impatience. "Is this the girl Debbie wanted to rescue so bad?" Chutsky said.

I looked at my brother, who was practically hopping on one foot in his eagerness to be gone. I looked back at my sister, draped across Chutsky's shoulder, and I sighed. "That's her," I said.

Chutsky shifted Deborah's weight slightly so he could reach over with his one real hand. He put it on Samantha's throat and held his fingers there for a few seconds. Then he shook his head. "Too late," he said. "She's dead. Debbie's going to be very upset."

"I'm awfully sorry," Brian said. "Can we go now?"

Chutsky looked at him and shrugged, which made Deborah slip a little bit. He caught her—fortunately not with his steel hook—readjusted her weight, and said, "Yeah, sure, let's go," and we scurried for the ramp off the boat.

Getting down the wobbly gangway was a bit tricky, especially since Chutsky was using his hand to hold on to Deborah, leaving only his hook to hold the guide rope. But we did manage, and once we were on terra firma we headed quickly for the gate.

I wondered if I should feel bad about Samantha. I didn't really think there was anything I could have done to save her—I hadn't even done a very good job of saving myself, which had a far higher priority—but it made me uncomfortable just to leave her body there. Perhaps it was because of all the blood, which always unsettles me. Or maybe it was just that I was always so tidy with my own leftovers. Certainly it was not because I thought her death was tragic or unnecessary—far from it. It was actually a small relief to have her out of the way without having to take any of the responsibility for it myself. It meant that I was in the clear; there was no piper to be paid, and my life could slip back onto its well-oiled and comfortable rails without any more worry about frivolous court proceedings. No, on the whole, it was a very good thing that Samantha got her wish, or most of it. The only thing gnawing at me was that it made me want to whistle, and that didn't seem right.

And then it hit me—I was feeling guilt! Me, Deeply Dead Dexter, King of the Unfeeling! I was wallowing in that soul-crushing, time-wasting, ultimate human self-indulgence—guilt! And all because I felt secret happiness from thinking that the untimely end of a young woman was a good thing for my selfish self-interests.

Had I finally grown a soul?

Was Pinocchio a real boy at last?

It was ludicrous, impossible, unthinkable—and yet, I was thinking it. Maybe it was true—maybe the birth of Lily Anne and my becoming Dex-Daddy and all the other impossible events of the last few weeks had finally and fatally killed the Dark Dancer I had always been. Maybe even the last few hours of mind-numbing terror under the reptile glare of Alana's dead blue eyes had helped, stirring the ashes until a seed sprouted. Maybe I was a new being now, ready to blossom into a happy, feeling human, one who could laugh and cry without pretending, and watch a TV show without secretly wondering what the actors would look like taped to a table—was it possible? Was I newborn Dexter, ready to take his place in a world of real people at last?

It was all fantastically interesting speculation, and like all such navel-gazing, it almost got me killed. As I blindly marveled at myself, we came through the park all the way to the go-cart track, and I had wandered slightly ahead of the others, unseeing because of my ridiculous self-absorption. I slid around the shed at the edge of the track and very nearly stepped on two party-hearty pirates who were kneeling on the ground trying to start a thirty-year-old go-cart. They looked up at me and blinked stupidly. Two large cups of punch stood on the ground beside them.

"Hey," one of them said. "It's the meat." He reached into his bright red pirate sash, and we will never know whether he was trying to get a weapon or a stick of chewing gum because, happily for me, Brian stepped around the shed just in time and shot him, and Chutsky came around and kicked the other one in the throat, so hard I could hear it crack, and he went over backward making gacking noises and clutching at his windpipe.

"Well," said Brian, looking at Chutsky with something like affection. "I see you're not just eye candy."

"Yeah, I'm terrific, huh?" Chutsky said. "Really useful." He sounded a little bit down for somebody escaping unharmed from a cannibal orgy, but perhaps getting Tasered left an emotional afterglow.

"Really, Dexter," Brian said. "You need to watch where you put your feet."

We made it to the main gate without further incident, which was a relief, since sooner or later our luck was bound to run out and we would stumble onto a large number of pirates, or enough who were sober, and we would have a very hard time. I had no idea how many shots Brian had left in his borrowed shotgun, but I didn't think it could be many. Of course, there were presumably plenty of kicks left in Chutsky's foot, but we couldn't count on being attacked by any more bad guys thoughtful enough to charge us from a kneeling position. Altogether, I was very glad to get through the gate and back to Debs's car.

"Open the door," Chutsky said to me in a demanding tone of voice, and I reached for the car's door handle. "The *back* door, Dexter," he snapped. "Jesus Christ." I made no attempt to correct his manners; he was too old and grumpy to learn, and after all, the strain of his failure this evening must have been taking some toll on his always basic etiquette. Instead I simply shifted to the car's back door and pulled on the handle. Naturally enough, it was locked.

"For fuck's sake," Chutsky said as I turned around, and I saw Brian raise an eyebrow.

"Such language," my brother said.

"I need the key," I said.

"Back pocket," Chutsky said. It gave me just a moment's hesitation, which was silly. After all, I was quite well aware that he had been living with my sister for several years. But still, I was surprised at the thought that he knew her this well, that he automatically knew where she kept her car keys. And it occurred to me that he knew her in other ways that I never would, too, knew other small domestic details of her life, and for some reason the thought made me hesitate for just a second, which was not, of course, a very popular choice.

"Come on, buddy, for Christ's sake, get your head out of your ass," Chutsky said.

"Dexter, please," Brian added. "We need to get out of here."

Clearly, I was going to be everybody's whipping boy tonight, a complete waste of protoplasm. But raising any objection would just take more time. Besides, anything that could get the two of them to agree was almost certainly inarguable. I stepped over to Deborah, where she lay across Chutsky's shoulder, and slid the keys out of the back pocket of her pants. I opened the back door of the car and held it wide as Chutsky put my sister down on the seat.

He began to go through a quick paramedic's exam of Deborah, which was harder than it should have been with his one hand. "Flashlight?" he said over his shoulder, and I got Debs's big police Maglite from the front seat and held it as Chutsky thumbed up her eyelids and watched her eyes react to the light.

"Ahem," Brian said behind us, and I turned to look at him. "If you don't mind," he said, "I would like to disappear?" He smiled, his old fake smile again, and nodded toward the north. "My car is a half mile away in a strip mall," he said. "I'll just ditch the gun and this corny robe, and I'll see you later—tomorrow for dinner, perhaps?"

"Absolutely," I said, and believe it or not I had to fight down a very real urge to give him a hug. "Thank you, Brian," I said instead. "Thank you very much."

"You're very welcome," he said. He smiled again, and then he turned away and walked off into darkness.

"She's gonna be okay, buddy," Chutsky said, and I looked back to where he still squatted beside the open back door of the car. He held her hand, and he looked overwhelmingly weary. "She's gonna be all right."

"Are you sure?" I said, and he nodded.

"Yeah, I'm sure," he said. "You should still take her to the ER, get her checked out, but she's okay, no thanks to me and—" He looked away from me and for a very long moment he didn't say anything, long enough that I began to feel uncomfortable; after all, we were agreed that we needed to get out of here. Was this really the time and place for quiet contemplation?

"Aren't you coming along to the hospital?" I said, more to move things along than because I wanted his company.

Chutsky didn't move or speak. He just kept looking away, off into the park, where there were still scattered sounds of revelry and the mindless thump of the music wafting toward us on the night breeze.

"Chutsky," I said, and I felt real anxiety growing.

"I fucked up," he said at last, and to my very great horror, a tear rolled down his cheek. "I fucked up big-time. I let her down when she needed me the most. She could have been killed, and I couldn't stop them, and . . ."

He took a deep and very ragged breath. He still didn't look at me. "I've been kidding myself, buddy. I'm too old for her, and I'm no fucking good to her or anybody else. Not with . . ." He held up his hook, and thumped his forehead against it, resting his head there and looking down at his fake foot. "She wants a family, which is stupid for a guy like me. Old. A mess, and a cripple—and I can't protect her, or even— It's not me she needs. I'm just a useless, old fuckup—"

There was a shriek of female laughter from inside the park, and the sound brought Chutsky back to the here and now. He snapped his head around to the front, took another deep breath, a little steadier, and looked down at Deborah's face. Then he kissed her hand, a long kiss with his eyes closed, and stood up. "Get her to the ER, Dexter," he said. "And tell her I love her." And then he marched to his car.

"Hey," I said. "Aren't you going to . . ."

Apparently, he wasn't going to. He ignored me, got into his car, and drove away.

I did not linger to watch his taillights flicker off into the night. I secured Debs in the backseat the best I could with a seat belt around her middle, and got in. I drove two miles or so, far enough to be safe, and then pulled over. I reached for my phone, then thought better of it and instead picked up Chutsky's phone from the seat where Debs had thrown it. His phone would be shielded from little things like caller ID. I dialed.

"Nine-one-one," the operator said.

"You all better get a whole lotta boys over to that ol' Buccaneer Land right fast," I said in my best Bubba voice.

"Sir, what is the nature of this emergency?" the operator asked.

"I'm a veteran," I said. "I done two tours in Eye-rack and I know gunfire when I hear it and that's sure as shit gunfire in Buccaneer Land."

"Sir, are you saying you heard gunshots?"

"More than jes' heard it. Went and took a look in there, and they's dead bodies everywhere," I said. "Ten, twenty dead bodies, and folks dancin' 'round 'em like a party," I said.

"You saw ten dead bodies, sir? You're sure?"

"And then somebody took a bite outta one and started to *eat* it an' Ah run. Never seen nothin' so groo-sum in mah life, an' Ah wuz in Baghdad."

"They—*ate* the body, sir?"

"You all best get all them SWAT boys over there pronto," I said, and I hung up and put the car in gear. They might not round up everybody in the park, but they would get most of them, enough to get a picture of what had happened, and that would be enough to get Bobby Acosta, one way or another. I hoped that it would make Deborah feel a little better about Samantha.

I nosed the car up onto I-95 and began the drive to Jackson. There were several closer hospitals, but if you are a Miami cop, you tend to home in on Jackson, which has one of the best trauma units in the country. And since Chutsky had assured me that the visit was precautionary only, I thought it best to go with the experts.

So I drove south as fast as I dared, quietly for the first ten minutes, and then just before the turnoff for the Dolphin Expressway, I heard sirens, and then more sirens, and a column of emergency vehicles long enough to deal with a major invasion went by in the opposite direction. They were followed closely by a matching column of satellite trucks from the local news departments—all headed north, presumably to Buccaneer Land. Moments after the noise had faded, I heard movement in the backseat and a few seconds later Deborah spoke. "Fuck," she said, not really a surprising first word, considering the source. "Oh, fuck."

"You're all right, Deborah," I said, craning my neck to see her in the mirror. She lay there with her hands clasped over her middle and a look of numb panic on her face. "We're on our way to Jackson, but just to check. Nothing to worry about; you're okay."

"Samantha Aldovar?" she said.

"Um," I said. "She didn't make it." I glanced again in the mirror; Debs closed her eyes and rubbed her stomach.

"Where's Chutsky?" she said.

"Well, ah, I don't really know," I said. "I mean, he's okay, you know, not hurt. He said, 'Tell Deborah I love her,' and then he drove away, but . . ." A large truck jerked in front of me, even though I was in the HOV lane, and I had to swerve and brake. When I looked back in the mirror again, her eyes were still closed.

"He's gone," she said. "He thinks he let me down, and so he got all noble and left me. Just when I need him most."

The idea of needing Chutsky at all, letting alone "most," seemed like stretching credibility to me, but I played along.

"Sis, you're going to be all right," I said, searching for the right reassuring words. "We'll get you checked out at Jackson, but I'm sure you're fine, and you'll be back at work tomorrow and everything will seem all right, and—"

"I'm pregnant," she said, which really left me nothing at all to say.

EPILOGUE

CHUTSKY REALLY WAS GONE—DEBORAH WAS RIGHT ABOUT that. After a few weeks it became clear that he wasn't coming back, and there was nothing she could do to find him. She tried, of course, with all the single-minded skill of a very stubborn woman who was also a very good cop. But Chutsky had spent a career in black operations, and he swam at a deeper level. We didn't really even know if Chutsky was his real name. After a lifetime of espionage, he probably didn't know either, and he vanished as completely as if he had never existed.

Deborah was right about the other thing, too. It soon became very obvious to everyone that all of her pants were suddenly too tight, and her usually bland shirts had changed into loose-fitting, Hawaiian-patterned things, the kind that she would normally never willingly accompany even to the drunk tank. Deborah was pregnant, and she was determined to have the baby, with Chutsky or without him.

I worried at first that her new status as an unmarried mother would hurt her standing at work; cops are generally very conservative people. But I had apparently not kept up with the New Conservatism. Nowadays, Family Values meant that getting pregnant when you were single was fine, as long as you stayed that way, and Deborah's prestige at work actually went up as her belly got bigger.

You would have thought that a pregnant detective would have been sympathetic enough to convince anyone of a person's wickedness, but at the bail hearing for Bobby Acosta, the lawyers played up the fact that Joe had just lost his wife—Bobby's stepmother, who had raised him and meant so much to him, now tragically departed, and they somehow forgot to mention that she had died in the act of torturing and murdering a few sundry people, like wonderful precious me. The judge set bail at five hundred thousand dollars, which was chump change for the Acosta family, and Bobby skipped happily out of the courtroom and into the arms of his ever-loving father, as we had known all along he would do.

Deborah took it better than I thought she would. She did say a bad word or two, but after all, she was Deborah, and all she really said was, "Well, fuck, so the little shit walks," and then she looked at me.

"Well, yes," I said, and that was pretty much that. Bobby was free until his trial, which could be years away, considering the caliber of lawyer his father brought to bear. By the time Bobby actually went before a jury, all the lovely headlines about "Cannibal Carnival" and "Buccaneer Bloodbath" would be forgotten, and Joe's money would get the charges reduced to hunting out of season, with a sentence of twenty hours' community service. A bitter pill to swallow, perhaps, but that's life in the service of that old whore Miami Justice, and we had certainly expected it.

And so life settled back into its normal rhythms, measured now by the growth of Deborah's waist, the fullness of Lily Anne's diaper pail, and the Friday-night dinners with Uncle Brian, now a highlight of our week. Friday was an ideal night, among other reasons, because that was when Debs had a birthing class, reducing the chance that she would drop in unexpectedly and embarrass my brother; after all, he had, speaking from a purely technical point of view, tried to kill her a few years back, and I knew very well she was not the kind to forgive and forget. But Brian planned to hang around for a while; apparently he truly enjoyed playing uncle and big brother. And, of course, Miami was his home, too, and he was quite certain that even in this economy it was the best place to find a new job that suited his unique skill set, and in any case he had enough money to tide him over for quite a while. Whatever her other faults, Alana had rewarded talent quite generously.

And to my very great surprise and growing unease, one more rhythm had begun to assert itself, even over the slow and steady blooming of my new human self. Gradually, at first so subtly I did not even notice it, I began to feel a tiny tugging at the back of my neck—but not my physical neck, not really my physical anything, just . . . something slightly behind and . . . ?

And I would turn and look, puzzled, and see nothing, and shrug it off as imagination, no more than a delayed case of nerves from all I had suffered. After all, poor battered Dexter had truly been through the mill. It was perfectly natural that I should be uneasy, even jumpy, for a while after so much physical and mental trauma. Completely understandable, normal in every way, nothing to worry about, don't think twice. And I would go about my ordinary human business of work time–playtime–TV time–bedtime in its endless unchanging cycle without a care until the next time it happened and I would once again suddenly stop what I was doing and turn around at the call of an unheard voice.

So it went for several months as life got duller and Debs got larger, until she was big enough to set a date for her baby shower. And the night I held that invitation in my hand and wondered what perfect gift I could get her for her Blessed Event I felt the tug of that unvoiced sound again and turned around behind me and this time, framed in the window at my back, I saw it.

Moon.

Full, bright, saucy, lovely moon.

Calling, compelling, shining and beaming, wonderful bright loudmouth moon, whispering sweet nothings in its reptile tones of steel and stealth, saying the two soft syllables of my name in its same old shadow-loving dark-eyed voice, so very well known from so very many times before, so familiar and so comfortable and now so oddly welcome once again.

Hello, old friend.

One more time I feel the leathery wings rustle and unfold in the dark basement, hear once again the joyful whisper of a Passenger brushing off neglect and calling for happy reunion.

It's time, it says, with a small cold thrill of seeing just how things must be this one more time like always. *It is very much time.*

And it is.

And so although I thought I had gone beyond all this, away from the rattle and slash of the Passenger, I was wrong. I still feel it, feel it now stronger than ever, pulling at me from that great fat blood-red moon hanging in the window with its leering, mocking grin, daring me to do what must be done and do it now.

Now.

And in the tiny still-wet corners of my new human soul I know that I cannot, dare not, must not—I have family obligations—I am holding one in my hand, the invitation to Deborah's baby shower. Soon there will be a new Morgan, a new life to care for, an obligation not to be taken lightly, not in this wicked and dangerous world. And that molten brassy moon-voice, ever louder, whispers slyly that this is true; of course it is. The world is wickedness and danger, very true; no one would ever deny it. And so it is a very *good* thing to make the world a better and safer place, one small slice at a time, and especially when we can do this thing and meet our family obligations at the same time.

And yes, the thought comes slowly and uncoils with a sharp and perfect logic. It *is* true, very true, oh, so true and oh, so very neat as well, making perfect sense of so many messy little pieces that need to be nudged into line and made to behave and after all there are those family obligations and in any case there is that voice, that beautiful wailing siren-song voice, and it is calling far too strongly in its fat happy brassy voice for me to say no to it now.

And so we go to my dusty office closet and put a few small things into a gym bag.

And so we go into the living room where Rita and the children are watching TV and on Rita's lap is Lily Anne—

And for just a moment I stop dead, looking at her, face snuggled down into the warmth of her mother, and for several long heartbeats the sight of her is louder than any song the moon could sing. Lily Anne . . .

But eventually we breathe, and the deep melody of this perfect night rushes back into me with the air and I remember: It is for her sake that we do this tonight. For Lily Anne, for all the Lily Annes, to make a better place of the world they will grow into, and the wild happiness comes back, and then the cold control, and we bend down to kiss my wife on the cheek. "I need to go out for a little while," we say in a very good imitation of Dexter's human voice. Cody and Astor sit up straight when they hear our voice and they stare wide-eyed at the gym bag, but we stare them down and they are silent.

"What? Oh—but it's . . . All right, if you're— Could you get milk on the way . . . ?" Rita says.

"Milk," we say. "Bye." And as Cody and Astor goggle in awe at what they know will happen now we are out the door and into the warm blanket of metallic moonlight that has clamped over the Miami night and holds it now in taut readiness for us, for our Night of Need and Necessity, for the thing we will do, *must* do; we slip once again into the welcome darkness for that one perfect present for a baby shower, the wonderful gift for a special sister, the one thing that only her brother knows she wants, the one thing only he can get for her.

Bobby Acosta.

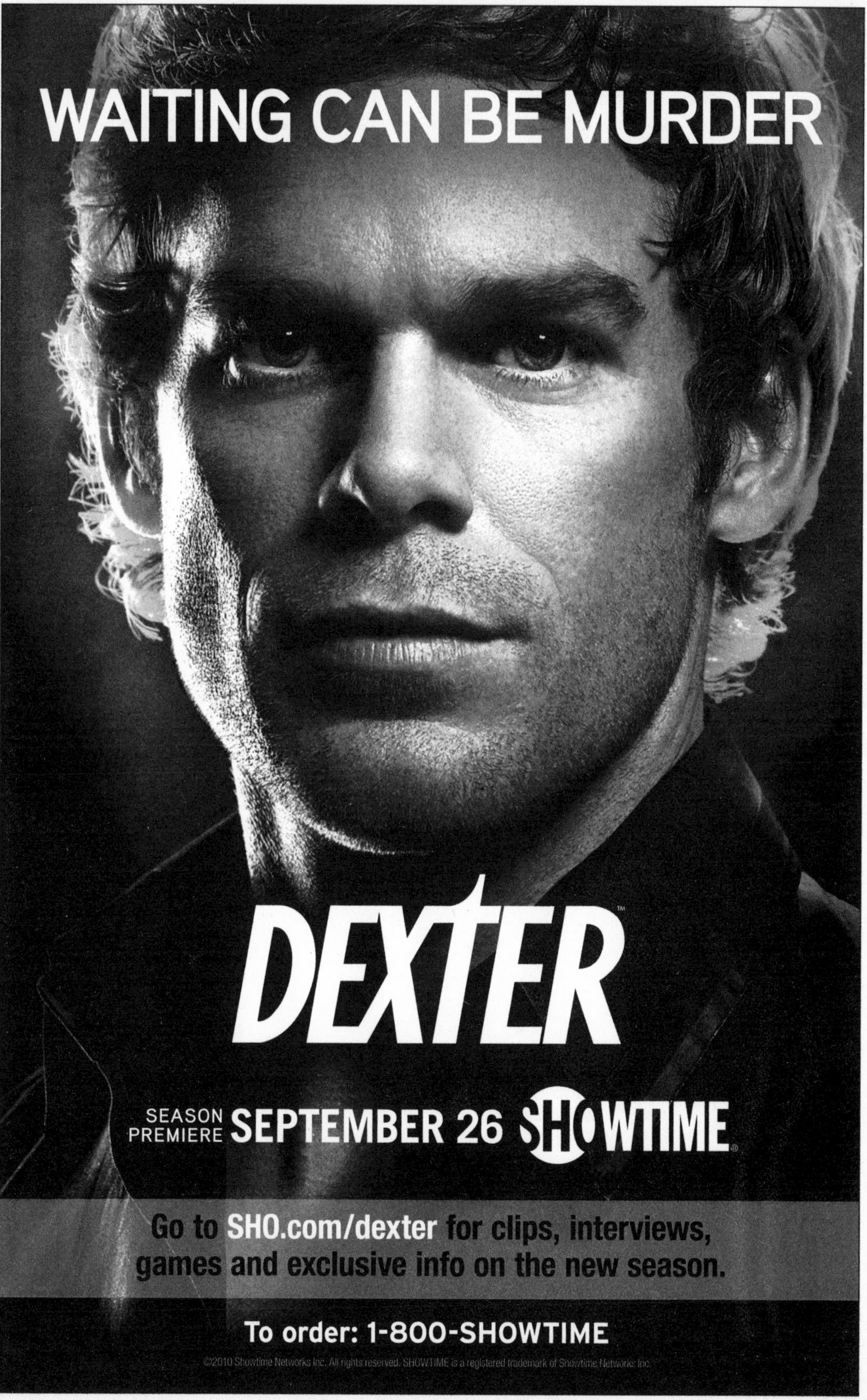
WAITING CAN BE MURDER
DEXTER™
SEASON PREMIERE SEPTEMBER 26 SHOWTIME®
Go to SHO.com/dexter for clips, interviews, games and exclusive info on the new season.
To order: 1-800-SHOWTIME
©2010 Showtime Networks Inc. All rights reserved. SHOWTIME is a registered trademark of Showtime Networks Inc.

HE'S ONE KILLER DAD!

Even more killer on DVD and Blu-ray!
Season 4 Available Now!